More praise for
TANGLED ROOTS

"Cannon's take on the nuts-and-bolts of social entropy in Southern California is right on and rapier sharp!"
—ABIGAIL PADGETT
Author of *Turtle Baby*

"Cannon juggles a nice array of motives and suspects as her sharp, extremely appealing sleuth unravels the underlying story of revenge."
—*The Wilson Library Bulletin*

"[Nan Robinson is an] intelligent, gently cynical, and endearing series sleuth. . . . Taffy Cannon excels at capturing the flavor of her Southern California settings, as well as at creating complex, fascinating characters and intriguing stories, and the fans and reviewers who hailed her debut will be equally delighted with the second Nan Robinson mystery."
—*Grounds for Murder* (Newsletter)

"This is an A+ book. . . . The drama unfolds amidst the fragrant beauty of the flower industry, in poignant contrast to the ugliness of human behavior."
—*Booknews from The Poisoned Pen*

By Taffy Cannon:

Fiction:
CONVICTIONS: A Novel of the Sixties

Nan Robinson mysteries
A POCKETFUL OF KARMA*
TANGLED ROOTS*

Young Adult Fiction:
MISSISSIPPI TREASURE HUNT*

*Published by Fawcett Books

TANGLED
ROOTS

Taffy Cannon

FAWCETT CREST • NEW YORK

A Fawcett Crest Book
Published by Ballantine Books
Copyright © 1995 by Taffy Cannon

All rights reserved under International and Pan-American Copyright Conventions. Published in the United States by Ballantine Books, a division of Random House, Inc., New York, and distributed in Canada by Random House of Canada Limited, Toronto.

Library of Congress Catalog Card Number: 95-90702

ISBN 0-449-22390-6

This edition published by arrangement with Carroll & Graf Publishers, Inc.

Manufactured in the United States of America

First Ballantine Books Edition: February 1996

10 9 8 7 6 5 4 3 2 1

In memory of my parents,
who loved roses . . .

ACKNOWLEDGMENTS

Many members of the San Diego County flower-growing community generously shared their time and expertise. I am particularly indebted to Eric Larson of the San Diego County Flower & Plant Auction, Dave Pruitt of Sea Coast Greenhouses, and Bob Echter of Dramm and Echter. Additional information and advice came from Capt. Dennis Tico of the Oceanside Fire Department, Dr. Katharine Sheehan, Dr. William Ackerman, and David R. Thompson. These good people bear no responsibility for any errors I may have made in using and adapting their information for this book.

Special thanks, as always, to Bill Kamenjarin.

CHAPTER 1

The last twenty minutes of Shane Pettigrew's life were filled with bureaucratic twaddle.

He was tired and a bit drunk, and he found himself unexpectedly saddened by the spicy scent of the luxuriant pink-and-white stock that perfumed his greenhouse office. Amelia had loved stock, giggled over its old-fashioned name "gillyflower," called the winter smell of them " 'picy."

Ah, Amelia. Shane looked up at the framed portrait of the five of them that still hung in the corner of the office, where his father had left it. Amelia and Shane and Cassie sat in front of their parents, blond urchins scrubbed into respectability for the photographer. Cassie looked a bit sullen, careening headlong into puberty. But Amelia was a sweet little pixie, all big blue eyes. Shane didn't remember when the picture had been taken, didn't have all that many specific memories of Amelia, either. But whenever he smelled stock, he could picture her running through the pink-and-white fields behind the house, laughing. Those were better memories than the later ones, than the last one—the tiny patent-leather shoe washed away from the roots of the peach tree, his father's primordial howl when he realized they had finally found her.

Amelia.

Shane shook himself and forced his attention to the papers on the desk. That last beer was a mistake. It was going to be hard to stay awake, and all this crap had to be done by morning. This was the part of his work he hated most, the chore he always avoided till the last possible moment. But he'd promised Margaret, and he didn't dare break that promise. The force of Margaret's disapproval could revert him instantly to the ten-year-old boy in the portrait hanging on the wall.

His battered wooden desk was cluttered with invoices, receipts, and government forms. Bookkeeping made him crazy, and Margaret handled most of it, but he had to at least look at everything. And sign the checks, of course. Tomorrow morning this big wad of paper was due at the accountant's.

But the worst was unquestionably the government forms.

This first one, at least, was easy. Margaret had already filled in the federal Work-Day Report, listed all the reportable workers and their INS numbers. A strange form, allowing equal column spaces for *Sod, Sugar Cane,* and *All Other Crops*. He kept thinking sometime he'd have to read all that fly-speck print on the back. But quarter after quarter, he never quite got around to it.

That completed form went to Jeffersonville, Indiana. Wherever that was. What did bureaucrats in Indiana know about Oaxacan natives cutting greenhouse roses in Floritas, California?

Shane signed the Work-Day Report, then stared glumly down at the Monthly Pesticide Use Report. Already late. The stack of greenhouse spraying sheets was barely decipherable and depressingly high. From them he'd have to compile the three-carbon form for the State Department of Food and Agriculture, another piece of paper nobody'd ever read, but God help the sap who didn't file it.

There must be some way Margaret could get the computer to do this part. He'd ask—no, beg—her, with a two-pounder of See's nuts and chews to sweeten the pot. Or, even better, maybe Jeff could take it all over. He actually seemed to *like* this kind of stuff. Ask Jeff in the morning, then.

But it was already morning, wasn't it? Shouldn't have stayed so late at Ernesto's. He could forget his earlier idea of catching a few hours' sleep and then surfing at dawn. At this rate, he'd still be here at six when the greenhouse workers started coming in. And all those miserable little boxes on the wretched form would still be empty.

He sighed and picked up the first form, routine Orthene spraying on the roses in greenhouse seven, signed by Juan Verdugo. At least this one was neat; Juan had been educated by a very persnickety order of nuns back in Tehuantepec.

Shane was barely a quarter through the stack when he heard footsteps on the gravel path outside. He glanced at his watch in surprise. One forty-five. Who on earth would be coming by at this hour of the morning? And where were they coming from on foot? He hadn't heard a car.

The door opened and Shane stared, startled. "What are you . . ." he began.

His eyes widened as the gun barrel lifted swiftly to point straight at him. Before he could react, the quiet night was broken by three shots fired in rapid succession. Shane clutched at his chest and stared at his assailant in confusion, unable to ask the questions racing through his mind. Other thoughts pushed the questions aside, other images flashed through his brain.

They're right, he thought suddenly. Your life *does* pass in front of you. . . .

A bubble of blood trickled out the corner of his mouth as he tried to speak. The taste was strange, unexpected.

Then it faded.

By the time the sixth shot was fired, Shane Pettigrew slumped dead in his chair, eyes wide in glazed astonishment.

As time passed, the spicy aroma of the flowers in the tiny office slowly gave way to the ugly odors of death.

. . . She was riding the tractor when the engine started acting up, giving that rhythmic THUNK that always signaled trouble.

Colleen appeared suddenly beside her, smiling in her denim overalls. "I'll fix it, Mom," her daughter told her, reaching into an enormous toolbox. "We don't need to bother Daddy." But the engine grew louder and louder. . . .

THUNK! THUNK! THUNK!

Julie shifted her weight as she slowly opened her eyes, groggy and disoriented. The noise continued and she recognized it now as somebody banging on the front door. How long had she been asleep? The clock over the fireplace read nine-fifteen. She didn't even remember lying down after breakfast. . . .

"I'm coming!" she called as the banging continued. She slowly sat up. She felt all fuzzy. The dream had been so vivid, the field freshly turned and pungent all around her, furrowed and ready to plant. The daughter had appeared with perfect clarity, too, that pigtailed competent little girl ready to take on the tractor engine.

Colleen.

But Colleen wasn't born yet, still slumbered peacefully in her mother's body, a tiny organism only a few inches long. Maybe it wasn't Colleen at all, but Colin.

She crossed the hardwood floor and swung open the front door. Two men stood there, one in the uniform of the Floritas police. Her heartbeat sped up dramatically.

"Mrs. Chandler?" The man who spoke wore a tan sportcoat and had short thick brown hair. He was about six feet tall, no more than forty, and in good physical shape. Not a hint of paunch. He wore the kind of utilitarian wire-rimmed glasses that were supposed to give one an aura of authority. On this guy they were redundant.

Julie nodded, puzzled. Surely he could hear her heart pounding. "Yes."

"I'm Detective Woodward, from the Floritas police," he told her, holding up identification. She barely looked at it, clutched at the door frame to steady herself. What was going on? "Is your husband at home?"

"Adam's out in back," she answered carefully, liking this less and less. "Is something wrong?"

The detective ignored her question. "We'd like to speak to him, please. May we come in?"

"Yeah, sure." What did they want with Adam? What could he possibly have done?

"What *is* it?" she asked again, a definite edge of fear in her voice this time. There was something in their attitude and formality that frightened her, pushed all her paranoia buttons. She involuntarily pulled her bulky white cardigan closed, clasped her hands in front of her slightly swollen belly. In general, pregnancy seemed to have raised her body temperature a good five degrees. Now, however, she felt cold.

"We'd like to speak to Mr. Chandler," the detective repeated, stepping past her. He exuded a sense of man-talk-don't-worry-your-pretty-little-head that made her feel like slugging somebody, preferably him. Which was, she realized suddenly, the biggest surge of energy she'd felt in weeks. Being pregnant was exhausting.

As he moved into the room, Detective Woodward swept his eyes carefully back and forth, up and down, running some kind of internal camcorder. Julie was acutely aware of scattered magazines, dust-bunnies reproducing in corners, abstract artworks in dog slobber on the windows, animal hair everywhere. Two of the cats slept curled in a pool of sunlight on the floor.

"This way," she said abruptly, turning to lead them through the kitchen, past dirty dishes piled on the counter. She saw the phone receiver lying on the counter and remembered taking it off the hook before lying down. Absently she hung it up, then continued outside.

She blinked in the sudden bright light as Arlo raced over, growling lightly. He wasn't much of a watchdog, just a pound mutt, but he made an effort at appearances. The frantically wagging tail gave him away every time. "It's all right, boy," she told him, reaching down to scratch his ears.

But was it?

The greenhouse loomed on the left, dark-green shadows of plants vaguely visible through heavy plastic sheeting that covered the building's sturdy wooden frame. On the right, the Chandlers' large vegetable garden was filled with tidy rows and beds of winter brassicas and lettuces, trellises of sugar snap peas. Winter tomatoes in wire cages were beginning to blush faintly pink.

Adam was straight ahead, fifty yards into the nearest flower field, bent down harvesting gypsophila into white plastic buckets to take to the Flower Auction later in the day. He wore his customary faded jeans and a dark-gray sweatshirt, his long brown hair pulled back in a ponytail at the back of his neck. He looked up as Julie called, then loped toward her, frowning at the sight of her companions. Adam had his own paranoia buttons regarding police.

Julie listened numbly as the detective introduced himself and asked Adam where he had been the night before.

"Right here," he answered shortly. "Why?"

"Have you seen Shane Pettigrew recently?"

Adam shot Julie a guarded look, then turned back to the policeman. Julie felt her heart race. "Last week, I guess."

"When was that?"

"I don't remember."

"I saw him at the Auction," Julie said quietly. Stay calm, act normal. "Day before yesterday."

Adam glared at her, his message clearly to shut up. The cops exchanged glances and Julie felt her pulse surge again.

"Did Shane have an accident?" she heard herself asking, ignoring Adam's glare. Later. She'd deal with Adam later. "What's going on?" she asked, in what she tried to keep an even tone. In her mind she saw Shane's truck wrapped around a power pole, his body crumpled over the steering wheel.

The detective focused on her now, his eyes suddenly more intense. "What sort of accident?" he asked.

"Why, automobile," she answered, surprised. Shane was a notoriously bad driver. Everybody knew that. His cars always had crinkled fenders and his insurance rates were astronomical. But the cop's response was wrong. If Shane had cracked up on the highway, they'd just tell her, wouldn't they?

If Shane had cracked up on the highway, she realized suddenly, there'd be no reason in the world for any cops to come and tell the Chandler family. This was something else. And it wasn't good.

"No, he hasn't been in an automobile accident," the detective answered. "You say the last time you saw him was . . . when?"

"I took a load of flowers over to the Auction on Tuesday," Julie answered when it became clear that Adam wasn't saying anything. Just as well, probably. What was going *on?* "Shane was just leaving when I got there." Hurriedly, pretending not to see her. Shane could be a real coward sometimes.

"I see. Do you own a gun, Mr. Chandler?" the detective asked conversationally.

Adam's frown deepened. "Why?"

Julie moved closer to Adam, clutched his arm. Now she was really frightened.

"Is there some reason you don't want to answer that question?"

"Is there some reason you won't tell me why?" Adam shot back.

Adam was getting angry now. Julie could see a little vein

pulsating in his temple. She shivered and tightened her grip on his arm.

"Adam," she said gently.

"I want to know what's going on," he said irritably. "You're upsetting my wife."

"We don't mean to upset anyone," Detective Woodward replied blandly. "But I don't understand why you're unwilling to answer the question."

"Everybody around here has guns," Adam said evenly.

"Including yourself?"

Adam inhaled. "Look, I'm really busy right now. I have to get these flowers picked and over to the Auction, my wife is pregnant and not feeling well. You're playing some kind of game with us and I don't like it."

Detective Woodward's eyes darted back and forth from Adam to Julie, then settled on Adam.

"It's no game, Mr. Chandler," he answered finally. "Shane Pettigrew was shot to death last night."

Shane. Dead. Julie felt light-headed, dizzy. *Shot to death.* She stumbled the few steps to the glide rocker nearby, sat down.

"Are you all right, ma'am?" The detective's voice was downright solicitous. Belatedly, Adam moved to her side, put a hand on her shoulder.

"Easy does it, Julie," Adam told her softly, as his hand bit into her shoulder.

"I'm all right," she said quietly. "But what—" She looked up at the detective, wished she could see Adam's face.

"Mr. Chandler," the detective went on, as if there'd been no interruption, as if they were discussing the Padres or the Chargers. "Do you own a gun?"

Shane dead. How could it be?

Adam moved abruptly and sat down beside Julie. "What happened?" His voice was shaky. She could feel his body vibrating with tension and shock.

"That's what we're trying to find out." Detective Woodward's voice was surprisingly gentle. There was a pair of Adirondack chairs nearby. He pulled one over and sat facing them. Too close. "You can help us by cooperating."

Adam shook his head, as if to clear his mind. "A gun. You asked if I have a gun?"

The detective nodded. Beyond him, Julie noticed, the uniformed officer was wandering around the yard. Very casual, very informal, yet somehow it felt orchestrated. And threatening.

"My dad's old thirty-eight," Adam said. "We've had some problems with rats in the greenhouse. It's registered," he added defensively.

"Could we see it, please?"

Adam heaved an irritated sigh and stood up, turning toward the greenhouse. "It's in here," he said over his shoulder, walking through the enclosed end section, past the work tables where Julie trimmed flowers and assembled bouquets. Julie stayed seated, uncertain that her legs would work. She noticed the uniformed officer stop at Adam's bike hanging just inside the door, look at the tires.

Adam went to the far wall, to the cupboard where the .38 lived on the top shelf, behind an odd lot of ceramic pots.

It wasn't there.

Detective Woodward became suddenly and crisply formal. "I'm afraid you'll have to come with us, sir. You have the right to remain silent," he began, and Julie felt her world crumpling around her as she heard the familiar litany, the staple of a thousand TV cop shows. It had always seemed silly before.

Now it was terrifying. Adam stood with his eyes half closed. All color drained from his face and he swayed slightly.

"Call Ramón," Adam told her, when the warning finally ceased. "Tell him to get down to . . ." He turned to the cops. "Where are we going?"

"The Floritas police station," Detective Woodward answered. "Will you be all right, ma'am? Would you like us to call someone for you?"

Ma'am, indeed. It was laughable. Would they change their minds and leave Adam if she said no, she wouldn't be all right? Then, right around the moment that she thought she would scream or faint or maybe both, she felt her fear solidify into cold competence. The emergency reaction. Julie was always a real champ in an emergency.

"I'll be perfectly fine," she answered icily. "Thank you for your concern." She hoped it made them feel like the banana slugs they were. She stood up slowly, walked to Adam, and leaned up to kiss him quickly on the lips. His were cold. Adam wasn't good at all in emergencies. Adam panicked, forgot things, lost control.

"Don't worry, honey," she told him softly, soothingly. He was shaking now, and ashen. "Whatever nonsense this is, Ramón will take care of it. I'll call him right now."

She watched them go through the house, out the front door, get into the blue-and-white Floritas P.D. cruiser. Adam sat in the back, the two cops up front.

This couldn't be happening.

She sat at the kitchen counter, closed her eyes for a moment, and took a couple of deep breaths. Then she looked up Ramón Garza's office number in downtown Floritas and called him, fighting a momentary surge of her own panic. What if he was in court or something?

But he wasn't. And he didn't take her seriously at first.

"Come on, Julie," his rich voice came through the receiver. "Bad joke."

"It's no goddamned joke, Ramón! Shane's dead, somebody killed him and they think it was Adam. You've got to straighten it out. They've *arrested* Adam!"

"Shane? Shane dead?" Now Ramón's tone was full of wonderment, denial. Julie was suddenly aware that Ramón and Adam had both grown up with Shane, had known him since boyhood. Marrying Adam had been, in some ways, like joining an overaged Boy Scout troop. Adam, Shane, and Ramón had more shared history than many conventional siblings. "What happened? Why haven't I heard anything about it?"

Julie fought back anger. "They wouldn't tell us what happened, only that somebody shot him."

"He must have interrupted a burglar or something."

"Then why did they make a beeline here and ask to see Adam's gun?"

"They what?"

Julie repeated the statement, told him everything else the cops had said. She reminded herself that learning of Shane's murder had to be a horrific shock for Ramón, even as it had been for Adam.

Even as it had been for herself.

"Julie, this is crazy. I'll get right down there," he promised.

"Thanks, Ramón." She had never believed that stupid saying about a burden shared being a burden halved. Even so, she felt better now that Ramón knew. A teeny, tiny bit, almost too infinitesimal to measure.

Ramón was full of reassurance for a moment, then abruptly put her on hold. "Adam's on the other line."

When he returned he was brisk and businesslike. "I told Adam to keep his mouth shut till I get there. Julie, don't worry about it. But do one thing, and do it fast."

"What?"

"They're likely to come back with a search warrant. Think about whether there's anything at your place that you wouldn't want the police going through."

Julie hung up the phone and felt a surge of panic. That had to be a veiled reference to drugs, but she and Adam didn't have any, hadn't even smoked grass for years. But wait—The letter. What had Adam done with it?

She carefully locked all the doors, then went to the

bedroom. She dug through his drawers frantically, poked in the pockets of his jeans and jackets, tried to think of places he might have put it. It wasn't anywhere.

She sat on the edge of the bed and took several deep breaths. How could this be happening?

Shane Pettigrew was dead. Somebody had shot him.

The police believed it was Adam. That meant they knew. They *knew*.

She threw herself on the bed and sobbed.

CHAPTER 2

In the office of the California State Bar Trial Counsel, Nan Robinson was trying very hard to put herself into the mind of Bruce Lancaster. Not to figure out what he had done; that was appallingly clear. But to try to fathom *why*.

Here was a guy who had worked his way through college and law school, hung a shingle, and developed a successful small general suburban practice. He had a house, a family, and no extraordinary debts. There was no indication that he abused alcohol or drugs.

Yet he had risked it all in a penny-ante scam complicated enough to require both considerable forethought and accomplices in Hong Kong. On at least three separate occasions, he had filed claims for the loss in transit of expensive electronic equipment shipped to the United States. The sealed boxes had weighed in properly on shipment and arrived empty in California.

The first two times, insurance paid with only a cursory investigation. On the third occasion, however, an alert Long Beach Customs agent, recalling scuttlebutt from a buddy in San Francisco, investigated further.

The "electronic equipment," it turned out, had actually been dry ice, carefully packed in Hong Kong and dissipated into the atmosphere somewhere over the Pacific.

Nan felt confident that this wasn't a one-time lapse in judgment. People didn't toe the line for forty-seven years and then suddenly hatch a scheme of such sophistication. A thorough enough investigation would undoubtedly show that Bruce Lancaster had been pulling off low-level scams his entire life.

He'd be the upperclassman who sold locker passes to freshmen, the magazine salesman whose subscriptions never arrived, the joker who disappeared after collecting security deposits from a dozen different people for a vacant apartment which wasn't his to rent. He'd buy designer suits still bearing department store tags at ninety percent discounts out of seedy garages, ask no questions about the dirt-cheap stereo installed in his car.

He could, of course, have been worse. He wasn't defrauding old ladies of their retirement nest eggs, or selling bogus cures to cancer victims. His were technically victimless crimes. Still, while it was difficult for Nan to sympathize with insurance companies as victims—difficult, indeed, to even *think* of insurance companies rationally—she conjured up hideous punishments for such scammeisters every time she paid an inflated premium.

But it wasn't Nan's responsibility to track down Lancaster's seamy past, only to look into the current issues of criminal fraud that threatened his license to practice law. Her investigations as an attorney for the California State Bar weren't intended to be a substitute for standard legal remedies, either criminal or civil. Rather, they were designed to protect the public from lawyers of Lancaster's highly dubious integrity.

Then the phone rang. Julie.

Nan had been cruising on autopilot through the morning, but the phone call from her sister brought her to full alert.

The mere fact of the call was significant; Julie had never before phoned Nan at work. More to the point, she sounded mildly hysterical.

"What's wrong?" Nan asked in alarm.

"Adam's been arrested for murder!"

The notion was so outrageous that Nan would have laughed out loud if Julie hadn't so obviously been serious.

"Easy does it, Jules," Nan soothed. Adam? *Murder?* "Let's start at the beginning."

"God, I don't know where to start," Julie wailed. To hear Julie in this condition was alarming. Her sister was not the sort who fell to pieces.

"Just the facts, ma'am." Somebody had to stay calm.

That brought a faint chuckle. "But I don't know what the facts *are!*"

"Hey! Something's happened, right? Just tell me whatever you do know."

As Julie explained the morning's events, Nan flipped through her calendar, shuffling and rearranging her schedule. It was midmorning on Thursday and the rest of her week's obligations at the State Bar could be put off or taken over by someone else. She obviously would have to go down to Floritas, and the sooner the better.

Even if this were all the simplest misunderstanding, Nan knew that cops were far more likely to make mistakes than to admit or rectify them. Assuming that Adam had done no wrong—an assumption Nan was prepared to make, at least for the moment—it was important to get him released quickly. Every minute he was in custody, his position grew shakier. The longer you leave somebody in a cell, the guiltier he looks.

Besides, regardless of what Adam had or hadn't done, Julie obviously needed Nan right now.

After she hung up, Nan called Moira Callahan to cancel their literacy tutoring session and left a message on Tom Hannah's machine that she was going out of town and wouldn't be able to make dinner the next night. She got her responsibilities covered at the office and was on the Santa Monica Freeway heading west from downtown L.A. in less than twenty minutes.

Venice was cold when she pulled the '67 Mustang into

the alley behind her walk-street home. The early-morning fog had lifted but the marine layer still hung damp and chilly and murky around Nan's little house. There was a dank quality to a beach-town winter that manifested itself in mildew creeping along closet walls, windows swollen shut, telephone-wire corrosion that made even the closest crosstown connection sound like it was patched through Prudhoe Bay.

And the little black cat was sitting on the doorstep again, meowing pitifully.

Nan grimaced at the animal. It had showed up about two weeks earlier and seemed to be living under the house. Any time Nan made an appearance, the cat was waiting: imploring, thin, and pathetic. She kept hoping it would go away, get itself adopted by some neighbor. Its very presence made her feel guilty, though not yet guilty enough to let it in or give it food. Presumably it was foraging in the trash.

"I can't help you," she told the cat, brushing it aside to get in the house. The cat shivered and gave one last plaintive meow.

Inside, the house was nearly as cold as outdoors. She'd run the wall heater in the bathroom for half an hour this morning before leaving and then shut it off. Nan moved around purposefully, pulling a small suitcase from the back of the closet, neatly folding clothing into it. Julie's was a jeans-and-sweater kind of existence, but this sounded like Dealings with Authorities. The suit she was wearing would be fine in court, and she hurriedly chose another work outfit in case things dragged on. She tossed in the book from her bedside table, recalling that her last thought before drifting off the night before had been that the world's most hazardous occupation was being Travis McGee's girlfriend.

Nan set the lights on timers, left a message for her neighbor Shannon to keep an eye on the place, locked the house, and was quickly on the Marina Freeway, once briefly known as the Richard M. Nixon Freeway. That name had

later been dropped, probably when officials realized the
road wasn't long enough to be sufficiently crooked.

Traffic on the 405 heading south could never be described as light, but at least now, at midday, it was moving.
As a jumbo jet swooped across the freeway at LAX, Nan
realized with a start that it was exactly two weeks, almost
to the hour, since she'd last made this same trip to Floritas.
That had been a joyous, celebratory occasion, heading
down on Christmas Eve to be with family for the holiday.
The flower business was doing well and Julie's pregnancy
was vicariously thrilling.

What on earth had happened?

Adam Chandler was not one of Nan's favorite people,
though she loved her sister far too much to ever share her
reservations. And there'd never been real reason to, at least
till now. Still, whatever his flaws, Adam hardly seemed the
sort of man who would kill a lifelong friend.

Nan considered her relationship with Julie and Adam one
of the true constants in her life, an anchor. They had been
together nearly ten years, and for the most part theirs had
appeared to be a comfortable and happy relationship. They
had met up north, where Adam was working for a begonia
farmer and Julie drifting through a succession of low-level
jobs while she diffidently wondered what she would do
with her life. They'd been married in a grove of redwoods
in Santa Cruz. A couple years later they moved to San
Diego County, where Adam had grown up.

They were complementary, Adam and Julie, each filling
in the other's gaps. Where Adam was somewhat moody
and introspective, Julie beamed and bubbled. Where Julie
might flit from one project to another, Adam began something and followed it through. Where Adam was a loner,
awkward in groups and ill at ease with small talk, Julie was
effortlessly gregarious. The differences were strong and undeniable, but in a way they explained the long-term success

of the relationship. "We complete each other," Julie had said once. And in large measure it was true.

Nowhere was it truer than in their floriculture business. Adam was the farmer at one with his land, content to work the soil while Julie dealt with the public, took the flowers to market, went to Flower & Plant Association meetings.

They never had a lot of money—Julie had once listed their occupation as "dirtscrabble farmers" on a government form—and there was even less now that Adam's mother was in a nursing home with Alzheimer's. Adam grumbled about their financial woes, but Julie never seemed to mind being poor. She had become in adulthood a nester, a creative woman who refinished ratty old furniture into gleaming beauty, whipped up watermelon pickles and slipcovers with the same ease that Nan wrote memos. When times got tight, Julie took short-term jobs without complaint.

She and Adam had been saving for years, trying to get together enough to buy some land of their own. Doris Chandler's nursing home costs put the kibosh on that plan, at least for now. But for the past three years they'd been happily ensconced in a pleasant little house they leased complete with greenhouse and contiguous flower fields. The place had needed a lot of work when they moved in, but they worked together—replacing the leaky roof, shoring up the sagging greenhouse, painting and refinishing the interior as if it were their own place. Adam was a good carpenter and skilled all-around handyman.

What they didn't have, and had seriously quarreled over, was children. Adam had two teenage sons from a failed marriage, living with their remarried mother in Stockton. He had given himself a Father's Day vasectomy after the birth of his second child.

At first, Julie had confessed to Nan, she didn't think it really mattered. Like Nan, she felt great ambivalence about the idea of having and raising children. But as time went by, Julie had realized that it did matter to her. A lot. She badly wanted a child of her own. It had taken years to get Adam to agree to try to reverse the vasectomy. Finally, last summer he consented and Julie became pregnant with gratifying promptness.

God, what if Adam *had* killed Shane Pettigrew? It would make a hideous mess for Julie and the baby both.

Nan swung into the number one lane and passed a Mayflower moving van, trying to summarily dismiss the image of Adam as murderer. She was startled to discover that she couldn't.

The crime Julie had described seemed quite coldly premeditated, and Adam Chandler certainly knew how to nurse a grudge. His view of human nature was that everyone was out to get everyone else. With Adam it wasn't a question of his glass being half full or half empty; it was half *stolen,* and cracked to boot. People jerked other people around a lot in Adam's universe. Nan suspected that if he didn't do such essentially isolated work, his life would be considerably more complicated.

Even so, he didn't seem the sort of man who could slip out of his marital bed in the dead of night and go blow away one of his best friends. And Shane Pettigrew hadn't seemed the kind of man to provoke such calculated rage.

Nan had met Shane a few times over the years, and her memories of him were all pleasant. He was an attractive, charming fellow, an interesting conversationalist, a good listener. He had that aura of health and fitness that comes only from actually performing physical labor in the out-of-doors. He was divorced and, Nan suspected, a bit of a chaser.

She had seen him just this past Christmas, when she went with Julie and Adam to Angus Pettigrew's annual Boxing Day open house. Angus was Shane's father, one of the Grand Old Men of San Diego County floriculture, and his Boxing Day open house was his way of repaying all social obligations incurred through the course of a year.

Angus Pettigrew's house could accurately be described as

a spread, a vast, rambling place atop a hill overlooking his greenhouses and what remained of his flower fields. That night it had been filled with people of all ages, most of them strangers to Nan.

Shane was leaving with his sons, good-looking boys of perhaps eight and ten, when they arrived. Nan was pleasantly surprised when he later returned and sought her out on the lower deck where she sat by herself in a sea of massive potted poinsettias, sipping a fairly volatile eggnog.

"Boxing Day, round two," Shane told her with his endearing, crooked grin, explaining that he'd dropped the boys at his ex-wife's house. "Aren't you cold?" He dragged over a portable heater and sat down in the redwood chair beside Nan's own.

He was tired of holiday joviality, he claimed. "It used to be magic, watching the kids rush out and attack their stockings. But now . . ." His voice trailed off and Nan braced for one of those interminable divorced-father mea culpas, all self-flagellation and anguish over laundry lists of missed opportunities.

He surprised her then by changing the subject altogether, asking about Nan's work and showing what certainly seemed to be a genuine interest in her answers. They drank more eggnog and he disappeared inside, promising to find something solid to eat.

He returned with two nicely arranged plates of buffet food, trailed by Adam and Julie.

"They're trying to sneak away," Shane said. "I promised I'd see you home, if that's all right."

"It's just that I'm so tired," Julie explained apologetically. Adam, who'd come to the party with all the enthusiasm of a collie being dragged into a veterinary office, remained silent and put a protective arm around his wife's shoulders.

"If you're sure . . ." Nan told Shane, realizing that she'd be quite happy to spend more time with him.

"I wouldn't offer if I weren't," he answered, and there was a certain low undercurrent in his voice. Routine sensuality, she'd thought at the time, even while she felt flattered.

After Julie and Adam left, Shane began talking about the threat of offshore production to the American floral industry. "The worst is Colombia," he groused. "They've virtually wiped out the U.S. carnation business."

"Oh, come on," Nan answered. She was feeling the eggnog by then. It radiated warmly outward through her body, gave her fingers and toes a pleasant tingle in the cool, starry December night. "Colombia produces coca leaves and coffee and drug lords, in no particular order."

"And flowers," Shane added. "Lots of flowers. They export a billion carnations a year. That's with a B, and it's about three-quarters of the entire U.S. carnation market. And that's just carnations. One terminal at Miami International does nothing but process incoming flowers, half a dozen seven-forty-sevens a day full of them."

"How come I've never heard of this?" Nan asked skeptically.

Shane smiled, revealing a crooked eyetooth that kept him from looking too Southern-California perfect. With his slightly shaggy blond haircut, dark blue eyes, and light permanent tan, he could have easily passed for an aging surf bum. Which, actually, he was.

"Beats me," he said. "I'm not what you'd call a heavy reader, but I've been waiting for years for the media to pick up on it, some movie or cop show. It's such a natural. Great visuals. But it's never happened."

"Seven-forty-sevens full of nothing but flowers?" It seemed incredible.

"Yep. Of course every now and then something else turns up on board. There was a seven-forty-seven confiscated one time after they found cocaine in the carnations."

"But why do they grow flowers?" Nan asked. "It can't

be because there's not enough money going into the country."

"A suspicious person might say it was to launder drug money. A suspicious person might note that the industry is subsidized by cocaine, might even wonder if workers on coke get more done. Of course the labor is much, much cheaper. Somebody there might make in a week what he'd get in an hour here. And they have a lot of good microclimates."

He paused and shook his head. "Pettigrew Nurseries used to do maybe two-thirds of our greenhouse business in carnations. Then the Colombians started exporting flowers below cost. Look at it this way: If it costs you fourteen cents to raise a carnation in Floritas and Colombia can *sell* them at nine cents a stem, who do you think is going to get the business? Florists don't care where the product comes from and the consumer doesn't know. There's no U.S. loyalty in the flower business." His grin was wry. "I guess you could say the Colombian dumping was a blessing, that it made us diversify."

"Can't somebody do something about it? The dumping?"

Shane shrugged. "We've tried. We've got studies that show exact correlations between Colombian government subsidies and the Miami market price. But it's tough to prove, and tough to enforce."

Nan half expected a pass when they left, and felt a little twinge of disappointment when he drove her directly back to Julie's and kissed her cheek instead. She came away from the evening liking him a lot, looking forward to seeing him again on some future visit. That was twelve days ago.

And now he was dead.

She stopped for lunch at the In-N-Out Burger off the Avery Parkway exit. As she chomped into a gooey double cheeseburger, she felt vaguely guilty at taking this one last flesh fix before entering the vegetarian purity of the Chandler residence.

Nan often went days without eating red meat, or regular meals of any sort. But she was a child of the Corn Belt, raised on sirloin steaks so big they slopped off the side of her plate. And being denied brought out a fundamental carnivorous bent in her. Julie was really quite an excellent cook, but despite all the holidays Nan had spent with the Chandlers, she'd never quite adjusted to the notion of spinach lasagne for Christmas dinner. Her ambivalence could be neatly summed up by a newspaper food section headline she'd once seen: "Meatless Meal Meets Flavor Expectations."

Nan was still burping slightly forty minutes later when she drove up the curved road to Julie's house in Floritas, through an orchard of leafless fruit trees which would shortly burst into glorious blossom. The road was lined with big seafoam statice plants shooting up their vivid purple flowers.

She parked outside the house beside a late-model gold Cadillac. In the bright light of midday, the old frame house was definitely ready for the coat of paint Adam was planning to put on come summer. But the house was the last thing an arriving guest noticed. The flowers were simply too overwhelming.

Katsumi Nashimora, from whom the Chandlers leased the property, had returned from the European theater in 1945, collected his family from a Japanese internment camp in Poston, Arizona, and returned to San Diego, where he eventually managed to buy this property. In the fields behind the house he raised strawberries in winter and tomatoes in summer. He planted the orchard. He put huge beds of flowers in front of the house, designing the gardens so that there was something in bloom in every bed in every month. Down by the road, at a wooden stand, his family sold the bounty of their land.

Adam had grown up with Mr. Nashimora's children, who didn't follow him into the family business. When the elderly Nisei developed a degenerative bone disorder, he stubbornly continued to work his land, until he fell and broke a hip that never properly mended. After the wheelchair became a permanent part of his life, he conceded defeat and moved into an apartment in town.

The Nashimora legacy was everywhere now. Masses of cheerful flowers bloomed in the gigantic beds where another house might have featured a lawn. An enormous jade bush beside the driveway was covered with delicate pink blossoms and a pyracantha trained up one side of the porch was ablaze with thousands of scarlet berries. On the other side of the porch a hardenbergia dripped clusters of violet flowers off a trellis. Other trellises held vines which would provide their own bright and fragrant magic later in the year.

Julie had the door open before Nan reached it, and wordlessly dissolved into tears as Nan hugged her. Julie was several inches taller than Nan and, at thirty-four, two years younger. Today she seemed shrunken and aged. Nan held her sister, nodding hello over Julie's shoulder at the handsome, impeccably dressed man just inside the living-room door. She had met Ramón Garza a few times over the years, on the same kind of occasions where she'd met Shane Pettigrew.

When Julie finally broke away, Nan shook hands with Ramón and they all went into the living room. Ramón was about five nine, sinewy, and very intense. His skin was golden bronze, his glossy black hair thick with a slight wave, his penetrating eyes like obsidian. He was a lithe, energetic man, a fitness fanatic who'd once been a Navy SEAL. Ramón maintained a solo general practice in Floritas and had recently been listed by *San Diego* magazine as one of the county's most influential people.

He usually treated Nan with the wariness she had come

to expect from attorneys first meeting a State Bar investigator. It wasn't necessarily that any of them had done anything wrong, just that Nan was a reminder that they *could,* with disastrous results.

Today was no exception.

"I've been telling Julie about Adam's situation," Ramón began rather stiffly. "Of course, the police have made a ridiculous mistake, but, unfortunately, they have some rather compelling evidence."

"Such as?" Nan asked.

Ramón glanced at Julie, who huddled in a corner of the couch with her hands clasped around her knees. Her long straight hair, which normally gleamed and cascaded past her shoulders, looked matted and unkempt.

"Adam's gun was found a hundred yards from the office where Shane was shot, tossed into some oleanders. They haven't run ballistics on it yet, but it was recently fired and empty. Then there's a gum wrapper that was found outside the office door. For XyliFresh cinnamon-flavored."

Nan winced. Adam constantly chewed XyliFresh cinnamon, an import from Finland, of all places. He bought it by the carton from a health-food store in Leucadia.

"Fingerprints?"

Ramón nodded. "Adam's prints are on the gum wrapper."

"Damn! What about the gun?"

"I couldn't find out about prints on the gun, but I'll know in a day or two. I have some sources I can use."

"Have you talked to Adam?" Nan asked.

He nodded again, rather wearily. "I just came from the Vista jail. He'll be arraigned in the morning and until then, he's being held without bail. He says he doesn't know anything, that he was here all night."

"Do they have a time of death?"

"Somewhere between midnight and three A.M. Shane was

at Ernesto's over in Leucadia until eleven-thirty and he left alone. Said he had to work."

"Ernesto's?" Nan frowned. "Isn't that the drive-thru Mexican restaurant?"

Julie smiled faintly and shook her head. "That's Alberto's. Ernesto's is this funky little bar down at the beach, been there forever. Ernesto is actually this big surfer who used to be called Bad Ernie till he broke his pelvis and about eighty other bones in a motorcycle accident. He bought the bar with his insurance settlement when he had to give up surfing."

"And this was somewhere Shane used to hang out?"

Ramón nodded. "For many years. Before Ernie bought it, it was a dive that didn't check I.D.'s. We all went there as kids, Shane and Adam and me."

"Do you still go there?" Nan asked.

Ramón shook his head with a frown. "Not since I've been married."

"Okay," Nan said. "So Shane was at Ernesto's and he left at eleven-thirty. Was he drunk?"

"Ernie says no. Says he just had a couple of beers."

That meant nothing, Nan knew. Bartenders could be held liable if they served drunks who caused later trouble or accidents. And any patrol cop in the country would tell you that drivers so blotto they'd pissed their pants would claim only to have had two beers. Nobody ever told an arresting officer he'd had three fast martoonies or five single-malt Scotches.

"And he left alone?"

"That's what Ernie says. He was found about quarter to six this morning when his office manager got to the greenhouse."

"And Adam didn't go out at all between eleven-thirty and six A.M.?" Nan asked Julie.

She shook her head emphatically. "He was here that whole time. We both were."

"Asleep?" Nan asked. The Chandlers were early risers who generally turned in by ten.

"Yes," Julie answered, rather defiantly. "We both were. We got up about six and had breakfast."

"Do you remember waking up at all during the night?"

Julie shrugged. "I went to the bathroom a couple of times. Something about the way the baby's positioned right now, I have to go all the time. But my clock doesn't light up. I don't know what time it was, just that it was dark."

"Adam was there when you went to the bathroom?"

Julie nodded.

"And in bed when you woke up?"

Julie stared angrily at Nan. "Of course he was! Whose side are you on, anyway?"

"Hey, take it easy! I'm just trying to get some idea of what's happened." Nan's voice was gentle, but she could see the alibi as hopelessly flawed. From the carefully controlled expression on Ramón's face, she guessed that he agreed.

The phone rang and Ramón jumped to his feet. "I'll get that. Julie, I don't want you taking any calls or talking to any media people." He left the room and Nan could hear the low murmur of his voice on the phone in the kitchen.

"Have there been many calls?" Nan asked.

"I guess," Julie answered numbly.

"Have you said anything to the press?" Nan tried to keep the alarm from her voice.

Julie's guilty look gave her away. "Not really."

Nan groaned. "Jules, you can't say anything!"

"All I said was that it was a big mistake. Then I hung up."

Nan knew that a clever reporter could wrest an entire story out of even the simplest statement of denial. "We need to get you an answering machine right away. Or change your number. Maybe both."

"But Adam . . ."

"Adam hates machines. I know." Message machines were just one of the issues Adam was dictatorial and opinionated about. "Adam doesn't get a vote on this, Julie. He's in the pokey." When Julie winced, Nan was instantly contrite. "Oh, honey, I'm sorry."

Ramón had come quietly back into the room and was shifting his weight near the door, clearly anxious to leave. Nan turned to him. "Can we see Adam?"

"I could probably get you in if you really think it's necessary, Nan. But he told me very specifically not to let Julie come to the jail."

"I just couldn't . . ." Julie mumbled.

"And you don't have to," Nan told her firmly. "For that matter, since Ramón's obviously doing all he can, I don't guess it would serve any purpose for me to go, either."

"I really need to leave now," Ramón apologized. "I have a meeting with a client. I left the phone off the hook, Julie. If you need to have it on, Nan should answer. Call me, either of you, if there's anything else I can do. I'll check whether there's anything more I can do for Adam before the arraignment. Call me at home tonight and we'll set up tomorrow."

He bent down in front of Julie on one knee and took both her hands in his own. The gesture was warm, almost courtly. "Be strong, Julie. We'll take care of this."

"I don't know what to say, how to thank you," Julie told him.

"Adam's my friend, he's like a brother to me. I'll do everything within my power for him, you know that."

After Ramón left, Julie remained scrunched up on one end of the couch. One of the cats, a long-haired calico, jumped up behind her and sniffed tentatively. Guinivere, this one was named, and she was young and pretty, covered with random patches of butterscotch and black and cinnamon. She was also in the way. Nan waved a hand to shoo the cat away as she sat beside her sister, then stroked Julie's quivering arm.

"Julie, we'll work this all out. Everything will be all right."

Julie looked up, started to look at Nan, then shook her head and stared straight ahead. "I don't think so," she answered grimly.

"Oh, come on." Nan made her tone light, reassuring. "There's some circumstantial evidence, that's all. It seems like somebody set Adam up, and I have to admit that worries me. But let's look at this objectively, Jules. There's three things you look for in a murder—motive, opportunity, and means. The gun was obviously stolen out of the greenhouse. That greenhouse is never locked, is it?"

Julie shook her head.

"And you can just walk around the house to get to the greenhouse," Nan went on. "Or come in through the fields." One side of Mr. Nashimora's property was bordered by a greenhouse compound that raised seedlings, but the other was open flower fields, owned by a major grower. "Now, we know what kind of a watchdog Arlo is. He'd probably hold the gate open for a burglar. But anyway, that takes care of the means. On to opportunity. You told me yourself that Adam was here all night, so he didn't have the opportunity."

She was really getting into it, gaining confidence as she spoke. Yes, there was something very hinky going on here, but they'd deal with that later. "And what possible motive could there be? Adam and Shane have been good friends forever."

Julie sat there looking lost, vulnerable, heartbroken. If anything, she seemed in worse shape now than when Nan had arrived. Not much of an endorsement for Nan's function as Chief of Morale.

"There's a motive," Julie mumbled dully, after a moment's silence. "Only Adam wouldn't have . . . I'm *sure* he wouldn't." She swallowed.

Nan felt a queasiness in her stomach that had nothing to do with the double cheeseburger. "What?" she prompted after a moment.

"Oh, Nan, I don't know how to tell you."

Nan looked at her sister and said nothing, rubbed Julie's arm in a gentle, aimless rhythm. Guinivere jumped suddenly into Julie's lap and she buried her face in the cat's fur.

After a minute or two, Julie raised her head, eyes squinched shut in pain. "Last year I . . . I had an affair with Shane."

CHAPTER 3

Nan was stunned.

She felt as if she were whirling on a carnival midway ride, plastered to the wall by centrifugal force while the ground suddenly disappeared beneath her feet. Until this very moment, the idea of any infidelity in the Chandler marriage had seemed utterly impossible to her.

Nan's own marriage had ended with more of a whimper than a bang, and her track record in subsequent relationships was somewhat less than inspirational. She was now at a point where she had begun to accept that not everyone was meant to be paired, that there was a certain dignity to maintaining total control over one's life.

She still believed in happy endings and the possibility of lasting, meaningful relationships. She even believed in white picket fences, and lived behind one. But she'd bought the house herself and lived there alone.

Adam and Julie, however, represented another type of life together, one that Nan had always subconsciously believed she would live herself.

There were virtually no specific details of their life that Nan coveted. She didn't want to live out in the country and raise flowers. She didn't want to anguish from month to month whether she could pay the light bill. She didn't want a small herd of pets, a freezer full of homegrown veggies, original needlepoint pillows, or slipcovers crafted for secondhand chairs. She most certainly didn't want to drive a twelve-year-old pickup truck.

But—at least until now—she had always been profoundly envious of the fact that Adam and Julie coexisted so gracefully.

"Does Adam know?" Nan asked quietly after a moment or two.

Julie nodded grimly. "He found out last week."

Swell. "Did you tell him?"

Julie's eyes widened in horror. "Good God, no!"

"So who did?"

"I don't know. He ... He got a letter in the mail. Unsigned. I was out in the greenhouse making up bouquets and he came storming back, waving this piece of paper and yelling. I couldn't figure out what he was talking about and then it just hit me like a knife in the gut."

This was getting screwier and screwier. "Did you see the letter?"

Julie nodded. "Later. At first ... well, it got kind of complicated."

Undoubtedly. "What did the letter say?"

"It wasn't really a letter. Just one line typed on a plain sheet of paper."

Nan waited. And waited some more. "Saying?"

Julie squinched her eyes closed tight. " 'The baby is Shane's.' "

"Oh, no!" Adam was legendarily possessive.

"Oh, yes. I mean, yes that's what it said. But it's *not* Shane's baby, Nan. There's no question about that. It was all over with Shane for months before I got pregnant."

"But you told Adam anyway? About you and Shane?"

Julie seemed chagrined. "I suppose I could have just brazened it out. Maybe I *should* have. You know, laughed and made out like it was some kind of prank. But I was so stunned—I just spilled my guts, Nan. I told him everything. And it was really awful."

"Did he . . . get physically upset?"

"You mean, like did he beat me up? No. Adam's never hit me, Nan. He's punched out a wall or two, but he never laid a hand on me. It was Shane he was ready to throttle." She put her fingers over her mouth, hearing her words. "But he wouldn't *kill* him, Nan! I *know* he wouldn't."

Nan decided to leave that one alone for the moment. "What happened then?"

"He stormed out of here and went to find Shane. He didn't come back home till late, and he was real drunk. I don't know where he'd been. I was afraid to ask. He wouldn't talk to me for days. Not a word." Julie shook her head sadly, tears rolling down her cheeks. "Oh, Nan, what you must think of me!"

Nan looked at her sister, a competent easygoing woman reduced to sobbing semihysteria, and she inwardly cursed Adam Chandler. And Shane Pettigrew. And men in general.

"I think," Nan answered drily, "that you aren't exactly the first person I've ever known who had an extramarital affair." Julie looked startled. Nan smiled and forged on. "That I happen to fit that same description myself. That we could probably fill a good-sized hall with residents of Floritas who also fit that description." She considered a moment. "For that matter, we could probably fill a good-sized room with women who had affairs with Shane Pettigrew. If I'd stayed here any longer at Christmas, I might have been one of them."

"I wondered about that," Julie admitted. Her mouth almost smiled. "He's hard to say no to."

"But eventually you did?"

"Oh, yeah. I always knew it could never come to anything. It was never meant to be any kind of . . . I don't know, Nan. It was just one of those things that happened, and then once it did happen, it was easier the second time. You know."

Nan did indeed. "How long did it go on?"

"A couple of months last spring." Julie shook her head. "You have no idea how difficult it is for me to talk about this."

"Listen, everybody's done things they wouldn't want to have to talk about. Including me. Maybe especially me. Why don't we make some tea or something? Have you eaten anything today?"

"I had breakfast. But that feels like months ago."

Later, sitting at the kitchen table drinking Lemon Zinger and nibbling dispiritedly at a bran muffin, Julie resumed her story. She seemed less hesitant now, almost eager to have Nan understand.

"I was feeling kind of low and unappreciated," she explained. "It wasn't that there was anything dramatically *wrong* between me and Adam, other than the business about trying to get him to reverse the vasectomy, and that had been going on for a long time. You remember."

Nan nodded. Julie had first confided her longing for a child at least three years earlier.

"Anyway, we'd started growing some alstroemerias, or rather I had. Adam isn't very interested in them, but I think they're really neat flowers, and florists like them because they last practically forever. So it seemed to make economic sense to grow some. Shane had been doing a lot of work with alstros for years. He's done some really exciting stuff with hybridization."

Julie's face clouded and she took a sip of tea. "You know, it's so strange, Nan. There's this sense of shock and horror I have about Adam being arrested, but that seems real in a way that Shane being dead doesn't."

"You can only process one thing at a time."

Julie shook her head. "It isn't that. When somebody older dies, it may be unexpected, but there's a sense of inevitability to it. Like when Dad died, even though the circumstances were so ghastly. But Shane was so *young*. He was the kind of guy you'd expect to live forever. That was part of his attraction, I guess." She gazed out the window at the flower fields, but Nan knew her sister was seeing something else altogether.

"So you started seeing Shane about the—what kind of flowers was it?"

"Alstroemerias. You may not recognize the name, but I know you'd recognize the flowers. I've got a few of them, I'll show you later. Yeah. We were in his greenhouse one afternoon and he was talking about the hybrids and . . . something changed."

"He came on to you?"

Julie shook her head. "No, not really. You know how sometimes when you first meet somebody there's this instant sense of sexual tension? Well, I'd known Shane for years by then and never felt anything like that. I used to really disapprove when he was screwing around on Sara, before he got divorced. And since then, I'd tease him about his girlfriends. But it was just a brother-sister kind of teasing. And then all of a sudden there was this . . . like a change in barometric pressure. Zap! Everything was different. He felt it, too, I could tell. So I did the only thing I could think of to do."

She paused, then grinned for the first time since Nan's arrival. "I got the hell out of there. I left in such a hurry I just abandoned a bunch of stuff I was planning to take home."

Julie poured herself some more tea. "I dreamed about Shane that night, Nan. Erotic dreams. It was just like being fifteen again, having a wild passionate crush on somebody totally inappropriate. I didn't know what to do, but I figured if I ignored it, it would go away. The next day when I went to pick up the stuff I'd left behind, I was kind of brusque and businesslike. I never looked him in the eye, I just didn't dare. But I could tell he was just looking at me and knew exactly what was going through my mind. He walked me out to the truck and the next thing I knew we were at a motel up by Camp Pendleton."

She made a silly face of contrition, looking for all the world like an errant puppy caught beside the overturned trash.

Nan shrugged and laughed. "So? These things happen, Julie."

"But not to me!" Her indignation was so pure that Nan couldn't help laughing again. "No, really, Nan. I'd never done anything like that before, not since Adam and I first got together. I mean, sure, there were a lot of guys before Adam, but then I always felt as if I were looking for something. Once Adam came along, I was certain I'd found it. That was what shook me up so much when I found myself wanting somebody else."

Nan decided to cut to the chase. "Why did it end?"

"It was too complicated and too much trouble, and I felt too guilty."

That pretty well covered the map. "Did Shane feel guilty?"

"I don't think so. He didn't want Adam to find out, of course, and he and Adam still went on their weekend bike rides and stuff. Sometimes I'd go, too, and it was just like always. There was something kind of jarring in realizing how duplicitous we were. I know Shane really loved Adam. And he was still seeing other women, at least publicly. It was when I realized that made me jealous that I knew I had to end it."

"So who knew?"

Julie spread her hands, palms upward. "I don't *know*. I liked to think that nobody knew. I *assumed* nobody knew. We were always really careful where we went and who saw us. It wasn't like this was the only thing happening in either of our lives. Sometimes a week or more would go by when I wouldn't see him at all and then there'd be three days in a row. It all depended."

"Where did you go?"

"Usually to his place. He has . . . had a condo with a really private entrance." Julie's grin this time was wry. "No accident, I'm sure. A couple of times we went to a motel, but that usually seemed sort of . . . tawdry."

They both jumped at a loud knock on the front door. Nan opened the door just far enough to determine it was a fresh-scrubbed young man from the *Blade-Citizen* and to send him briskly on his way. When a *San Diego Union-Tribune* reporter came by half an hour later, Nan decided it was time for action.

"We're going out," she announced to Julie, who recoiled at the very notion. "We're getting chain locks for the doors and an answering machine."

"I don't want to leave," Julie protested. "What if somebody comes by?"

"That's the whole point, Jules, avoiding people who come by. But I guess you're right, that somebody ought to be at the house. Is there anyone you could ask to come over just for a little while? What about the whozits next door?" Nan nodded toward the side of the house where the neighboring greenhouses stood.

Julie shook her head. "Out of the question. They're very weird and *very* unfriendly." She considered a moment. "But Lisa's not far away. I'll try her."

Nan brought her things in and had changed into jeans and a heavy cotton sweater by the time Lisa Tudor arrived half an hour later. Lisa was a plump and breathless young woman with frizzy black hair, a baby in a carrier, and a bag of infant paraphernalia that could probably have gotten ten the Donner party through the winter.

"Julie, I feel so *awful* about this," she said, setting the baby carrier on the floor by the fireplace and tossing the bag onto the couch, where it narrowly missed a gray cat. He'd arrived as a kitten named Frisky, but had grown into an adult who might more properly be called Comatose.

Frisky/Comatose rose, stretched languidly, took one appalled look at the baby, and split. "Brad's on late tonight,"
Lisa went on, "so there's no rush getting back. Stay out as
long as you want."

"I don't want to go at all," Julie grumbled.

"But she is, and we'll be back soon," Nan said firmly,
pushing her sister out the door. "The phone's been off the
hook, Lisa, and there are probably people who've been trying to get through. Like reporters. Don't answer anything
unless we call. I'll give it three rings, hang up, and call
right back."

"Aye, aye, ma'am." Lisa saluted crookedly. Brad was career Navy.

"Was I really that bossy?" Nan asked as Julie settled in
the Mustang.

"You always are," Julie answered. "It's part of your
charm."

Nan stuck her tongue out, turned the car around, and
started down the drive. "She seems really nice. Where do
you know her from?"

Julie explained that Lisa had been a coworker a few seasons back in an Encinitas candle shop during the Christmas
holidays. Julie had held a lot of odd, temporary jobs over
the years as she and Adam leased flower fields and tried to
save money for a down payment on the land they might
never get to own. Many of those jobs were in local greenhouses, including Pettigrew Nurseries. She'd also been a
dog groomer, waitress, receptionist, and salesclerk in half a
dozen disparate shops. Once, briefly, she'd driven a chase
car for hot-air balloon rides. Everyone she ever worked for
wanted to hire her permanently.

Julie was too nervous about being recognized in public
to leave the car, so Nan dashed inside a discount department store and made the necessary purchases while her sister slouched in the front seat under a wide-brimmed canvas

garden hat. Then they found an Alberto's drive-thru, loaded up on Mexican takeout, and headed for the beach.

Nan parked facing the ocean at the scenic viewpoint on the bluffs north of Floritas. The shoreline was far below, and posted signs warned that the cliffs were unstable. The previous winter's rains had washed away big chunks of land. Pedestrian traffic was forbidden along the cliff edge, but a few foolhardy folks strolled cliffside anyway as Julie and Nan ate in the car.

The short winter day was already ending and a few wispy clouds drifted across the tangerine sunset. Nan was so accustomed to L.A. smog that the routine year-round splendor of North County sunsets invariably took her by surprise.

"What about Mom?" Nan asked, when she'd polished off her enchiladas. It was a subject she knew they'd both been consciously avoiding.

"What about her?" Julie wiped her hands on a napkin. Despite protestations of little appetite, she'd practically inhaled her tostada.

"We need to call."

"No we don't."

"She'll be really upset and hurt if we don't let her know."

"So?"

"What am I supposed to tell her when she calls me?"

"Nothing."

"And what about when she calls you? And gets the machine?"

"I'll tell her we've decided it's time to enter the twentieth century."

"And when she asks to talk to Adam?"

"She won't. She never does. You know as well as I do that she doesn't like him."

Nan was not prepared to argue that one, which happened to be true. "Julie, there's no way this thing is going to end without her finding out about it sooner or later. You *know* that."

"She doesn't read the San Diego papers." Julie sounded a little giddy. "This won't be big news in Spring Hill, Illinois. I vote for later rather than sooner."

"Like when?"

Julie grinned. "Well, maybe when she comes out to help with the baby. You know. 'Where's Adam, Julie?' 'Oh, he's up in San Quentin, Mom. But he'll be back in twenty years.' "

They both laughed then and Nan felt enormously relieved. If Julie was making slammer jokes, she was probably going to be all right. Black humor had gotten the Robinson sisters through a lot over the years.

But it wasn't funny at all when they called Spring Hill.

"I'm down at Julie's, Mom," Nan began brightly. "She's fine, but there's a bit of a problem." *Other than that, Mrs. Kennedy, how did you like the parade?*

Nan could practically feel June Robinson stiffening, and she could hear the sound of inhalation as her mother lit a cigarette. Two thousand miles away, Mom was unconsciously shifting into the everything-is-just-fine-and-there's-no-problem-thank-you-very-much mode she had perfected over three decades of marriage to an alcoholic.

The initial response, after Nan's brief, upbeat explanation, was predictable. "It's too late to fly out tonight," Mom said, "but I'll leave first thing in the morning."

"Gosh, Mom, no, there's no reason at all to do that." *Told you so,* Julie mouthed. Nan stuck out her tongue and carried on. "We've both talked about this and we agree that there's absolutely no need for you to come right now." Nan recapped what she considered her most persuasive arguments, then put on Julie.

Julie stressed just how self-sufficient she was feeling, that everything was going to be just dandy, *really,* that her own health was excellent and the baby was fine, that this was all just a silly, outrageous mistake, that they'd call every night with an update.

"She's going to come, I just know it," Julie announced flatly after hanging up. "She's marching down the basement stairs at this very moment to get her luggage. Four pieces minimum, plus the carry-on bags." June Robinson's idea of traveling light was no foot lockers.

"Nah," Nan answered, opening a second Carta Blanca. Her first had somehow disappeared during the call to her mother. "She'll stay put. You almost had *me* convinced there was nothing to worry about. So now. Is there anything we need to do around here?"

Julie's eyes widened. "Oh, Lord, everything! I haven't even looked in the greenhouse today, and we were supposed to pick for the Auction tomorrow, and Arlo must be starving . . ."

"Lisa fed all the animals, she told me. I think they were circling the baby like sharks. Why don't you just figure out what absolutely positively *can't* be put off and then we can either do it really fast or forget about it. After that, I have a special treat."

"What?" Julie asked suspiciously.

"Later."

Julie shook her head firmly. "Forget it. I'm not handling surprises very well today."

Nan smiled sweetly. "If you insist. I brought along *White Girls With the Blues*."

"You still *have* that!?!"

"I do indeed. Now. Chores?"

"Rock bottom minimum," Julie promised, shaking her head in wonder. "I can't *believe* you still have that."

So they retrieved the buckets of gypsophila Adam had been picking that morning, now wilted and unsalvageable. On their lightning run through the greenhouse, Nan followed instructions blindly. Her knowledge of horticulture was strictly academic; she knew the names of all sorts of

things, and couldn't grow any of them. Even allegedly in-
destructible houseplants, things with names like Cast Iron
Plant, croaked automatically under Nan's roof. She'd once
managed to kill a spider plant and all of its offspring.

When everything was finally finished, it was totally dark
and really cold. Nan layered on another sweater and made
hot chocolate while Julie built a fire in the fireplace.

Finally, with a flourish and a deep bow, Nan started the
tape.

CHAPTER 4

Linda Ronstadt belted out the opening lines of "When Will I Be Loved," as the sisters settled back in their chairs. Nan noted with satisfaction that Julie was actually smiling.

Julie had assembled *White Girls With the Blues* a dozen years earlier in Santa Cruz at the end of a romance with a talented manic-depressive sculptor. One of the ends, actually. It was a relationship that took longer to conclude than it had actually lasted.

On moving out of Franco's studio, Julie crashed with friends possessing an extensive record collection, and in an exercise she later acknowledged as pure masochism, systematically compiled a tape that combined several dozen classics of the hurt-woman genre. Joni Mitchell was heavily represented, along with Carly Simon, Joan Baez, Janis Ian, Maria Muldaur, and many others. It was a powerful collection, working clear through to Janis Joplin's plaintive wail on "A Woman Left Lonely."

Years later, when Nan was going through her divorce, Julie had sent her the tape. At first it didn't seem particularly relevant, since Nan was the one who wanted out of the marriage, but she was surprised to find how much it all hurt anyway. The music eased the mourning she had never expected. There was certainly no sisterhood more universal than that of women in pain because of men.

Now there was a soothing familiarity to the music, a continuity that reminded Nan—and hopefully Julie as well—that the sisters had weathered quite a lot of nasty turbulence over the years, and would undoubtedly make it through this squall as well.

"Okay," Nan said. "Let's see if we can't figure out what's going on here. We'll take it as a given that somebody killed Shane Pettigrew and went to a fair amount of trouble to frame Adam." Actually, Nan wasn't taking that as a given at all. But it wouldn't help Julie to know that her own sister had serious doubts. "Now, about the letter Adam got. When did it come?"

"Thursday," Julie answered grimly. "New Year's Eve."

Ouch. Nan thought back to her own New Year's Eve, a quiet dinner for half a dozen dateless women at Shannon's. She had gotten quietly blasted, then rolled across the sidewalk and fallen into bed, resolving that this would be the year she developed a bona fide personal life. It had seemed, at the time, a lonely and mildly sad way to ring in the New Year. She had even thought a few times of Adam and Julie, never dreaming their world was exploding.

"Do you still have it?" Nan asked hopefully.

Julie shook her head. "I never saw it again after he left that afternoon. And . . . I looked for it today. I couldn't find it."

"Then tell me everything you remember about it."

"It was on plain white paper," Julie began, wrinkling her brow. "Like it was a photocopy machine. The words were typed in a single line in the middle. *The baby is Shane's.* Properly punctuated, no typos. It looked like an old typewriter, not a printer. You know, the letters weren't perfectly aligned. It definitely wasn't laser printing. Nothing else on the page. It was folded in thirds and it came in a plain white business envelope with a typed address to Adam and no return address."

"Postage stamp? Metered? Correct address?"

"Down to the ZIP code. And it was stamped with one of those ordinary flag ones that come on a roll." Julie put her hands over her face and pulled them backward through her hair. "It seemed odd at the time and it seems even odder now. An anonymous letter? Puh-lease!" She picked up a passing cat, who obligingly draped its furry body across her lap. "But it by God got the job done."

"Have you and Adam talked about it since that first day?"

Julie shook her head. "Not really. It seemed to me the most important part was that he had to *know* the baby was his. The rest, well, time would help smooth it out. I thought he believed me about that, but sometimes it's tough to tell with Adam. He's kind of deep."

So's a septic tank, Nan thought in annoyance. Yes, Adam had been wronged, but he was hardly an innocent victim. If he hadn't been so moody and withdrawn, Nan felt fairly certain Julie would never have taken up with Shane.

"Let's set aside motive for the moment," Nan suggested, "and talk mechanics. Who might have gotten into your trash to get one of Adam's gum wrappers?"

"Anybody, I guess," Julie answered. "We leave it down by the road on Wednesday nights and it gets picked up early Thursday. But you know, Adam's always chewing that gum and he leaves a trail of wrappers wherever he goes. Somebody might have gotten one at the Flower Auction, maybe. I guess," she said slowly, "that's the most likely place. He wouldn't litter on a bike ride or anything. He'd stick it in a pocket and bring it home."

"Okay. The gun is trickier. Do you ever shoot it?"

"I have, but not for years. When we first moved down here, Adam took me to the shooting range a few times. He said if we were going to have a gun that I should know how to handle it. But I didn't like it very much, and after a while he let me quit."

"Okay, then. How often does Adam use it? Does he ever take it with him anywhere?"

"Only to the target range, but he doesn't do that very

often anymore. He just uses it for the rats that get into the greenhouse sometimes. There was one last summer got into a bag of *real* expensive sunflower seed and ate nearly ten pounds. Adam was just furious but he got the little sucker."

Nan was puzzled. "Surely there's some other way. . . ."

"Well, yes and no. You can't use any kind of poisons because they generally kill by causing internal hemorrhaging. So if one of the cats caught and ate a poisoned mouse or rat, it could kill the cat, too. Food chain and all that. And traps . . . I don't know. They're fine for mice, but awfully messy for bigger rodents."

"A gun's not messy? Seems to me if you hit a rat with a thirty-eight, you'd end up with a lump of hamburger. Or maybe just a red smear."

Julie permitted herself a ghost of a grin. "Well, yeah, but if Adam does the shooting, then he does the cleanup and disposal, too. I know, it sounds crazy. But that's just how he's always done it, the same way his father did. As a matter of fact, the gun belonged to his father."

"And who knew about it?"

"I don't know. Guys at the target range, I guess. Ramón could probably tell you better than I can. He and Adam still go over to this range in Escondido sometimes. Ramón has a carry permit because he's had some death threats."

"Really?" Death threats to lawyers driving Cadillacs weren't something Nan liked to think about much. Death threats to *any* lawyers.

"Uh huh. Most of his practice is fairly routine, but he's taken some pretty unpopular cases now and then, particularly the migrant stuff. A lot of people are *very* unhappy about the illegals in North County."

"When was the last time you remember seeing the thirty-eight?" Nan asked.

"Just before Thanksgiving," Julie said, after a moment. "I was in that cupboard looking for vases and pots to use for fall arrangements for a friend who was having a big family dinner. The gun was there then. I don't recall the last time I saw Adam with it, though."

"Let's assume for now that whoever took the gun did it when both of you were gone. How often does that happen?"

"Often enough, I guess. We'll go to the Auction, or on bike rides, though I haven't been doing that for a while because I feel sort of overbalanced on the bike. Parties once in a while. We go to the movies sometimes, even out to dinner." Julie's face darkened. "Not much anymore, with Doris in the nursing home."

"Okay, then," Nan said. "We've established that somebody who paid attention could get in here with both of you gone, and that the gun might have been missing for up to six weeks. Let's move on. Who might have reason to want Shane dead?"

"I can't imagine," Julie answered slowly. "I've been thinking about it all day, even when I was trying not to. And I just can't come up with any answer. Shane could be exasperating, but everybody liked him."

Except, presumably, the cuckold. Or cuckolds. Shane Pettigrew sounded like a man who left no wife unturned. "At least one person didn't," Nan reminded. "And maybe more. So. If there's nobody obvious, let's try a different approach. Pettigrew Nurseries is a big business. Is there some business rival who'd want to be rid of him?"

Julie shook her head. "Flower growers aren't like that, Nan. It's a major industry here, of course, the biggest one in Floritas. But it's a small community of growers, not at all cutthroat. Nice people. For the most part, everybody knows everybody and we all get along."

"Then what about somebody at Pettigrew Nurseries who felt slighted, or put upon, or angry?"

"Not that I know anything about. Margaret Whiting would be the one to ask about that. She's . . . I guess you could call her an office manager, but that really doesn't fit.

She's been there forever, used to work for Shane's dad, then stayed on when Angus retired."

"What will happen to the business now?"

"What do you mean?"

"Is it the kind of thing where with Shane gone, everything will fall apart?"

Julie laughed. "Heavens no! Sure, Pettigrew Nurseries was dependent on Shane, but it's not like it will crumble without him. It's been family-run all these years, and there's actually another family member working there now. Cassie's son, Jeff."

"Who's Cassie?"

"Shane's older sister. She lives up in L.A. Cassie's an artist, and I think she's pretty successful. Evidently she used to be a real hell-raiser. Angus disowned her ages ago and they don't speak. But when her son said he was interested in the family business, Shane put him right to work." Julie smiled. "Jeff's a really bright kid. It made a bit of a stir when he came, and it was a little awkward, too. It's his other grandparents who own this house."

Nan blinked. "The Nashimoras?"

"Yep. The oldest Nashimora boy and Cassie had a very brief early marriage. Quite the scandal, apparently. Angus doesn't hold much with mixing of the races. But Jeff decided he wanted to learn the flower biz, and he certainly has the right bloodlines for it. Academic credentials, too. He's got a business degree from USC."

"What does he do at Pettigrew Nurseries?"

Julie shrugged. "I really don't know."

"Any other Pettigrews lurking in the shrubbery?"

"Not that I know of. Certainly not in the business."

"Who *is* in the business?"

"Well, the laborers are mostly Mexican, and most of them have been around a long time. It's a pretty stable work force."

"What about management?"

"There's a couple of guys who work different angles. Ned Wannamaker handles all the shipping, Will Drake does marketing and sales. On the production side, there are a couple of guys who run the greenhouses and somebody else who oversees the field production. Pettigrew doesn't do very much field production anymore, though."

"So the show can go on?"

"Oh, sure. It'll be a bit of a mess for a while, but in the long run, the only thing that's likely to fall by the wayside will be Shane's hybridizing."

"Is there anybody who'd want to sabotage that?"

"What for? If somebody comes up with some exciting new species of something, the whole industry ultimately benefits. And it's not like it's particularly secretive. We're not talking atom bomb here, Nan. These are *flowers*. Like the alstroemerias. Shane isn't the only one who's hybridizing them." She smiled with an almost maternal pride. "Shane has done some really good work, though. He has one really nice-looking white alstro, virtually no freckling."

"Come again?"

Julie explained patiently. She had plenty of experience trying to horticulturally educate her sister, generally without notable success. "Alstroemerias usually have splotches on their petals. Freckles, so to speak. I personally find them kind of charming, but in terms of versatility for the floral industry, the freckling can work against it."

"Why?" Nan could feel herself tuning out, asking questions to be polite, not paying much attention to the answers. On the tape, Janis Ian's "Jesse" segued into Rosanne Cash's lament on "Seven Year Ache."

"Florists want dependable, versatile flowers. Special holidays have special demands, like red roses for Valentine's Day. But most of the time, when florists do their general buying, they need flowers that they can use in different ways, take the same things and arrange them differently and come up with something for a luncheon centerpiece or a new mother or a funeral arrangement. When you've got one flower that can do all three, you're ahead of the game, less likely to get stuck with flowers you can't use. Flowers are highly perishable, after all, which is another plus for alstros. They last a long time. But pure colors of anything are valuable, and a really good white is a plus for any variety."

"And you say Shane's developed a white alstroemeria?" Julie was too eager to get off the main topic. Nan wanted to stay focused.

Julie nodded. "Sort of. But it's got problems. The flowers are small and there aren't very many of them. Actually, I think he's had better luck with his yellow trials. A pure yellow alstro would be almost as valuable as a white."

"Are these things ready to market?"

"God, no! They're all still really experimental. When you hybridize, you can't depend on plants grown from seed to be true to the parents. No, there isn't any way to mass-propagate Shane's alstros right now short of tissue culture. That's really expensive and Pettigrew isn't set up to do it anyway. Shane was probably years away from having anything valuable in a commercial sense."

"So you can't think of anything business-related?"

Julie frowned. "Well, there *is* that Fairy Tale World business, but I don't see how that could have anything to do with this."

Nan brightened. "Isn't that the theme park you were talking about at Christmas? Does that have something to do with Shane?"

"Well, not directly," Julie answered. "Fairy Tale World started out in Georgia, I think, around Atlanta, and they've got another one in Dallas. It's a theme park aimed at families with little kids, and they're looking to expand into Southern California. Everything is still really tentative, but there's a contingent in Floritas—Chamber of Commerce types—who've been really gung ho about getting them to put it in Floritas. They want Angus Pettigrew to make some of his undeveloped land available for it."

"Is he going to?"

Julie shook her head. "Not a chance. Angus hates the idea. *Hates* it. He says there's too much development around here already and enough is enough. I think he kind of regrets having sold off as much of his property as he has already." She cocked her head thoughtfully. "Actually, Shane was the one who was pushing for it, but as far as I know, the property all belongs to Angus."

Nan frowned. "Surely there's other land available around here. That's one of the things that's so nice about this area, all the open spaces. Why does it matter if Angus says no?"

"I suppose it doesn't, really. It would just make it easier for the developers, and that would make it easier to sell the Fairy Tale World people on Floritas. Angus is the biggest single landowner in town, and the sale could be a clean and easy transaction. The rest of the areas that are big enough for what they have in mind have multiple owners. Like, say, if somebody wanted to put it where we are here. They'd have to get not just the big tracts, like Spencer Growers' flower fields, but also the smaller landowners, like Mr. Nashimora, and the Ellisons, who own the greenhouse next door. Plus others down the way."

"But didn't you tell me that your place here was being pushed for some kind of a mall?"

Julie nodded. "That, too, but not very hard, because I know Mr. Nashimora will never sell. There's always somebody slinking around trying to put together a deal, but as long as there are holdouts, it can't happen."

"Yeah. But let's back up here. You say that Shane wanted his father to sell to Fairy Tale World and Angus refused?"

"You make it sound like more of a confrontation than it's really been. At least more than I know of. Once Angus makes his mind up, that's that. He wrote the book on stubborn, Nan. He's even worse than you. And I don't think this was something Shane cared about enough to go to the mat for."

It did suggest possibilities, though. You had to start somewhere. "Okay, then. Is there anything else you can think of about Pettigrew Nurseries that might be relevant here?"

Julie shook her head glumly.

"All right," Nan went on. "If the business doesn't suggest any obvious answers, what about Shane's personal life?"

"Messy," Julie answered promptly. "Always messy."

"Women?"

"That's a big part of it. Shane was married to Sara when I first met him, but I think he always had a roving eye. I'm not sure when he started seeing other women, but I'd heard rumors. I'd mention it to Adam and he'd just laugh it off, but looking back, I'm sure he knew. The first time *I* knew for sure was when Shane's younger boy started school. Sara'd been staying home with the kids and suddenly had a lot of time on her hands. Shane had some girlfriend and Sara found out about it and raised holy hell."

"Publicly?"

"Oh, no. But I remember she came to Adam and me and she wanted to know did we know about it and why hadn't we told her and a lot of other shit."

"*Had* you known?"

Julie shook her head. "I told you I didn't. Adam said later that Shane had mentioned it, which kind of surprised me. I'm not sure what part surprised me more, that Shane had told Adam or that Adam hadn't told me."

"Boys can keep secrets, too."

Julie's smile was wry. "I guess so. You know, I'd forgotten about this, but Sara has this awful brother, who's been in and out of jail most of his life. Frank . . . what's his last name? Reid. He beat up Shane pretty badly around then. Broke his nose and a couple of ribs."

"Sounds like somebody with a grudge against Shane." Nan found the prospect cheering.

"Oh, I don't know. He's kind of a scumbucket, the kind of guy who beats people up for fun. You know, a day without an aggravated assault is a day without sunshine."

"But he's worth looking into."

"I guess." Julie sounded doubtful.

"So let's get back to Shane. Sara found out he'd been stepping out. After that there were other women?"

"After that there were other women. In droves. And maybe there had been all along, I really don't know. I do know that as long as the marriage was technically in force, he stayed pretty discreet. But once Sara threw him out, he was the Stud Prince of North County for a while."

The tape moved on to Maria Muldaur's version of "Any Old Time."

"How long ago was that?" Nan asked.

"Hmm. Maybe two or three years. Then he settled down a bit. Not really with one woman, just not so rampantly polygamous."

"His business didn't suffer because he was so busy tomcatting?"

"Not that I ever knew about. Like I told you, there are other people who handle most of the nitty-gritty at Pettigrew. And he always had time for his own stuff. He probably surfed two or three times a week, year round, for instance. Sometimes Adam'd go, too, but not as often, only when there was an Alaskan storm or something that made really great surf here. A lot of our work has to be done in the early morning when the surf's best."

"So who's Shane been seeing lately?"

Julie considered. "There was a banker he was dating last year, I don't know where he ran across her. She was nice in a kind of stuffy way. When he stopped seeing her I asked what happened and he told me she couldn't get used to the idea of a boyfriend who wore jeans to work and had dirt under his fingernails."

"What about since then?"

"I've heard some rumors about a new assistant he had, this girl fresh out of horticulture school up at Davis, Kimberly something. She's real bright and cute and earnest. I'd be astonished if he didn't have something going with her. Propinquity and all that."

"Anybody else?"

"Not that I know of. He didn't have a date at Boxing Day, you may recall."

Nan smiled. "Would he normally?"

Julie cocked her head and pursed her lips thoughtfully. "Now that I think about it, no. He may have regarded that as 'bringing somebody home' even though he hasn't lived with Angus for ages. I don't think he's brought anybody to Boxing Day since he split up with Sara. And of course he had his kids there earlier."

"He mentioned something at Christmas about a lawsuit against him, some automobile accident?" Nan had been trying to remember the details without much luck. People felt obligated to share their legal travails on meeting attorneys, in much the same way socializing physicians were always treated to symptom recitals. Often she paid only enough attention to appear polite; unfortunately, this had been one of those times.

Julie snorted. "*Some* automobile accident? Shane's life was an endless succession of automobile accidents. Usually nothing major, but he was in the assigned-risk pool and he mostly paid people off on his own."

"He could afford to do that?"

"He couldn't afford not to."

"And people didn't sue him for personal injury?" In Los Angeles County, Nan knew, one out of every two automobile collisions resulted in litigation.

"Nah. Just that one lady and she was genuinely hurt. Oh, I think somebody tried to squeeze some money out of him awhile back, but it was a real weak claim and it settled cheap."

"So what happened to the lady who really got hurt?"

Julie leaned back and yawned, stroking the cat in her lap. This was a different one, sleek and black, not unlike the cat who'd been hanging around Nan's house.

"Shane made a bad left turn," Julie said, stifling another yawn. "The woman broadsided him and went into the windshield."

Nan winced. "No seat belt?"

"No seat belt. She was hospitalized for a few days, had some broken bones, a concussion."

"And the case is still pending?"

"As far as I know. Listen, Nan, I really want to help. But I'm so tired I can hardly see straight."

"Then for heaven's sake go to bed," Nan told her sister. "I'll make up the couch in the office."

"Sheets are in the—"

Nan waved Julie silent. "I can find the sheets. Don't worry about me. Go to bed!"

Nan was wrestling with the hide-a-bed in the office when Julie reappeared a few minutes later in a red plaid flannel nightgown. Her face was scrubbed, her hair brushed. She looked like a page from the L.L. Bean catalog.

"I don't think I ever said thank you for coming," Julie said. "Nan, I really appreciate it."

"How could I not come? You're my sister."

"Adam has a sister, too," Julie pointed out, "and I think I can safely say we won't be seeing her." Adam's sister was married to a stockbroker in Portland and a subject of great irritation in the Chandler household. Her contributions to their mother's nursing home upkeep were invariably late, if they arrived at all. She hadn't set foot in Floritas for years.

"Are you going to call her?"

Julie shook her head. "Nope. And this is the first time I'm glad Doris Chandler has Alzheimer's. At least she doesn't need to know about it."

"We'll work everything out, Jules, don't worry," Nan reassured as she hugged her sister good night. She then closed the door and made a careful inspection of the room's nooks and crannies. More than once she had fallen asleep at Julie's house and wakened with some animal in her armpit.

Finally satisfied that she was alone, she stopped to look at two framed photo collages hanging on the wall, both assembled by Julie. One featured Julie and Adam, beginning up in Santa Cruz in a field of gaudy begonias and continuing through their wedding and move to Floritas. Julie often clowned and mugged for the camera, but Adam was more often than not serious in the shots, almost sullen. There were pictures of Adam's sons at different ages, lanky boys Nan had met only once, at the wedding. The other pictures were mostly homey: Adam on a ladder patching the greenhouse roof, Julie holding a bushel basket of ripe tomatoes, Julie with a litter of kittens.

The second collage mostly predated Julie and Adam's marriage. This one included shots of Adam as a boy, with and without his family. There were pictures of Shane and Ramón, too—teenagers in Shane's red convertible, young men camping in the mountains, beach shots with surfboards. Nan looked for a long time at a picture of the three friends sitting under a thatch-roofed table on some golden beach, probably in Baja. All were tanned and young and fit and smiling, dressed in T-shirts and cutoffs, holding beer bottles aloft. There was a Butch-and-the-Kid quality to the photograph.

How had they come from that carefree moment to this unfolding nightmare?

Shaking her head, Nan crawled into bed. As she wiggled on the uncomfortable mattress, she knew she'd be confused and disoriented when she awoke in the morning. She thought about Julie, who would wake up alone tomorrow in the bed she normally shared with Adam. Adam, who would wake up in the Vista Jail, facing arraignment for murder. And Shane Pettigrew, who wouldn't wake up at all.

CHAPTER 5

Nan and Julie met Ramón Garza for breakfast the next morning at a cheerful chain restaurant near the Vista courthouse. Ramón was glum.

"We've got some problems, Julie," he began. He was dressed nattily, pinstriped and power-tied, but he didn't have the air of calm authority Nan remembered. He seemed nervous, fidgety.

A bouncy young Latina waitress with an improbable long black braid resembling twisted rope came and took orders, brought coffee and a teapot for Julie. Nan watched Ramón, who grew increasingly antsy. He must have found out. When the waitress left, he took a deep breath and stared hard at Julie.

"Julie, I've learned that Margaret Whiting told the police you and Shane were . . . involved." He turned to Nan. "Mrs. Whiting is the office manager at Pettigrew Nurseries."

Julie said nothing, dropped an herbal teabag she'd brought along into the small steel teapot full of water. She wore a blue denim maternity jumper with a white turtleneck underneath. Her hair was pulled back at the nape of her neck in a simple silver barrette.

"Adam told me he confronted Shane last week at the nursery," he went on. "Apparently quite a few people heard."

"Look," Julie said quietly, "I really don't want to talk

58

about this. It wasn't anything important and it was over a long time ago."

Ramón looked as if he'd been chewing something truly nasty. "I'm sorry to have to bring it up," he told her, "but the D.A.'s office is pretty keyed up about this. It gives Adam a wonderful motive."

"Adam was angry, sure," Julie protested, "but he didn't kill Shane." She put a spoon into the teapot and irritably pushed around her teabag.

"We have to find a way to convince a jury of that, then."

"Why do you sound so doubtful?" Now Julie was really indignant, her eyes flashing angrily. "Adam was home in bed with me. And he's *not* a killer."

"Julie," Ramón began calmly. He had regained his gentle, impassive demeanor. "Adam is my friend. I want to do everything possible to help him, and you. But we have to look at this from the prosecutor's point of view. The husband is always the most logical suspect when his wife's boyfriend gets killed, even when there *hasn't* been a public confrontation."

Nan saw Julie's jaw clench.

"Shane was *not* my boyfriend," Julie snapped. "He and I had a brief physical relationship last year. He was never my *boyfriend*. We realized it was a mistake and we stopped it. No hard feelings, no broken hearts. That's all. Everything was over a long time ago. And I want to make it absolutely clear to you that this baby is Adam's."

"I never suggested . . ."

"You didn't have to."

"Julie, Julie." His voice was soft, almost crooning. "I'm sorry that this is happening, that we have to talk about it at all. I feel for you and Adam. But you need to know that this is going to come out at the arraignment this morning. I'd strongly suggest that you not be in the courtroom."

"I want to go," Julie announced.

"How long will the arraignment take?" Nan asked.

Ramón frowned. "I really don't think you people should go."

"There's nothing that could keep me out, short of a direct order from the judge," Nan told him. "As for Julie, that's her decision."

"I'm going," Julie said shortly.

"So," Nan resumed, "how long will this take?"

"Not very long, once Adam's case comes up. It all depends on how many cases are ahead of us, how many lawyers need priorities, that kind of thing. They run arraignments pretty efficiently here. Most of them are done via TV monitors with the accused and his attorney both in the jail. Public defenders generally do it that way. But I always bring my client out and into the courtroom. Now let me tell you what to expect, Julie. Or has Nan already gone over all this with you?"

"I couldn't have." Nan smiled wryly. "I don't know myself. I've never practiced criminal law."

Nor had she ever felt the slightest interest in doing so, though she refrained from telling Ramón. It fascinated Nan that the general public so glamorized criminal law. Probably a reflection of TV, dating back to *Perry Mason*. But real-life criminal law didn't have much to do with dramatic courtroom revelations. It was plea bargains and not getting paid and clients who were usually guilty.

Ramón Garza smiled back, and Nan was struck again by his classic good looks. "It's really quite simple," he began. "Now, Adam's been charged on what's known as a 'righteous one-eighty-seven.' That's a generic murder complaint and it leaves the degree open. There are four possible degrees of murder—first or second degree and voluntary or involuntary manslaughter. The D.A. likes to leave it open because that gives them more room to maneuver and bargain later."

As he went on, outlining the courtroom procedures, Nan thought ahead. Ramón was a nice guy and by all accounts his practice was successful. But he didn't specialize exclusively in criminal law, and that worried her. Sure, he was probably an okay lawyer if you'd been caught dealing a little coke or sticking up a 7-Eleven. But Nan wanted a really first-class criminal attorney for Adam. The kind of man or woman that you *could* base a TV show on. This was almost certain to be a capital murder case, and a juicy one at that. Adam needed every conceivable legal advantage.

Nan would have to make some phone calls, find out who was really good in San Diego criminal law circles, meet with possible counsel. Maybe Ramón could work out some kind of co-counsel arrangement.

She hoped he wouldn't have his feelings hurt.

When Adam Chandler entered the courtroom, he glanced around once, glowered for a single hurt moment at Julie, then turned his eyes away and never looked at the Robinson sisters again.

He looked awful. His hair drooped lank and stringy and there were dark circles under his eyes. His blue jail jumpsuit was too large and hung on him awkwardly. Which of course didn't help his appearance—or aura—a bit. Put the pope in a jailhouse jumpsuit and leave him to rot twenty-four hours in a holding cell and he'd look like a hardened felon, too, by the time he shuffled into court.

Nan squeezed Julie's hand and whispered not to worry, realizing how absurd the statement was. Julie's fingers were icy and her grip intense.

Adam's case was called early, and the actual proceedings went quickly. Bail was set at an outrageous $500,000. Half a million dollars.

Ramón had already pointed out a couple of reporters, one of whom Nan recognized from the Chandlers' front door the day before. "I need to talk to them," he warned the sisters, "but I don't want either of you with me." He had showed them a back exit earlier and they agreed to meet later at his office.

Nan hoped he knew what he was doing as she hustled Julie out into the gloomy gray January morning.

"There's no way I can raise that kind of money," Julie sniffled later, when they were all safely back in Ramón's office in Floritas.

The office was spacious, in a small stucco building with half a dozen miscellaneous professionals on either side: lawyers, accountants, a dentist. Each office had its own street entrance. Ramón's inner office featured French doors that could open in warmer weather onto a private patio area. The patio had some planters of purple geraniums and a small round table with four chairs, white-painted wrought iron. Thick evergreen hedging surrounded the patio, gapping occasionally to reveal a two-foot stucco fence and the parking lot behind.

Inside, everything was handsomely furnished, with glass-fronted oak bookcases and an imposing burgundy leather chair behind Ramón's massive oak desk. Very traditional, with a definite scent of prosperity. His diplomas were expensively framed and there seemed to be a lot of them. Clients who came in here would be reassured both by the opulence and by the fact that Ramón seemed so at ease in his surroundings. People don't particularly want to pay their lawyers a lot, Nan knew, but they want to believe that others have. And that the others considered the money well spent.

Ramón frowned now and leaned forward, elbows on the desk, as he listened to Julie.

"We don't own anything but the pickup truck," she went on, "and we've dipped into what little savings we have to pay for Doris Chandler's medical expenses. Never mind the bail, I don't even know how we can pay *you*, Ramón."

"I wouldn't take your money, Julie." He sounded formal and a bit huffy.

"Don't be silly. We'll pay you, I promise."

He focused on Julie, and smiled ingratiatingly. "When this is all over, you have Victoria and me for dinner."

"Oh, come on, Ramón."

"Julie, let's take care of what needs to be taken care of now and worry about my fee later." He smiled again. "All right?"

Julie hesitated. "All right. Ramón, how long is he going to have to stay there in jail? He looked so lost, so terrible. And I really *can't* think of any way to raise that bail. Half a million dollars? If it were for anything else, we could maybe go to Angus Pettigrew, but obviously . . ."

"We'll get the bail reduced," Nan said firmly. She stared at an expensive but tacky little brass-plated figure of blind-folded justice on the desk. Ramón's business cards rested in the scales. "It's a truly ridiculous amount."

"Undeniably," Ramón agreed. "And I'll certainly move for a reduction. What happened today was a reflection of the standing of the Pettigrew family. Angus Pettigrew has been a major force in North County for a long time."

"At least Angus wasn't there, in court," Julie said. "I couldn't have faced him in public. I'm not sure how I'm going to be able to face him at all." She sighed. "But I know I have to."

Ramón was reflective for a moment. "So do I." He grimaced. "I'm in a slightly awkward situation here."

A bit of an understatement, Nan thought. According to Julie, Angus Pettigrew had raised Ramón and put him through school. So that as an adult he could defend Shane's accused killer.

The situation was beyond awkward. It was untenable.

"First things first," Nan said. "We'll have to get Adam's bail reduced. Whatever it ends up being, we'll need ten

percent in cash?" Ramón nodded. "And the rest can be col-
lateral?"

He nodded again. "Property, stocks or bonds, that sort of
thing."

Which didn't help much. Julie probably had forty-three
bucks in the bank and Nan's equity in her house wouldn't
even cover the ten percent. Nan took a deep breath. There
was no easy way to broach this, but it had to be done.
"Ramón, we need to get a really top-notch criminal attorney to represent Adam. Who would you suggest?"

Ramón bristled predictably. His gaze was dark and impassive, a trifle defiant. "Adam wants *me* to represent him."

"I'm sure he does," Nan agreed, "but let's be reasonable
about this. You said yourself that you're in an awkward
situation, too close to everybody involved. Surgeons don't
operate on their own family members."

"This isn't the same," he argued, annoyed. "And I may
not be a big-name lawyer, but I have something some hot-
shot wouldn't. Loyalty to Adam. To Julie. And to Shane, to
see that he's avenged."

"I'm not sure vengeance is what we ought to be con-
centrating on," Nan responded evenly. "This is an ethical
question."

"Are you saying that the State Bar disapproves?" Ramón's voice held an edge now. He seemed genuinely angry.
But his anger was refreshing in a way. Most lawyers were
too afraid of a State Bar attorney's power to talk back.
Ramón's refusal to be cowed was commendable, even
touching.

"I'm saying that the sister-in-law of the defendant wants
to be certain he has every possible legal advantage, that's
all. And that perhaps Adam's interests would be best served
if he's represented by someone with no personal ties to the
victim *or* the defendant."

Ramón turned to Julie. "Julie, when I saw Adam yesterday, when I saw him this morning, he asked me to help

him, to take care of him, to use all my legal training and skills to find the truth and set him free." He was addressing the jury now, and he was good, really good. Nan could see that Julie—who had earlier agreed that another lawyer should be found—was wavering. "Do you trust me, Julie?"

"Of course," Julie answered without hesitation.

"Do you believe me to be a competent criminal attorney?"

"Yes."

"Julie, I want to help you, I want to help Adam. Let me. Give me the opportunity. You know how we grew up together, Adam and Shane and myself. We were like brothers. I don't want to let that brotherhood go now, to abandon Adam when he really needs me."

"Oh, Ramón," Julie said, starting to sniffle. "Of course I want you to defend Adam."

Nan knew it was over, that she'd lost this round decisively. In a way it was reassuring that Ramón could be so persuasive. But she wasn't going to let go easily.

Ramón seemed to sense that. "Julie, thank you. And I promise you this. Any time you feel I'm not doing the absolute best possible for Adam, you can fire me, no questions asked. Bring in any lawyer you want. Is that fair?"

Julie nodded.

"Good. Now. What you said before about seeing Angus. I think we both should go to him. He has to be in terrible pain."

The Latina who opened Angus Pettigrew's front door was barely five feet tall and whippet thin. It was hard for Nan to judge her age. Fifties, probably. Her face was swollen from crying and she wore a simple cotton dress in unrelieved black.

"Tía Guadalupe," Ramón greeted her, reaching down to hug the tiny woman.

The woman wrenched out of his grip and let loose an

explosive barrage of accusatory Spanish. Ramón answered her, speaking rapidly and, to Nan's extension-class-trained ear, incomprehensibly. The only word she was sure of was *Shane*.

"Could you excuse us for a moment?" Ramón asked Nan and Julie, leading the woman out of the room. The stream of rapid-fire Spanish continued, her voice rising and vituperative, his low and persuasive.

"C'mon," Julie said, turning out of the tiled entry hall into a large living room.

Picture windows looked out onto lushly landscaped grounds, a wide lawn surrounded by shrubs and flower beds. A large double red poinsettia bush was still in full flower. After all these years in Southern California, Nan still felt startled by the six-foot poinsettia bushes that sprang into blossom every winter.

Outside was more cheerful than inside, however. At the Boxing Day party, this room had been crowded with convivial, festive people. Hearty carols had played out of speakers mounted high on the walls and everything was very jolly.

Now, empty, the room had an oddly dated and abandoned look.

Everything was waxed and polished and in perfect order. The sisters left footprints in the fluffily vacuumed plush carpet as they crossed to chairs beside the fireplace. The furniture had probably been the last word from Scandinavia when it was purchased a quarter-century earlier. Now it was just awkward and angular. Nan was not surprised to find her chair uncomfortable.

"Did he call her 'Aunt'?" Nan asked.

Julie nodded. "I don't think she's a blood relation, but she's worked for Angus since Ramón first came here. They're very close. His own family was killed in an accident when he was young, something gone wrong with a heater in the migrant housing."

"An explosion?"

Julie shook her head. "A gas leak, I think."

Before Nan could ask for further details, Ramón returned alone. He seemed troubled.

"Guadalupe says Angus has been holed up in his workshop. He's sent away everybody who's come to see him and offer condolences. She says he doesn't seem to be doing anything but brooding. She doesn't want us to go out there, but I told her we really have to. He's locked in, but she gave me the key. Come on."

Julie was pale and seemed unsteady on her feet as they walked through the house and out through a large and immaculate kitchen—*Better Homes and Gardens*, from the same general era as the living room. Ramón led them down a curved path lined with massive oleanders and stopped outside a large windowless metal building. It had the look of something put up hurriedly by government in wartime.

Ramón hesitated for a moment outside the door, then turned a key in the lock. He walked cautiously inside, followed closely by Nan and Julie.

Nan's first reaction was that the room was stiflingly hot. She blinked in wonder as she looked around. Huge, oddly shaped pieces of metal sat on various workbenches and the place was pervaded with a sense of permanent disarray. Charts, some tattered and yellow, hung on the walls. In the center of the floor stood what looked like a small rocket ship.

What *was*, in fact, a small rocket ship. For twenty years now, according to Julie, Angus Pettigrew had been diligently applying himself to a project that—in light of NASA's budget, resources, and accomplishments—seemed quixotic at best.

Angus Pettigrew sat at a long work table. He turned at the sound of their arrival and his face darkened in rage, turned almost burgundy.

"*OUT!!!*" he roared. "Traitors! Out of here, all of you!"

Presumably Nan was included by virtue of companionship, since her Boxing Day meeting with Angus Pettigrew had been so cursory she was certain he wouldn't remember her.

"Uncle Angus," Ramón began. "We had to come to—"

"How did you get in here? That damned Lupe—I'll wring out her brown hide. You're trespassing. *Leave.*"

The back of Ramón's neck flushed briefly. "We need to talk to you," he continued, in the same persuasive tone that had worked so well on Julie in his office. It wasn't having much effect here.

"Whatever you think you may have to say to me," Angus thundered, "I don't want to hear it. You are trespassing, all of you. Leave immediately before I have you arrested."

Beside Nan, Julie began to sway. "Dizzy," she murmured, as her knees buckled slightly.

Nan grabbed her. "Ramón! Help me!" The two of them ignored Angus as they helped Julie to a utilitarian daybed on the side wall. Julie let herself be led, let herself be laid down on the brown corduroy cover. She never lost consciousness, though for a moment or two, Nan was sure she was on her way out.

Angus Pettigrew rose to his full six feet four and glared. "Is there some purpose to this charade?" he snarled.

Nan whirled to face the old man, furious herself now. "It's no charade, you fool. This woman is almost six months pregnant and she's under an incredible strain right now. Her husband is in jail for a crime he didn't commit and she felt obligated to see you and set matters straight. I can't imagine why she wanted to bother, if this is the way you treat her."

Angus Pettigrew had a full head of white hair and big bushy eyebrows to match. He raised them both now. "And just who the hell are you?"

Nan realized through her rage that Julie's color was better, that her sister was actually trying to sit up. She could also see that Ramón was horrified by Nan's outburst. The old man seemed taken aback. Apparently people didn't normally cross Angus Pettigrew.

Well, tough.

Ramón stepped forward, between Angus and the sisters, extended one outspread palm toward each of the adversarial parties. "Please," he said, "please. Let's all be calm here. Julie, are you all right? Do you need a doctor? An ambulance?"

Julie turned sideways and propped herself on an elbow. "No, please no, Ramón. I'm fine, honest. I didn't mean to be so dramatic." She really did look much better.

"Uncle Angus," Ramón said, "this is Nan Robinson. She's Julie's sister and a very important attorney with the State Bar."

Nan found the introduction irritating, not to mention inaccurate. But Angus Pettigrew stopped fulminating and began to listen, so she let it pass. The old man sat back down at the table and nodded almost imperceptibly to Nan, who decided this was not the appropriate time for a firm handshake and a pleased-to-meet-you.

"Nan is right," Ramón went on. "It *was* Julie's idea to come here today. I knew I should, too, but I was afraid to, afraid of what you must be thinking."

"I think," Angus said firmly, "that I raised you as a son and now you've cast your lot with my blood son's murderer."

"Adam didn't kill Shane." Julie's voice from the daybed was firm and clear. She seemed to be making a remarkable recovery. For one fleeting moment Nan wondered if the faint had actually *been* a charade, Julie's way of dealing with someone she knew quite well. She dismissed the thought immediately. Nobody could fake the total loss of color that had preceded the near-collapse.

"Then who did?" Angus Pettigrew asked.

Who indeed?

* * *

When Nan and Julie arrived back at the Chandlers' house, Julie noticed immediately that the bushes were mussed up, some of the flowers broken off in the beds beside the house.

"Oh, no!" Julie wailed. "What *happened?*"

"At a guess," Nan answered, "the police came out with a search warrant. I hope Lisa did everything the way Ramón told her."

Julie was starting to look weak again and her eyes filled with tears. "I hate the idea of somebody pawing through my things."

"Believe me, it's better that you didn't have to watch it happen," Nan assured her as they approached the door. The assurance sounded false. Nan herself would be livid at the idea of a search of her own home in her absence.

As she raised her hand to offer the code knock, the door swung open. An attractive sixty-two-year-old woman wearing a stylish Italian sweater and black wool slacks smiled graciously at them. Her brown hair was short and styled in wings that swept down either side of her carefully Cliniqued face. A cigarette dangled from her right hand.

Julie looked at Nan.

Nan looked at Julie.

They spoke together.

"Hi, Mom."

CHAPTER 6

Nan had never seen a church so crammed with flowers.

Massive arrangements featuring mums the size of canta-loupes filled the outer lobby. Giant wreaths marched along the outside aisles of the nave, no doubt a fire hazard. The altar and pulpit were engulfed by a sea of gargantuan vases full of large blooms, many of them quite exotic. Behind the altar, a large stained-glass Jesus gazed down, bemused. Someone unaware of Shane Pettigrew's connection to the floral industry might easily have assumed the demise of a major mafia don.

Nan and June Robinson sat midway up the left aisle with Ramón Garza and his wife, Victoria. Nan had gotten over her irritation that her mother—who had never known Shane or any other of the legitimate mourners—had insisted on tagging along. She was prepared to fight until Julie pulled her into the hall of the rapidly shrinking Chandler house and hissed that if Nan didn't get Mom out from underfoot there was likely to be another murder.

It had always been understood that Julie would stay home.

Under other circumstances, Ramón would undoubtedly have been considered family and seated up front. In his cur-rent uneasy position bridging the Chandler and Pettigrew camps, however, he chose discretion and distance. His black suit was superbly tailored, his manner grave. He had agreed to attend with the Robinson women only because of

71

Nan's insistence that she needed him to identify Shane
Pettigrew's friends and coworkers.

Ramón's wife, Victoria, was a knockout, the kind of Latino beauty featured on posters promoting travel to
Andalusia. Her shoulder-length hair gleamed ebony and
curled under in a sleek pageboy. Her enormous eyes were
a rich chocolate brown, and her soft, sensuous mouth was
carmine, an exact match for perfect long fingernails and the
scarf she wore at the neck of a simple black sheath. But the
tranquility of Victoria's posture was belied by her hands.
Her long, lovely fingers twisted and twined continually in
her lap, fidgeted with her purse, picked at imaginary lint
on her skirt.

Nan watched carefully as mourners filed into the hushed
church, not entirely certain what or whom she expected to
see. She assumed that there were police present somewhere,
though she couldn't spot them. Nan vividly recalled the de-
tectives at Debra LaRoche's memorial service. That had
been a significantly more subdued affair, a quiet gathering
of friends who shared their memories of Debra in a bucolic
outdoor setting.

The cops hadn't learned anything at that funeral and Nan
was relatively certain they'd learn nothing here. Maybe
they hadn't bothered to come at all. Nothing had been
heard from the Floritas police since they'd searched the
Chandler house and removed Adam's bicycle. There was
no indication that any investigation was continuing, that
any other suspects were under consideration.

Ramón provided a quiet running I.D. as the mourners
filed into the church before the service. The large group of
Latinos seated together at the rear across the aisle were, he
believed, mostly employees of Pettigrew Nurseries. He recognized about half of the other mourners as being from the
floriculture industry, mostly flower growers and their families. There were a lot of folks he couldn't identify, many of

whom were probably thrill seekers with no connection whatsoever to Shane Pettigrew.

The first row on the right was empty and cordoned off. The two rows behind held top employees of Pettigrew Nurseries.

Ned Wannamaker, head of shipping, was a wizened fellow in his late fifties, mildly stoop-shouldered, with aviator glasses and thinning gray hair combed carefully across his bald spot. He wore an ill-fitting brown sportcoat and a large turquoise-and-silver bolo instead of a tie. He had, Ramón said, been with the company for decades.

Marketing manager Will Drake was newer to the operation. Around forty-five, he had a lot of coarse sandy hair and a salesman's reflexive pearly grin. He'd probably been barrel-chested at one time, but his center of gravity was heading south. He gave off an aura of robust cheer, and Nan was quite certain he had a dozen funeral jokes at his fingertips, simply as a matter of habit.

Far more intriguing was Margaret Whiting. She was trim and sixtyish, with an air of quiet, ladylike competence. Her light-brown hair was styled short and simple, her glasses were becoming but unremarkable, and she wore a black wool suit with a crisp white lace blouse.

Ramón maintained that Margaret Whiting had been secretly in love with Angus Pettigrew for years, and the assertion was entirely plausible. Even ravaged by time and sorrow, he was a handsome man with great presence. It seemed to Nan, however, that Ramón's assertion missed the point.

Margaret was the kind of woman who ran small businesses—usually with insufficient recognition—all over America.

Such women handled personnel problems, kept inventory, knew where to find everything, and possessed elephantine memories for obscure business details their male bosses had long since forgotten. They came to work early

and stayed late. They were intensely loyal and could recall
with great clarity the days when the boss was young and
hungry and the entire operation ran out of a single room.
Because they managed the payroll, they were likely to have
forced confrontations at some point—often around the time
the company computerized—about the inequity of their
own pay scales. The ones with truly smart bosses saw their
salaries appropriately adjusted.

There was a stir among the congregation as Shane
Pettigrew's immediate family entered from the right of the
pulpit and took seats in the first row. Angus Pettigrew
loomed large on the aisle, his florid face a sharp contrast to
the thick shock of white hair. This was the second time the
widowed Angus had buried a child. Julie had told Nan
about his daughter Amelia, missing for a decade before her
body was discovered. Angus looked terrible, lost and be-
fuddled.

Beside Angus sat Shane's young sons, uncomfortable in
suits and ties. Both were blond and blue-eyed, strongly resembling their father. The younger one's face was red and
swollen and the other was trying so hard to be nonchalant
that it broke Nan's heart.

Their mother sat on their other side, impassive in a royal-
blue dress patterned with abstract white irises. Her brown
hair was twisted into a French knot and secured with a
fancy white hair ornament that might have passed for a hat.
Sara Pettigrew's stony composure was in sharp counter-
point to the effusive sorrow of Angus Pettigrew's housekeeper, Guadalupe Morales. Lupe, at the end of the family
row, was swathed in black and sobbed ceaselessly.

Between Sara and Lupe sat a solemn Eurasian boy of
perhaps twenty, dressed in a dark suit and ignoring everyone. This, Ramón whispered, was Jeff Nashimora, son of
Angus Pettigrew's prodigal daughter Cassie.

The burial would be private and the body wasn't in the
church—might not, Nan realized, even have been released

yet by the medical examiner's office. Just as well, actually, since there didn't seem to be room for it, what with all the flowers.

As the minister entered and moved to take his place at the pulpit, there was an unrelated stir throughout the congregation. Nan watched a striking blonde stride confidently up the center aisle, past the Pettigrew employees and the family pew. She was tall and tan and her thick hair fell straight just past her shoulders. She wore a long, loose black blouse belted over black leggings.

"Cassie," hissed Ramón. "I had no idea she'd be here." He sounded stunned.

A brother's funeral seemed like a command performance to Nan, but the Pettigrew clan apparently operated in some parallel universe. Nan watched Cassie Pettigrew pass her father without so much as a nod and come to a stop directly in front of Sara and her sons. She leaned down and spoke softly to all of them. Jeff Nashimora, seemingly unsurprised, had risen on her arrival and kissed his mother graciously before sitting again.

But it was Lupe whom Cassie embraced as she came around the end of the pew and entered from the side aisle, and Lupe she kept an arm around as she seated herself.

Only then did the minister begin.

The service was short and simple, making no reference to the circumstances of Shane's death, only to the fact that he had been snatched from life in his prime. There was a lot of sniffing, some of which could probably be attributed to a pollen level that the Air Quality Management District would regard as catastrophic.

Everything was moving along smoothly when Nan saw Angus Pettigrew clutch at his left arm and grimace. She had a good angle on his ruddy face and could tell that he was startled. His hand moved to his left shoulder and a spasm of pain crossed his face.

Then he pitched sideways into the aisle.

* * *

Guadalupe screamed and the church erupted.

The next few minutes were chaotic. The congregation roared as the minister made futile pleas for people to remain calm and seated. He cued the organist, but any soothing music was drowned out by the pandemonium. Murmurs and rumors swirled and babbled through the congregation. Hoarse whispers of "murder" and "poison" were met by others saying "heart attack" and "stroke."

As Victoria Garza crossed herself, Ramón leaped up and ran down the side aisle toward the front of the church. He moved fast, but by the time he neared Angus, there was already an impenetrable crowd of people surrounding the stricken man.

"Please let Dr. Merrill through," the minister pleaded. A silver-haired man in a beautifully tailored navy chalk-striped suit tried to push his way up the center aisle. He was clearly unaccustomed to rude physical contact. "Let the doctor through."

By the time the doctor beat a path to his patient, police officers had materialized from among the congregation, waving their shields and pushing people rather roughly out of the way as they hurried up the aisle and raced to block the exits. The cops ordered gawkers back into their pews and the crowd slowly and reluctantly retreated.

Except for Ramón. He stood behind Angus and the kneeling doctor, holding Guadalupe in his arms as she moved into full-blown hysteria. Cassie and Sara and their sons remained in the pew.

A distant siren grew louder and then paramedics came rushing up the aisle with a gurney. More sirens were followed by the appearance of several uniformed police officers who stationed themselves at the doors.

When Angus Pettigrew was rolled down the center aisle to the waiting ambulance five minutes later, Nan felt quite certain she would never attend a more dramatic funeral.

* * *

"I'm going to take Tía Lupe to the hospital," Ramón told them outside the church. "Nan, could you possibly give Victoria a ride home?"

After forty-five minutes, the police had finished preliminary questioning of just about everybody who had been in the church. From the speed with which they processed the mourners, Nan assumed that nobody had noticed anyone lurking in the floral arrangements with blowdarts and curare. Her own examination had been extremely perfunctory: name, address, the observation of Angus clutching his arm before falling.

There was, Ramón had told them with a wry half-smile, some problem, because a number of the greenhouse workers had bolted at the first sign of trouble. But the police recognized that this probably had more to do with insufficient INS documentation than any likely guilt. This was, after all, Floritas.

"Of course," Nan answered. "I'll be happy to give her a lift. Just promise you'll call as soon as you hear anything definite."

"They probably won't let us anywhere near him," Ramón said. "But I promised Lupe . . ."

"Promises, promises," came a husky voice off to Nan's right. Shane's sister Cassie swept Ramón into a major embrace before turning to give Victoria a polite air kiss that neither woman seemed too keen on. She wore a musky designer perfume and quite a lot of gold jewelry—bracelets, cascading earrings, a breastplate-styled necklace reminiscent of ancient Egypt. No tears had damaged her heavy eye makeup. Up close it was obvious that this woman put hours every day into exercise. She was all lean muscle, with terrific legs showcased in the tight leggings. She wore very high heels and towered over everyone, particularly Lupe and Victoria, who were each maybe five feet tall.

"Cassie, this is Nan Robinson, Adam's sister-in-law,"

Ramón introduced carefully. He sounded a little strained. "And her mother, June Robinson. Nan, June, I'd like you to meet Cassandra Waterford."

"Not Waterford," she announced, putting an arm around Guadalupe again. Lupe looked withered and dazed next to this vibrant Valkyrie. "I got sick of all those last names my ex-husbands kept saddling me with and went back to Pettigrew. Actually I'm thinking of going to court to be just Cassandra. Would that be hard to do, Ramón?"

"Not in L.A.," he answered. "Cassie, Lupe, and I are on the way to the hospital. Do you want to come with us?"

"You must be joking," Cassie said with a gravelly laugh. She had one of those film noir bourbon and cigarette voices. "That'd be likely to take the old bastard out for good." She smiled down at Lupe. "I know you're worried, Lupe, but Angus has the constitution of an ox. He'll bury us all."

Guadalupe's only response was a muffled grunt as she crossed herself for the hundredth time. Now a tall blond man with bright blue eyes walked up, offering a hand to Ramón. He wore a light-gray suit and flashed a lot of white teeth.

"Terrible, terrible things happening," the man said, with a shake of his head. He was somewhere in his forties, fit and tanned pretty well considering that it was midwinter. "I'm just stunned by what happened to Shane. And now this . . ."

"We're all stunned," Ramón told him, inching toward his car. "Were you in the church?"

The man nodded. "I came in late, just in time for the excitement. Poor Angus. I sure hope he's all right." He turned to Victoria, leaned down, and gave her a brief hug. Then he turned to Cassie, extending his hand again. "I'm Pete Hobbs. I don't believe we've met."

Cassie shook his hand and looked him up and down. "Cassandra. Just Cassandra."

"My pleasure, Just Cassandra," he told her. "I'm sorry about your brother."

He turned next to Nan, who smiled politely. "I'm Nan Robinson and this is my mother, June Robinson."

Wheels seemed to be going around in Pete Hobbs's eyes. He had to be wearing contacts; real irises weren't issued in such vivid shades. "I'd have sworn you were sisters," he said with a twinkle.

Mom preened. "How you flatter me!"

"It's an easy mistake," he went on, while Nan stifled her gag reflex and watched Cassie's eyes roll quietly skyward. "You're Julie's family, right?" At Nan's nod, he continued. "We're all just reeling from the ridiculous idea that Adam would have ever hurt Shane."

Ramón was helping Guadalupe into his car at the curb. "We need to get to the hospital, Pete, if you'll excuse us."

"Well, of course! Listen, tell Angus we expect him to be up and frisky, toot sweet. And Ramón, I know this is a bad time, but later this week let's talk. Give me a call and I'll buy you lunch."

"Sure thing," Ramón agreed, without notable enthusiasm. He kissed Victoria. "I'll call as soon as I know anything, honey. We'll see you all later." He got in the car, started the engine, and drove off.

"And I need to run on, too," Pete Hobbs announced, with another big smile. The guy was a champion grinner. "Can I give anyone a lift? No? Well, good to meet you, ladies. Victoria, take care of yourself and don't let that guy of yours work too hard." He ambled away, still smiling.

"Whoops, my son's trying to sneak off," Cassie Pettigrew announced suddenly. "Bye!" And she, too, was gone.

Nan led the way toward her Mustang, trying to process the afternoon's events and not really paying much attention to her mother's chatter at first. June Robinson was normally quite good at the sort of meaningless gabble that fills awkward silences and puts folks at ease. But she made a serious misstep before they even reached the car, and there was no way Nan could stop her in time.

"Do you have children, Victoria?" Mom asked.

Nan saw Victoria inhale as the color drained from her face.

"No," Victoria answered shortly. Julie had told Nan of Victoria's half-dozen miscarriages, that she and Ramón were now embroiled in the nightmarish rituals and high-tech humiliations of fertility medicine.

"Oh, well, you have plenty of time," Mom prattled on. "I used to think I'd never get to be a grandmother, before Julie finally came to her senses. Now, Nan here, I don't know what I'm going to do about her."

"Actually, Mom, I don't think it's your input that would make the difference," Nan told her, rather sharply.

But Mom refused to be derailed. "I know, I know. It's none of my business. But you can't blame me for being wistful about being a grandmother."

"You'll be one in April," Nan reminded her. "You can spoil Julie's baby absolutely rotten." She paused a moment, then tried to move to a more neutral ground. "Victoria's an English professor, Mom. She teaches at San Diego State."

"How interesting," June Robinson effused. "I may be old-fashioned, but I do think it's important for people to learn the language of the country they live in. My own grandmother spoke nothing but French when she came to this country, and she became absolutely fluent in English. You'd never have known it wasn't her first language, except that she had the most lovely little accent."

They were at her car now. Nan unlocked the passenger door and held the seat forward for Victoria to get into the backseat, resisting an urge to kick her mother sharply in the shin. A paragon of restraint, she glared fiercely at Mom instead. June Robinson chose to remain oblivious as she settled into the front seat while Nan slipped behind the wheel.

"Victoria doesn't teach ESL, Mom," Nan said carefully. "Her field is English literature. Shakespeare, isn't that right, Victoria?"

"Yes," Victoria answered shortly.

June Robinson raised a hand to her face in horror. "I'm *so* sorry," she said, turning to smile sheepishly at Victoria as Nan moved away from the curb. "I just can't seem to open my mouth today without putting both my big old feet in."

"Don't worry about it," Victoria answered politely. "Ramón's involved in so many causes that it's a perfectly natural mistake."

But it wasn't, and Nan knew it. It was just another instance of the rude stereotyping her mother specialized in. There were more Latinos in the Chicago area now than there had been in Nan's childhood, when a Spanish surname was as uncommon as a saguaro cactus in the suburban town of Spring Hill. But June Robinson's understanding of Latinos—or of the Cambodians and other ethnic minorities now well represented in the Midwest—remained limited and provincial.

Now Mom lit a cigarette. Nan glared sideways at her but said nothing. They'd been through this before. Mom rolled down the window.

"You might want to see if the smoke bothers Victoria, Mom." It was an awkward spot to put Victoria in, but too bad. The point needed to be made.

"Oh, dear, I'm sorry," Mom said. Unapologetically. "You don't mind my dirty little habit, do you, Victoria dear?"

"Of course not," came the answer from the backseat.

"I do hope poor Angus Pettigrew will be all right," Mom said, pointedly exhaling out the open window. "Do you suppose somebody really tried to kill him, too? Right there in church, for goodness' sake, in front of God and everybody?"

"I think he had a heart attack," Nan replied. "And he seems to have the constitution of an ox, so I imagine he'll be just fine. Victoria, who's Pete Hobbs?"

"He has a restaurant down the beach," Victoria answered. "Hobbs House. Maybe you've eaten there?"

Nan remembered seeing the place, a New England-style building facing the ocean. "No. Usually when I'm here we eat in or go out for Mexican food. Adam and Julie are pretty particular about what they eat. So that's his place, huh? Do you like it?"

"The food's quite good," Victoria said carefully. "And he seems to be doing pretty well. Ramón said he's thinking about opening another place, too."

"Pretty ambitious in a shaky economy."

"True enough. Actually, I think he's put the plans on hold for a while." Victoria frowned slightly. "You know, I was kind of surprised he showed up today."

"Why?"

"Oh, nothing," Victoria said. "I'm really speaking out of turn here."

Nan's favorite kind of speech. She twisted her head to look into the backseat. "Come *on,* now! Don't tease, Victoria. How come?"

Victoria hesitated. "Well, Pete's been dating Sara Pettigrew. Shane's ex-wife."

Really? "Oh, yeah? Is it serious?"

In the rearview mirror, Nan watched Victoria shift her weight uneasily. "I really don't know," she said finally. "And I shouldn't have said anything. You know, it's gotten awfully cloudy in the last hour or so. Wouldn't it be great if we got some rain?"

The latest California drought brought conversation back to neutral, even boring, ground. June Robinson was having major difficulty adjusting to the water conservation routines practiced at Julie's. At the kitchen sink last night she'd used a veritable geyser to rinse off each individual lettuce leaf before her daughter produced a bowl in which to dip the produce. She was offended at the idea that a toilet might go unflushed through more than one use. And she was absolutely flabbergasted when Julie popped the cork back into the tub after her mother's bath and began bailing with a bucket to water the recently trampled flower beds out front.

"But you had all that rain last winter," Mom had protested. Correctly. The preceding winter had been a mighty soggy one. This year, however, there'd barely been a heavy dew.

"This is a *desert*," Julie replied in exasperation. "A desert which every once in a while gets a lot of rain. We don't have much in the way of reservoirs down here, either. Once the rain stops, it's over. There has to be snow in the Sierras—lots of it—to make a real difference, and that hasn't happened in years."

But Mom was learning. This morning she had, unprompted, shut off the tap while brushing her teeth. And she was charmingly self-deprecating now as she described her crash course in water conservation to Victoria.

Conversation remained banal until they reached the Garza home, in a spanking-new subdivision of Oceanside. The houses here were large two-story California-Spanish, with red tile roofs and uniformly nondescript landscaping. They sat relatively close together with minimal yards, a technique used to shoehorn a few extra homes onto each block. In keeping with the times, these abbreviated yards were billed as water-wise and low maintenance. Several homes on Ramón and Victoria's block featured nothing out front but gravel and the occasional agapanthus.

Hardscaping, it was called, to differentiate it from honky-tonk parking lots.

Several boys were playing softball in the cul-de-sac at the end of the street and a teenager whizzed by on a skateboard, wearing the year-round sidewalk surfer uniform of baggy shorts, oversized T-shirt, and backward baseball cap. Little girls jumped rope in front of one house and two shiny new bicycles lay momentarily abandoned in front of another.

It seemed an awkward neighborhood for people yearning to be parents.

"Would you like to come in for some coffee?" Victoria asked politely but with no measurable enthusiasm.

"Oh, I'd just love that," June Robinson burbled before Nan had a chance to make excuses. "I'm absolutely parched."

Inside, the Garza home was spacious and airy, featuring cathedral ceilings and filled with contemporary furniture in pastel shades of blue, mauve, and cream. Large modern prints hung on the walls. The living room was dominated by curved cream leather sofas arranged around a low black stone coffee table. There was little to suggest who might live there, apart from a bookcase filled with leather-bound editions of literary classics. Certainly there was no evidence of Ramón's political activism. It might have been a model home.

"I'm afraid everything is a terrible mess," Victoria apologized as they followed her into a kitchen with gleaming pink granite counters and a virginal butcher-block island. The only possible cause for her apology was an ironing board set up in one corner. The Marimekko cover wasn't even scorched.

"Don't be silly," Nan told her. "It's absolutely lovely. Have you lived here long?"

They talked real estate then, changing markets and over-development and the relative disparities between Los Angeles and San Diego. Neither Nan nor Victoria was crass enough to discuss the specific market values of their own homes, though Nan felt quite certain that her Venice bungalow—in all its shabby charm—had probably cost more than this place with its four bedrooms and cathedral ceilings and shiny new appliances.

At a guess, Nan's whole house would fit comfortably into the kitchen and family room here. With room left over for her car.

"I'm curious," Nan said as she and her mother perched on stools at the pink granite breakfast bar while Victoria ground beans and used a European coffee press. "How did you and Ramón first meet?"

Victoria smiled. "It was a blind date."

"You're kidding!"

Victoria nodded, with a faint blush. "It's true."

Nan shook her head. "I can't think of a single blind date I've *ever* had that wasn't an unmitigated disaster. Starting with high school and heading right into the grim present. I'm really impressed, Victoria."

Victoria laughed for the first time. "I guess it was kind of lucky," she admitted, "and it almost didn't happen at all. What happened was I was new to California and a little overwhelmed by the whole place."

"Where had you been living?" Nan asked.

"Back East. As a matter of fact, I'm as midwestern as you are. I was born and raised in Lawrence, Kansas. My father was a professor at the university."

"For heaven's sake," said June Robinson. "Do you suppose you girls could talk just a little louder while I stand out here on the patio and smoke a cigarette?"

"You don't need to do that," Victoria protested. Feebly.

"Of course I do," Mom said, to her credit. And she did it, too, opened the door and stood just outside, carefully blowing her smoke away from the house. "Now, you were telling us about your blind date with Ramón."

"I had a friend on the faculty who was involved in migrants' rights issues," Victoria explained, "and he kept talking about this amazing lawyer up in North County. Ramón Garza. Ramón had taken on such-and-such government officials, Ramón had lobbied in Sacramento, Ramón was spearheading a drive to set up hiring halls. Ramón defended indigents unjustly accused. Ramón this, Ramón that, etcetera, etcetera.

"I figured he'd be horribly intense and humorless and, well, probably kind of grubby, too," Victoria went on. "Plus I'd had a couple of bad experiences dating lawyers. No offense, Nan."

Nan laughed. "I've had some bad experiences dating lawyers myself. A bad marriage to one, too."

June Robinson frowned at the mention of her erstwhile son-in-law. By now most of her friends were dealing with their children's divorces, child custody battles, and messy cohabitations, so there was no reason for her to act defiled by a simple no-fault divorce. But she did anyway.

"So what happened?" Mom prompted.

As a relative newcomer to the dating arena herself, Nan realized suddenly, her mother had more than a passing interest in tales of successful blind dates. June stubbed out her cigarette in a potted ficus and came back inside, careful to dispose of the butt under the sink in the trash. Nan was impressed.

"Well, Luke, that's my friend, just wouldn't let up. He kept insisting I had to meet this guy, that he was really special, that we'd get along beautifully. By now I was absolutely certain that nothing could ever come of it. Luke and his wife set up a whole dinner party just for me to meet him and then I got sick and couldn't go. Probably psychosomatic. Afterward, Ramón called me up and told me how disappointed he was, blah-blah-blah, and couldn't we just get together for a drink sometime? It was the first time I'd ever actually spoken to him, and he was so insistent that I ended up saying yes just to get it over with."

While she'd been telling the story, Victoria poured coffee into three delicate Mikasa cups and set out a matching cream and sugar service. She produced a plate of fresh assorted Pepperidge Farm cookies. Nan could tell that her mother, who appreciated such niceties and despaired of her own daughters ever embracing them, was enchanted.

Now Victoria paused and gave a radiant smile. "That was seven years ago."

"What a lovely story," June Robinson sighed wistfully.

"It does have a fairytale quality," Nan agreed. "My own experiences are more on the order of the princess and the frog. Only the frog is never a prince in disguise. He's just some horny old toad."

They finished coffee and moved out to the living room, where they sat around the massive black stone coffee table. Nan was wondering if they shouldn't just go on back to Julie's. Mom was certainly holding her own conversationally and Victoria didn't seem quite as uncomfortable, but still. . . .

June Robinson was in the middle of a complicated tale of her misadventures with her latest cockapoo at obedience school, a venture neither of them seemed remotely suited for, when the phone finally rang. Nan jumped in relief.

"They're keeping Angus in the CCU overnight," Ramón told her, "but everything is stable now. The doctors all seem to agree that it was a mild heart attack, nothing sinister. They want to keep him here till at least Tuesday, but already he's feeling well enough to be kicking up a hell of a fuss. Hates the hospital gown, wants some real food, says they're all a bunch of money-grubbing quacks." He chuckled. "In other words, vintage Angus."

"So the doctors and police don't think it was anything other than his own body acting up?" Nan asked carefully. "I'd hate to think anybody would try to kill him, too, but it *would* be convenient for Adam's defense. He's got an iron-clad alibi."

"They won't rule anything out absolutely," Ramón answered. "And of course they're doing all kind of blood work and toxicology testing to be on the safe side. But

Angus has had high blood pressure and all sorts of cardiac problems for years, and he's been under incredible stress these past few days."

"I see. Listen, I haven't talked to Julie about this yet, and we left the phone unplugged. But I think it's time to get back to her, and I'll fill her in then. Is there anything you want us to do?"

"I can't think what. Lupe insists on spending the night here, so I'm going to take her to the house to get a few things. I want to see if I can't get some food into her, too. She passed out on me once already, and as far as I can tell, she hasn't eaten properly for days."

"Okay," Nan told him. "And I'll talk to you later tonight about that other thing."

That other thing was June Robinson's earlier suggestion that if Ramón could manage to get Adam's bail reduced, she would be willing to post bond for him.

Julie was fighting the offer tooth and nail.

CHAPTER 7

"I can't do it," Julie insisted. Her fingers flew, working cobwebby white yarn with needles barely thicker than hatpins.

"Not *can't*," snapped Nan. *"Won't."*

"Spare me the semantics, Nan. I know Adam wouldn't want to."

"And just what *would* Adam want? To rot in jail for God knows how long while you risk your health and the baby's trying to be Wonder Woman? You can't do everything, Jules, run the business singlehanded and have a baby at the same time. Not to mention worrying about the trial and trying to figure out who actually killed Shane."

"Lots of women work right up to the minute they give birth."

"Lots of women stick up banks. Turn tricks for crack. Beat their kids. We're not talking about lots of women, Julie. We're talking about one woman. One extremely pigheaded woman. You."

"Girls, girls, don't squabble." Juno Robinson snuggled inside the afghan she had wrapped around herself in the chair she'd pulled close to the fireplace. Both sisters were amused that a lifelong midwesterner was being such a wimp about ordinary Southern California chilly winter nights. They'd also figured out that with a little wine in her, Mom didn't complain so much. Nan had stopped at Trader Joe's in Oceanside coming back from the Garza house to replenish the Chardonnay supply. "Julie, Nan's right. And it's not as if I won't get the money back."

"Adam doesn't want to take your money, Mom. And neither do I."

"You won't be taking it, darling," Mom cajoled. "You'll just be borrowing it. If it makes you feel better, think of it as a loan to the baby." To underscore her point, Mom picked up her own fluffy knitting, another impossibly tiny garment with lime and lemon stripes, and began clicking needles briskly.

"Nothing's going to make me feel better," Julie said grimly.

"Things will get better, honey. They always do." June Robinson spoke with absolute sincerity, and Nan knew that her mother meant every word. It was just another variant on the denial which had taken her through decades of marriage to an alcoholic. But Nan wasn't about to bring that up now.

"Look, Jules." Nan softened her voice, made it persuasive. "You're making essentially the same arguments I did when Mom wanted to loan me money so I could buy my house. And that was something that could rightly be regarded as frivolous. I didn't *need* to buy the house, after all. I just *wanted* it. I already had a perfectly acceptable place to live."

"An apartment," Mom sniffed, refilling her wineglass and leaning forward to top off Nan's.

Nan couldn't help smiling. Mom's snobbery about condominiums had led to the offer in the first place. After Nan's realtor friend Shannon showed her the little house on a Venice walk street, Nan had offhandedly mentioned the visit during a routine Sunday phone call to her mother. But she wasn't seriously considering a move at the time. The math was all wrong. Her equity in the condo and State Bar salary couldn't be crunched in any realistic fashion to yield an affordable mortgage payment.

Mom's totally unexpected offer to supplement the down

payment had made it manageable, possible. But Nan hadn't asked for money, hadn't even considered asking, and had resisted mightily at first.

"I was afraid I'd lose my independence somehow if I let her help me. I was just like you. Everything I had I'd earned, either on my own or as community property with Leon. Hell, I wouldn't have even had the condo if we hadn't gotten so much out of the house in Brentwood when we got divorced. The market went up like crazy while we owned it."

"And I haven't meddled, either," Mom announced proudly. She peered down at her knitting through little half-glasses and counted stitches. "Why, I haven't even seen the house yet, and it's been ages since Nan moved in." She shifted her weight slightly. It was just about time for another stroll around the grounds to smoke. Here inside the house, Julie had laid down the law. Never mind secondhand smoke and possible damage to the baby. Being in the same room with cigarette smoke made Julie throw up.

"Months, anyway," Nan answered glibly. Actually, she was a bit nervous about her mother's first visit to her investment, which would probably take place tomorrow. Mom knew the statistics, knew the square footage. Had even seen pictures. Nevertheless . . .

"You're both missing the point. This isn't some damn real estate transaction," Julie sniffed. She picked up a new ball of luminous white yarn and carefully removed the paper band, joined the almost evanescent strands.

Nan felt klutzy and excluded, her own fingers busy with nothing more demanding than the stem of her wineglass. Her mother and sister belonged to a sorority she would never join. It was probably twenty years since Nan had last attempted any sort of needlework project. Everything she had ever tried—knitting, crochet, needlepoint—turned out lumpier than institutional oatmeal. Except, of course, the popcorn-knit hat, which was flat, full of holes, and sized to fit a rodeo bull.

"But that's precisely my point!" Nan told Julie. "This is much more important, and you're kicking Mom in the face for trying to help."

"Julie, I've been trying for years to get you to allow me to help you and Adam. I've told you and told you that I'd loan you the money for a down payment on a house." Mom looked wistful for a moment, and Nan was sure she was thinking about the spiffy new Garza place. Adam and Julie would hate a house like that.

"When we can afford a house, we'll buy one," Julie answered stiffly. "What Nan chose may be right for her, but we aren't comfortable with the idea of borrowing money we can't pay back. It's all we can do to make our rent."

"But you told me yourself that old Japanese gentleman is sick. And that once he passes on, his children are likely to sell this place, lickety-split."

"So far Mr. Nashimora is holding his own. Mom, *please*. Can't we just drop this? I don't want to argue anymore."

"I'm not arguing, darling, and I won't say another word about the house. But for heaven's sake, let's be realistic about getting poor Adam out of jail. Do you know what goes *on* in those places?"

Julie looked like she was ready to cry. Again. "Mom, *please!*"

June Robinson shook her head. "Julie, you're just being silly about all this. Your father left me very well provided for. Sooner or later whatever I have will go to you girls anyway. What's wrong with sharing it now, when you can really use it? If I live to be a hundred, you'd be old ladies before you got anything."

Nan sipped her wine and felt a shudder pass through her body. In the back of her mind, Nan carried an image of her mother, debilitated and bedridden, quite possibly senile and incontinent, a permanent resident in Nan's guest bedroom.

And it would be Nan's guest bedroom, not Julie's. The unmarried daughter invariably took care of the invalid parent.

Already it was happening to some of her friends and none of them were prepared for it. Right around the time they finally started to grow up themselves, their parents were becoming dependent. The problems varied from family to family, but they all drew from the same core pool: widowhood, failing health, botched personal finances, previously unstated expectations. Add large doses of guilt and stir well. Staggering leaps in medical science kept people alive far longer than Social Security—or their children— had expected to support them.

The grandmas in sweat pants, as typified by June Robinson, were active and healthy now. But the countdown was on.

"If you live to be a hundred, Mom," Julie said deliberately, "you'll need every penny yourself."

"But I have a lot of money!" Mom sounded so indignant that Nan laughed out loud.

By Spring Hill standards her mother undoubtedly was a very wealthy widow, with a paid-for house, a new car, and a stock portfolio. But Nan's Los Angeles frame of reference for "a lot of money" was quite different: Iranian exiles plotting the return of a Shah; coked-out actors paid millions for a few days' work on sophomoric movies; egomaniacal rock stars in gold spandex and marabou; crass businessmen buying their way into society by endowing art museums; the ultra nouveaux riches who bought famous historical mansions in Beverly Hills and razed them to pursue their own tawdry visions of architecture. Like the TV producer who built a place so egregious it featured an entire floor for his wife's tacky wardrobe.

"Mom, I haven't taken any money from you since I was twenty," Julie said, "and I don't intend to start now."

Phil and June Robinson had promised their daughters full support through whatever education they chose. In Nan's case that had lasted through law school and allowed her to begin her career free of the crippling debt carried by so many of her classmates. Julie, however, had always been the family rebel. She'd dropped out of the University of Illinois in her junior year and headed west in her own version of manifest destiny.

"Honey, I know you're proud, and I respect that. But I also know how hard you and Adam work and that sometimes money gets a little tight."

Nan hadn't realized her mother capable of such diplomacy. The fact was that the Chandler household ran on a never-ending austerity budget. Julie often joked that she could squeeze a nickel till the buffalo tap-danced, though Adam never acknowledged that there were any financial problems and got sulky if anyone else mentioned them. Right now, however, with baby expenses looming on the horizon, simple frugality wasn't going to be enough.

"Why don't you just sleep on it, Julie?" Nan finally suggested. "Mom's already talked to the people back home and we're set to move in the morning." There were definite advantages to the kind of small-town setup where your banker and broker and attorney were all folks you'd known for decades, saw routinely, and called by their boyhood nicknames. Like Binky Hart, the bank president. "Maybe we'll think of some other way. But frankly, unless Rumpelstiltskin happens to be in the neighborhood, I can't imagine what it will be."

On Monday morning, Julie was mopey and the circles under her eyes were deeper and darker.

"I don't want to do this," she said flatly. "Every instinct I have tells me not to. Adam will be furious. But, Mom, if you're still willing to put up his bail, I'd be grateful for your help."

Then she went out to the greenhouse, tears streaming

down her face. Nan and June Robinson knew better than to follow her. Instead, they swung into action.

By midmorning, they had finished their business with Ramón at the courthouse and were headed back down El Camino Real toward Floritas.

"Why are all those Mexicans just standing around like that?" Mom asked at a red light in Carlsbad where a clot of migrant workers waited patiently. All male, they wore resigned expressions and a ragtag collection of thrift-shop clothing. One of the nattier fellows was sporting a brand-new Naval Academy sweatshirt and a companion had on a Cubs cap. Several were listening to Walkmans.

"They're looking for work. Though this late in the day, it's not likely anybody's going to pick them up."

"I don't understand. How can you be looking for work if you're standing on a street corner?"

"People who need unskilled laborers come by and pick them up," Nan explained. "Contractors, mostly, or folks who need heavy yard work done, digging or that kind of thing. They get paid cash off the books and then they send most of the money back home to their families in Mexico."

June Robinson nodded knowingly and blew smoke out the window in the general direction of the men. "So they're wetbacks."

Nan shook her head, cringing. Of course the migrants didn't understand, probably weren't even close enough to hear. But *still*. "Pejorative term, Mom. Undocumented workers."

"Well, they don't belong here, no matter what you call them. And how on earth do they get in? Why, I remember when I was here one time and Julie and I drove down to Tijuana, it took forever to get back across the border."

"Only because you were crossing at an official customs point. It's a long border, Mom, and it's a sieve. Illegals come in by the thousands. If somebody really wants to get across, they can."

"Are you telling me they just let these people swarm across the border?"

"Not officially. Officially the U.S. government is appalled. *Appalled!* They've tried ten-foot fences, helicopter patrols, freeway median barriers, checkpoints, floodlights. Everything but land mines, which I think are favored by some of the more conservative local politicians. And of course they do catch a lot of people. But all that happens is they're sent back. The smart ones say they're from Tijuana. That's where the Border Patrol sends them, then, and they don't have as far to go next time."

"But I thought this was all taken care of. That there was some kind of amnesty."

"The amnesty's long since over, and it was only good for people who'd already been here for more than five years." Nan thought of her friend Maria Perez, whose parents had become legal during the amnesty. The Perezes had lived in East Los Angeles for over fifty years, raised a family and lost a son in Vietnam. All without benefit of citizenship, or even genuine green cards. "It's no help to anybody who wants to come now."

"Well, I'm sorry. If these people aren't here legally, I don't see why the Border Patrol doesn't just pick them up and send them right back. It's not like they're being the least bit discreet."

Nan chuckled at her mother's naive faith in government. "There isn't enough money or manpower. Of course, if one of those mint-green vans pulled up right now, those guys would move like missiles." The migrants along El Camino Real might appear to be hanging cool, but they all had a sixth sense for *La Migra*.

"But where do they live?"

Nan waved a hand to the east. Shrubby grayish brown hills rolled into the distance beyond a few vivid fields of bright-green strawberry plants marching in rows along glistening sheets of plastic. There was no sign of civilization. "Back there."

June Robinson squinted, puzzled. "But there's nothing there!"

"Not that you can see, no, which is the whole point. The most basic kind of shelter is what they call spider holes. A lot of guys dig little caves into the side of the hill, facing the road so they can see *La Migra* coming. The openings are covered with brush. There are full-blown encampments, too, hundreds of them scattered around San Diego County. They move from time to time. Nobody knows how many people are living in the hills, but estimates run around fifteen thousand."

June Robinson grimaced and clutched her shoulders in a shiver. "What a horrible way to live! And it's so cold at night. What happens when it rains?"

Nan remembered a small encampment she and Julie had come upon one time hiking in the hills high behind Julie's house. The place was deserted when they arrived, though people were clearly living there. Nan had felt uneasy, certain they were being watched. Mildewed mattresses lay on filthy scraps of discarded carpet, sheltered by torn agricultural plastic stretched over odd bits of discarded lumber and the occasional length of PVC piping. A stove had been rigged out of a rusted oil drum. There was a lot of trash around, empty milk bottles and plastic wrappers from *mucho grande*-size tortilla packages. There was no obvious water source, no discernible sanitation arrangement.

"They get cold and wet, Mom. You're right, it's a disgrace. But nobody can agree on what to do about it. Ramón Garza works with a group trying to arrange for housing, but it's an uphill battle. You know, not in *my* backyard."

June Robinson shuddered again. "I can't imagine living like that. I'd just go back to Mexico."

"Not if your family was starving there, and this seemed

like the only way you could feed them. Or if you already
had your family here and you were all living in an encampment."

"You mean they have *children* living like that?"

Nan nodded. "Not a lot, but some."

"That's outrageous. There must be something that can be
done. Surely somebody's *responsible*."

"You figure out who, Mom, I'm sure Ramón would like
to know."

Two hours later, Julie and Nan left the greenhouse in the
Chandlers' old pickup, its camper shell full of flowers.
Emmylou Harris sang on the tape deck, very upbeat and
ethereal. Nan was casually nonchalant as she fastened her
seat belt and leaned back. Julie drove like an automaton,
hands clenched on the steering wheel.

Just another perfect day in paradise.

The truck was loaded with buckets of gypsophila and
sweetheart roses to be dropped off at the Flower Auction,
as well as smaller orders of mixed bouquets for delivery to
Julie's regular customers. Julie had worked at a frantic pace
in their absence: cutting, stripping, and bundling flowers,
then assembling dozens of bouquets. Therapy, she called it,
though Nan didn't believe therapy was supposed to leave
you hyperventilating.

The Chandlers sold primarily wholesale, moving the
bulk of their flowers through the grower-owned cooperative San Diego County Flower & Plant Auction in nearby
Carlsbad. Adam's attitude was simple: get the crop to market efficiently and economically, just as you would cabbages or sorghum. He particularly liked gypsophila, or
baby's breath, because it could be field-grown on short-lived perennial plants, had a lengthy growing season, and
was in continual demand by the florist industry. Baby's
breath made a great filler for all sorts of bouquets and it
never went out of style.

He was unconcerned that it was also, in the long run, fairly boring.

Julie brought an artistic touch to Adam's operation, a connoisseur's delight in fragrance, texture, and hue. While Adam's father had been producing crops of carnations and sweetheart roses as Angus Pettigrew's field and greenhouse foreman, Julie's was carrying home peace offerings of perfumed posies to his tight-lipped and long-suffering wife. It was barely possible—though extremely unlikely—that some of the Chandler-grown flowers had ended up in Robinson vases.

While Julie and Adam generally concentrated on a few basic crops—gypsophila and roses, currently, one crop for the field and another for the greenhouse—Julie delighted in experimenting with different flowers. She had begun years ago with a casual contract to provide table flowers for a friend's natural-foods restaurant. Through word of mouth she had gradually expanded, selling prepared bouquets wrapped in lace-printed cellophane for resale by assorted local entrepreneurs.

The bouquet biz didn't bring in much money, but Julie adored it, loved selecting and creating and arranging different bouquets from whatever flowers she had available at any given moment. Because Mr. Nashimora had planted so many different types of flowers on the property, often all she had to do was wander around with a bucket and shears. And maybe fill it out with a little baby's breath.

After an hour and a half of bouquet deliveries, Nan felt fried, but she was a picture of equanimity compared to Julie.

"There's no reason for me to be so nervous," Julie chided herself as they drove into the parking lot just off Palomar Airport Road and I-5 at the Flower Auction. "Everybody's really been pretty nice."

Yeah, Nan thought, the way people are nice when they

hear you failed your mammogram, or that your drunken father wrapped himself around a telephone pole down on Washington Street, no survivors. Awkwardness had pervaded every stop they made.

The lone exception was a Floritas antique shop proprietress dressed in an odd amalgam of Colonial Williamsburg and sixties Haight-Ashbury, with a fabulous head of billowing, shoulder-length white hair that curled and swirled around her shoulders. The woman had rushed forward from the back of her store, clutched Julie to her massive soft bosom, and held her closely. She had offered counsel and solace, warnings not to let the bastards get Julie down. "You take *care* of yourself," she ordered fiercely as the sisters left. Nan appreciated the woman's genuine concern, felt unneeded enough to browse around the shop and grateful enough to purchase an interesting glass paperweight.

"Oh, dammit!" Julie slapped her hand in irritation on the steering wheel as she rounded the corner of the massive building. A big white Pettigrew Nurseries truck was backed up to the unloading door of the Flower Auction. Great timing.

"Just stay calm," Nan told her. "We'll get in and out as fast as we can."

"I don't think I can do it," Julie moaned. "And it's just going to get worse. I've got to be in here all the time in the next couple of months. We're moving into our most important season."

The cut-flower industry was theoretically year round, with a steady and predictable call for weddings, funerals, birthdays, and anniversaries. But the reality was that most business revolved around three major floral holidays: Valentine's Day, Easter, and Mother's Day. Valentine's Day, which drew on the Chandlers' two major crops, was crucial. Their goal was to have as many roses as possible available for early February. After mid-May, Nan knew, it would be a downhill slide through the rest of the year.

Timing was critical. Growers caught with an overabundant or badly timed crop or one that came too early or too late faced a real dilemma: sell cheap, even below cost, or turn a magnificent crop into compost. Almost every grower had a personal horror story about sending mountains of beautiful blossoms to the dump. The market was rigid and predictable. Folks wanted bronzes and yellows and oranges through November, for instance, but the day after Thanksgiving everything had to be red and white.

As they began unloading the flowers onto portable carts, Julie seemed to disintegrate before Nan's eyes. Her hands were shaking and she dropped two white plastic buckets of roses in a row, splashing her jeans.

"Take it easy," Nan told her gently. But Julie didn't seem to hear. She just chucked the roses back in the buckets and worked blindly on.

As always, Nan found the inside of the cavernous warehouse breathtaking, the aromas intoxicating. There were flowers everywhere, hundreds of mobile carts loaded with buckets of mums, roses, gypsophila, and a dozen others. Most were locally grown, but there were exotics, too, flown in from Hawaii: ginger and lobster-claw and anthurium.

Afternoon was the slowest time in the Auction, taken up primarily by growers dropping off product. Many growers would bring in their flowers in the predawn hours the next day to ensure maximum freshness. The actual auctions, attended mostly by San Diego and Orange County florists, began each morning at six-thirty and were generally over by eight.

Julie transacted her business with a woman who wore the same noncommittal expression they'd been seeing all afternoon. Nan hovered nearby, pretending far greater interest in a cart of pale-yellow spider mums than she felt. Right now she didn't care if she never saw another flower.

When Julie finished, they headed for the door. Suddenly a female voice called from across the room. "Julie! Hey!"

A solidly built woman in jeans and a sweatshirt was waving from the area near the shipping doors. Boxes of prepacked flowers were stacked, awaiting loading onto refrigerated trucks. The flowers would go to Lindbergh or LAX airports or, in some cases, be trucked to their far-flung final destinations.

Julie sighed and started toward the woman, who met them halfway, beside four carts stacked with boxed ferns. Julie introduced her as Laura Belton, a rose grower.

"I'm so glad to see you," Laura said matter-of-factly. She looked to be around fifty and had a folksy, no-nonsense air. "I've been worried. How's Adam doing?"

"He's supposed to be released on bail this afternoon," Julie answered.

"Well, that's good news! I don't care what anybody says, there's no way Adam Chandler would hurt a fly, and I mean that literally as you well know. I always get a kick out of thinking about him trying to grow flowers organically!"

"We do compromise," Julie pointed out mildly. "Everything gets a whiff of poison at least once before it comes to market."

"Well, I should hope so. You can't very well have ants crawling all over the roses somebody gets for her anniversary. Or some big juicy worm crawling out of the bride's bouquet as she walks down the aisle."

"True enough," Julie agreed. They'd obviously had this conversation before.

"Listen," Laura said, lowering her voice, "did you hear about Kimberly Wilkes leaving Pettigrew?"

Julie's eyes widened. "No. What happened?"

"Seems she announced this morning that she's taken a job over at Transbloom."

"Transbloom? The people in Vista who do the tissue-culture work?"

Laura Belton nodded. Her wide-set gray eyes matched

the streaks of silver in her collar-length hair. The haircut itself was utilitarian and might have been done with hedge clippers. She shifted her weight and spoke conspiratorially. "I for one would have thought that she'd stick around Pettigrew and take over Shane's hybridizing. That'd be a great opportunity for her and they really don't have anybody else to do it. Unless the Nashimora boy is interested."

Julie shrugged. "I doubt it. Jeff seems more interested in the business side. But maybe Transbloom made Kimberly a better offer. She's ambitious, not the kind to stick around one place if something better came along."

Laura narrowed her eyes slightly. "And with Shane gone, she'd have a lot less incentive to stick around, I daresay. I was a little nervous that she and Sara might have some kind of dustup at the funeral."

"Sara wouldn't care about Kimberly," Julie said.

Laura gave a deep, hooting laugh. "Don't be so sure about that. Remember the scene Sara made at the Boys and Girls Club benefit?"

Julie frowned. "What are you talking about?"

"Back in November, it was. The Floritas Boys and Girls Club had a big fund-raiser, the kind of dinner-dance thing where you have to dress up and make nice. I hate that kind of shit, but I'm on the board, had to go. Anyway, Sara's on the board, too, has been for years. Shane came with Kimberly, and I thought Sara was going to rip her throat out. She was shrieking at her, made one hell of a fuss."

"Hard to believe," Julie muttered, looking more and more confused.

"Well, you better believe it," Laura told her. "Thought for a few minutes we were gonna have us an old-fashioned hair-pull. Then Shane came along, separated them. He grabbed Kimberly and got the hell out of there."

"Was Sara with Pete Hobbs?" Nan asked.

Laura and Julie both stared at her. Both women seemed to have forgotten Nan was even there.

"As a matter of fact, I believe she was," Laura answered. "It was Pete got her settled back down afterward. Good with people, Pete is. Course he deals all day with the public." She glanced back at the shipping door and stiffened. "Hey! Wait a minute!" she yelled. "They're messing up, Julie, gotta go."

Julie, slightly dazed, watched Laura dash off.

"So tell me," Nan asked, "is this Kimberly the one you were telling me about?"

"Yeah. Shane's latest squeeze. But I hadn't heard anything about that scene of Sara's. It doesn't sound like her."

"I want to talk to Sara."

"She won't be real eager to see any sister of mine," Julie said.

"Wait a minute. You keep telling me that Sara was cool about the divorce, that it was all over. She has a boyfriend who's at least good-looking and maybe more. Is Hobbs House a pretty successful restaurant?"

"I guess so," Julie answered, looking around nervously.

"But despite the handsome restaurateur at heel, she makes a public scene about her ex's new girlfriend. And now you say she won't want to see me because of you. Inconsistency always intrigues me."

"Whatever. Nan, I want to get out of here."

"Sure, Jules."

Nan started toward the door and Julie followed. Nobody seemed to pay any attention as they left the warehouse. Just outside, however, they passed a middle-aged Latino man getting into the Pettigrew Nurseries truck. He stared at Julie, narrowed his eyes, and spat on the ground.

"*Puta,*" he snarled. "*Puta.*"

Julie froze, burst into tears, and ran for the pickup.

Nan got there in time to take the keys and insist on driving home, a true adventure. The pickup handled like a runaway buckboard. While her sister snuffled in the corner of the cab, Nan thought about the visit to the Auction. Of course Julie would find it distressing that rank-and-file Pettigrew employees—one, anyway—considered her a whore.

Far more intriguing, however, was Kimberly Wilkes's sudden job change. And Sara Pettigrew's public animosity toward Shane's girlfriend. The icily controlled woman who had sat in the front pew at Shane's funeral didn't look the type to make vulgar public scenes.

Nan would definitely have to meet both women. Soon. And it might be interesting to visit Hobbs House, too.

CHAPTER 8

The sniper in the eucalyptus grove waited patiently, seated with back against the peeling bark of a tall old tree.

Everything was ready. The rifle was loaded, laid gently across the army blanket. The light came from behind and the view was clear, to the curve in the road below where the car would inevitably slow and make a better target. A quick lifting of the rifle and sighting verified that this was indeed the perfect location.

Traffic passed below at intervals, never very much of it. Wayfarer Road was generally quiet, off the main transportation arteries. People on this road were headed toward specific local destinations. A station wagon full of children coming home from school. A pickup with a bed loaded with potted palm trees. An older couple in a big new car, the man driving slowly, peering ahead uncertainly, hands locked on the wheel at ten to two.

It might be hours before the target came. Or minutes. It was important not to stop paying attention, not to lose the few moments of opportunity.

Now came the smooth purr of another car engine and the nose of the gold Cadillac rounded the bend. The rifle swung into position.

Crack! The shot shattered the afternoon calm as the rear window of the Cadillac splintered. The car lurched forward instantly, raced away as the second shot fired. That one went into the rear fender and then the car was gone, speeding away into the afternoon.

It remained only to collect the expended shells, wrap the rifle in the army blanket, and leave.

Nan and Julie had been home barely half an hour when Ramón and Adam arrived. They pounded on the door, and when Nan admitted them, simply stood there a moment, looking angry and scared.

Adam was a mess: sallow, drained, and gaunt, hair hanging dark and greasy down his back. Julie emitted a little shriek and ran to him. Nan held her breath, braced for Armageddon. But they wrapped their arms around each other in a strong and binding hug. Nan had dreaded the possibility that Adam would create an immediate scene. That one would occur eventually seemed certain.

He kept one arm around Julie's shoulder and looked around cautiously. He still looked furious, and somehow shaken.

"What is it?" Nan asked. She knew he wished they would all evaporate. But this seemed like more.

"Somebody took a shot at us," he said shortly, drawing Julie close. "On Wayfarer Road."

June Robinson drew her breath in sharply. Nan reached for her, felt her mother tremble. "Just now?" Nan asked.

"Forty-five minutes ago," Ramón told them. "But I'm sure it was an accident." His voice lacked conviction. And rightly so. This wasn't South Central L.A.

Adam led Julie to the sofa, sat down beside her. She had started to cry, tears running silently down her face. The others followed them into the room and Nan settled her mother into a chair. She remained standing, turned and faced Ramón.

"What happened?"

"We came around the curve on Wayfarer, just off El Camino Real," Ramón said. He stayed on his feet. Paced.

"Maybe half a mile from here. No warning. All of a sudden the back window just exploded. I heard another shot after that, but by then we were out of there."

"Do the police know?" Nan asked.

Ramón nodded. "I drove straight to the Floritas police station. They're sending somebody out to check. I told them I'd bring Adam back here and meet them where it happened."

Nan was stunned. What in the devil was going on? "Can I see the car?"

"Of course," Ramón told her. He turned first to Julie and her mother. "This probably has nothing to do with Adam," he began.

Then the phone rang. Nan raced to the kitchen to answer it, hands shaking.

A low guttural voice said only, "Ramón."

But he was already at her side. She handed him the receiver wordlessly. He listened for a moment, then hung up. He stared at the phone for a moment before turning to her. Adam had joined them now.

"I don't know who it was," Ramón said. His voice was a bit uncertain.

"What did they say?" Nan prodded.

"That I should have left Adam in jail."

Damn! There were a thousand things to say, but Nan didn't feel like talking in front of her sister and mother. "Show me the car," she suggested, and started for the door. "Adam, you stay with Julie and Mom."

Ramón followed Nan outside. Late-afternoon sun glinted on the gold Cadillac. The car was clean, waxed, lovingly cared for. Nan stared at the shattered rear driver's side window, saw shards of glass glistening all over the backseat. "A foot farther forward and it would have gotten *you*," she observed. She stepped back and checked the rear fender, saw the clean hole in the center of the panel.

"I don't think they were trying to hit me," he told her. "Or face it, they would have."

"But how would anyone know you were coming this way?"

"It was on the radio," he said. "Local news, Adam Chandler to be released on bail. Anybody who heard that would realize that sooner or later, Adam and I were going to go down that road. Adam's address is in the book, you know."

"And his phone number," Nan added slowly. Which explained the call. Unless, of course, someone already *knew* the address and number. "Were you followed, do you think?"

Ramón pondered for a moment. "It's barely possible that we were followed from the jail. I honestly wasn't paying much attention. But anyone who followed us wouldn't have been able to get in position to shoot. And I *know* we weren't followed from where it happened till we got to the police station. Then I really *was* watching the rearview mirror."

"I have to go back to L.A. tonight, and I really don't want to leave my mother here. Do you think Adam and Julie are safe?"

He considered. "Probably. The threat was directed at *me*, after all. But I can get a guard out here if you'd like."

"I'd like," Nan answered without hesitation. "Do it."

He looked at his watch. "I promised them I'd be right back," he said, "so I think I'll just take off. I'll use the carphone to set up a guard for tonight." He managed a smile. "Don't worry."

"*Don't worry?* Do you honestly think I'm dumb enough not to worry when somebody I care about gets shot at?"

The smile was stronger now. "I guess not. But it was, pardon the expression, worth a shot. Nan, say my good-byes, and I'll call to let you know about the guard."

Back inside, Nan found Adam, Julie, and her mother sitting in the living room, with the look of folks waiting out a loved one's emergency bypass surgery. She told them where Ramón was going, and announced his plans to hire a guard.

"We don't need one," Adam growled.

"Maybe not," Nan told him, "but humor me at least this first night. I'd feel better, actually, if the two of you don't stay here at all. You could come up to L.A. with us." She heard her own words in horror. What if they said yes? There was no room for Julie and Adam in her tiny house. There'd barely be room for her mother.

"Absolutely not," Adam declared. "We stay here. We have a business to run. I couldn't leave anyway. I have to stay in San Diego County."

"Julie could come." Mom's voice was strong, unexpected.

But Julie shook her head. "I'll stay with Adam," she said. "We'll be all right." She sniffed. "Mom, is that pie starting to burn?" The rich smell of cinnamon pastry filled the air, all but forgotten.

"Oh, my Lord, the pie!" June Robinson raised her hands in exaggerated surprise and hustled to the kitchen. She opened the oven door, frowning. "Oh, dear, it's browning *much* too fast. Julie, you *really* ought to get an oven thermometer." She fussed with strips of aluminum foil, topped the pie, and reset the timer. The others followed and watched, somehow relieved to be coping with trivia. The kitchen seemed suddenly shrunken to Lilliputian proportions.

"Sour cream apple," Mom told Adam, who responded with a thin-lipped smile.

When Mom was stressed, she cooked. Whole-wheat rolls rose plumply on the counter and the components of a broccoli-and-cheese frittata awaited final assembly. Sour cream and fresh herb salad dressing sat in a small bowl. Nan found it sweetly touching that her mother had labored so diligently to stay within the parameters of the Chandler family's vegetarianism. Back home, she considered no meal complete unless it incorporated a substantial chunk of animal protein. On the other hand, tonight's artery-cloggers weren't likely to win any Heart-Smart awards. And Nan herself was suddenly without appetite.

Then Adam spoke. "The pie isn't the only thing that smells here. I need a shower." Which was certainly true. He was downright gamy. As he moved, the Robinson women, as if choreographed by Balanchine, glided back, aside, and out of his way.

After Adam left to shower, Nan turned to Julie. "You're welcome to come with us," she told her sister. "Or to come up any time you want."

The phone rang again. Nan hesitated, then answered.

"I've got a guard coming at six," Ramón announced. "He'll stay a twelve-hour shift, and somebody else will come on in the morning."

"Adam won't like it," Nan warned him.

"Tough shit," he replied. "I need to go now. We're out at the corner where it happened and we've found the place where the guy waited. But there's nothing there, no shells or anything."

Not surprising, Nan supposed. Only in fiction were criminals careless enough to accidentally drop the key to a bus-station locker.

"I'll call you in the morning," Nan told him. "And I want you to think very seriously about who we could retain to take over this case."

"I won't be frightened off," he said, and hung up.

Then Adam returned, wet hair combed neatly onto the shoulders of an ancient Greenpeace sweatshirt. "I wasted a bit of water there," he said wryly, "and I let it all go down the drain. I want every speck of that jail dirt *gone*."

Nan told him about Ramón's call, the impending arrival of a guard. He didn't seem happy. But he did manage a smile when he opened the refrigerator. "Moosehead. I can always tell when you're in town, Nan. Mind?"

"That's what it's for," Nan answered. "Get me one, too. Maybe one for each hand."

He opened two green bottles, handed one to Nan, and turned to his wife. Julie seemed dazed, unfocused. Nan wished she'd sit down again.

"I need to get my hands in some dirt," Adam announced. "Real dirt, not jailhouse grime. You want to show me what's happening in the greenhouse, Julie?"

As the kitchen door closed behind them, Nan exhaled slowly. "You'd better get your stuff together," she told her mother. "We're leaving right after dinner, as soon as that guard shows up."

"But we can't just abandon them!" June Robinson protested. "Surely we can wait until morning."

"You keep forgetting I've got a job, Mom. I have to go to work in the morning. I've already been gone too long. And besides, what good would it do to have all of us here? There'll be a guard."

"I don't like it," Mom said. "Not one little bit."

"You think I do?"

"No, of course not, dear." Mom thought a moment. "I could stay here a day or two and then come up."

"Oh no you couldn't," Nan said firmly. "Even if this whole shooting thing hadn't happened, they need to be by themselves. This place is too damn small. The walls started closing in the minute those two fellows walked through the door."

"But I don't want Julie to feel we're deserting them."

"Mom, they've got enough problems without having to put any social energy into being nice to us."

June Robinson gave one of her patented mother-of-all-martyrs smiles, but she did shut up.

* * *

Just before dinner the guard arrived, a young man in his thirties with a carry permit and a crisp paramilitary air. Nan showed him around the property while Adam sulked inside. Hiring a guard wasn't much of a solution, she realized, but for a day or two it couldn't possibly hurt.

At dinner, Nan gingerly broached the subject of Adam's legal representation. He firmly opposed any change.

"If Ramón is willing to stay on after this," Adam said, "I'd never dream of asking him to quit. It would be a total slap in the face. I've known Ramón all my life, Nan. You want me to just cast him aside?"

"But this isn't personal, Adam," Nan argued. "People change their legal counsel all the time, even when nobody's threatening anybody. I realize that Ramón's your friend, that you think of him as a brother. But you know, if you had a medical problem and Ramón were a surgeon, he wouldn't operate on you. Ethically he *couldn't*. He's emotionally involved. This is a really nasty situation, getting worse by the minute. You need the best lawyer we can find."

Adam shook his head. "I need somebody I can trust. Case closed." He heard his own harshness, looked around the table. "Look, I'm in a hell of a spot and you've all been better than I had any reason to expect. Better than we deserve." The last was an obvious dig at Julie, and it made Nan uneasy. Would their departure trigger a firestorm?

"Adam, even if nothing had happened on your way home, let's not forget that somebody hates you enough to set you up for Shane's murder."

"You've got it backward, Nan," he said, shaking his head. "It's *Shane* that somebody hated."

"And you think it's just a coincidence that you're the one left holding the bag? Holding the gun, actually. *Your* gun."

He shook his head again. "It has to be a coincidence. Besides, Ramón says there's no fingerprints on that gun. Not mine, not anybody's."

Good luck selling that to a jury, Nan thought.

* * *

Freeway traffic was light when Nan and her mother headed north at seven-thirty. "We *are* doing the right thing in leaving," Nan said as they merged onto I-5. "And I don't want to talk about it anymore."

June Robinson sniffled, but she didn't say anything. And Nan made a determined effort not to think about the mess they were abandoning.

The Mustang sailed through Floritas and Carlsbad and Oceanside into Camp Pendleton, which occupied some of the most prime oceanfront real estate in Southern California. If the government ever really got serious about balancing the federal budget, they could make a nice piece of change by selling off Camp Pendleton in little bitty lot-sized chunks.

"I have so much trouble with all these Spanish names." Mom spoke up for the first time as they passed the Las Pulgas road exit. "How can you keep track of what they mean?"

Nan shrugged. "Mostly you can't, and it doesn't really matter. I do know *Las Pulgas,* though, and it's a personal fave. *The fleas.*"

A signed warned: ENTERING PEDESTRIAN ACCIDENT AREA, NEXT 8 MILES. Mom was disconcerted by the yellow caution signs that began appearing in abundance. Each featured silhouettes of a man, woman, and child running. The child appeared almost airborne.

"Why on earth would anybody try to cross this on foot?" Mom asked, in genuine amazement. Pedestrian carnage was probably the only problem that the beleaguered Chicago expressway system didn't suffer from.

Until the past few days, seeing Southern California through her mother's eyes, Nan hadn't really noticed the ubiquity of the local immigrant problem. The migrants were like eighty-degree Christmases, purple-haired sales clerks, countless signed glossies of unknowns on every L.A. dry cleaner's wall: initially jarring, but quickly passing into easy familiarity.

"It's illegal aliens again, Mom," she explained. "We're coming up to the Border Patrol checkpoint. A lot of illegals riding north get out of the vehicles they're in, cross the freeway, and walk this stretch to avoid car checks. Then they have to cross the freeway again to hook up with their rides."

"Well, surely they realize how dangerous that is!" Midwestern indignation echoed in June Robinson's voice.

"Not really. A lot of them haven't got a clue how fast the freeway traffic is. You come from some tiny town in Mexico with dirt roads, you don't have much frame of reference for a Buick doing seventy-five on cruise control. And it's not exactly a new problem. Adam says when he was growing up they used to call this stretch Slaughter Alley."

Nan slowed the Mustang, allowing herself to be passed by almost everybody. There'd been a recent rash of tragedies along this strip, people wiped out in an instant by motorists who didn't believe the signs till too late. A notably insensitive Texan Nan knew likened it to armadillos.

Another sign came up, with lights blinking across all lanes of traffic: CAUTION: WATCH FOR PEOPLE CROSSING ROADS. Now other cars were slowing down, and not just out of caution. "This could take a while, Mom," Nan warned. "The checkpoint seems to be open."

For five minutes they crawled forward. When they finally reached the checkpoint, a Border Patrol officer standing between two lanes barely glanced at Nan's Mustang before waving them through. Others were not so fortunate. Off on the side in the large checkpoint/weigh station lot, officials were opening trunks and questioning half a dozen drivers. What they mostly had in common was brown skin, black hair, and shabby vehicles. On either side of the checkpoint, mint-green vans sat with back doors open, awaiting the unlucky. In the final quarter of the previous year, San Diego area Border Patrol had apprehended nearly 150,000 illegals.

"Why, he barely looked at us!" Mom exclaimed. "We could have had a whole family in the trunk and they'd never know."

"They work on instinct, Mom. And on profiles, though they'd never admit it. Two Anglo women traveling alone are pretty low risk for alien smuggling. Besides which, I don't think we could fit a legal pad in the trunk, what with all your luggage."

As they drove on, the San Onofre nuclear power plant loomed on the shoreline to the left. Its twin reactors looked like mammoth moonlit mammaries, each with a glowing red nipple. Now came the last sign: LEAVING PEDESTRIAN ACCIDENT AREA. Nan kept the Mustang at fifty for another five miles, allowing herself to be passed by almost everyone. North of the checkpoint, migrants were likely to be even less cautious as they jubilantly recrossed the freeway. Nan's daily existence carried enough built-in guilt trips without inadvertently killing someone whose only offense was seeking a better life.

As they moved into Orange County, Mom began sniffling. Nan wasn't really surprised. The miracle was that she had lasted this long before falling apart.

Nan reached over and touched her hand. "It's going to be all right," she soothed. How often had she made that statement in the past few days? Not nearly enough times to convince herself. And that was *before* this afternoon.

Suddenly June Robinson burst into full-blown tears. "How can it?" she caterwauled. "Poor Julie, it just breaks my heart to see this happening to her." She was sobbing now, totally out of control. "And Nan, I could never say this to Julie, but what if it's *true?* What if Adam did kill that Shane?"

Indeed. What if?

"Mom, I've thought about that, believe me. And I just can't see it. Adam doesn't operate that way."

"But Julie and that Shane . . . you know." Suddenly Mom's voice was less hysterical and decisively angry. "How could she have *done* that?"

All too easily, Nan wanted to say. Shane had been a mighty appealing man. Instead, she tried to find a response that would assuage her mother without opening any further cans of worms. Confessing her own marital infidelity at this point seemed a poor response, one unlikely to comfort a small-town midwesterner.

"Mom, it just happened. These things do. And then it was over. Don't blame Julie. There's no point in blaming anybody."

"In all the years I was married to your father, I would never have *considered* . . ." Mom shook her head, as if to clear it. "I didn't raise you girls for this," she stated defiantly.

True enough. But what June Robinson *had* raised her daughters for no longer applied, had ceased to apply even before they left Spring Hill for college. Neither one was ever likely to be a small-town burgher's wife, wrapped up in bridge and volunteerism.

"Do you want to stop for coffee?" Nan asked.

"Heavens, no! I must look a fright. Nan, I don't mean to carry on like such a baby. I'm just so worried, and I feel so *helpless*."

"I know."

"And I'm angry, too." Mom's voice was surprisingly harsh. Then it broke again. "I just wish I knew who to be mad at."

When Nan exited the Marina Freeway two miles from her home, her mother awoke from the troubled nap she'd been taking for the past eighty miles.

Driving up Lincoln Boulevard, Nan found herself growing

increasingly nervous about her mother's first vision of the little Venice bungalow. Nan usually felt a certain sinking sensation on returning to L.A. from Floritas, was unpleasantly reminded that the mashed-together urban setting grew more surly and congested by the minute. But the feeling always quickly passed, usually by the time she was safely settled in her own home and had flipped through the accumulated mail and opened the latest *L.A. Times*.

Tonight felt different. Lincoln Boulevard seemed particularly busy and tacky, full of big vulgar lighted signs and rude drivers and a welter of unpalatable fast-food options. It didn't help when Mom began shifting around, asking in the manner of an impatient four-year-old if they were there yet.

Nan pulled into the alley behind Glorioso Way, extremely conscious of the rampant graffiti, the indecipherable scrawlings of youngsters who had failed to achieve literacy in either English or Spanish. She was grateful at least to have the new garage-door opener Shannon had provided as a housewarming gift; it eliminated lingering in the alley one second longer than necessary. An electric opener might seem like overkill for a crummy little one-car frame garage, but these were perilous times.

With the garage door safely closed behind them, Nan opened the side door into the sanctuary of the yard. The alley was invisible from the yard, concealed behind a solid eight-foot wooden fence. Nan found herself chattering nervously to fill the awkward silence and divert attention from the roar of traffic on nearby Lincoln. She knew her mother was too polite to say anything derogatory, at least at first.

But Nan also knew that Mom was making mile-a-minute comparisons. The two-story Spring Hill brick house where June Robinson had spent the last thirty-odd years was a formidable dwelling, with extra bedrooms, big screened porches, a sewing room, a formal dining room seating twelve, an attic, a fully finished basement, and a walk-in pantry the size of Nan's garage. The memory of Ramón and Victoria Garza's spanking-new split-level was fresh, and for all its ramshackle untidiness, Julie's house was roomy and surrounded by flower fields.

Nan's house was minuscule and surrounded by neighbors with overpriced alarm systems and large dogs who responded only to commands in German. Not to mention alley marauders wearing hairnets and brandishing cans of spray paint.

But at least the house was freshly painted, a soft pink with pristine white trim. The side yard, swathed in brilliant magenta bougainvillea that climbed a redwood trellis, was well lit. Mom's breath had been fast and shallow in the alley, but she quickly regained her composure and began commenting brightly on how cheerful the flowers were, how charming the little house looked, what a perfect shade of pink the paint was.

Then the damned black cat showed up, jumping onto the doorstep and meowing pitifully.

"How sweet!" Mom gushed, reaching down to pet the cat, who rubbed against her legs and continued crying plaintively. Nan could practically feel the wheels turning in her mother's mind: *Pets—safe territory—can't go wrong here.* "Why, you poor little thing, you must be freezing. Nan, you never told me you had a kitty."

"I don't," Nan answered shortly, deactivating the alarm system and entering the house. "It's a stray, and for heaven's sake don't encourage it." She blinked as she surveyed the kitchen counter, empty and gleaming. Surely she'd left the dish drainer out, full of glasses and odd plates that never quite made it to the cupboard.

As Nan moved through the kitchen into the front of the house, she grew increasingly disoriented. A large ficus stood in the dining nook. It looked terrific, custom-grown to grace that very spot . . . but it hadn't been there when she left for Floritas. An unfamiliar crystal bowl of perfect navel oranges and bright-green Granny Smith apples sat on the dining table. The browning and decrepit spider plant in the bay window had metamorphosed into an effusively robust Boston fern. And a vase of lilies graced the coffee table.

Had the place been burgled? By the staff of *House Beautiful*?

Then she saw the note by the fruit bowl. *Welcome Back! Call me when you get in. Shannon.*

Of course. Nan had called from Floritas just before dinner and left a message on Shannon Revell's machine that she and Mom were headed north. Now her friend, neighbor, and (not coincidentally) the realtor who had sold her the house was making sure that Nan's mother saw her investment in its best possible light. In keeping with that general plan, Nan immediately turned on the heat and popped in a CD of Linda Ronstadt's *Lush Life*.

Mom was not about to be distracted. Safely inside, she lunged for the phone and called Julie. Meanwhile, Nan retrieved her mother's luggage. By the time she'd hauled in her own nylon bag and Mom's five heavy matched Hartman suitcases, she was crabby and nervous again. The wretched cat was underfoot every time she passed through the door. She'd been joking earlier that Mom's luggage barely fit into the Mustang, but the second bedroom wasn't much roomier.

Mom hung up the phone and turned to her. "She says she's fine. Nothing more has happened."

"And it won't, I'm sure." Nan forced a broad smile. "Aren't you even going to look around?"

Startled, Mom giggled. "I can't believe I haven't! Why, Nan, it's just delightful." She began her inspection in earnest now. "Oh, just *look* at how the walls curve right up to the ceiling, so wonderfully Spanish. And stuccoed interior walls, how *interesting!* What a marvelous bay window! And that archway back to the bedrooms! It's all absolutely lovely, darling. Gracious, I need to do something about my haggard old face, after all my fussing back there." She wandered off to the bathroom humming "Sophisticated Lady," then called back in delight at the shamrocks painted on the ceramic tile.

Great. Mom was all wired now, perky from her nap and putting on fresh makeup. While Nan was utterly wiped out, yearned only to collapse into bed. Her *own* bed, with no bars across her ribcage, no springs that shrieked at the slightest movement.

Shannon rescued them.

Her brisk code knock on the front door was welcome beyond all reason. She bustled in cheerfully, wearing stonewashed jeans and a black, vaguely Oriental jacket over a chartreuse turtleneck, with every hair in place and full makeup on. Nan had once counted forty-three lipsticks in a basket in Shannon's bathroom, and often wondered what her friend would look like without makeup. In six years, she'd never even seen her with lipstick smudged.

While Nan hunted up matching towels for her mother, Shannon set about charming June Robinson. The two were, Nan decided as she half listened, pretty evenly matched. They rattled on and on about what an absolutely precious, *fabulous* little house it was: cozy, delightful, charming. Both were utterly oblivious to Nan's presence.

Nan took the opportunity to unpack, undress, and put on the powder-blue flannel nightgown her mother had sent at Christmas. She deliberately rumpled it so it wouldn't appear so obviously unworn. The nightgown was long-sleeved and high-necked, with prim little rows of lace on the yoke. During Nan's marriage, her mother had given her frilly, filmy lingerie that often bordered on risqué. There was a message in there, somewhere.

"I picked up some milk and eggs," Shannon was saying when Nan rejoined them in the living room, "and a couple of croissants to tide you over in the morning."

Nan meandered behind the chair where her mother sat facing Shannon and yawned pointedly, looking at her watch.

Shannon's formative years had been spent as the perennial pixie on *Our Family,* a popular TV series that painted an impossibly rosy portrait of the domestic condition. She took her cue immediately, stood and pulled her jacket closed. "June, you give me a buzz in the morning and I'll take you out for whatever else you want to pick up. I don't work till afternoon tomorrow. Will you be staying in town long?"

Nan held her breath and raised a thumb in appreciation to Shannon. Years of trying to qualify fast-talkers trying to scam their way into the real-estate market had trained Shannon to make tough questions sound offhand.

Mom hesitated, "I really don't know. I have an open ticket home, but I hate to leave when . . ." She glanced covertly at Nan.

"Shannon knows all about it, Mom. I talked to her the other night from Julie's." Nan turned to Shannon. "There was some excitement this afternoon, though." She briefly outlined what had happened, trying to cast it in the best possible light. Though there really wasn't one.

When she had finished, Mom sighed. "If I just had some idea what I could *do*."

"Let's start with a good night's sleep," Nan suggested, "and talk about it in the morning. I think you'll find the daybed's a bit more comfortable than Julie's hide-a-bed."

"A mountain stream strewn with boulders would be more comfortable than Julie's hide-a-bed," Mom announced. Even teetering on the brink of emotional breakdown, she was a dab hand at putting on a happy face. "You look exhausted, darling. For heaven's sake, get some rest."

Mom already had coffee brewed when Nan got up in the morning. "Such a selection," she burbled. "Eleven different kinds of beans! I barely knew how to begin. Your freezer's like a coffee shop, Nan. I hope Kona's all right." As she spoke, she popped two croissants in the microwave.

Nan yawned. "Coffee's the easy gift for singles, Mom." Actually, there'd been a lot more—miscellaneous Christmas gifts Nan had already taken in to work. If she tried to drink her entire holiday haul before it lost its potency, she'd be awake till April. Ricocheting off walls.

She sipped the cup her mother set before her. In the last gray moments before falling into dreamless sleep, Nan had planned the get-Mom-out-of-town campaign. Verbal communication in the early morning was not her strong suit, but this was urgent.

"The best thing we can do for Julie right now is just keep out of the way down there," Nan began. "If it looks like she's in any danger, then of course I'll insist that she come up here. And it goes without saying that you're welcome here for as long as you'd like to stay. We can rent you a car if you want. I'll need mine to drive to work."

"I'm sure I can just walk around and find whatever I need in the neighborhood." Unless Mom required seat-covers, periodontal work, or an auto battery, that seemed unlikely. "But, Nan, you've got to *do* something."

"I'm not sure what I *can* do, Mom."

June Robinson frowned. "That Ramón seems like a nice enough fellow, and I'm horrified that anyone would try to hurt him, but . . . is he really the best lawyer for Adam?"

Nan sighed, wishing she could wholeheartedly answer yes. True, Ramón Garza had much to commend him. He was poised, successful, and well regarded, with good connections in the community. His loyalty to Adam seemed absolute and he appeared to regard his friend's defense as a holy crusade, even in the face of gunfire.

But Ramón also had a lot of other commitments. Could he muster either the time or resources to mount a properly aggressive defense? Julie and Adam seemed relieved that

Ramón wanted no money up front, but the Garza family had to eat. Not to mention office rent, mortgage and car payments, insurance, and Victoria's wardrobe, which probably ate up every penny of her professorial salary.

"I hope so," she answered noncommittally. "For now there's probably nothing more anybody can do. There are some people I want to talk to up here and then we'll see."

After getting her mother's solemn promise that she wouldn't blindly wander off until Shannon had properly oriented her, Nan grabbed her untouched croissant and fled.

It always amazed Nan how quickly she could get behind at work, even when she planned her time off carefully. An unexpected absence like this one was a hundred times worse. She got in early and worked frantically through the morning, figuring that at least it would take her mind off Adam and Julie.

It didn't. The papers on her desk kept blurring, replaced by sepia-toned images of stony-faced jurors, hostile witnesses, a hanging judge. Adam being led from the courtroom to take the long bus ride north to Death Row. Ramón being picked off by a sniper on his way to deliver the final appeal.

By late morning, when Nan called her mother, she was a wreck.

Mom burbled on about what a lovely girl Shannon was and how the two of them had walked down to the beach for brunch at the Oceanfront Cafe, right by that lovely little Small World Books. She was absolutely enchanted by the walk streets, the idea of having only a sidewalk between the houses that faced each other. Nan was intrigued by the notion of two such sedentary women walking anywhere.

"Such a beautiful day," Mom went on. "Scarcely a speck of smog. And when I think what it's like back home ..." Back home, according to this morning's *L.A. Times*, featured fourteen inches of snow and a wind-chill factor of minus eleven degrees. "Sometimes I think you girls have the right idea after all and I ought to just get myself a little place out here somewhere on the beach."

Nan let her ramble on a bit, hoping that Shannon had curbed her entrepreneurial instincts. A little place—a *very* little place—on the beach in Southern California was likely to run a million plus. Besides, it wouldn't be fair to uproot her mother after decades in the same friendly little midwestern town. Absolutely not, no sirree bob.

After hanging up, Nan tried to reach Ramón, who was out of the office, or at least not taking calls from Nan Robinson. Next she called Moira Callahan, the Culver City woman she tutored through an adult literacy program. She tried to cancel their regular Thursday evening dinner *cum* lesson and found herself steamrolled into accepting an invitation for herself and her mother. Swell. They could all eat pot roast and discuss how incomplete Nan's life was, how desperately she needed a husband and children. Moira was nearly as tiresome on that subject as Mom.

Her call to Rosalie O'Brien's pager was more successful. Rosalie was a homicide detective with L.A.P.D., an intelligent and perceptive woman Nan had met the previous year.

"Have you got time for lunch?" Rosalie asked.

"Yeah, but no appetite."

"Well, I'm starving," the detective told her, "and I'm at Parker Center. Meet me in fifteen minutes at the entrance to Olvera Street and I'll buy you a burrito."

Rosalie O'Brien was standing under a massive Moreton bay fig tree with an elaborately fanfolded trunk when Nan arrived. She was a slim, silver-haired woman in a pale-gray suit with a royal-blue blouse and matching crystal teardrop earrings. She was a striking figure, and might have easily been mistaken for a bank executive or attorney. Except for her eyes. Rosalie had cop eyes, always on the move.

"Look at that," Rosalie said, nodding at the moth-eaten old burro guarding the entrance to Olvera Street. A busload of Japanese tourists wearing nametags and a dazzling array

of photographic equipment had converged on the mangy
old donkey. "My parents honeymooned in L.A. and they
had a picture taken on that same old burro. Talk about a
low-overhead business!"

They got food and sat at an outdoor table overlooking
the plaza. A ballet folklorico company in elaborate cos-
tumes entertained the tourists, most of whom would never
get any closer to Mexico than this re-creation of the original El Pueblo de los Angeles. The female dancers wore
wonderful dresses with full skirts in vibrant colors, their
dark hair skinned back into buns that cascaded ribbons.
They resembled exotic tropical butterflies as they danced.

Rosalie listened carefully while Nan explained the situation in Floritas. She really knew how to listen, one of the
many talents that made her such an effective detective.

"I don't like the sound of it," Rosalie said finally, "and
the sniper yesterday is particularly disturbing. But if the
whole thing's really a setup, it sounds like an awfully good
one. I know he's your brother-in-law, Nan, but have you seriously considered the possibility that he did it?"

The question *did* keep coming up.

Nan sighed. "Yeah. And I wish I could say it's flat-out
impossible, but I can't. Adam's moody and possessive and
jealous. Plus a bit paranoid. I could picture him charging in
there when he first found out and blowing Shane away. All
too easily. But the premeditation? I don't know. It fits with
the idea of stewing and obsessing about Shane's betrayal,
yeah. But Adam's not stupid. I can't believe he'd leave
such an obvious trail to himself."

"Even the brilliant make dumb mistakes," Rosalie noted.
"My daughter married an actor."

Nan laughed. "True enough. But how'd he get there?
The place is a good six miles away. Julie filled the truck
and wrote down the mileage just before she came home
that afternoon. They keep some kind of goofy record, for
taxes, I think. She says it hadn't been driven."

"And there's *no* other way he could get there?"

Nan thought of the impounded bicycle. Adam had been riding bikes through those hills for thirty years. "He's got a bike," she conceded. "But Julie swears he never left that night."

Rosalie waved a dismissive hand. "Wives lie for their husbands, cop rule number four ninety-three. But, okay. Say your brother-in-law *didn't* do it. Then you're dealing with somebody devious enough—and informed enough—to set him up for it. What do the cops say?"

"I haven't talked to them directly yet. But I plan to this weekend when I go back, particularly after yesterday. So far, Adam's lawyer's the only one who's really dealt with the police."

"I keep hearing what sounds like uncertainty in your voice. About the lawyer."

Nan laughed. "You ought to be a detective." There seemed no reason not to share her reservations about Ramón, so she did, feeling guilty and racist.

"You aren't going to want to hear this," Rosalie said, "but it sounds to me like the best bet would be pleading out to manslaughter. The scenario fits: Adam's tossing and turning, anguished over his wife's affair. He decides to go see Shane, have it out. He takes along the gun to scare him. They struggle, the gun goes off, Adam realizes what's happened, he panics and leaves."

Nan listened grimly. This was not the kind of suggestion she'd been hoping for. "I don't think that fits the evidence, Rosalie."

Rosalie chuckled. "That's where your buddy the local criminal lawyer comes in. He probably cuts deals all the time with the D.A. down there and they just grind the evidence to fit. And if he's got people shooting at him, he'd probably be happy to unload the case." She cocked her head. "No go? Okay, then, let me think about this. I don't know anybody in Floritas, but I've got a friend in

Escondido. Let me talk to him. Tell me about the detective who's working the case."

Nan passed along what little information she had on Detective Larry Woodward. "I only saw him in court, Rosalie, but he struck me as cold. The kind of guy who makes his mind up and that's that."

"Hell, we're all like that. It's the only way you can ever clear anything."

"Give me a break. I've seen how you work. Now, C.J., on the other hand, there's a case of close-minded." C.J. Bennett, Rosalie's young partner, had been imprinted in the cradle by Dirty Harry. In C.J.'s universe, everyone was felonious until proven otherwise, and he didn't convince easily.

"C.J.'s okay," Rosalie defended mildly. "Listen, let me see what I can find out." She smiled and touched Nan's hand across the table. "But, Nan, what you're saying about the lawyer, that he's too close to it, too emotionally involved?"

"Yeah?"

"The same holds true for you, toots."

CHAPTER 9

When Nan arrived home that night, she found a litter box in the bathroom, a ceramic bowl full of cat kibble in the kitchen, and a black cat curled up on her couch. It was snoring softly with just the hint of a wheeze.

"Don't say a word," her mother admonished as Nan began to splutter. "You can cast the poor little foundling out the moment that I leave. But I just couldn't bear to see her starving out there."

"Alley cats don't starve in Venice, Mom. People feed them."

Mom shook her head sadly. "Nobody's been feeding poor little Nefertiti. The sweet thing's skin and bones."

Nefertiti?

Patience. "Mom, there's a very good reason why I don't have any pets," Nan said gently. Sort of. "I don't *want* any pets. It can't stay."

"Nefertiti won't be any trouble at all, I promise. Why, she's got perfect manners. She knows all about the sandbox and she hasn't scratched the furniture or anything. I think she's got a little cold, though. Shannon promised to take us to the vet tomorrow."

Seething, Nan opened a St. Pauli Girl from a six-pack that had miraculously appeared in the refrigerator during the day. Shannon must have left it as penance for the vet offer. Grossly insufficient penance.

"Isn't it supposed to be the other way around?" she

asked after a few healthy gulps. "The kid brings home a pet and asks 'Can I keep it?' and the stern mother says 'No'? And what's this Nefertiti crap, anyway?"

"She has such a regal profile," June Robinson explained. She was at the kitchen counter busily stuffing mushrooms with some kind of cheese and herb mixture. "And of course the Egyptians revered cats."

Look where it got them, Nan thought. But she had vowed not to get embroiled in any meaningless arguments with her mother. The meaningful ones were quite difficult enough. The cat might have a few days' respite, but it would damn sure go back out where it belonged when Mom went home.

"I just talked to Julie," Mom said. "Everything's quiet and she sounded better."

Than what? "They still have the guards on?"

Mom frowned. "Yes, but Adam wants to get rid of them. I talked them into another day, anyway."

"Good. Is this dinner?" The question seemed superfluous. A big slab of sirloin was marinating in wine. A bowl of salad greens from Julie's kitchen garden looked like the cover of *Sunset* magazine. Not to mention the mushrooms, the first legitimate hors d'oeuvres prepared in the kitchen since Nan had moved in. One couldn't really count chips and salsa.

Mom giggled sheepishly. "I suppose this sounds silly, and for heaven's sake don't tell your sister, but I've had the most incredible craving for steak ever since I got to California. Isn't that awful?"

Nan gave her mother a hug. "Of course not. And as a matter of fact, there's something about visiting Julie that brings out the carnivore in me, too. Is that whole thing for us?" The piece of meat was truly enormous.

Her mother smiled conspiratorially. "Every single bite. Anything that's left can go into a steak salad later; I have a wonderful new recipe. But first I figured we'd eat until we belch ourselves into oblivion, just like Henry the Eighth."

The phone rang then, and June Robinson answered it reflexively. Her eyes widened as she listened. "Why, yes, yes, it is! Well, for heaven's sake! . . . No, I'm just here for a little visit . . . Just lovely, thanks. It's so horribly cold back home this time of year."

By now Nan was frankly baffled. Who on earth was her mother chatting with so familiarly? Mom's only local acquaintances were people she knew through Nan.

And then she realized exactly who was on the other end of the line, moments before her mother held out the receiver and announced sweetly, with an honest-to-God wink, "It's Leon, darling."

"I'll take it in the bedroom," Nan told her through clenched teeth, as she picked up her beer bottle and left the room.

Leon! What could *he* possibly want? It was ages since she'd heard from him, nearly a year. The L.A. legal community was big enough—and Nan's circle of friends small enough—that she could be reasonably certain not to unexpectedly encounter her ex-husband.

She sat on the bed, counted to ten twice, took a swig of beer, and picked up the phone. "You can hang up now, Mom," she said first, and waited for the click before she spoke again. "Hello, Leon."

"It caught me by surprise," he said, "having your mother answer the phone." His voice was instantly familiar, pitched just a little higher than he would have liked. When they were married it hadn't been annoying. At first.

"Not nearly as much as it surprised her, I suspect. How're you doing?" And do I care? But of course she did. She had loved Leon, after all, loved him enough to once believe they'd spend their whole lives together.

"Things are going well," he said. He sounded uneasy.

"McSweeney Lane is opening a D.C. office, maybe you heard."

"Well, of course I did!" One of the McSweeney Lane senior partners had recently become a major muckety-muck in the current administration, and the firm had announced its plans for a satellite office within a week of his appointment. An astonishing coincidence, of course. "Are you going?"

"You bet," he answered enthusiastically. "I've been sort of commuting for a couple of months now while this was in the works, but it's time to settle down. I've got an offer on thc townhouse and I've made a down payment on a place in Georgetown."

Was this what a civil divorce ultimately reduced itself to? Real-estate babble?

"I'm very pleased for you," Nan said, realizing that she meant it. "It should be terrific." Leon had grown up a lobbyist's son in Sacramento and was a lifelong political groupie. He would never be an elected official himself; he lacked the requisite crowd-pleasing congeniality and tolerance for banality. Plus, there was that voice. But he routinely worked seventy-hour weeks without flinching and he'd make one hell of a behind-the-scenes puppeteer. The Great and Powerful Oz.

"Would you like the fish?" he asked. Leon had retained, in their property division, his massive saltwater aquarium, with its dozens of improbably shaped and tinted species. He'd sunk a fortune in the setup. At least once a week something chartreuse or cerise was discovered floating belly up, at around fifty bucks a pop.

"Not really," she answered, "but Nefertiti might."

"Nefertiti?"

"A stray cat that my mother seems to be adopting on my behalf."

"Nan!" He sounded horrified. Well, he *was* devoted to those fish, the only form of pet life suited to his hours.

Leon liked dogs, too, though he hadn't owned one as an adult. Now, however, he probably visualized himself throwing a Frisbee to a golden retriever in Rock Creek Park.

"I'm sorry," she told him. "We're under a bit of a strain here. Adam was arrested for murder."

"Adam!" There was a moment's silence. "Who'd he kill?"

Not "What happened?" It was interesting that Leon had no trouble accepting Adam as a killer, without even knowing about Shane and Julie. Of course he'd never liked Adam much. Adam was a little too physical for Leon, with unsettling working-class tendencies. Leon preferred to view the blue-collar world in abstraction.

Nan sighed and told him the whole story. He listened, making no gratuitous comments, not even about adultery, a subject on which he held antediluvian views.

"Sounds to me like he's guilty as hell, Nan. Sorry. Of course I don't know squat about criminal law."

"Me, neither," she conceded dispiritedly. "I'm sorry, too, Leon. I didn't mean to dump this on you. I know how you feel about Adam."

"The hell with Adam," he snapped. "It's you I don't like seeing hurt. And I don't like the idea of that sniper." He paused for a moment, cleared his throat. "Actually, Nan, there was something else I called about, but I feel like kind of a shitheel bringing it up."

"Don't let that stop you," she told him, suddenly exhausted. "What?"

Another pause. "I'm getting married, Nan." He spoke a little too quickly. "And I wanted you to hear it first from me."

Somehow it was unsurprising. Nan realized that she'd known instinctively from the beginning just what this call was about. And maybe it was just the brain drain of the past couple of days, but she couldn't summon any emotion at all.

"Congratulations," she told him. "Who's the lucky associate?"

"How'd you—" Leon laughed. "Damn, Nan, you're too sharp for your own good. She's Marisa Christianson. Yale Law. I think you'd like her."

"Undoubtedly. She's in the D.C. office?"

"She will be. We're hiring her away from a D.C. firm. She's been working with me on a couple of things for over a year, long before we opened our own office." Nan had a fleeting image of the courtship, a sense of déjà vu that was surprisingly wrenching.

"Love on an expense account." She chuckled. "Well, it worked well enough for us." Leon and Nan had been a very junior partner and a very junior associate, respectively, when McSweeney Lane assigned them together to a major case in San Francisco. They returned to L.A. eight months later, engaged. In between came a succession of marvelously plush hotel rooms and some of the most memorable meals of Nan's life. Well seasoned with fog, cable car rides, and the kind of joyous lovemaking that accompanies a courtship awash in extremely fine wine. "I wish you all the best, Leon. Really."

And she did.

In a way his announcement tied a loose thread in her life, a life that was currently a veritable pompom of loose ends. Even so, it took nearly ten minutes after she hung up before she felt sturdy enough to go back out and face her mother.

Who had, of course, been giddily fantasizing a reconciliation.

On Wednesday, Nan tracked down Louise Bannigan, a classmate from UCLA Law School now working for a blue-chip San Diego firm in the securities department. Louise didn't know Ramón, but she lived in Solana Beach and was familiar with his name.

"He's an activist, that's all I know off the top of my

head," Louise said. "Gets his picture in the papers whenever some local town turns down a proposal for migrant housing, that sort of thing. Always being recognized when anybody honors Hispanic leaders in the community. I imagine you can get anything about his background out of Bar records."

"Uh huh," Nan answered noncommittally. She had already checked. Ramón was clean with the Bar. He'd graduated from UCSD, spent six years in the Navy, gone to Southwestern Law School, and passed the bar on his first shot. There were no complaints on file against him.

"Let me ask around," Louise told her. "I used to date a guy in the D.A.'s office who might know something. Call me in the morning."

The next day, Louise gave her the number of Ed Malloy, a former prosecutor now in private practice. Malloy was affable. "So you knew Louise when she was wet behind the ears," he said.

"As far as I remember, Louise was *never* wet behind the ears. Not even damp," Nan told him. "She always bristled competence."

"Still does," he agreed. "And she tells me you want to know about Ramón Garza."

"He's representing my brother-in-law in a big ugly case, and I need to know if that should worry me."

"You mean the Pettigrew murder?"

"Uh huh."

"I can't imagine why you'd be worried," he answered without hesitation. "Garza's good, no doubt about it."

"Do you have any personal experience with him? Like when you were a prosecutor?"

"Only the Jesus Alcazar business. You know about that?"

"No," Nan admitted.

"Jesus Alcazar was an illegal," Malloy told her, "one of a bunch of guys who used to hang around a gas station in Encinitas looking for work. The gas station owner, a guy named McGovern, got fed up and tied Jesus to a telephone pole with a sign around his neck saying 'Vamoose.' When somebody called the cops, McGovern told them he was holding Alcazar for Immigration. Cops left, very dumb. Immigration took their sweet time getting there. Meanwhile, a crowd gathered and there was a bit of a ruckus. When the cops came back, they arrested half a dozen locals and migrants for disturbing the peace."

"Sheesh. When did all this happen?" Nan asked. It sounded vaguely familiar; Julie had talked about it at the time.

"Two, maybe three years ago. Anyway, McGovern was arrested and charged. It was my case and it was looking to be an ugly trial. McGovern decided to plead out to misdemeanor false imprisonment and we dropped the felony charges. There were some protests when we did that."

"Major?"

"Not really. Just awkward. Garza represented Alcazar, who had special dispensation from INS to stay in the country till the criminal case was resolved. That put me and Garza more or less on the same side. Once McGovern pleaded out, Garza filed a civil suit against him on behalf of Alcazar, who then went back to Mexico. Got him a pretty good settlement, I understand. McGovern did six months in County Jail."

"How'd you feel about Ramón Garza as Alcazar's lawyer?"

"He was good. Competent, prepared, really on top of things. He was also . . . I guess you'd have to call it tenacious. Had a commitment to Alcazar that seemed to go beyond the case."

"Was that the only time you dealt with him?"

"He does some criminal work, but I never came up against him on anything. His reputation's solid, Nan. That's it, really."

"Thanks," Nan told him. "I really appreciate the input.

Just one more thing. What do you know about Peter Swenson?" Swenson was the prosecutor in Adam's case.

"This is all off the record?" Malloy asked hesitantly.

"So far off I'm forgetting it as you tell me," Nan assured him. "I just want a sense of what's going on. I guarantee your name will never arise anywhere."

"Okay. I guess. You've got to understand that when you work in the D.A.'s office, you get a kind of a combat mentality. People burn out. God knows I did. But Swenson doesn't seem to suffer burnout the way the rest of us do. He doesn't make bad cynical jokes. He's a real tightass, actually. He does it all by the book and he doesn't let go."

And sure enough, Peter Swenson was brusque when Nan reached him at his office. He took just long enough to determine that there was nothing official about her call, told her it would be unethical to discuss the case, and hung up.

By Saturday morning, when they set off at eight for Floritas, Nan felt qualified for some kind of Family Togetherness Survival award. They could throw in a commendation for grace under pressure, too. It wasn't that she didn't love her mother dearly, or that her mother was a particularly difficult house guest.

On the contrary, Mom had been remarkably obliging. She'd filled the empty planter boxes under the front window with cheerful pansies and primroses, located a shower curtain that dramatically upgraded the bathroom, charmed Nan's friends, and cooked a string of remarkable meals.

It was simply that . . . that what? That Nan was accustomed to having her own way in her own space? Unsuited by nature and habit to sharing her free time? A busy professional, consumed by work and other responsibilities?

A selfish brat?

Well, one thing she'd learned from her sessions with Adult Children of Alcoholics: nobody has to be perfect.

Imperfection might be a tough task, but Nan was getting better and better at it.

The Mustang seemed to fly south on the San Diego Freeway that morning. They sailed past the airport and down through the smelly refinery squalor of Long Beach, which Nan and her mother both agreed was reminiscent of the East Chicago neighborhoods they had passed through years earlier on family outings to the Indiana Dunes. As always, Nan wondered about the sign for the Oil, Chemical & Atomic Workers International Union. It was a group that would have plenty of trouble finding insurance coverage, she was sure. And did anybody survive long enough to get a pension?

As they moved into Orange County, they practically had the road to themselves. Around El Toro, they passed an orange VW Beetle converted into a pickup truck, an oddity even by Southern California freeway standards. They reached Floritas by nine-thirty, with time to spare. Nan's appointment with Detective Larry Woodward was at eleven.

Adam and Julie were out in front pruning fruit trees when they arrived. Arlo, their enthusiastic but pea-brained dog, was running giddy laps, chasing something only he could see.

Apart from a certain edginess, Adam was outwardly unchanged by recent events. Julie, for her part, suddenly looked a lot more pregnant, and Nan was shaken to realize that she was due at the end of April. Only three months away.

"I've been thinking about your flowers all week," Mom announced, as Adam hauled her luggage inside. "Trying to remember what was where. It's so amazing to me to think that all these things are blooming right now, when my poor yard is under a foot of snow."

"Well, then, come look around," Julie told her, "and figure out what you'll want to pick tomorrow to take back with you." Mom's Sunday flight was at four-thirty, and Nan would have given even odds that Adam and Julie both knew exactly how many hours away that was. Nan certainly did.

Mom's eyes brightened. "What fun!"

Adam emerged from the office/guest room just as Mom and Julie headed out to the greenhouse. He started back out to the orchard and Nan followed, trailed by the dog. Adam didn't seem particularly pleased to have her along.

"No more guards?" she asked, leaning on an already-pruned plum tree.

He shook his head. "What's the point? Somebody wants to get me, they will."

An interesting form of fatalism. "And what about Julie?"

"She's okay. Nobody's threatened her, after all. Or me, either, technically. Just Ramón, and he says he's used to it."

Even third world dictators, Nan suspected, never got used to death threats. But she let it go. "And how are you doing?"

He looked at her impassively. "How do you think?"

"I think it's probably really awful," she answered easily. "I'm sure the jail part was nasty, and then being home, with the guards and the uncertainty, well . . ." She shrugged.

"It sucks," he said shortly. "The whole thing. And it doesn't help having it on the TV and in the papers, all these assholes calling up wanting some kind of inside info, like what I really want to do is talk to some dipshit reporter."

"Just stonewall and they'll go away," Nan suggested. "At least with the machine you can screen your calls."

"Terrific. I got me a goddamned message machine." He made it sound as if the hot-water tap had started running pure dioxin.

"Did you talk to Sara Pettigrew?" Nan had asked Adam to grease the skids for a session with the grieving widow.

"Yeah. She'll be home all afternoon, suggested you come by around three."

"How did she seem about talking to me?"

Adam waved his free hand. "Willing. Sara's a good lady, Nan, and she's worried. She says she doesn't believe I killed Shane, which was kind of a surprise. I thought everybody had me nailed for it."

"Hardly everybody, Adam. Ramón's busting his hump for you, and plenty of others, too. You're not alone in this."

"Well, I *feel* pretty goddamned alone. Like who can I trust, anyway? I trusted Shane, and look where that got me." He kept pruning as he talked, angrily clipping away at errant branches with long-handled loppers.

"Adam, what happened when you went to see Shane? After you got that letter?"

He stopped pruning for a moment and stared at her, eyes cold with anger.

"Look," she said softly, "I know you feel like I'm prying and it's none of my business. I wish it *wasn't* my business. But I can't help if I don't know what happened."

"Help? How can *you* help?"

"I can try to figure out who killed Shane. If you didn't."

"What do you mean, *if* I didn't?"

"Just what I said," she told him, struggling not to scream in frustration. "You're not acting like somebody who's innocent and framed, Adam."

"Oh?" He sound petulant now. "How would somebody like that act?"

"Well, for starters he'd probably be loudly protesting his innocence."

Adam leaned back his head and bellowed. "I'm innocent!" Then in a normal tone he asked, "Now what?"

"How about some kind of effort to help us figure out who *isn't* innocent?"

"Look," he said after a moment, "*nobody'd* want to kill Shane. He wasn't that kind of guy. Even when I went storming over to see him, tracked him down in the greenhouse, started throwing plants around . . ." He paused, almost startled. "Damn, I *did* that. Swept a whole row of one-gallons right off the table in there." He shook his head in amazement. "But once he started talking to me, I couldn't stay mad at him. It woulda been like, I don't know, like kicking a puppy. He kept telling me it was all his fault, too, that I shouldn't blame Julie, that she never wanted to in the first place and she's the one who cut it off."

Not a particularly compelling argument for Adam's innocence, all told, that his adulterous wife had been forced.

"Were there witnesses when you had this, uh, discussion?" Nan asked.

Adam frowned and gathered a pile of prunings. "That Kimberly girl was working with him when I got there, but she split right off, soon as the sparks started flying. And later on, when I'd settled down a bit, Jeff Nashimora stuck his head in, acted like he was looking for Kimberly. But I think he was checking up on us."

"Did you go straight to the greenhouse when you got there?"

He shook his head. "Nah. I went to the office first. They told me where Shane was at."

Nan groaned. Witnesses everywhere to a major confrontation barely a week before the murder. She thought of Leon's reaction when he learned of Nan's affair during the waning days of their marriage. Unequivocal fury, just like Adam, a man he believed he had nothing in common with. Of course that was different. Nan had been looking for a way out of what had become a tedious and unsatisfying relationship. And she knew Leon considered infidelity unforgivable.

"What about afterward?" she asked.

"I got a bottle, went down to the beach. Stopped by Ernie's at one point, but it was New Year's Eve and everybody was partying. Couldn't quite get into it. So I just went down and sat there, watching the waves. Maybe I passed out awhile, I dunno. Then I went home."

Happy New Year.

The Floritas Police Department was housed in a huge bunkerlike building that sprawled atop a hill east of El Camino Real. There were no windows on the first floor and the ones upstairs were shielded by heavy curved metal. The complex had been built during a period of frenzied North County development and frankly seemed like a lot more law enforcement than Floritas could possibly need. A sweeping road led up to the complex, bordered on both sides by wide expanses of cerise ice plant just coming into bloom. Tall pyracantha bushes outside the building were still loaded with crimson berries.

Detective Larry Woodward fetched Nan from the lobby in shirtsleeves, then brought her upstairs to an office with a view of the largely empty weekend parking lot. There were two other desks in the room, but on a Saturday morning he had the office to himself.

Woodward had a brisk air to him, a crisp cop rigidity. At the same time, he seemed to make a deliberate effort to appear uninteresting, ordinary. Perhaps seeming dull was a legitimate job skill here in the semirural suburbs. Rosalie O'Brien's Escondido friend had said that Woodward was a good cop, with the kind of urban background that made a gig in Floritas a form of retirement.

"I don't see how I can help you," Detective Woodward said, rather formally. "Our evidence has been turned over to the district attorney's office. It's in their hands now."

"Because you told them the investigation was completed," Nan reminded him. Politely. Graciously. Adam couldn't possibly be helped if she further alienated his chief accuser. Adam had undoubtedly done plenty of his own alienating.

"Ms. Robinson, it *is* complete. We have motive, opportunity, and means. Now, I understand you have friends in L.A.P.D. Homicide. Up where you live, things are a bit wilder than down here. You have your gangs and your major drug dealers and your drive-by shootings. Homicide in L.A. is a growth industry. Down here, things are a lot quieter. We like it that way and we do everything we can to keep it that way. Something happens, we can give it all the time and attention it needs. We've done that here."

"But what if you're wrong?" Nan asked.

He just looked at her, dark eyes piercing through pale-gray lenses.

Nan smiled ingratiatingly. "It *is* possible," she said. "We both know that. Certainly the obvious answer is usually the right one when somebody gets killed. But it isn't *always* the right answer. What I've heard is that you're a good cop with a lot of experience where things aren't so quiet. And it seems to me that this situation might hit you as being a little too neat and tidy, a little *too* obvious."

"A matter of opinion, really."

"But if Adam killed Shane Pettigrew, why was somebody shooting at him on Monday?"

"Nobody was hurt," he noted.

Nan stared, felt anger rising. "You mean you'd take it seriously if Adam and Ramón were in intensive care? But since they were lucky enough to get away it doesn't count?"

"Not at all, Ms. Robinson," he assuaged. "Not at all. There's been a history of threats on Mr. Garza and we take them all seriously. He's not a popular man in some circles. We dug a couple bullets out of his car, but without a rifle to match them to, we're pretty much stuck. Unless you have some suggestions?" He remained excessively polite.

"Adam didn't shoot at himself," Nan pointed out. "Doesn't this make you wonder a bit?"

"Like I told you before, we investigated thoroughly. I

shouldn't even be talking to you now, Counselor, as you well know. Garza's the lawyer, and there's no reason to talk to him, either. This little meeting is a courtesy, a favor for a friend of a friend. Please don't try to push it too far."

"I won't. And I can appreciate that the Pettigrews are a pretty major economic force in Floritas."

"This is true," Detective Woodward agreed mildly. "I was thinking much the same thing this morning as I drove down Pettigrew Road past Pettigrew Park to work out at the Pettigrew Y. It's like the Eckes in Encinitas, done in miniature."

"Even so," Nan said, smiling carefully, "if I were to find evidence that showed Adam *didn't* do it, or that somebody else did, everything I've heard about you says you'd follow up on it."

He narrowed his eyes, and for the first time Nan could see that he was as uncomfortable about this little dance they were performing as she was.

"I was on the force in St. Louis when I started out," he said slowly. "There was a stickup at a mom-and-pop convenience store in a changing neighborhood, three punks. Old couple ran the place, Kratzel their name was. Mr. Kratzel tried to be a hero and they shot him. Mrs. Kratzel fainted or they probably'd've whacked her, too. She I.D.'d a kid from the neighborhood, said he was one of the ones did it."

Detective Woodward smiled for the first time. "Bobby Robinson, his name was, probably no relation to you being as how he was of the African-American persuasion. Now Mrs. Kratzel was old, lousy eyesight, failed her driver's license eye test the year before. But she was sure it was Bobby and he didn't have much of an alibi, just his mama saying he was home, and we all know what *that's* worth."

About as much as your wife saying you were home in bed all night, Nan realized. *Nada.*

"Bobby got convicted," Woodward went on, "sent up

twenty-five-to-life, swearing all the while he's innocent. Just like they all do. So about three years later, I pop this other punk. We've got him cold on a string of armed robberies—videotapes from store security. And we've got him on video pulling the trigger on this Pakistani sap thought his brother-in-law'd be pissed if he opened the till. Punk's sitting in jail looking at consecutive sentences go up higher'n he's ever learned to count and he gets religion. Starts copping to a lot of stuff, including the Kratzels. Took me nearly six months, and more aggravation than a man's meant to take. But I got Bobby Robinson out of the joint."

"A lot of cops would have let it go," Nan observed. Despite herself, she was impressed. "Most cops. What happened to him? After he got out?"

Detective Woodward suddenly looked tired. "He'd done his GED in the joint, started college. There was a certain amount of publicity at his release. He got a scholarship, finished college. Went to work managing a government-funded community development project and bled it so bad even the bureaucrats couldn't help notice. After he got out of prison the second time, I kind of lost track of him."

"Shit," Nan said involuntarily. "I wanted you to say he got elected to the City Council."

Woodward's grin twisted. "Like that would mean he was honest?"

They laughed together. Nan still wasn't entirely comfortable around this guy, but she'd lost the presumption that he was a small-town bozo.

"What about the rest of the Pettigrew family?" Nan asked.

The detective looked at her, eyes suddenly narrowed. "What about 'em?"

"Are they all accounted for on the night of Shane's murder?"

"His ex-wife and kids were at home. His old man was out in the workshop building space ships." Woodward's expression and tone remained determinedly neutral, as befit one who took Pettigrew Road to work out at the Pettigrew Y. But Nan felt quite sure that the detective had little patience for rich retired flower farmers who dabbled in rocketry. "His sister was at home in L.A. unalibied. And her son, the Nashimora boy, had dinner with his paternal grandparents and then went home to his apartment in Floritas by the beach. No verification there. He lives alone."

"Ramón Garza says that Cassie and her son don't gain financially from Shane's death," Nan noted, hoping for some kind of offhand and revealing response.

Fat chance. The detective turned one hand upward. "Then there you are."

"There's no other possible motive for Cassie or her son?"

"The sister's been gone from here for twenty years. Bad blood between her and the old man, but she and Shane seemed to get along fine. And Shane was the one who brought the kid, Jeff, into the business. The old man wasn't superthrilled about that, but he did like the idea of having somebody from the family come into the business. Very family-oriented man, Angus Pettigrew."

"Hmm," Nan said mildly. "And I imagine you've checked out Frank Reid." Reid was Sara Pettigrew's brother, the original bad seed.

Woodward cocked a finger at her. "You've done your homework. Yeah, we checked out Frankie. His parole is up, so there's nobody keeping official tabs on him right now. But we believe in preventative law enforcement around these parts. Frankie's been living in Oceanside since he got out of Chino. He was at an all-night poker game the night Pettigrew was killed."

"Is that a firm alibi?"

The detective grinned. "There's nothing very firm about

Frankie. The par-*tic*-ulars of his alibi aren't any more stable than the rest of his life, I suppose."

"Where was the poker game?"

"Oceanside, and yeah, I know what you're thinking. A hop, skip, and jump away from Floritas. But his buddies all swear he never left, that he was on a winning streak."

Nan considered. The death of Shane Pettigrew might seem like a major win to Frank Reid. "These guys are reliable?"

Woodward laughed. "Reliable? Yeah, like a stopwatch from Sri Lanka that you buy off the back of a truck at a swap meet."

"So they could be covering for Frank Reid."

"It's possible, yeah. But these aren't the kind of gentlemen who keep secrets well. Even an eight-ball like Reid probably wouldn't be dumb enough to trust them."

"Hmm." It sounded promising anyway. "Does Frank Reid have a job?"

"He does some body work at an auto repair place in Oceanside. Don't know how regular it is."

"I understand he made a lot of trouble when Shane and Sara were divorced, that he beat up Shane pretty bad at one point."

"No charges were brought," the detective said laconically.

"But you're aware of it."

"He was still on parole then. If Pettigrew turned him in, he knew we'd be happy to Fed Ex Frankie back to the joint. He didn't, so we couldn't. There were no witnesses. So Reid was the one owed Pettigrew, all things considered."

"You knew about the fight at the time?" Nan asked.

Larry Woodward just smiled. Nan suddenly had a sense that very little happened in Floritas—or North County—without this guy being aware of it.

"Are you the one who busted him when he got sent up?" Nan asked.

Woodward shook his head. "I didn't have that pleasure. Escondido got him. He was running a crystal meth lab with a couple other gentlemen. Mixed clientele. Used to do a lot of business out of his girlfriend's beauty parlor in Escondido. Carrie's Cut 'n' Curl." He chuckled. "The last thing Carrie cut was a deal with the prosecutor. She'd been Frank's old lady on and off, but seems it was off by the time of his trial. Something to do with another girlfriend being in her seventh month. I heard that when Carrie got out of Frontera and came back to Escondido, somebody busted her up pretty good."

"Frank?" Nan asked hopefully.

"Frankie was a guest of the State of California at the time. Carrie claimed she didn't have any idea who did it, and she left town once she got out of the hospital."

"Did Shane Pettigrew have anything to do with his brother-in-law's crystal meth operation?"

Detective Woodward shook his head. "Not even a whisper to suggest anything. It was looked into, gingerly. Very gingerly, the Pettigrews being who they are. But everybody agreed that Shane and his wife hardly ever had any contact with Frankie. They were both clean."

"So Shane himself never had any trouble with the law?"

"He was a lousy driver," Woodward said. "His DMV printout makes depressing reading. But apart from fender-benders and speeding—the automotive variety—the only time he ever had anything to do with us was when he'd be in here bailing out one of his Mexican workers."

Nan frowned. "Did that happen often?"

"Not really. But there was a kind of flurry back around the amnesty. Not just Pettigrew, a lot of the other growers, too. You get some guy who's been Mr. Meek Little Illegal, Señor Meek Illegal, for years. Keeping a low profile, nose squeaky clean. Suddenly he's got a green card and we can't ship him back to Oaxaca. He goes a little nuts. Public drunkenness, disorderly conduct, assault. There was a lot of that for a while, but then the dust settled. Caught the growers kind of by surprise."

"What we need to find out now," Nan said firmly, "is who caught Shane Pettigrew by surprise the night he was killed."

"Ms. Robinson," Larry Woodward said politely, "I believe we've already done that. Adam Chandler isn't a total stranger to violence, you know. He had a juvenile record in Floritas, and he's been arrested twice as an adult for assault, once in Oceanside and another time up north."

"But no convictions," Nan said without expression. She was fishing here. This was news to her, unpleasant news. She was aware of a Santa Cruz arrest a dozen years earlier, some kind of parking-lot brouhaha. "Tell me about Oceanside. And when was that, anyway? I forget."

Detective Woodward looked at her. "It was fifteen years ago. There was a misunderstanding at a bar. The charges were dropped because there was some question about who actually threw the first punch. But everybody agreed on what happened. Adam Chandler thought somebody was trying to snake his date. And he made a serious effort to throw the guy through a plate-glass window."

CHAPTER 10

Sara Pettigrew's house was set far back on a half-acre of avocado trees, within earshot of I-5. The gnarled old trees looked as if they'd been there a lot longer than the house or, for that matter, the freeway.

Nan guessed that the original house had been similar to the humble, single-story frame dwellings on nearby lots. Somebody had dramatically upgraded this place, attaching a three-car garage, sweeping a wing forward into the yard, topping it off with a second story, and then stuccoing the works. The only discordant note was a cobalt-blue tile roof, probably intended to make the house look modern. Instead, it gave the impression of a fantasized picture in a child's coloring book.

All told, a massive project. If the remodelers were Shane and Sara, with an already rocky relationship, a project like this might easily have done their marriage in.

High up in one of the larger avocados, boyish shouts and laughter came from the kind of treehouse most kids only dream of. Split-level, it sat firmly in the tree and sported a hinged Dutch door, sloped roof, shutters, and a two-tone paint job. It, too, had a cobalt-blue roof; maybe the kids had picked the color scheme for both places. The treehouse had a defiantly professional look. At a guess, it was an ancillary project during the house makeover.

The doorbell played the "Hallelujah Chorus." Sara Pettigrew answered the door in black jeans, a pink-and-orange horizontally striped turtleneck, and big sheepskin slippers. Her dark-brown hair had been twisted into a knot at the back of her neck at Shane's funeral. Now it hung loose on her shoulders, giving her a younger, less severe look. She was in her early thirties, starting to thicken slightly through the hips. Her skin was fresh and clear, with no makeup. Little lines radiated from the outer corners of her eyes, and there was a deep frown furrow between her brows.

"Come in," she said warmly. "Did you have any trouble finding the place?"

"None at all," Nan assured her. She'd expected a certain amount of hostility, but this woman seemed friendly, open, easygoing. It was hard to believe she'd made a public scene at a formal dinner dance.

Sara took her into a small, charming room that opened through French doors onto a rose garden. Compared to the carefully tended flower beds and grounds at Julie's place, the rose garden looked ragged and neglected. The bushes were unkempt, with a few late blowsy blossoms and scattered bright-orange hips, badly in need of their winter pruning.

But the interior of the room more than compensated. There were lots of hanging ferns and a pair of huge fiddleleaf figs. Forest-green wicker furniture had plump cushions covered with chintz patterned in cabbage roses that matched the wallpaper. A bottle of white zinfandel matched the cabbage roses and sat on a small wicker table, with cheese and crackers and two glasses. One glass was already full. Sara poured the second without asking and handed it to Nan.

"Have they found out any more about who shot at Ramón and Adam?" Sara asked, sipping from her glass.

"Nope," Nan answered, "and I'm not sure anybody official cares. I was at the police station today and they were amazingly indifferent."

"I wonder why?"

"Maybe for the same reason everybody's so sure Adam killed Shane. Only I can't figure out what that is."

Sara cocked her head. "Well, the obvious answer is because Shane was sleeping with Julie. Who ought to have known better, I'd have to say. But mostly I suspect it's because Angus is satisfied it was Adam."

"Angus has that much power?" And that much anger?

Sara nodded. "That much and more. There was a time when Angus Pettigrew owned maybe a third of Floritas. He sold off a lot of it over the years, not always at the best times in terms of profit, but still. When he needed money for his goofy rocket ships, he'd sell off a chunk. Good old Project Icarus. He's blown up at least three *major* rockets out in the desert since I've known him, bought property out there just for a launch pad. If one of them ever really went into space, I think we'd all keel over in shock. It used to really frost Shane that his dad spent so much time and money on something so pointless. But even with all the money he's poured into that, Angus is still a very rich man."

"Who thinks Adam killed Shane."

"Apparently."

"Do *you* think so?"

Sara shook her head slowly. "No, but I can understand how people would. Adam's always had this dark, moody side to him. I can imagine him stewing over it till he just exploded."

"But I understand he already *had* exploded when he first found out. You have any idea how that happened, by the way, Adam finding out?"

"Ramón said he got a letter."

"I know, but who sent it?"

"Beats me," Sara said. "Nobody ever sent *me* any letters when Shane was running around on me. And apparently I could've gotten a whole sackful."

An interesting point. "Tell me about Adam and Shane. How did they get along?"

Sara laughed. "Like brothers, in all the good and bad ways that can mean. Shane kind of looked up to Adam, 'cause he was a few years older. Mostly they were pretty tight, particularly when I first knew them."

"Which was when?" Nan asked.

Sara thought for a moment. "Let's see. I never actually *met* Shane until I was out of college, but I knew who he was. I grew up in Oceanside, but I dated guys from Floritas High sometimes. Shane was two years ahead of me in school, so he'd been out of college a while, was working for his daddy by the time I met him. There was a big barbecue down on the beach. Adam and Shane were there stag. I went home with Shane that night and the rest, as they say, is history."

"But not happily ever after?"

Sara looked pained. "I tried. God, how I tried! And I never stopped loving him, even after I figured out that he was probably the most horribly unfaithful husband who ever lived. I guess he just couldn't help himself. Anyway, that's what he told the counselor I dragged him to, back when I thought I could somehow patch up the marriage."

"It wasn't patchable?"

"Not by me. I . . . I finally just decided I couldn't take it anymore, that I had to cut my losses and get on with my life without him. The divorce was hard on the boys, of course."

Nan nodded. "It always is, no matter how cool the parents are. Anyone who says divorce can be easy hasn't tried it."

"You?"

Nan nodded again.

"Kids?"

"No. But I've watched too many of my friends go through it. How are the boys handling Shane's death?"

"They aren't. They're in such deep denial that it frightens me. Clark, he's the younger, seems more in touch with his emotions. But Christopher's just got it all locked up inside himself."

Sara seemed to take comfort from this shared confessional. She poured herself more wine and added a bit to Nan's glass, which still sat untouched on the table.

"It fascinates me," Nan said, "the bond between those guys. Adam and Shane and Ramón."

"You have to remember," Sara explained, "when they were growing up, Pettigrew Nurseries was way out in the country. The other nurseries were all clustered down around the coast. Angus set up his operation farther east, where he could get more land to grow vegetables, too. Tomatoes, mostly, and strawberries. He's very feudal, Angus. The kind of man who likes being master of all he surveys."

"And the boys?" Nan prompted.

"All they had was each other. Adam's dad managed the field operations for Angus, and the Chandlers lived in their own house on the property. Ramón, well, he lived in the big house, but that was because of what happened to his family."

"They were killed in some kind of accident, weren't they?"

Sara nodded. "It was all before my time, of course. Ramón's family were migrants. Angus used to have . . . I guess the INS would call it a smuggling operation now. Back then, it was just a pipeline, kind of a feeder system. There was a little town somewhere in Mexico, and when Angus needed workers, he'd pony up to get however many people he needed into the country. The border was a lot more open then."

"But if they were all so close, that makes it seem all the more incredible that Angus would believe Adam killed Shane."

"It beats me. All I can figure is that he can't bear to have any more uncertainty in his life. Poor Angus. He's had so *much* uncertainty, so much sorrow. All those years when he didn't know what happened to Amelia, they really marked him."

"What *did* happen to Amelia?"

"You mean you don't know?" Sara sounded shocked.

"Only vaguely," Nan admitted. "I know she was kidnapped when she was a little girl and her body turned up years later. But it was all before Julie and Adam got together."

"Amelia's kidnapping," Sara said slowly, "was one of those experiences that marks you for life. It marked *me,* and I didn't even know her. She was two years younger than I was when she disappeared. Eight. Just like Clark is now." She shook her head. "God, can it be that long ago?" She leaned back and drank some more wine. The bottle was going fast.

"It happened on a Sunday," Sara continued. "The Pettigrews had all been to church. Very pious, Angus was back then. They had dinner and then Angus and his wife, Carol, went out to visit friends. They dropped Cassie off at a girlfriend's. Shane was grounded for some reason and couldn't leave his room. He was twelve. Amelia had a dog who was her constant companion. She and the dog would wander all around the flower fields and greenhouses. The Pettigrew property was huge, flower and vegetable fields stretching all over the place.

"Amelia and her dog went out to play and nobody ever saw her again. She just vanished. The housekeeper was supposed to be watching her, but she was used to Amelia going off with the dog, so she didn't get worried. It wasn't till Angus and Carol got home that anybody realized she was missing."

"The housekeeper. Was that Guadalupe?"

Sara shook her head. "Somebody else, who was fired on

the spot. Probably drawn and quartered, too, knowing Angus."

Nan thought a minute. "But what about the dog? Surely it would have defended her."

"He was found a day or so later behind the greenhouses in a trash can. Poisoned with some kind of pesticide."

Nan shuddered. "Where was Adam's family when all this happened?"

"Camping in Baja, if I remember right. Out of town, in any case."

"Well, there must have been a huge fuss, wasn't there? A giant hunt?"

"Oh, there was," Sara told her. "That's what I meant when I was saying that it marked me as well as the Pettigrews. The papers had these enormous photographs of Amelia on the front page. She was blonde with a Dutch-girl haircut. She looked a lot like Shane." Sara shivered, remembering. "My parents wouldn't let me out of their sight for months after that, and it was the same with all my friends. North County was horrified. It was a real loss of innocence. We'd always felt so safe, so insulated here."

Nan did some rapid calculations. "Wasn't that during Vietnam? A lot of people would have been passing through Camp Pendleton."

"Oh, they were, and plenty of Navy men, too, all over San Diego. Thousands and thousands of guys were going through basic, getting advanced training, all of that. That was the big theory, that it was one of them, some outsider. And of course there was the possibility of hippies. Shane said that was Angus's favorite theory, some kind of Manson family thing."

It would have been everyone's favorite theory, Nan realized. There couldn't be such sickness in their own tightly knit community. Better to blame outsiders, dissidents, even Marines.

"Angus paid a ransom, too," Sara went on. "A few days

after Amelia disappeared. There'd been all kinds of man-hunts, Boy Scouts combing the hills, that kind of thing. No trace of her. Then Angus got a phone call from some guy asking for a lot of money. The FBI didn't want him to pay, but Angus insisted and he went alone."

"That would fit with everything I know about him," Nan said.

"It sure would. Only the FBI followed him anyway, and they nabbed the guy who picked up the ransom. He was a long-haired Nam vet with a heroin habit. The perfect villain. Angus was furious when he realized that the FBI had tricked him, said they were responsible for Amelia being killed. Only problem was, the guy hadn't kidnapped Amelia at all. He was just trying to cash in."

Nan frowned. "For sure?"

Sara nodded sadly. "For sure. You can imagine they did everything they could to pin it on him. Once he realized they were going to really nail him, he came up with an alibi that nobody could break. All they could get him for was extortion. And Amelia was still missing, only now they'd lost a week in looking for her. The hunt went on, but it was hopeless."

"But they did find her later."

"Ten *years* later," Sara emphasized, "and purely by accident. It was right after Shane and I got married. We'd just been through a drought cycle and then it started raining. Rained and rained and rained. Angus had sold off a big tract of land to some developer and they'd graded a new road through his peach orchard to bring in construction equipment. The body was buried in that orchard, right by where the road cut through. The rain washed away enough dirt to . . . expose it."

Nan grimaced. "How horrible!"

"Angus and Shane found her," Sara said, "if you want to talk horrible."

"What were they able to tell from the body?"

"Not much. Her neck was broken. They guessed she'd probably been killed right away, that first day when she disappeared. But there was no way to know for sure after all that time. It just destroyed Angus. By then Carol was dead, too. Cancer."

"And they never learned anything more about who did it?"

Sara shook her head.

"What about why?"

"That was even stranger. There didn't seem to be any reason. It wasn't possible to tell after all that time if she'd been molested, but there were the remains of clothing on the body, what she was wearing the day she disappeared. A pink taffeta dress, little patent-leather shoes. Finding her body just shattered Shane. He used to obsess on it, trying to figure out why. Amelia was a shy kid and nobody believed she'd have gone with a stranger."

"What about somebody she knew? One of the migrant workers, maybe?"

"There were a bunch of workers on the property, yeah. In a kind of shanty-town arrangement off back, out of the way. But it wasn't anywhere near the peach orchard, and you have to figure they really grilled them all."

"There was never any other attempt at ransom?"

"Only that one guy."

"What happened to him?"

Sara looked unhappy. "He died in prison. Some kind of race thing."

"Hmm. Tell me about Cassie."

Sara laughed. "Ah, Cassie. Everybody's favorite bad girl."

"Meaning?"

"Cassie's pretty amazing. She's the only person I know who ever stood up to Angus and didn't get totally mowed down. Disinherited, yeah. But she's got money of her own. At least one of her husbands was super rich, and her paintings sell for a lot these days. Cassie's done okay for herself."

"How did she and Shane get along?"

"Great. We didn't see her real often, 'cause she lives in L.A. She had a condo in Palm Springs for a while and we'd go out there sometimes. Shane really liked Jeff, of course. Cassie'd bring him down to see his other grandparents and Shane would take him over to see Angus. And when Jeff first came down here last June after he graduated, he stayed here till he found his own place."

"Do you think he really wants to go into floriculture?"

Sara considered. "I don't think he's really interested in the flowers as much as the business end. Which was fine with Shane 'cause he was just the opposite. I hope Jeff'll stay."

"Why wouldn't he?" The job market in Southern California for newly minted business majors was pretty grim of late. Jeff Nashimora's other job prospects were likely to involve flipping burgers.

"Because he turned down a bunch of other offers, including some in Tokyo, to go to work at Pettigrew. Jeff was at the very top of his class at SC. And Angus always treated him like dirt. But he seems happy here. Here, have some of this Brie. It's really wonderful."

Nan dutifully spread cheese on a cracker and sipped some of her wine. "I understand Shane had a number of automobile accidents."

Sara smiled. "He sure did. But so what?"

"Looking for motives."

"Well, I don't think anybody'd sneak up on him with a gun in the dead of night because he dented their fenders," Sara said.

"They weren't all fender-benders, though, were they? Wasn't there an older woman who was rather seriously hurt?"

"That was Esperanza Alvarez. I'm not sure just how

badly she was really hurt, but she got hold of a good lawyer and really shook Shane down. I hate lawyers." Sara rolled her eyes. "Oh Lordie, listen to me. No offense. It's just that . . ."

"No offense," Nan answered easily. On job respect surveys, lawyers were usually ranked below used car salesmen and drug dealers, occasionally above axe murderers. "Most people don't like lawyers."

Sara frowned. "I wonder why that is?"

Nan had given the question considerable thought. "The average person only comes in contact with a lawyer when something is going seriously wrong in her life," she explained. "Her kid's been busted, the business is going belly up, her husband has a DUI, somebody's rear-ended her. Or, even worse, *she's* rear-ended somebody. The lawyer is associated with something really stressful *and* expects to be paid for it. Some professionals have it a lot easier that way. Your obstetrician, say, associated with the glorious moment of birth. But your lawyer's the guy who does your divorce."

Sara was smiling now. "I guess that makes sense."

"So what about this Alvarez woman's lawsuit?"

Sara shook her head. "It was after Shane and I were separated, and I don't know very much about it except that it was Shane's fault. As usual. Of course. And that she was genuinely hurt, though probably not as much as the settlement she got. That was the accident that finally landed Shane in assigned-risk. You wouldn't believe what our car insurance premiums were when we were married. Or how often we'd get dropped and he'd have to hustle and find some other carrier. That Shane." There was a wistful tone as she said his name, a definite lingering fondness.

"How'd he ever get that name, anyway?"

"His mother was a big Alan Ladd fan," Sara answered with a quick grin. "Or so the story goes. Angus tended more toward Jack Palance."

Nan took a deep breath. This next part wasn't going to be easy. "What can you tell me about Kimberly Wilkes?"

Sara's smile and tone both turned tight and bitter. "She was Shane's latest, that's all. His assistant at the greenhouse, all very cozy. For the Shanes of this world, there's an endless supply of Kimberlys."

"You don't think the relationship was anything special?"

Sara shook her head. "I could be wrong. God knows he fooled me long enough with enough women. But I don't think she meant anything much to him."

"Still, I understand there was some kind of . . . misunderstanding at the Boys and Girls Club Benefit," Nan said carefully.

Sara looked truly chagrined. "Oh, Lordie, you heard about that?" Nan nodded. "I'd, uh, had a bit of wine. And I was really pissed at him because the boys told me Kimberly stayed over the weekend before when they were at his place. I didn't like that, didn't think his sons needed to be party to his promiscuity. But it was nothing, really. It's just that Shane never took too well to responsibility."

"He *did* marry you," Nan pointed out.

"We were young and in love. In hindsight, though, I'm not sure Shane should ever have married anybody."

But if he hadn't, Sara wouldn't be ensconced now in a half-million dollars of prime real estate. Without career, job, or, according to Julie and Adam, the slightest interest in finding either.

"Did you know about Shane's affair with Julie?" Nan asked.

Sara's eyes widened, then narrowed abruptly. "I sure didn't, and it's hard for me to believe somehow. For all of his . . . tomcattery, I'd never have suspected him of messing with a friend's wife. And not just any friend, either. *Adam.*"

"That hadn't happened before?"

"Not that I know of, not that that means anything. It seems there were an awful lot of things about Shane's private life that I was never aware of." She filled her wine-glass again and drank.

"I met Pete Hobbs after the funeral," Nan said quietly. "He seemed like a nice guy."

Sara smiled lopsidedly. "That he is, old Peter. That he is."

The front door banged and a deep male voice called out. "Sara? Hey, Sara, you here?"

A flash of anger passed over Sara's face as she stood. "Back here," she called. "I'm busy."

A moment later, a fortyish man stood in the doorway. He wore faded jeans and a black T-shirt under a black leather jacket featuring ten pounds of hardware. He had a gut, a swagger, and an attitude.

Sara looked unhappy. "I'm busy now, Frank," she said pointedly.

Ah, of course. Frank Reid. There wasn't much of a re-semblance, except maybe in the eyes.

"So I see," he said. "Who's your pretty friend?"

Nan could tell this wasn't the kind of guy who'd expect to shake hands with what he'd probably call a "babe." "I'm Nan," she said, staying curled in the corner of the loveseat, smiling sweetly.

"This is my brother Frank," Sara said guardedly. "Frank, we're in the middle of something." There was an edge of warning in her voice. Interesting.

"We were talking about Shane," Nan put in quickly. "I understand that you were unhappy when he and Sara split up."

Frank Reid's eyes narrowed suspiciously. "What are you, a cop?"

"I'm a lawyer. Julie Chandler's sister."

"Well, Julie Chandler's sister, me and Shane got on just fine. We understood each other real good."

"That's odd," Nan told him. "I heard you were plenty pissed with him. Even beat him up."

Frank Reid switched tacks, assumed a lazy smile. "I guess you heard wrong." He turned to Sara. "Just popped in to see if you needed anything, Sis."

"I'm fine," Sara answered, tight-lipped. She was still standing and she was slightly unsteady on her feet. The wine bottle was nearly empty.

"I'll run along then," he said. "Don't want to spoil your girl talk." He turned to Nan and nodded, a glint in his eye. "Nice meeting you."

Nan watched Sara as her brother went back out to the front of the house. Only when the door slammed again did the woman exhale.

"I'm sorry if I upset him," Nan began awkwardly. "Or you."

"I'm not upset," Sara said shortly, "but I think you'd better go now. I hope you can help Adam." Something passed across her eyes. "Adam's always been really good to me. He didn't deserve Julie fucking Shane. And he doesn't deserve this."

Nan followed Sara, who wove slightly as she walked to the front door. This was ending on the wrong note, and she wanted to stay in Sara's good graces.

"I really appreciate your help," she said, "and I know Adam does, too. Thanks for being so candid with me. If you think of anything that could help, could you call me?" She handed Sara a business card, with her home phone written on the back.

Sara stuck the card on a pile of mail that looked as if it hadn't been touched in weeks, then opened the front door warily.

Frank Reid had vanished and her sons were stalking each other in the front yard, skulking behind avocado trees. They held enormous water guns. As Nan watched, one of them hit the treehouse a hundred yards away with what looked like firehose strength.

"They're good-looking boys," Nan said.

"They favor Shane," Sara responded. "Poor little guys. They don't even realize how bad they've been hurt. It comes to them in little bits and pieces."

"They'll be well provided for, though, won't they?"

"That's only money," came Sara's bitter reply. "Only money."

Still, Nan reflected as she dodged the water warriors on the way out to her car, money could be a powerful motivation for all sorts of things.

Murder included.

CHAPTER 11

Julie took June Robinson to the airport on Sunday afternoon, insisting that she was perfectly all right to drive home alone—"Fine, just fine, *really* I am!"—in a tone that bordered on hysteria but brooked no argument.

Once they'd left, Nan and Adam went to visit Katsumi Nashimora, the Chandlers' landlord.

Adam drove Nan's new vintage Mustang, admiring it as effusively as he had at Christmas. And with good reason. The car was a silver '67 V-8 fastback and really cherry, right down to the lighted Mustang grille ornament. It was a replacement for the '66 model totaled in an accident the year before.

Nan preferred to consider herself somewhat removed from the rampant automania that infected the Los Angeles basin, but she spent too much time behind the wheel not to want a car she could truly enjoy. For years now, that had meant old Mustangs, which represented one of the more glorious memories of her youth as the daughter of a midwestern Ford dealer. Like her youth, the cars were far from headache-free. Still, she was generally philosophical about the inconvenience, reasoning that once you put a few decades on *any* car, you have to expect the mechanical systems to start punking out. So far, however, this one hadn't given any trouble.

Now Nan sat with a large bucket of mixed flowers at her feet and looked over at Adam, taking the curved back roads of Floritas with the relish of a Grand Prix test driver. Had he killed Shane? Rosalie O'Brien's admonition about not letting her personal relationship cloud reality kept echoing in Nan's mind.

Adam was moody, no question, and he had a temper. There were those assault charges, for one thing. He could explain each of them away, but there was an undeniable pattern. No way around it, the temper was there. Even Nan who rarely visited had seen it flare up. And he freely admitted racing over to Pettigrew Nurseries for a confrontation that had included at least raised voices and trashed plants.

She also remembered the time they'd been out to dinner and emerged from the restaurant to find the truck's window smashed and his tape deck missing. Adam was furious, pounding his hand into the back of the driver's seat. It was, she remembered glumly, the invasion of his space that angered him most.

An affair with one's wife constituted an invasion of space, all too literally.

Katsumi Nashimora and his wife lived in a ground-floor apartment in Encinitas, not far from the ocean. Mrs. Nashimora, a tiny woman with delicate Japanese features, let them in. She critically eyed Nan as she greeted Adam with genuine warmth. "We have been so worried," she told him. "Are you well?"

It was an interesting question, and Adam responded in the affirmative as he handed over the bucket of flowers. Before he could introduce Nan, a wizened old Nisei in a wheelchair rounded the corner. He didn't seem much larger than his wife.

"It was good of you to come," Mr. Nashimora said formally, "even in your time of trouble. The flowers are lovely. Please sit down, both of you." As he moved his chair into an empty space beside a small lacquered table, his wife disappeared with the bucket and Adam introduced Nan.

"I can see the resemblance to Julie," the old man told her. "She is a lovely woman, your sister." He turned dark, puzzled eyes on Adam. "But I cannot understand what they are saying, Adam. About the strange death of Shane Pettigrew."

"I don't understand it myself," Adam answered. He sounded almost as formal as his host. "But I wanted to tell you myself that I would never have hurt Shane."

"That is what Jeffrey said, and what he told the police. He told me officers talked to everyone at the nursery."

"Jeff's doing a fine job there," Adam told him. "Shane was really pleased with his work."

"He is a very smart boy," Mr. Nashimora agreed. "A college degree before his twentieth birthday. Richard was hopeful that he might go into medicine, but Jeffrey says he prefers the flower business." Richard Nashimora was Jeff's father and Cassie Pettigrew's first husband, a Brentwood plastic surgeon.

As the two men moved into a discussion of horticultural technicalities, Nan flirted with a new theory. Was it possible that the death of Shane was purely incidental, a stepping-stone to frame Adam so he'd be forced to leave the Nashimora property? Jeff Nashimora sounded like a pretty shrewd young man. Might he be looking to build his own floral empire on the base provided by his paternal grandfather?

Shane's death and Adam's arrest had pretty effectively cleared the younger generation out of two floriculture businesses all at once. Granted, Julie and Adam's operation was strictly mom-and-pop beside the complexities of the Pettigrew spread. But *somebody* would eventually have to take over Pettigrew, too, and Angus favored relatives.

After Mrs. Nashimora reappeared with a vase of exquisitely arranged flowers and a tea tray, Nan carefully broached the idea. "It's my understanding," she began, "that the reason you're leasing your property to Adam and

Julie is that Richard and your other children have pursued careers outside the floral business." The old man nodded slowly. "And I know it's certainly been a wonderful opportunity for Julie and Adam to take over a place that was already producing so much so beautifully. But I can't help wondering something that really isn't any of my business."

Adam looked at her curiously, and Mrs. Nashimora raised one eyebrow. Mr. Nashimora's leathery face remained impassive.

"I would imagine," Nan went on, "that your property is quite valuable in today's market, and that you've probably been approached from time to time about selling it for real-estate development."

Mr. Nashimora's gaze grew stonier. This was obviously nothing he wanted to discuss with a total stranger.

"Julie told me she'd heard rumors that a shopping mall might go in nearby, either on your land or those flower fields beside it. And I know that a lot of business people in Floritas would like the town chosen for Fairy Tale World, the children's theme park." It was a proposition that civic bean counters would relish: a tourist attraction aimed at families with young children and disposable income. Such a place would bring in immediate income to local motels, restaurants, and related businesses even while it enhanced the town's revenue base. "It occurred to me," Nan went on, "that if somebody wanted to get you to sell your property now, losing your tenants might influence you."

"The land is not for sale," Mr. Nashimora said slowly and deliberately. "Yes, they come to me now and again, but always I say that the land will not be sold while I am alive. And surely nobody would kill me for my few small acres."

The implication was clear enough, and exposed a glaring flaw in Nan's reasoning. If anybody'd be bumped off under Nan's theory, it would be the old man.

"I'm grasping at straws," Nan conceded. "And I must admit that I don't have a lot of respect for developers as a general class of people, so I'm always willing to assume the worst of them." Pond scum was an analogy that came to mind. "I'm just wondering, though, have you heard anything about the proposed shopping center, or Fairy Tale World?"

"I was approached a year or so ago," Mr. Nashimora admitted, "about the shopping center. And yes, there have been people who have talked to me about this Fairy Tale place. But I give them all the same answer, that I have no interest in selling. Perhaps Spencer Growers would sell the fields by my land, I don't know. That couple who bought the Sakai greenhouse, they might sell. I did not speak to them much ever."

If they were as peculiar as Julie claimed, that made sense. As the conversation moved back to more neutral territory, Nan decided she would visit Julie's next-door neighbors first thing in the morning.

And it was interesting that Katsumi Nashimora hadn't even mentioned his grandson in the context of the property's future.

That night, with Mom safely on an O'Hare-bound flight, life seemed much calmer. After dinner, Julie and Nan set up the Scrabble board and Adam reluctantly agreed to join them, grumbling good-naturedly that he'd be trounced.

As Julie placed the letters F-E-L-I-N-E on the board, she smiled wickedly at Nan. "So tell us about Nefertiti," she said sweetly.

Nan rolled her eyes. "I feel sandbagged," she said. "She'd been hanging around, the way Venice cats do, and I kept thinking—hoping—that she'd find a home somewhere. So then Veterinarian's Best Friend Mom brings her inside and the next thing I know she's got a little velvet bed and all her shots and Mom keeps saying in that cutesy, little-girl voice, 'You *can't* just cast her out again.'"

"Well? Can you?"

"I don't know," Nan admitted. "But I really don't *want* a cat. I don't even *like* cats."

"Yeah, I know," Julie said, mimicking her sister. " 'They're sneaky and suspicious and independent and smug and sly and they climb all over the kitchen counters.' Which, except for the kitchen counters, is a pretty accurate description of *you,* big sister."

"They also claw the furniture and yowl all night long. They pee on everything and poop in your shoes. If I wanted a pet, which I don't, I'd want one with some pet virtues: loyalty, obedience, enthusiasm."

Adam gave a deep guffaw. He seemed immeasurably relieved by his mother-in-law's departure. "Sounds like you want a boot camp Marine."

"If you're so concerned about Nefertiti, I could bring her down here," Nan offered.

"We've got four cats already," Julie said. "No way. Why don't you just give it a try, Nan? You can always cast her out again. Or take her to the pound. Of course if you take her to the pound, they'll probably have to kill her."

"All *right*," Nan answered irritably. "That's just exactly enough!"

With a flourish, she built B-I-T-C-H onto Julie's I.

At eight-fifteen on Monday morning, Nan crossed the barren orchard to the greenhouse next door to meet the elusive people who had bought the old Sakai greenhouse. They were a brother and sister named Kevin and Lucille Ellison who operated a "plug" business, starting flowers from seed and selling the tiny seedlings to other growers once they were firmly established.

As she approached the door, Nan could hear Beethoven playing inside. Loud. She knocked, waited a minute or two, then stepped inside and called, "Hello?" Louder.

A bespectacled woman who might have been anywhere from forty to sixty came out of the back of the greenhouse.

She wore overalls and an orange T-shirt and had stringy mouse-brown hair hanging listlessly on either side of a long, thin face. Nan's first thought was that she'd misplaced her pointed hat and broomstick.

"Yes?" the woman asked suspiciously.

Nan introduced herself and explained that she was trying to find out if either Lucille or her brother might have noticed anything unusual happening at the Chandler place in the weeks before Shane's murder.

"We pay no attention to them," Lucille answered rather shortly. "Except when we have to drive that dog off our property. It leaves its messes everywhere."

"I'm sorry to hear that," Nan apologized. How did it happen that *she* of all people had to defend Julie's nitwit dog? "Are you usually here most of the day?"

"It varies," Lucille said. "We have another greenhouse in Leucadia and we split our time. What we do here is very labor-intensive, however. Starting seed is an extremely exacting business that requires close supervision and great concentration." Presumably mere mortals couldn't possibly handle it.

"Are you ever here at night?" Nan asked. Julie had said not, but it couldn't hurt to check.

She shook her head. "Never."

"So you'd have no way of knowing if anybody came or went from the house next door on the night of January sixth?"

"I said I wouldn't. I've spoken to the police at some length about all of this already. I can't tell you any more than I told them."

"Do you see much of Julie and Adam?"

Lucille Ellison glared. "You don't listen very well, do you? I told you *no!*"

"I'm sorry to disturb you," Nan apologized. "And there's just one more thing I'm wondering about."

"Lu?" A male voice came from the back of the

greenhouse. "Lu, where are you?" The masculine counterpart to Lucille Ellison came around the corner carrying a flat of tiny green something-or-anothers. He ignored Nan and spoke to his sister. "Will you just *look* at this!"

Lucille gasped as she stared at whatever horror the seedlings offered. To Nan they looked perfectly swell.

"I'm Nan Robinson," she told the man. "You must be Kevin." It was an easy enough guess. He was the geek to his sister's geekette. His hair was as stringy as hers, though not as long and a lot thinner on top. His T-shirt was gray, but the blue denim overalls were the same style as Lucille's. It was the glasses that really amazed Nan, however. Both wore little wire-rimmed granny glasses, perched low on their noses, in a style that had been out of vogue for decades.

They might have been identical twins, one of whom had undergone sex-change surgery.

"Yes?" he answered, with his sister's surliness.

"I've been speaking to Lucille about my sister Julie and brother-in-law Adam next door," Nan said, watching Kevin's eyes narrow. "She tells me that you don't have much contact with them."

"I've never spoken to either of them in my life," he announced, turning to go back into the greenhouse. The Ellisons weren't long on social skills.

"There's just one more thing I'm curious about," Nan said to his receding back and his sister's sullen front. "I understand that there's talk of developing the land here, a shopping mall or maybe even Fairy Tale World. Do you know anything about that?"

"And what if I did?" Lucille snapped. "It wouldn't be any business of yours, then, would it? You'd best leave now. We have work to do."

Lucille held the door open and Nan walked through it. Julie was right: this pair was unlikely to notice anything larger than a mealybug.

* * *

Nan went back next door, had another cup of coffee, and then set off for Pettigrew Nurseries. The greenhouses covered several acres off El Camino Real, well down the hill from the house where Angus Pettigrew was holed up in the big windowless workshop with his earthbound rocket ships. There couldn't be much joy, anymore, in being master of all he surveyed. All that was left was the land.

Fields gently rolled between the greenhouses and the house, planted with something just starting to break through the dark soil in defiant emerald sprouts. It was impossible for Nan to tell now what the field would look like when it came into its glory in a few months. She felt safe in assuming, however, that Angus Pettigrew wouldn't much care.

Being here on the Pettigrew land was oddly unsettling. Superficially everything looked healthy and prosperous. But underneath it all, there was a sense of . . . she wasn't sure what. She couldn't help feeling that there was definitely something wrong, something far more than the simple murder of a philandering flower grower.

Nan remembered reading about a giant fungus discovered on thirty acres of the Michigan Upper Peninsula. *Thirty acres.* The largest living thing in the world, it was, silently reaching out and twisting and expanding for millennia, just below the surface of the forest floor. No human had ever realized it was there, its tentacles tangled in the roots of everything that grew above, around, and through it. It had survived all that time by feeding on the remains of dead and decaying plant life, things that had once been as marvelously vibrant and alive as the exotic flowers growing in these greenhouses by the King's Highway.

There seemed to be some kind of subterranean force here, too, and Nan wished she could figure out what it was.

As she drove along the concrete roadway between the tall, plastic-shrouded greenhouses, the place seemed deserted. Inside some of the greenhouses, she could barely make out the shapes of tall green plants. Big heater hoses on the outside looked like gargantuan clothes dryer exhausts.

But when she turned left beyond the last building, the employee parking lot was full. It might be Martin Luther King's birthday and a national holiday, but the flowers didn't know that. As Julie had expected, the Pettigrew operation seemed to be in full swing. The cars were primarily American, battered old junkers that probably belonged mostly to the Mexican workers and could only have survived so long in a desert climate where metal rarely rusted.

Nan got out of her car and stopped a moment to look around.

According to the map Julie had drawn, Shane's office with its private outside entrance was right around the corner there. That patch of oleander, then, over by where the nicer, newer, imported cars were parked—the nursery's equivalent of an executive lot?—must be where the police had found Adam's gun. It was a ridiculous spot to discard something you didn't want found immediately, which made the idea of a frame more plausible.

She wished she knew, really *knew*, that Adam was innocent. But she couldn't quite make the final leap of faith required. And if he *was* guilty, she wanted to find out for certain now and make the best of a bad situation. Why squander time, hope, and energy in a futile attempt to clear him? Nan had always been a firm believer in taking bad medicine and getting it over with.

She walked over to the entrance to Shane's office, now tightly closed and presumably locked. She considered. Working late at night, Shane would surely have heard any unusual noises from outside. There were no houses around here, just the hushed greenhouses and his father's lonely place far up the hill. An approaching car would sound like a freight train. The gravel path crunched under Nan's feet;

it would be difficult to sneak up without making some kind of noise.

Yet Shane hadn't gotten up to investigate, was still sitting at his desk when he was shot. He might have been expecting his killer, of course, at an assignation set for some other reason. Did he ever bring women here at night? Good luck at this point getting anyone to speak to *that* subject.

The autopsy had shown him to be legally drunk at the time of his death, something else nobody was talking about. Maybe it was too much trouble for Shane to get up and investigate an arriving car. Maybe he was passed out. Or maybe his visitor had come in and stayed a while, then killed him.

But these last two ideas seemed unlikely. There was a pen in his hand, according to Ramón's police contacts. It seemed more likely that he'd been taken totally by surprise by someone who slipped up the path and came in suddenly.

There was no reason to assume, though, that the killer arrived after Shane did. Someone might have been biding time, waiting to be sure Shane showed up alone. Hiding here at night would be easy. There were plenty of places where a car could be tucked unnoticed between the greenhouses, and there were literally thousands of spots where a person could find cover for hours. Nor was a car essential; slipping away on foot might take a while, but it could certainly be done.

Getting in and out by bicycle would be even easier, she realized grimly. Particularly for someone like Adam, who knew every inch of the property and surrounding hills, had been traveling this route since El Camino Real was barely paved.

But enough of that.

How had the killer known Shane would be working late that night? He might have mentioned his plan to any number of people. Apparently it was well known that he liked to handle paperwork and administrative chores at night when there'd be no interruptions. Of course, anyone who had known that Shane planned to be in his office the night he was killed wasn't admitting it now.

Nan went back to the warehouse entrance. A medium-sized white refrigerated truck bearing Arizona plates and the logo of a Phoenix floral company was backed up to a wide loading door. As Nan watched, two Latino men loaded boxes of flowers onto the truck while an Anglo driver ticked things off on a clipboard.

She walked around the truck and saw other employees inside, across the warehouse packing more boxes of flowers. Buckets and carts loaded with flowers were everywhere and fresh floral scents filled the morning air. At a table on the far side of the room, four women deftly stripped and bundled roses.

Nobody paid the slightest attention as Nan crossed to the open doorway leading to a small suite of offices on the west side of the warehouse.

The executive offices of Pettigrew Nurseries had a strange ambience: part small-town hardware office, part turn-of-the-century feed store. Scarred wooden desks didn't match each other or their chairs, and the wooden mail pigeonholes in one corner were so old the paint was flecking off. The walls were paneled in unvarnished, highly pitted dry wood that seemed likely to spontaneously combust. Framed eleven-by-fourteen pictures of flowers provided the sole ornamental touch, and those were badly faded. One had been knocked slightly off center and the paneling revealed underneath was much darker.

Anachronous dry erase boards on the walls charted the current prices of various flowers, mostly esoteric. What on earth was ministrictum, Nan wondered idly, and how did it differ from maxi? Just inside the door a clear plastic gallon bottle of Kooler Kleaner and Bucket Bath sat on the stained brown industrial carpeting.

Directly ahead, a man in shirtsleeves talked into a phone

that rested on his shoulder with a padded extender. Nan recognized him from the funeral as Will Drake, the sandy-haired marketing manager. He gave a hearty salesman's chuckle as Nan passed through to Margaret Whiting's office.

If anything, the office manager's lair was more Spartan than the outer office. The floor in here was linoleum, circa 1953. A coffee maker and computer were the only modern touches; a scrivener in an eyeshade on a tall stool would look right at home.

"Can I help you?" Margaret Whiting looked up from the papers she was working with on a desk. She had the no-nonsense look Nan remembered from Shane's funeral. But she also looked tired. Her pale hair was flat and lifeless, her eyes wary behind lenses in plain plastic frames. She reminded Nan of somebody. Who?

"I hope so," Nan answered warmly. This was going to be tricky. She identified herself fully and watched the woman's eyes narrow suspiciously.

"I don't see what I can possibly—" Margaret Whiting began.

Nan held up a gentle hand. "If you could just hear me out for a moment? May I sit down?"

Manners triumphed over hostility, as Nan had hoped they would. Margaret Whiting gave the shadow of a nod, and Nan pulled a padded metal chair from the wall. She set it near the office manager's desk and sat down.

"I know this has all been terribly difficult for you," she began. "I met Shane several times and had the opportunity to talk with him quite a while on Boxing Day. I thought he was a remarkable person." Maybe she was laying it on too thick, but everyone agreed that Margaret was fanatically loyal to the Pettigrews. Nan noticed a slight flicker when she mentioned Boxing Day. "Perhaps you were at Mr. Pettigrew's party, too? It was terribly crowded and I didn't know many people . . ."

Margaret Whiting nodded slightly again.

"Anyway," Nan went on, "I find it absolutely appalling that somebody would kill Shane. He was so very much alive, and seemed like such a genuinely nice person. Now I know that the police think my brother-in-law killed him, and that there's some circumstantial evidence to support that idea. But I'm personally worried by three things. One, I don't think Adam killed Shane. Two, if Adam didn't, then somebody else did and is getting away with it. And three, who shot at Adam and Ramón last Monday?"

"The police seem entirely satisfied," Margaret Whiting said stiffly. "Surely that's more their department than yours."

Nan smiled. "Strictly speaking, of course you're right. But you see, I'm an attorney who works in investigations for the California State Bar. Of course that's hardly the same as investigating a murder, but the work I do has given me a sort of sixth sense about when a situation just doesn't seem right. And frankly, Ms. Whiting, this situation seems totally wrong."

Margaret Whiting regarded Nan sullenly. She wasn't about to volunteer anything, not even a cup of coffee.

"Were you here on New Year's Eve when Adam came by to see Shane?"

Margaret sniffed. "Well, I guess so! He was ranting and carrying on like a madman. He stood right there in that doorway and swore he'd kill Shane." Swell. Nobody'd shared that charming detail with Nan before. "And before I could do anything, he ran off to the greenhouse."

"Did you think Shane was in danger at the time? Enough to, say, call the police?"

"Well, I didn't call the police, for heaven's sake. But I did ask Jeff to go make sure they were all right." As Adam had said.

"Did you have any indication before that Shane was . . .

involved with my sister?" Nan continued, marching briskly into the quicksand.

"I don't see what possible business of yours that is." Which sounded like *yes* to Nan. "Or what it has to do with the price of peas."

Aunt Aggie, Nan thought suddenly. That's who Margaret was like: Mom's cousin from Davenport, Iowa. Aunt Aggie who handled everything but the drill in Uncle Jack's dental practice.

"It's my business because Adam has asked me to help him, and because if somebody has framed him for something he didn't do, there must be a *reason*. That reason may have to do with Adam or it may have to do with Shane or it may not have anything to do with either of them. I just don't know. Ms. Whiting, I realize this is painful for you, but surely you want justice done."

"She had no business carrying on with him," Margaret stated firmly. "She was married to one of his best friends."

So Julie was cast here as the malevolent temptress. Interesting.

"And apparently they were indiscreet. Was the affair common knowledge?"

Margaret shook her head. "I don't believe so."

"But you knew about it."

"Only by chance." She spoke reluctantly, and a slight flush rose on her neck. "I . . . overheard a telephone conversation. I picked up the phone to make a call without pushing the button to a clear line first. She was . . . telling him she couldn't make it that afternoon, that it would have to be another time."

Interesting again. Margaret was a telephone eavesdropper. Nan wondered just how much she knew about Shane's affairs, sexual and otherwise. Probably plenty. Of course she'd never admit listening on a regular basis. But Nan would have bet a truckload of sweetheart roses on it.

"You recognized Julie's voice?"

"Certainly. I've known her ever since she moved back here with Adam. She worked here on and off, you know, before they moved into the Nashimora place. When I had surgery a few years ago, she worked in this very office." The notion seemed to disgust Margaret, to warrant a belated Lysol hose-down.

"Did you ask Shane about Julie at the time?"

"Of course not!"

"So it might have been simply a meeting to discuss some kind of business."

Margaret hesitated a moment, torn between loyalty to the dead and the desire to firmly pin that red A on Julie's chest. "Shane's personal bills come to this office, ever since he and Sara separated. They included ... motel charges."

"I see." And Nan did. Margaret was the kind of woman who would backtrack on her accurate and detailed calendar to reconstruct the days when Shane charged a room at some hot pillow house to his MasterCard. "When Julie worked here earlier, did you notice any kind of ... improper relationship then? Or any other time before the phone call you inadvertently overheard?"

Margaret shook her head. "Shane and Sara were still living together back then. Poor Sara. Left alone with those two fatherless boys to raise." Evidently Margaret had never officially recognized the divorce. Sara had, after all, been left alone quite a while before Shane died. But if the woman nursed a devotion to Sara, that was an avenue of approach.

"I saw Sara on Saturday. She told me she's absolutely certain that Adam couldn't have, *wouldn't* have, killed Shane. She can't imagine why Angus Pettigrew is so certain that he did."

Margaret stiffened again at the mention of the patriarch's name. "Mr. Pettigrew has suffered beyond endurance. That poor man has lost everything—his wife, his daughter, and now his son. All he has left are his grandsons. I don't see how he can find the strength to carry on."

Perhaps by blaming an easy scapegoat. "Have you spoken with him since he got out of the hospital?"

"I'm sure that's none of your business. Mr. Pettigrew knows that the company can function in his absence."

In other words, no.

"And I'm sure you're carrying on quite well," Nan agreed. "Of course it must be difficult picking up on all the things that Shane was doing. For instance, I understand that some of the alstroemeria hybrids he was working with are missing."

Margaret Whiting emitted a faint gasp. "How on earth do you—I'm sure I don't know what you're talking about."

"Ms. Whiting, someone told my sister yesterday that the greenhouse where Shane was hybridizing was inventoried this week, and that several of his most perfect and highly developed specimens were gone. And that they haven't turned up anywhere else on the premises."

This was a truly hot scoop, one whispered to Julie last night on the phone by a source she declined to name. Nan hadn't pressed her on it, but suspected it was somebody here at Pettigrew. Jeff Nashimora, at a guess.

Margaret wasn't saying anything, so Nan went on.

"As I understand it, they're the flowers that he was working on with Kimberly Wilkes. Who also left here very recently. Did anybody see the alstroemerias after Kimberly quit?"

Julie's source said no. Margaret clammed up and Nan went on.

"I can't help but wonder if there's some connection between all these events. Could the flowers have been missing without Shane being aware of it?"

Margaret shook her head. "He worked in there every day."

"Could anyone who worked here get into that greenhouse?"

"Access was restricted. We keep the keys here in the office." She nodded at the wall just inside the door. An assortment of keys hung from pegs on a tole-painted wooden bed of tulips. "Shane generally kept that greenhouse locked because of the possibility of something being improperly pollinated. We have so many different species here, you see."

"But of course Shane could get in and out whenever he wanted. What about Kimberly?"

"What about her?" This lady wasn't giving an inch.

"I know she worked closely with Shane on that project. Did she have a key?"

Margaret nodded, her lips tightly pursed. She seemed to rank Kimberly somewhere between leaf miners and thrips.

It was hard for Nan to get a fix on Kimberly Wilkes. Was she just Shane's flavor-of-the-month, as Sara and Margaret both seemed to feel, or was she a dedicated young professional lucky enough to find a position of responsibility with a prominent grower? She certainly wouldn't be the first young woman whose mentor was also her lover. More important, perhaps, if she was Today's Young Career Woman, had the morality gene been bred out of her in grad school?

"Let me ask you a hypothetical question. If Kimberly, or somebody else with access to that greenhouse, wanted to remove some plants and not be noticed, how could they do it?"

"It wouldn't be difficult," Margaret said after a moment. "That particular greenhouse is on a corner and there's a door at the end of it. If she acted as if she wasn't doing anything wrong, nobody would pay any attention. Plants and flowers are always being moved around here. She could put a few specimens in a van or a truck. Even the trunk of a car."

"The plants that are missing, were there very many of them?"

Margaret shook her head.

"So Kimberly would certainly seem like a logical suspect. Isn't there some way you could have the police investigate, or press charges against her?"

"For what? Once a plant is repotted and relabeled there's no way to prove its identity. Even if we were certain that a plant in her possession came from this nursery, it would simply be our word against hers."

"So she could get away with it."

"She already has," Margaret Whiting said firmly. "And now, if you don't mind, I'm really quite busy. Can you find your way out?"

Will Drake was still on the phone when Nan carefully closed the door to Margaret's office. She hesitated a moment, then pulled a chair up and sat by the end of his desk. It was a mass of order forms and papers, all wildly jumbled. Which probably drove Margaret crazy.

He smiled a greeting and continued the conversation, something about gerbera daisies. There was a decided southwestern twang in his voice. In a moment or two he hung up and turned to Nan.

"I know we haven't met," he said, extending a hand, "because I never forget a face, 'specially not a pretty one. I'm Will Drake. What can I do you for?"

Nan introduced herself, omitting her relationship to the Chandlers. She explained that she'd been talking with Margaret about Shane's murder, which was true enough.

"I've been investigating," she went on, "and I'm concerned that there may be some motive that hasn't been readily apparent, something that would explain what happened."

"What happened," Will Drake said, "is that Adam Chandler found out Shane was diddling his wife and he blew him away." The implication, right at home with his accent, was that such behavior was both logical and justified.

"On the face of things that certainly seems plausible," Nan agreed. "But what about others who might have had a grudge against Shane Pettigrew? Someone in the business, perhaps?"

He shook his head. "Not that kind of business." He pronounced it *bidness.* "Everybody gets on just fine. And Shane, he got on with everybody."

"So I understand. He seems to have gotten on particularly well with women."

Will Drake chuckled. "Good-looking young fellow like that, can't say it's a surprise the ladies took to him. 'Course he shoulda known better'n to fool with a friend's wife. Nothing but trouble lies that way."

"How long have you worked for Pettigrew Nurseries?" Nan asked.

"Oh, I reckon it's been three, four years now."

"Have you been in the flower industry around here long?"

He shook his head. "No, ma'am. Came out here because my wife's mother was sick, never really intending to stay. Worked in the Rio Grande Valley before that, selling Ruby Red grapefruit out of Brownsville."

"So you haven't really known—"

"What on earth is going on here?" The voice belonged to Margaret Whiting and it was furious.

Nan turned to the doorway where the woman stood with her hands on her hips.

"I was just talking to Will here," she began.

"I really don't think you have any further business on the premises," Margaret informed her coldly. "I'd suggest you leave immediately."

"Why, Margaret," Drake said, standing up. "What's the problem? This lady's investigating—"

"This lady is Adam Chandler's sister-in-law and she's

got no business snooping around here." Evidently the only snooping Margaret sanctioned was her own.

Will Drake looked at Nan with a slightly hurt expression. "You didn't say . . ."

"I didn't really get a chance to," Nan apologized, standing up. "Ms. Whiting, I certainly didn't mean to disrupt anyone's work here, and I'll be happy to move along now." She put one of her cards on Will Drake's desk. "If you think of anything, please call me."

CHAPTER 12

On her way out of the Pettigrew Nurseries complex, Nan made a few deliberate wrong turns, looking for the greenhouse where Shane's missing alstroemerias had been kept. She never did find the place and emerged hopelessly confused, with a sense that someone who knew her way around could probably spirit away an entire building, not just a few rare plants.

Then she got lucky. As she turned toward El Camino Real, she saw Jeff Nashimora coming out of one of the greenhouses. Alone. He wore jeans, a black sweatshirt, and tennis shoes. She waved and beckoned to him, and he crossed to her car, looking puzzled.

When she introduced herself, he smiled. "I saw you come in and I wondered who you were."

"Well, I just got the bum's rush out of here," Nan admitted, "but I'd really like to talk to you. Is there someplace around here we could maybe go get some coffee?"

He glanced at an expensive watch. "I could duck out for a little while, sure, if you'll bring me back. And there's a place just up in La Costa where they roast their own beans." He crossed in front of the car and got into the passenger seat, commenting with pleasure on the Mustang. A few minutes later they were seated on a patio overlooking a new development of enormous, four-bedroom split-levels.

"So," Nan asked, "how'd you decide to come work at Pettigrew? It must seem kind of . . . tame after L.A."

He gave a disarming smile. He was a good-looking kid, appearing vaguely Pan-Pacific but not particularly Japanese. Cassie had strong genes. His hair and eyes were dark, but he was big-boned and nearly six feet tall.

"It was a couple of things," he answered, setting down his cappuccino. "I was planning to go into international banking, and I still may. But what happened was, junior year we were assigned to review an existing small business and spotlight its strengths and weaknesses. I did my study on Pettigrew Nurseries, kind of as a lark. But when I was down here doing the research, I found myself kind of . . . enjoying myself. Shane took me out surfing a couple of times like he used to when I'd visit as a kid. I had a lot of fun. Then when I finished the report and showed it to Shane, he told me any time I wanted, I could come back and go to work here. When I finished at SC, I had some pretty good offers, but I started thinking, maybe it would be kind of interesting to come here for a few years. Kick back a little, surf, enjoy myself. When it gets old or I get bored, I can always go back to banking."

Nan frowned. "Isn't banking kind of a shrinking field right now?"

He smiled with serene confidence. "True enough. But I speak fluent Japanese."

"A useful skill," Nan agreed. "So what exactly do you do at Pettigrew, anyway?"

"Whatever nobody else wants to do, actually. Shane was starting to have me do a lot of administrative stuff, which he didn't really like much. I've been rotating, working with the different parts of the business. Except growing. Neither one of my grandfathers would like to hear me say this, but I've got a real black thumb. Doesn't matter much, though, since there's so many others really good at that. But I've been kind of surprised to see how . . . well, bush league a lot of the operations are. You know, things done a certain way just because that's how it's always been done. There's a lot that could be done with shipping, for instance, to open new markets. And Pettigrew's marketing . . . well, it's okay, I suppose. But generally, when you get past cutting prices, folks in the flower industry haven't got a clue about marketing."

"You sound like you're in this for the long haul." Interesting.

"I guess it's possible." The disarming smile again, then a slightly darker expression. "I worked really well with Shane, but anything could happen now."

"Do you have any ideas who might have wanted Shane out of the picture?"

"Enough to kill him? None at all. It doesn't make sense to me, killing Shane. Of course they all say Adam did it, but that's awfully hard for me to imagine."

"You know Adam well?"

He shook his head. "Hardly at all, really. I see him mornings at the beach sometimes, but nobody talks much there. Other than that, I just know he was a friend of Shane's and my mom's. My mom doesn't get along very well with my grandfather Pettigrew, so we never visited him much when I was a kid. I know my other grandparents a lot better, really." He reflected a moment. "My grandfather Nashimora was really pleased when Adam and Julie took over his greenhouse."

Nan had ordered a truly sinful cafe mocha, with a mountain of whipped cream and sprinkle of cinnamon. She took a sip and asked, "What's it been like around the nursery since Shane's death?"

He considered. "Sort of like everything's . . . on hold. Like everybody's on some kind of NordicTrack trying real hard to move but not getting anywhere. Some folks think my grandfather Pettigrew's going to come down and take charge, but I doubt it, myself." Would the king descend from Olympus? Film at eleven.

"What have people said about the missing alstroemerias?"

That one brought a grin. "That they're sitting on Kimberly's patio."

"Would she do that?" Nan asked.

The grin widened. "Old Kimberly? I guess she'd do just about anything, if she decided it was what she wanted."

An intriguing response. Had she ever wanted this healthy and attractive young man?

"You know her well?"

Jeff shook his head. "Just to see at work. She was Shane's girl."

Shane's girl did not seem pleased when Nan found a pay phone after dropping Jeff Nashimora back at the nursery and called her at Transbloom in Vista.

"This is Nan Robinson," she told the young woman. "I'm investigating Shane Pettigrew's murder and I'd like to ask you a few questions."

"I've already told the police everything I know," the young woman protested.

"I understand that," Nan said officiously. This was dangerous territory. It would definitely not do for a State Bar investigator to be charged with impersonating an officer. "But there are a few things I'd like to clear up. I'll be there in about half an hour. Where can I find you?"

Nan followed a battered old pickup with a camper shell down Highway 78 to Vista. The license plate holder announced: MY OTHER CAR WAS REPOSSESSED. It was flanked by bumper stickers saying ORGASM DONOR and WORK: MILLIONS ON WELFARE DEPEND ON YOU and MY KID BEAT UP THE STUDENT OF THE MONTH. Emulating the old man, at a guess.

The night before, Adam and Julie had theorized about the implications of the missing alstroemerias.

"If I had my hands on a really unique flower," Adam had

observed, "and I wanted to cash in fast, I'd take it offshore. To Mexico, or maybe even Colombia. Then I'd set up a tissue culture lab and reproduce the hell out of it for my greenhouse operation. Tissue culture's expensive, but you can get a zillion plants in a hurry. Then I'd grow those plants and ship their cut flowers right back to the U.S. of A. A grower can get patent protection for a unique variety, but you can't enforce a patent on flowers imported from offshore. And for a really hot flower, the demand would be enormous."

"What would you consider a 'hot' flower?" Nan asked.

Adam thought for a minute. "It would have to be truly remarkable to make it worth all the trouble and expense. You'd have a *lot* of start-up costs. But it would be worth it for something like a genuine blue rose, or a black one. Roses take a long time to reproduce 'cause you can't use seed. So do bulbs. A blue amaryllis might be nice. With flowers that grow easily from seed it probably wouldn't be worth the trouble or expense. Like a blue zinnia. Or maybe a pink marigold."

Julie grinned and looked at Nan. "Remember when Burpee had that contest? To find a white marigold?"

Yeah, right. Nan shook her head with a polite smile.

Julie misconstrued simple courtesy for interest and continued. "Well, old man Burpee just loved marigolds, and what he really wanted was a white one. So they put up a reward for anybody who could produce a truly white blossom, ten grand. It was *great* marketing. You figure with millions of people growing marigolds every year, some of them are bound to have white mutations. People kept sending in their seeds, something like eight thousand of them, and after twenty years, a great-grandmother from Iowa won the prize. Now Burpee offers great big gorgeous white marigolds and they've even developed hybrids." She frowned slightly. "There aren't any more Burpees in the business anymore, though. Bought out by the big boys."

This was the most animated Julie had been since Shane's

death. Nan fed her a question, eager to continue the mood. "So what about pink marigolds?"

Adam shook his head. "No pink ones, Nan. Not even close. Species that cross over from the pink-white-lavender range to the red-orange-yellow one aren't all that common, and it's usually a big deal when it happens. Like when somebody came up with an orange-faced pansy. Even orange roses still aren't that common."

"Because they're ugly," Julie sniffed.

"Whatever," Nan said. "So would Shane's alstroemerias fall into that category? Worth setting up an operation in Mexico for?"

Adam and Julie shook their heads simultaneously. Nan was pleased to see them thinking this through as a team. Adam couldn't possibly realize they were talking about the flowers that first brought Julie and Shane together.

"He had some nice specimens," Adam said, "but nothing that spectacular. He had a long way to go before there'd be something to really knock out the industry."

"They'd make a nice calling card, though," Julie had pointed out, "for somebody looking to improve her position."

Kimberly's directions to Transbloom were accurate and precise. Nan had no trouble finding the low white buildings off Santa Fe Drive in Vista. A woman at a desk in the front office made a phone call, and Kimberly appeared almost immediately.

She was slight and pretty, with a cloud of russet hair, deep-green eyes, and a pale, almost translucent complexion. She looked very, very young. Julie said Kimberly was twenty-four, but this girl could easily pass for a high school JV cheerleader. Or Jeff Nashimora's steady girl, wearing his letter sweater. She wore a white lab coat over trim turquoise slacks and a matching silk shell. She seemed anxious to get away from the front office and quickly led Nan down an inside corridor.

"We can talk in my office here," she explained, opening the door to a small cubicle.

The inside wall was glass and overlooked an enormous room full of tiny green plants. This wasn't the standard North County wood-and-plastic-sheeting greenhouse, but a solid building with walls and a relatively low solid ceiling. Fluorescent lights were suspended not far above the young plants. At the distant end, beyond another glass wall, two figures in pale-green surgical gowns and caps worked busily at something Nan couldn't quite see.

"How interesting," Nan exclaimed, looking out through the glass. "What are you growing?"

The young woman looked at her in mild annoyance. "This is a tissue culture laboratory," she explained. "We take species of plants that are particularly strong or desirable and reproduce them asexually. The techniques we use allow us to make a million copies of a single plant in a year, where conventional rooting techniques might only provide a dozen."

"Very impressive," Nan told her. "So does that mean that all those plants down there are the same? What are they?"

Alstroemerias, maybe?

Kimberly shook her head. She seemed nervous. "There are a number of different plants being reproduced right now, but I'm afraid that I can't discuss the particulars. That's confidential information."

The young woman sat in the chair at her computer terminal, turned to face Nan, and smiled faintly. The computer screen behind her glowed green with statistics, as bright as the clones in the lab beyond. There was one other chair, hard-backed metal, just inside the door. Nan sat in it.

"I don't see what I can help you with," Kimberly said. "I've already told the other officers everything I know."

"Actually," Nan said, "I'm not with the police."

Kimberly started. "Then what—"

"Julie Chandler is my sister. I don't believe that Adam killed Shane and I'm trying to find out who actually did."

"You told me you were a cop!"

Nan shook her head. "Not at all. I only told you I was investigating Shane's murder, which is perfectly true. I know you were sleeping with Shane and I know you were working on his special hybridization program." She smiled and crossed her legs. "They've discovered that the alstros are missing, you know. And they know perfectly well what happened to them."

Kimberly tried to look indignant, without great success. She was braced for another kind of confrontation altogether. She started to say something, stopped, and then stood up.

"You came in here under false pretenses," she announced, "and if you don't leave immediately I'm going to call the police."

Nan chuckled. Thrown out of three different greenhouses by three different indignant women in a single morning. She'd have to look into charm school.

"I don't really think you'd want the police to know why I came to see you," Nan pointed out. "They're likely to start wondering just when those plants turned up missing. It might occur to them that maybe you stole them before Shane was killed, and when he confronted you about it, you shot him to keep your secret."

"That's nonsense!"

"Oh, I don't know. I understand you were with Shane on the night he died."

"We had dinner, not that it's any business of yours," Kimberly snapped.

"And sex, too." Ramón had sounded embarrassed during the phone call where he revealed that detail, based partly on the autopsy and partly on the presence of semen on Shane's underwear. Real men, Ramón had implied, didn't discuss the particulars of other real men getting laid. At least not with women.

Kimberly's eyes widened. She glared and said nothing.

"You were at your apartment, weren't you?"

"I don't have to talk to you about this or anything else."

Which was certainly true. Ramón had assured Nan that the police had verified Shane and Kimberly's dinner at a Greek restaurant in Oceanside. A neighbor had seen him leave her apartment around ten-thirty. If there were holes in the story, the police were in a much better position than Nan to find them. Of course, that presupposed that they were looking.

"Never mind all that, then. I'm sure it must be very disturbing to realize you were the last woman he was ever with. But I'm also sure he enjoyed it." The bitchy statement surprised Nan. Where had it come from?

Hatred blazed out of Kimberly Wilkes's deep-green eyes. "Get out of here," she ordered. She opened the door and pointed down the hall as if dismissing an errant student from a disciplinary session with the principal. The effect was lost, however. She looked more like a fourteen-year-old who'd just told her mother she never asked to be born.

"The thing is," Nan said, "there's the alstroemerias to consider." She stood and stretched languidly. "I understand that it would be next to impossible to identify the plants that are missing. And of course I have no way of knowing whether your new employers are part of this scam." She stretched again, moved to the inner window, and gestured down at the hundreds of thousands of tiny plants. "This job's a step up from what you were doing at Pettigrew, isn't it?"

Kimberly stared furiously. When she realized she was still pointing down the hall, she awkwardly dropped her arm.

"Right now," Nan went on, "I don't think anyone at Pettigrew is inclined to make too much of a fuss. For one thing, they're all still in shock, mourning Shane. What's a few flowers when you've lost someone you love? And ripping off a couple of plants might not initially seem like a big deal to somebody outside the industry. The police, for instance. But cops can be quick studies, sometimes. If those prize alstroemerias should happen to be down on the floor there getting ready to flood the market, they could probably make a nice case for felony grand theft."

Kimberly started to sputter, and Nan held up a hand. The girl fell silent.

"Right now, only a few people know about this. But I rather imagine that if the story made it into the papers, you'd be in a really touchy position and so would the people who run this lab. You're young and unproven, and a smart company would cut you loose in a twinkling, horrified to have been taken in by such a sweet young thing."

"You don't know what you're talking about," Kimberly asserted. There wasn't much starch left in her. "I'll show you out."

"Thanks for your time," Nan told her cordially. "It's been extremely educational."

Kimberly grimaced, her shoulders rigid under the lab coat. "Go to hell," she hissed.

The lunch crowd was thinning out when Nan arrived at Hobbs House at one-thirty, but there were still lots of people in the restaurant and the general air was bright and convivial. Hobbs House sat just across the coast highway from the Floritas beach. Windows all along the west wall offered magnificent views of wet-suited surfers, soaring aquatic birds, and a fishing pier to the south. This was the beach where Adam and Shane and Ramón had learned to surf as boys, where they still surfed a quarter of a century later.

A couple was just leaving a window table, and the hostess cheerfully signaled a busboy to clear it for Nan. The restaurant's interior was done in vibrant shades of pink and turquoise, and there were fresh flowers on all the tables. Nan blinked in sudden recognition. They were pink alstroemerias. With freckles.

A chipper waitress wearing shorts and a sunny smile brought iced tea and ran through an impressive list of specials. Every one sounded splendid, and Nan realized suddenly that she was incredibly hungry. She decided on the house seafood salad and asked if Pete Hobbs might be around. Still beaming, the waitress promised to find him immediately. The place was relentlessly cheerful.

A moment later, Pete Hobbs stood beside the table, in white pants and a bright pink-and-turquoise island shirt that matched the decor. The blue was pretty much the same color as his eyes, too. "Nan Robinson!" he exclaimed, as if even winning the lottery couldn't please him more. "I'm so *glad* you came by!"

"Everyone said this was a terrific place," she answered, "so I wanted to check it out. Have you got a minute?"

"For you—an hour. May I?" He had his hand on the back of the chair opposite Nan, and at her nod, he sat down. "How are Julie and Adam doing? I've meant to call, but . . ."

"But it's awkward. I know. They're doing all right, Pete, but this is a really tough time for them."

The waitress reappeared and set a glass of tea in front of Pete. He beamed up at her. "Could you bring us a plate of clam toasts, Mindy?" He turned to Nan. "I want to see what you think of these. We've just added them to the menu."

"I saw Sara on Saturday," Nan told him. "Maybe she mentioned it to you."

"She did indeed. Said she was real pleased you were working so hard to figure out what really happened."

Somehow Nan had a hard time believing this. But Pete Hobbs was the kind of guy who'd put a positive spin on anything: root canals, screaming babies, chemotherapy. The minor confrontation with Frank Reid and its aftermath still made Nan a little queasy. "Her brother came by just before I left. Have you met him, Pete?"

Pete put his head back and chuckled. "Old Frank's a real character, isn't he?"

Indeed. "I understand he didn't get along very well with Shane, particularly toward the end of the marriage."

Mindy set down a small platter heaped with tiny triangular open-faced sandwiches as Pete Hobbs raised his hands, palms up. "Thanks. He's a loyal guy, Frank. Looking out for his baby sister. I've got a sister, too, back in Ohio, and if I thought somebody did her wrong, I'd probably get upset about it myself."

To the point of aggravated assault? Nan tried one of the clam toasts. It was piping hot, cheesy and delicious.

"Mmm, *nice!*" she told him. "You know, I was glad to hear that you and Sara are together." She offered a saccharine smile of her own. It was catching in this place; pretty soon she'd be doodling happy faces on her napkin. "I guess she's been through a pretty hard time, even before Shane's death."

"The lady's a trouper," he reported with great admiration. "No doubt about it, Nan, a real trouper. And those boys of hers are pistols. I don't want to make it seem like more than it maybe is, but I consider myself one lucky fellow these days."

A lucky fellow whose girlfriend seemed quite nicely set up financially. "This is a wonderful place," Nan said. "Have you had it long?"

He shook his head. "Only four years now. I'm the new kid in town. I'll tell you what happened. I had a restaurant in Dayton and I came out to San Diego for a convention in January. The place just knocked my socks off. I told myself, Pete, you're only gonna go around once, that is where you oughta be. Six months later, I'd sold the steak house in Dayton and bought this place. It used to be a seafood house, but I thought that was too limited. Brought in a really fine chef, real talented little lady, and here we are. Got a great write-up in last month's *San Diego* magazine."

"I'm not a bit surprised," Nan told him, helping herself to her fifth or sixth piece of clam toast. She'd lost count and decided it didn't really matter. "Victoria told me you're thinking of opening another restaurant, too."

He held his hands up, the first two fingers on each crossed. "Hoping to. Hoping to. A lot will depend on whether or not we manage to get Fairy Tale World here. You heard about that?"

Nan nodded. "A little."

Nan's salad arrived, a massive glass bowl filled with delicate greens and topped with bay shrimp and what looked like genuine crabmeat. She tasted it. The house dressing was honey and mustard with just the right tang of lemon. "Delicious!" she told him, and he leaned back in mock relief. "So tell me about Fairy Tale World."

Pete Hobbs leaned forward and put both elbows on the table. Though he'd been nodding and waving and even exchanging a word or two with customers who passed the table all along, he managed to give Nan the sense that she was the most important person in the entire building. "I am so *excited* about the possibilities," he told her conspiratorially. "It would give Floritas just the economic kick in the pants we really need right now. These have been hard times around here lately, and Southern California tourism has been off everywhere. San Diego County has some really terrific attractions: Sea World, the Zoo, the Wild Animal Park. But we haven't had anything up here in coastal North County to draw overnight trade. We get the Canadian snowbirds every winter, and God bless 'em. But Fairy Tale World would pull in young families year round, and those are the folks we really need."

Nan nodded. "So it's pretty much a sure thing?"

He frowned slightly. "Not nearly as sure as some of us

would like it to be. We've got us a group of business people and merchants pushing really hard, and the City Council's pretty solidly behind us, except for one fellow, and he's kind of opposed to progress in general. But there's other places just as anxious as we are, and I'm not at all sure we've got the inside track just yet."

"It sounds like something that would take up a lot of space," Nan told him. "Where would it go?"

"That's the sixty-four-thousand-dollar question, Nan, right there. Angus Pettigrew has a really nice open tract in the southern part of town, but he's flat out against it. Even Shane couldn't soften him up, and I understand he took his best shot at it. There's a few other really good possibilities, though, but I don't want to risk a jinx speaking too soon. You know how that goes."

The hostess came over and spoke softly to him. "Nan, I wasn't raised to be rude, but there's a call just come in that I really ought to take. Could you excuse me?"

"Of course," she answered, not missing a beat on the salad. "I appreciate you giving me as much time as you did."

"The pleasure's all mine," he told her, standing up. When Nan asked for the check ten minutes later, Mindy told her that Mr. Hobbs had taken care of it.

Ernesto's was tucked into a eucalyptus grove along a stretch of old Highway 101 in Leucadia, a modest old frame building painted lemon yellow. A lovingly hand-painted sign featured a surfer in the curl of a magnificent wave.

Nan had changed into jeans, a casual cotton sweater, and sneakers, trying to look loose and unprofessional. *Non*professional, anyway. When she walked into Ernesto's just after four-thirty, the place was cool and dark, with Jimmy Buffett playing on the jukebox. A long rattan bar went down one wall, opposite a series of empty booths. Dozens of posters and large, framed color photos of surfers and perfect waves covered the whitewashed walls.

At the back of the bar, three guys played pool. Two of them had the standard beach-bum look, with sun-streaked hair and bleached-out baggy shorts. They probably belonged to the Toyota truck parked outside, loaded with surfboards. But they were older than Nan would have expected. One was nearly bald and both had saddle-leather complexions.

The third pool player was more burly, with a distinct paunch and unfashionably long brown hair that just brushed his shoulders. He wore old faded jeans with a rip in the knee and a T-shirt announcing SURF'S ALWAYS UP SOMEWHERE. This, Nan was certain, was Ernesto, aka Bad Ernie. The erstwhile surfer.

Nan slipped onto a barstool and examined the dozens of photos tacked onto corkboard behind the bar. The motif was surfing, with an occasional Harley-Davidson. A younger, slimmer version of Ernie was in many of the shots: Ernie in a wet suit, Ernie in gaudy Jams, Ernie holding various surfboards, Ernie having beer poured on his head, Ernie on a Harley, Ernie clowning by a restored woody, Ernie with a dazzling array of bikinied girls with killer tans.

Adam and Shane and Ramón were in some of the older pictures, too, mostly group shots. It was startling to see them in this context, but they fit in perfectly. There were a few more recent shots, too. It was hard for Nan to realize that there was no upper age limit on surfing in San Diego County, that grandfathers were out there in wet suits any morning of the year. A San Diego surfer had won the Nobel Prize in chemistry not long ago.

Out of the corner of her eye, Nan saw Ernie amble over, limping slightly. He went behind the bar, offered a bartender's insincere smile, and answered Nan's question by announcing he had Corona on tap. He filled a frosty stein at her request and set it in front of her with a mild flourish.

"You live around here?" he asked.

Nan shook her head. "Up in L.A. Venice."

He smiled again. "Great town, Venice. I've had me some fine times up there."

She sipped the beer. It was icy cold and wonderful. "You're Ernie, right?"

"Yeah."

She introduced herself and watched him move through wariness, caution, and uncertainty while she explained her relationship to Adam.

"Bummer, Adam being hit like that," Ernie said enigmatically. As a sometime biker and all-around hell-raiser, he'd probably seen the inside of a cell or two himself.

"Well, yeah. You know, Adam says he didn't kill Shane, and I believe him. But the cops, now, they see a guy with a ponytail and they don't bother looking any farther."

That registered. Ernie's nod shook his shoulder-length hair.

"I knew Shane," she exaggerated. "What I'm trying to do is get a sense of what he was up to that last night, see if maybe somebody he talked to here remembers anything important."

Ernie looked doubtful. As Nan's eyes adjusted to the dim light, she could see a faint web of scars on the left side of his face. He'd had a lot of reconstructive surgery.

"As I understand it," she went on, "Shane left his date around ten-thirty and then came here for a couple of beers. Would you say he was drunk?"

Ernie shook his head. "Nah."

"The reason I'm wondering is that he was legally drunk when he died." Ernie started to bristle, and Nan held up a hand. "Hold on, now. I don't know much about Shane's drinking habits, but I do know that somebody who holds his liquor pretty well can get *way* above the legal limit without being obviously drunk."

This was Ernie's out. As a bartender serving an

intoxicated patron, he could be liable for anything happening later. Except, presumably, murder.

"Shane could hold it pretty well," he agreed. "But he didn't seem wasted at all. He'd maybe had something before he came in here, but all I served him was a couple of drafts. He was bitching that he had to go back to the salt mines and do a bunch of bullshit paperwork, and he wouldn't've done that if he'd been wiped out. Couldn't've."

"You talked to him?"

"Well, sure."

"You've known Shane a long time, I guess."

Ernie nodded, with a wave at the wall of photos. "Mucho years."

"Did he seem different any way that last night?"

"The cop who came here asked me that, and I thought about it some more afterward. It shakes you up, you know, being the last person to see somebody alive." Ernie gave the impression he'd had the experience on more than one occasion. "But the answer to your question is no, pure and simple. He was just Shane, fooling around, talking about the Lakers. Me'n Shane used to play pickup basketball together, way back when."

"Did he talk to anybody else here that night?"

"Scott over there." Ernie nodded at the balding surfer at the pool table. "They shot a little stick. Hey, Scott!" The surfer looked up. "C'mere a minute."

Scott set down his cue and crossed to the bar, looking Nan up and down as he approached. His glance was boldly appraising, mildly dismissive, and irritating as hell. This guy had *loser* written all over him and he was rejecting *her?*

"This lady's a friend of Shane's," Ernie announced. "I was just telling her you'n him was shooting pool that last night."

"Yeah," Scott agreed reluctantly.

"Did he say anything about where he was going later that night?" Nan asked.

Scott shook his head. "Nah. Cops asked that, too. Honest to God, I was so wasted I barely remembered him being here at all."

"But he mentioned to you that he was going back to the greenhouse?" Nan asked Ernie.

"He was bitching about all the goddamned paperwork he had to fill out, stupid-ass forms. Pissed 'cause the surf was supposed to be pretty good and he'd be working. That's all."

"Hmm," Nan said. "Did you guys know somebody took a shot at Adam and Ramón last week?"

"Heard about it," Ernie conceded.

"You have any idea who that might've been? Or what it was about?"

"No idea," Scott said.

Ernie shook his head. "Haven't got a clue."

And so it went. Nan asked a few more questions, but neither Ernie nor Scott could remember anything significant Shane had said or done in the last hour before he went to catch up on his paperwork. Scott was relatively worthless, drunk as he claimed to have been.

But Ernie was quite certain that Shane had spoken to nobody else. He hadn't made or received any phone calls and was alone on both arrival and departure.

Which left Nan right back where she'd started. The entire weekend was a wash and the clock was ticking merrily along.

Adam kept moving closer to a capital murder conviction.

CHAPTER 13

Jeff Nashimora had given Nan his mother's unlisted phone number in Marina del Rey, along with an admonition not to call before dark. Cassie Pettigrew painted by natural light and she hated interruptions.

She was friendly enough, however, when Nan reached her on Tuesday night. "Jeff told me he talked to you," she said in her gravelly whiskey voice. "Do you want to come by now?"

Nan was exhausted, actually, but suspected that if she tried to go to bed early, she'd end up staring at the ceiling for hours. "Give me half an hour," she answered.

Cassie Pettigrew lived on the Marina peninsula, where cutesy nautically named streets ran alphabetically from Anchorage and Buccaneer clear through Yawl. Her penthouse was the third floor of a beachfront building between Spinnaker and Topsail.

"So," she told Nan, leading her into a living room full of black furniture in angular and asymmetrical shapes. The thick blond hair was in an untidy knot atop her head and she wore a loosely woven multicolored Guatemalan shift that stopped eight inches above her knee. She was barefoot, her long legs deeply tanned and just as deeply toned. "Jeff says you're trying to clear Adam. Is he innocent?"

The woman's frankness was refreshing after a long day at the State Bar spent on the phone with various masters of legal evasion. "I hope so," Nan answered, sitting in a triangular chair that faced the picture windows onto the balcony. Outside, a strong cold winter wind was blowing off the Pacific Ocean, rattling the screen and furiously clanking a bunch of wind chimes somewhere nearby.

"I hope so, too," Cassie told her. "I've always had a soft spot for Adam."

"You've known him a long time."

"My whole life," Cassie said, smiling. "We were babies together. Adam was the oldest of the boys. They were quite a handful, I must say. We called them the Unholy Trio. Did a lot of hell-raising, those guys."

"I hadn't realized till just recently that Adam had a juvenile record." Which Adam denounced as bullshit and Ramón considered inconsequential, being inadmissible.

"Only 'cause he wouldn't rat on his friends," Cassie defended spiritedly. Nan raised an eyebrow and she continued. "The three of them broke into a house in Floritas when the owners were gone and had a party. There were a bunch of us there, just a kid kind of thing. We weren't stealing anything, just cutting up. Acting out, getting drunk and high. The place was out of the way, but it was just our bad luck one of the neighbors happened to drive by coming home late and called the cops. Shane and Ramón and I got away out the back, but Adam got nabbed with a couple other guys who didn't move fast enough."

It sounded relatively harmless. At least no violence was involved. "You were all in school together, right?"

Cassie nodded. She was draped on a deep-black sofa with a back that rose like burnt toast points above a sea of pillows in animal prints: zebra, leopard, tiger, cheetah. Above her hung a large painting of a snarling tiger in a rich Rousseauian jungle. Her work? Nan squinted enough to make out the signature "Cassandra."

"Adam and I were the same age," Cassie explained, "and we went through together from kindergarten till I dropped out. Ramón was a year behind us, and Shane a year after him."

"Where did Adam's sister fit in here?"

"Oh, Pammy was a lot younger. Amelia's age." Cassie's face clouded momentarily. "It was the four of us who hung out together, in various combinations. Ramón ran around with some of the Mexican kids in junior high school and high school. But at first we were all stuck back out in the boonies together and we reacted differently to that. Me, I turned rebel. I was barely in junior high when I figured out there was a sexual revolution going on, and I wasted no time moving straight to the front lines."

Nan laughed appreciatively. Her generation's version of the good old days, free love and casual sex when all you had to worry about was getting pregnant. "You and my sister," she told her. "Julie was sneaking out at night for years when we lived at home. And somehow she never got caught."

"Interesting," Cassie said reflectively. "I guess that makes a certain amount of sense. Adam always said what he liked about me was that I was always trying to figure out what the rules were so I could be sure to break them all." There was an odd softness in her voice.

"Were you and Adam . . ." Nan let the question trail off.

"Lovers?" Cassie smiled fondly. "Yeah, we were. He was my first, as a matter of fact. Neither one of us had much idea what we were doing, as I think back, but it was sweet. My father did not approve, I might add. Even without realizing we were fucking like bunnies every chance we could get. Adam was a lower caste, he thought. The foreman's son. Strictly verboten." She gave a deep, throaty laugh.

"Did Shane know about you and Adam?" Nan had never had a brother, but she understood they were notoriously possessive.

Cassie shook her head. "I don't think he realized we

were getting it on, at least not at the time. Shane was the baby of the bunch, and we were all pretty young. Unless Adam or Ramón told him, which I can't imagine. He sure never learned from me. But he knew we were kind of girlfriend-boyfriend, me and Adam." She paused. "You know, I hate to say this, but Adam had a jealous streak even then. He was real upset about me and a guy I started going out with when we were supposedly a couple. Beat him up, even."

Terrific. "Do people know about this?"

"I don't think so."

"Was this before or after Amelia disappeared?"

Cassie's face clouded. "After. I think I always knew she was dead, really. And in some kind of twisted-up way, I decided I wasn't going to miss *anything,* because I might be dead tomorrow, too. Also, my folks really had me on a pretty tight leash. They wanted to know where I was every second." She gave a crooked grin that was startlingly like her brother's. "You'd be surprised how many places there are at a greenhouse where you can smoke a little dope and get laid. We used to hang out a lot in the walk-in flower refrigerator. Very romantic. Damn chilly, too."

There was something disconcerting about both Cassie's candor and sexual bravado, as if she didn't quite realize they were no longer shocking. That she was an adult with a grown son.

"But somewhere along the line you got involved with Richard Nashimora," Nan prompted. "Was he a classmate, too?"

Cassie gave another throaty laugh. "Richie was part of what we'd call a multicultural program today. Me balling all the major ethnic groups available. A black football player, Ramón, Richie Nashimora. Richie was valedictorian of our class at Floritas High. I never intended to marry him, but I waited too long when I got pregnant and I couldn't get an abortion. I'm not sure which set of parents was more horrified, mine or the Nashimoras. For sure, I wasn't what they had in mind for their brilliant overachieving firstborn son. Sansei Richie. And my father said a lot of truly hideous things about having a half-breed grandson. Charming man, my dad. Fortunately for everybody, Richie and I both knew there was no way we'd stay together. We split up when Jeff was a baby. After he finished med school, Richie married another Sansei and they all lived happily ever after. They even had custody of Jeff for a while."

"You didn't mind?" In Nan's admittedly vicarious experience, custody adjustments tended to be adversarial.

"Mind? Hell, I was grateful! I love Jeff dearly, but it took me a long time and three more marriages to get my act together. I'd hate to figure out how many thousands of hours of therapy I've been through. I may not be normal now, but at least I'm cured of worrying about it."

"What about Shane? Were you close?"

"You mean like incest?"

Nan was stunned. "Well, actually that wasn't what I meant at all. But since you brought it up . . ."

But Cassie was shaking her head. "Nope. Not that it didn't cross my mind, I'll tell you. Shane was a real hunk, and there was a time I'd do anything there was a rule against. But he would have been horrified at the idea. He got pissed off when my bikinis were too revealing, that sort of thing." So he *had* been a protective brother.

"What was his marriage to Sara like?"

"A disaster from the word go. She tricked him, you know, told him she was pregnant and then had a convenient 'miscarriage' after the wedding. I like Sara, don't get me wrong, but I think she set out pretty deliberately to trap him. Shane represented a lot of things she'd never had, starting with money. Her dad pumped gas at a Shell station in Oceanside."

And now she was a lady of leisure, driving soccer team shuttles and serving on charity boards. "Were they happy?"

"Who knows?" Cassie answered. "If there's one thing I've learned through my string of marital mishaps, it's that you can never know for sure what's going on in somebody else's marriage. Hell, it's tough enough to know what's happening in your own."

"So you weren't surprised when they split up."

"Not really. Shane was a pretty major-league womanizer, and eventually Sara had to acknowledge that."

"She says she never knew."

"Then she's lying," Cassie said shortly. "I remember her crying to me when she was pregnant with Christopher that Shane was fucking some little surf bunny."

"Does it surprise you that he'd have an affair with Julie? Being Adam's wife?"

Cassie shook her head. "Nothing really surprised me where Shane and women were concerned. 'I can't help myself,' he told me once. And I wasn't exactly the one to set him on the straight and narrow path."

"Had you seen much of him recently?"

"More than I had for a long time, actually. He always came up for my shows and openings. I have one this weekend and I kind of dread not having him there. He was like . . . the family representative. He'd kind of breeze in here, give me a big hug and say, 'So how's my much-married sister?' Damn, I can't believe he's really gone." She paused for a moment, choked back tears.

"Sweet, dear Shane," Cassie went on, control regained. "He was always so good to Jeff, too. Bought him his first skateboard, taught him how to swim and surf summers down there, all that Southern California boy stuff that Jeff's father never did 'cause he was studying or working all the time. I was kind of surprised, though, when Jeff decided to go to Pettigrew instead of taking some high-powered job. He speaks seven languages, you know. Four of them Asian."

"So it surprised you when he went to work for Shane?"

"Oh, yeah. He's a very urban, sophisticated kid, after all.

If he'd come of age in a different time, he'd have made a hell of an arbitrageur. But apparently it's worked out pretty well down there."

"So everybody says," Nan agreed. "If you'd been talking to Shane more lately, I was hoping you might have some idea what was wrong enough in his life for somebody to kill him."

"There's never been anything wrong in Shane's life," Cassie said, with what sounded vaguely like bitterness. "That was his problem, in a way. Anything he ever wanted he got. Any problems he ever had, he bought his way out of, or my father did. You know, boys will be boys." This time the bitter edge was unmistakable.

"Well, *something* was wrong," Nan pointed out, "or he wouldn't be dead. And maybe Jeff told you what happened last week."

Cassie frowned. "You mean Ramón getting shot at? I just can't believe it."

"Believe it," Nan told her. "I saw the bullet holes."

They talked the situation through from a dozen angles for another half hour, but Nan felt no closer to an answer than when she'd arrived. She left with an invitation to Cassie's gallery opening on Saturday and a growing sense of despair.

The next morning, Nan called her former neighbor James Walden. James had lived down the hall in the condo complex in Playa del Rey where Nan had moved after her divorce. He was an economic analyst and techno nerd. James had always been quite cordial to Nan, allowing her to use the miscellaneous office equipment he kept in his condo when she needed a fast photocopy or a nearby fax machine. Although he appeared curiously unburdened by any semblance of a personal life, he also seemed to nurse a little crush on Nan. She had never encouraged him, but he was sweet enough that she didn't have the heart to brush him off altogether.

"Are you familiar with a company named Fairy Tale World?" Nan asked him. "They've got theme parks in Georgia and Texas and they're looking to move into Southern California."

"Off the top of my head, no," James answered. "But I can certainly find out for you. Is this a company you're considering as an investment?"

Nan laughed. "I *live* in my investment, James. Since I moved out of the condo, my discretionary income is so discreet it barely exists." She explained that Fairy Tale World was scouting Floritas as a location, and told him that her sister was concerned that the property where she was living might be sold out from underneath her. It didn't seem necessary to explain about Shane, or Adam, or anything else. And it was a relief not to tell the story again.

"Something else, James. You know all those data bases you subscribe to? The ones that pry hopelessly into people's personal affairs?"

James paused, probably unsure whether he was supposed to laugh. "Yes?"

"How hard and/or expensive would it be to run a few names through?"

"Looking for what?"

"Well, credit checks for starters. Money, in general. Plus anything that seems out of sync, or unexpected. If I knew what I was looking for, it would be easier."

"True, but I can do a general scan," James told her. "Don't worry about the expense."

"Well, surely I can at least buy you dinner?"

"It will be my pleasure, Nan. Give me the names and I'll get right on it."

He was as good as his word. On Friday morning he called to say he was ready to report. "Ready to report" was his exact phraseology.

"Great!" Nan told him. "Where do you want that

dinner?" He picked Tandoori Palace, not far from the condo complex, and they agreed to meet at seven-thirty.

James was standing outside the restaurant when Nan arrived. She was five minutes early, but he looked as if he'd already been waiting an hour. He awkwardly switched his weight from one foot to another. He was very tall and very thin, all joints and angles. James was a nervous type to begin with, and the farther away he moved from his techno lair, the more unsophisticated he became. Tonight he was a mass of tics.

Inside the restaurant, however, he relaxed a little. This was mildly familiar territory for James, who had lived in India for a while as the child of a petroleum executive. After they ordered, he crossed his arms protectively and began to debrief. James wasn't the kind of guy who conversed, or even talked.

"Fairy Tale World is a wholly-owned subsidiary of a company called Enright Enterprises," he said. "They began in Georgia about twelve years ago, developing industrial parks. Then the head of the company fathered two sets of twins in three years and decided to build a children's theme park on land he'd acquired for a deal that fell through. From everything I can determine, it was a totally capricious decision."

James's tone made it clear what he thought about capricious financial decisions.

"Interesting," Nan murmured.

"Against all odds, the park became a success." Again, James's tone suggested that it should have failed, resoundingly. "He'd tapped into a specialized market, one that was just developing as relatively affluent baby boomers had their belated families. Fairy Tale World was unique in several respects. For one, it made absolutely no attempt to cater to anybody over the age of ten. There were no thrill rides, no fancy restaurants. No alcohol, smoking prohibited everywhere. A particular effort was made to offer nothing that might interest or encourage teenagers."

James folded his hands on the table, but they still twitched. "Secondly," he went on, "the emphasis was on *families*. The more children somebody brought, the lower the individual admission prices. And finally, the fairy tales themselves were bowdlerized to purge them of almost any kind of violent references."

"Really?" Nan found this vaguely disturbing. As a child she had devoured Grimm and Andersen, and yes, there *had* been an extraordinarily high level of violence in their stories. But so what?

James nodded. Nan wondered if anyone, at any stage of his life, had ever called him Jim. It seemed unlikely.

"The formula worked," he continued. "So well, in fact, that after four years, Enright expanded into Grand Prairie, Texas, between Dallas and Fort Worth. Same setup, same formula, same heavy family emphasis. They've continued to do well enough through leaner economic times because of the low admission rates and relatively low overhead. And, of course, because they're located in sufficiently mild climates to be very actively open year-round."

"And now they're coming to Southern California?"

"They want to," James said, "and apparently they've been playing several possible locations against each other. Ventura County, Floritas, Lancaster, even Palm Springs, though I can't imagine that they'd want to be in a location that's so beastly hot in the summer. Oxnard and Floritas seem to be the strongest contenders, and essentially Enright is sitting back and letting them try to outbid each other. Either location would be perfectly acceptable, from everything I can tell."

Their food arrived then. As James ate, he continued his report. "Those people you asked me about. They cover quite a spectrum."

Indeed. "What did you find out?"

"I did initial credit checks, and where indicated I delved more deeply. I'll begin with the most fiscally impressive of the lot." No question about *his* priorities. "Angus Pettigrew. He has substantial land holdings in San Diego County and owns a large nursery operation outright. It would be possible to probe his financial affairs in much more detail, but I had the impression you were primarily interested in financial irresponsibility or distress."

"True enough," Nan agreed.

"Now Shane Pettigrew . . . He died recently, did you know that?"

Nan nodded, repressing a smile.

"He left only minor assets, apparently. Some equity in a condo, a few bank accounts. Sara Pettigrew, who formerly was married to Shane, is more interesting. No employment record. She owes a lot of money—half a dozen bank cards charged to the max, some as high as ten and fifteen grand. Canceled by American Express and a few department stores. Title to a heavily mortgaged piece of residential property, and given the pattern of spending, there may be liens on that, too."

Very interesting. "Is she current on her debts?"

James shook his head and looked disapproving. "Not at all. And she's far past the point where the minimum monthly payment at least covers the interest. She's got a couple of judgments against her, too. Relatively minor ones, but still . . ." He shook his head again.

"How about Frank Reid?"

James rolled his eyes. "Terrible credit. Lots of judgments, all under a thousand dollars. No employment listed, though that's kept up badly as a rule."

He looked through his notes. "Peter Hobbs had a bankruptcy in Ohio thirteen years ago. But he rebuilt his credit well enough to own a business there later. He seems to be a restaurateur. Lived in Reno, Nevada, for three years and then came to Floritas four years ago. Owns Hobbs House Restaurant in partnership with a James Delgado of Reno."

"Really?" So Pete had embroidered the truth about his Southern California epiphany. Had flat-out lied, actually. And who was this silent partner in Reno? "Does he have debts?"

"Nothing major or current that I could determine. His last restaurant in Ohio was in Chapter Eleven, but he apparently pulled it together enough to unload."

Nan looked at James in wonder. "Boy, you're *good* at this, James. I'd like to think it's hard to get that kind of info about people."

"You'd be mistaken," James announced. "There's no privacy in America. None whatsoever. Now, who's left? Ramón and Victoria Garza. Solid credit, one thirty-seven K outstanding on a one-fifty K mortgage. And Adam and Julie Chandler are pretty much debt free, but with no discernible assets."

"What about the others?"

"Cassandra Pettigrew was listed as Cassandra Waterford. L.A. based, very solid financially. Ditto Richard Nashimora. Owns two medical buildings in Beverly Hills and part interest in a surgery center. Jeff Nashimora, his son, has a couple of new bank cards, no debts. Kimberly Wilkes owes twenty-four thousand for college loans. Katsumi and Miyoko Nashimora own a tract of land in San Diego County outright, no debts at all." He looked her in the eye. "Nan, what in the dickens is this all about?"

"Before I explain, do these people know you were checking their credit?"

He grinned slyly. "Even TRW doesn't know I was checking their credit."

Nan gaped. "You've cracked the TRW computer?"

He smiled benignly. "I've obtained access to certain materials, that's all. From a variety of sources. Oh, and if you're interested, all but Adam Chandler, Frank Reid, and

Miyoko Nashimora are registered voters. The three Nashimora men, Angus Pettigrew, Peter Hobbs, Kimberly Wilkes, and Sara Pettigrew are Republicans. The Garzas, Julie Chandler, Cassandra Waterford, and the late Shane Pettigrew are registered Democrats."

"Have you looked me up, too?" Nan asked suspiciously. It was truly disturbing to think that James—or anybody else with his equipment and expertise—could go waltzing through somebody's personal affairs this way.

"Not recently," he answered, with what he probably meant to be a devilish grin. "And there was nothing shocking or untoward on your record when I last looked."

She laughed, then told him briefly about the mess in Floritas. He listened attentively and promised to think further about the situation. At Nan's instigation then, the conversation became pleasantly banal. James talked at great length about a project he was working on, something complicated that had to do with energy depletion ratios. Nan listened politely. After dinner, she picked up the check, thanked him profusely, promised to be in touch again soon, and headed home.

The lights were on at Shannon's, and feeling restless, Nan crossed the quiet walk street for a visit.

Nan told Shannon about visiting the much-married Cassie Pettigrew. "Maybe I'm just sensitive because of Leon getting married," Nan admitted, "but I don't understand. How can somebody essentially my age manage to convince herself four times that she's found her one true love?"

"Only three," Shannon corrected. "You said she was knocked up the first time."

"But *still*. You've been married just as many times. Why bother?"

"So all right, I'm a hopeless recidivist. Who knows why? They say repeated marriages are the triumph of hope over experience," Shannon continued thoughtfully, "but in my case it's been more of an evolutionary process. Each time I got a little closer to learning about me, and what I wanted and what I was willing to give. Of course I might not have done so badly the first couple of times if I hadn't been a galloping alcoholic." She stopped a moment and thought, then giggled. "No, I take that back. My second marriage was tolerable *only* because I was drunk." She looked at her watch and frowned. "Where in the devil is Rebecca, anyway?"

Rebecca was Shannon's teenage daughter, and the subject of much consternation. Rebecca had a biker boyfriend and a rapidly diminishing interest in her studies. Now it was Shannon's turn to bitch and worry, Nan's to listen and console. Shannon had been right, Nan realized, when she'd touted her own proximity as a sales point for Nan's new bungalow. It was awfully nice to just walk across the lawn and have somebody to talk to: no cars, restaurants, freeways, public places, parking problems.

As for Shannon's current woes, Nan knew no advice was really wanted or expected. And it put her own angst in perspective. Compared to a daughter dating a tattooed biker, Leon's remarriage was a mere speed bump on the highway of life. It was nice, actually, that Nan's immediate life was relatively free of either crises or responsibilities.

Except trying to find a way out for Adam.

And except for Nefertiti, who followed her across to Shannon's house, waited patiently on the porch while Nan was inside, then came back expectantly at Nan's heel.

At the door Nan hesitated, sighed, and then let the little black cat in.

For the next week, Nan kept having the sensation that she was swimming under water, and maybe in Jell-O at that. Everything seemed slow and distorted and confusing.

She made a deliberate effort not to think too much about Adam and Julie, whose life had to be truly ghastly right now. She remembered Adam's barely civil withdrawal and Julie's numb acceptance and shuddered to think about their day-to-day existence.

Work fell into a mercifully manageable routine. She was able to move from task to task, from one naughty lawyer to the next, without getting too caught up in the whys and the wherefores. She did, after all, *like* her job, and she was good at it. There was a lot of satisfaction in keeping the legal profession relatively honest and moral.

True, her work bore a strong resemblance to Hercules cleaning the Aegean stables, and even dealt in some of the same materials. But there were definite payoffs, undeniable rewards: A scammer—felon in spirit if not outright deed—with his license suspended. A bona fide crook disbarred on his way to the big house. A substance-abusing baby boomer out of rehab with her practice and her life back in order. Those were the reminders of just why Nan had wanted to be in the State Bar Trial Counsel's Office in the first place.

Since Leon had called to announce his impending nuptials, she had given considerable thought to roads not taken.

She'd be a partner at McSweeney Lane by now if she had stayed with the firm, making a tremendous amount of money. Buying the Venice bungalow would have been no financial reach, and she'd probably have at least part-interest in a condo at Big Bear or Mammoth. She'd be able to stride into Bullock's or Nordstrom's and buy those really classy professional suits and dresses, the ones that made a statement before you ever opened your mouth, and she'd be able to do it without even looking at the price tags. She could afford to eat every meal of her life in restaurants if she wanted, and not just burger joints and neighborhood Mexican places. She could take off for a weekend in Hawaii or Aspen without booking her flight twenty-one days in advance.

If, of course, she could find a weekend when she wasn't working a good chunk of Saturday and much of Sunday.

Time was what she had bought herself by leaving McSweeney Lane, more than any single other factor. She was a bureaucrat of sorts at the State Bar, and her work didn't have a hell of a lot to do with the practice of law, but nobody expected her to put in seventy-hour weeks as a matter of course.

Actually, her work at McSweeney Lane hadn't had much to do with the practice of law, either. Whatever the practice of law really was. Nan had worked in civil litigation. At a major firm this meant big cases that usually involved multiple defendants and endless discovery and clients prepared to pay and pay and pay—just so long as Nan and her cohorts kept them out of the courtroom. Which McSweeney Lane was exceptionally good at.

Major corporations were terrified of going to trial in front of unpredictable L.A. juries, men and women who were—said corporations noted with regret—all too representative of their community. Jurors unlikely to truly understand the special problems of companies who might, for instance, resolve environmental compliance difficulties by closing local factories and relocating in some foreign clime where local rivers provided sewage disposal and the natives were thrilled to make three bucks a day. There was no telling when an L.A. jury might hit big old Ugly, Inc., with a multimillion-dollar verdict, issuing a warning to all the unfeeling big business bastards. No company wanted to risk being an object lesson.

Nan and Leon were midway through their divorce when she left McSweeney Lane to go to the State Bar. But that had been only a minor factor in her departure. Even while the marriage was good, they rarely saw each other at work, toiled in different departments on different floors and quickly gave up trying to commute together. After San Francisco, Leon had become an environmental specialist and Nan was handling employment discrimination cases, and both of them, so far as Nan could tell, were on the wrong side.

Leon didn't feel that way. For Leon, moral ambiguity never entered the equation. There weren't necessarily right or wrong sides, just *Us* versus *Them*.

Nan still didn't know for sure when she had stopped loving Leon. Or why she hadn't noticed it for so long, had mistaken familiarity and comfort for enduring bonds.

Maybe it was because the good times, while infrequent due to their ridiculous work loads, were so undeniably good.

Leon was smart, for one thing, really truly intelligent. Sometimes when they'd be talking Nan would feel a sort of synergy, as if each of them had been intellectually energized by the simple act of conversation. Ideas would fly, witticisms appeared from nowhere. The operation of Leon's brain could be fascinating, and fun. Sometimes Nan missed that, missed the long intense talks about politics and law and contemporary culture. Leon had a sociologist's view of the world around him.

And then there were Sunday mornings. Whoever woke up first would begin the slow and lazy process of lovemaking, gently rousing the other with the familiar caresses of fingers and tongue. It was their tacit denial of reality, as if they were the sort of people with nothing but time who really savored every moment.

Afterward they'd start on the Sunday papers, the *L.A. Times* and *New York Times,* scattering newsprint all over the king-sized bed in the king-sized Brentwood bedroom. Next would come a shower together, which often led to more lovemaking and the necessity of another shower, which Nan would take alone while Leon padded off, deliciously nude, to make *huevos rancheros.* It was the only dish he knew and the only meal he ever cooked.

She suspected that she would never be able to eat *huevos rancheros* again.

* * *

Julie called midmorning Friday all in a tizzy to say that somebody had cut Ramón Garza's surfboard leash. *Surfboard leash?*

"Slow down," Nan told her. "And start at the beginning. Is he all right?"

"Oh, sure," Julie assured her, "but that's not the point."

"So tell me what is."

"Adam and Ramón went surfing this morning," Julie began. "There was a big storm off the Aleutians, and the surf here has been really fantastic for a couple days. The guys have been out the last three mornings. Anyway, while they were out this morning, Ramón's leash broke. He didn't think much of it at the time, but when he got back to the office, he got a call from somebody saying the leash was just a warning. Drop Adam's case or next time he'd *really* be hurt. He went and checked the broken leash, and it turned out somebody had cut it almost all the way through."

Nan felt a surge of unexpected joy. Another threat to Ramón seemed further confirmation that Adam really *was* innocent.

"Forgive my colossal ignorance," Nan said, "but what in the hell is a surfboard leash?"

Julie giggled. "I forgot you're such a city slicker, Nan. A leash attaches to the surfboard at one end and the surfer's ankle at the other. With Velcro. It's heavy-duty quarter-inch rubber tubing, and the point is that the surfer doesn't get separated from the board after he goes down, doesn't have to chase the board all the way to shore."

"And somebody cut Ramón's? Wouldn't he notice it?"

"Not necessarily. It was only cut partway, so that as soon as a lot of pressure was put on it, when he went off the board, it snapped."

"And this is dangerous?"

Julie hesitated. "Well, yes and no. It's not really a big

deal for somebody who swims as well as Ramón. Some surfers are pretty poor swimmers, though. For somebody like that, it could be really dangerous. Most accidents with leashes have to do with getting tangled in something, like lobster traps. But that's not what's so important, Nan. Don't you see what this means?"

"That Adam's innocent?"

"Exactly!" Julie announced triumphantly.

Ramón, when Nan finally reached him, was nonchalant and irritatingly macho.

"It's no big deal," he told her. "Nothing for you to worry about."

"Wait a minute," she snapped, "of course it is. Does somebody have to actually kill you before you'll take this seriously? Somebody *did* kill Shane." She took a deep breath. "There's no question that the board was tampered with?"

"Not the board, just the leash, right by where it attaches to the back of the board. So it wasn't obvious. And yes, there's no question. It's a clean cut about two-thirds through, and then where it gave is kind of stretched and torn."

"Did you notice that at the time when it happened?"

He laughed. "At the time when it happened, I was tumbling around inside a huge wonderful wave. And then my board was gone. It was annoying, but these things happen. It didn't seem sinister."

"Until you got the phone call. Was it the same guy who called at Adam's?"

"Yeah. But like I told you before, I get calls like that a lot. I try not to let them bother me."

Depressing. And creepy, too. Nan wondered what Victoria Garza knew about the threats on her husband. A guy like Ramón would certainly downplay them to a high-strung wife. "What did he say?"

" 'Get off Adam Chandler's case. The leash was just a warning.' Then he hung up. And I went out and checked the surfboard, and damned if the leash hadn't been cut."

"You hadn't been home to change?"

"Sometimes when I go out in the morning and time is tight, I shower at the office," Ramón told her.

"You've got a shower in your *office?*" It slipped out before Nan realized how rude and incredulous she sounded. The notion was fascinating. Of course the big firms had showers, sometimes even full-blown gyms so that heavy billers wouldn't waste valuable time traveling to their health clubs. And—horrors!—maybe not come back afterward, skip out and go introduce themselves to their families. But Ramón was a solo practitioner in a small town.

"I had one put in," he said stiffly.

"So how could somebody have tampered with the leash?" Nan asked. "And when?"

"Well," he answered slowly, "the how's easy enough. A pocket knife would do it. And unfortunately, *when* is wide open, too. I keep my surfboard locked in the garage at home, in an old open-backed pickup that I use to get down to the beach. Somebody'd have to break into my garage to get at it at home. *But*—after we go out in the mornings, some of us generally have breakfast at the Maui Cafe. When we were there yesterday morning, the truck was parked around the corner. And then I brought it back here and it sat out back in the lot all day. Back home, I didn't unload the board or even look at it again till this morning. And I didn't really look very hard at the leash after it broke. Till after that call."

"It would have broken the first time you used it?"

"Or pretty soon thereafter. It might take a jolt or two before it went."

"But not a whole . . . session, or whatever you call it, of surfing."

"No way."

"So." Nan thought out loud. "So it couldn't have been cut before you went out yesterday morning or it would have broken then. But somebody could have gotten to it on the street or in your parking lot any time all day?"

"Yes." He sounded vaguely annoyed. Maybe because he was used to asking the questions.

"Could anybody have done anything to it when you got to the beach this morning?"

"No, it was never out of my sight. Nan, I've already thought this through."

"And have you told the police about it?" she asked pointedly.

"Yeah. It seemed prudent. But I'm not sure they care much."

Saturday night, Nan took Shannon to Cassie's opening at a very trendy gallery on the very trendiest stretch of Melrose. *Paintings by Cassandra*. The room was fairly crowded with the hip and the wealthy and assorted hangers-on. They were dressed for the most part in black and wore a great deal of jewelry, ranging from truly stunning to downright silly.

Cassie's paintings were acrylics, large and vaguely ominous. Well-camouflaged but menacing figures lurking in jungly settings. Predatory animals, mostly big cats. The overall effect was unsettling. These would not be easy paintings to live with, even in a large space. They had a definite obtrusiveness, an in-your-face quality remarkably like their creator. And they were outrageously expensive.

Cassie herself was in the next room, talking to her son. Jeff Nashimora was dressed to fit in—unstructured black jacket, silk turtleneck, black jeans. He looked young and handsome, the very picture of diffident ennui.

A couple wearing vests that looked like gold-plated chain mail came by, jostling Nan and sounding like a Halloween Haunted House. When Nan looked back a moment later, Jeff was gone and Cassie was bearing down on her.

"Nan! You came!"

"Well, of course I did," Nan answered. "I wouldn't have missed it. Cassie, this is my friend Shannon."

"Pleased to meet you," Shannon said, extending a gracious hand. It was a nice firm handshake on both sides, no delicate little ladies'-luncheon finger clasping here. "You do terrific big cats!"

"Thanks," Cassie said graciously. No self-deprecation here.

"My second husband," Shannon went on, "had two of your paintings in his office. Mountain Danger and one of the All Hallow's Eve series."

Cassie lifted an eyebrow. "From my dark and dangerous period. Was he dark and dangerous?"

Shannon gave her sleigh bell laugh, causing several nearby heads to turn, several surly sophisticates to smile. It was that kind of laugh. "He wished! He was a CPA. He *did* like the paintings, as a matter of fact. But he tended to buy art as an investment."

"Then he picked good stuff of mine," Cassie noted. "Those are worth a lot now. Sure they weren't community property?"

Shannon laughed again. "They were, my dear, a *business* investment."

Nan waved a hand around the room. "Lots of people here. Is this good?"

"In terms of business?" Cassie said. "Hard to say. People who would have bought a year ago, six months ago, aren't buying art right now. The market's kind of soft. Fickle, too. But we'll do all right. I'm considered pretty hot at the moment. Not spectacularly hot, but steady. And I just finished a big commissioned piece for a Hollywood producer's new place in Aspen. Where he has a lot more big rooms with empty walls."

"It was nice of Jeff to come up for this," Nan said.

"Oh, he always comes," Cassie answered offhandedly.

"Though this is the first time he's lived out of town. He's already headed back, actually. He just left."

Nan glanced at her watch. Seven forty-five. Jeff could be back in Floritas by ten, ready to party. Assuming he had anyone to party with.

Cassie looked across the room, and something flickered in her eyes. Dollar signs? "Listen, there's somebody I need to talk to. Don't leave without seeing me again, all right? I want to talk to you." And she strode across the room, smiling cordially in every direction as she passed the people assembled on her behalf.

Nan and Shannon paid a visit to the bar, scoring some really fine Napa Chardonnay and the new bottled water everybody was drinking these days. There was a nice selection of dim sum, too, tasty and varied enough that they decided to linger for a while by the buffet and call it dinner.

As did a lot of other people, Nan noticed. Some looked like they'd shortly be drifting off to other parties with various glitterati. Others had that slightly desperate look suggesting they *wished* they had somewhere else to go later. And some folks ducked in just long enough to see Cassie, then dashed back out again. Nan watched Cassie move from group to group. She seemed to know everybody, but there was no effusiveness in any greetings, no sense that any of these people were actually her friends. Shane Pettigrew would have been a real breath of fresh air in a setting like this.

After a while Nan and Shannon took drink refills out to the small courtyard at the back of the gallery. Even with a portable heater it was chilly. Cassie found them there when the crowd thinned an hour or so later.

Jeff had told her about the surfboard leash and she was worried. "Ramón would never admit he's scared," Cassie said shortly. "But what if something *does* happen to him?"

"It's worrisome," Nan agreed. "Do you think your father

could possibly have anything to do with this? Or with the sniper?"

"I honestly don't know," Cassie admitted. She sat on the edge of a raised planter full of pansies and crossed her spectacular legs. Tonight's minidress—black, of course—was breathtakingly short. But she didn't seem at all cold, despite a brisk wind that was raising goosebumps on Nan. "He can be such a gold-plated asshole, but I can't imagine him threatening Ramón. Or doing anything that might hurt him. No matter *how* pissed off he is at him."

"Then what this means," Nan said slowly, "is that somebody else *did* kill Shane, not Adam. And they've made a mistake. Maybe this means that somebody's getting nervous, that we're on to something."

But what?

CHAPTER 14

Julie fought back tears as she drove from the doctor's office. Everything was falling apart.

Everything.

She remembered a former housemate who was deeply religious, a zealot, really, though nobody was into labels then. This woman had changed her name to Magdalena, Maggie for short, because she felt Jesus had forgiven her so very much. Maggie hung a framed motto in the communal kitchen: GOD NEVER ASKS MORE THAN YOU CAN GIVE.

Yeah, right. It had sounded glib at the time and now it seemed truly preposterous. As far as Julie was concerned, God made more demands than two-year-old triplets.

There was simply no end to it, one awful thing piled up on another. Shane's murder had set everything in motion. And since that horrid morning when the police banged on the front door Julie hadn't had a moment's true peace or relaxation.

Of course it could be worse. It could *always* be worse, as Nan had been pointing out about various calamities for her entire life. Nan could always be counted on for words of cheer.

Adam might still be in jail, for starters.

But having him home hadn't provided the catharsis she was hoping for. He remained stiff and just barely polite. She had hoped that once the initial hubbub died down, once

Mom went back to Illinois and Nan to L.A., that their own life would somehow revert to normal.

Not quite.

In fact, she was hard pressed to remember what normal *was*. For so long, years now, there'd been one crisis after another, usually overlapping. If endless trauma was the new constant in her life, Julie was not at all sure she could manage.

The guards were gone, at least, and there'd been no threats to Adam since that awful experience with the sniper. They kept the doors locked all the time now, which was kind of sad, but Julie had never really felt their home was threatened. She wasn't sure why she thought that. Every thing *else* in her life was under siege. Even, now, her own body.

Adam had made efforts to communicate with his family. He visited his mother in the nursing home, though she no longer recognized him or anyone else. He returned from the visits drained and depressed. Aside from the mental deterioration, Doris Chandler's health was frightfully sound; she had no other medical conditions serious enough to warrant even minor medication and could conceivably linger in her private netherworld for decades. Expensive decades.

Shortly after being released, Adam had argued bitterly with Renee, his ex-wife in Northern California. Renee was refusing to send their sons, Dan and Jackie, for any visits at all, and had announced her intention of going to court if necessary. It shamed Julie that one of her first reactions had been relief at saving the boys' airfare. But the ultimate insult was that Adam's sister Pam had evidently powwowed with Renee and was publicly supporting the visitation denial. Pam's paltry contributions to her mother's upkeep were always late, and while she'd never considered taking Doris into her own Portland home, she still believed that Adam should have her in his. The self-righteous bitch.

As far as their own home life went, Julie might have

been running a boardinghouse, with Adam an immigrant new to the country, scrupulously polite but unsure of the language and thus reluctant to ever speak. He worked hard, spent long hours in the fields and greenhouse, did far more than his usual share of the harvesting and processing of winter vegetables. He swept floors, washed dishes, had even scrubbed the toilet for the first and only time in his life. He was pulling his own weight, and then some.

But he seemed to deliberately dodge Julie, to leave rooms when she entered, to find some other, more pressing, chore requiring his attention elsewhere whenever she appeared at his side. He had resisted her cautious sexual advances and initiated none of his own. He didn't even kiss her anymore, or touch her unless there was someone watching.

She had tried to talk to him about Shane, but Adam didn't want to hear. Refused to listen. And maybe he was right. There was probably nothing she could say that would make him feel better, and a total explanation could easily worsen matters. Adam didn't have a lot of imagination, and if she didn't force the issue, maybe he wouldn't think too much about Julie writhing naked in Shane's bed.

An image she herself focused on quite a lot lately.

The more she thought about the months of her affair with Shane, the more confused she became. Of course she never expected anything more than transitory pleasure, greater perhaps because it was illicit. It was a rebellion of sorts, and it wasn't supposed to matter. But it *had* mattered, had been important in ways she was only now beginning to admit.

Adam had been a real pain during that period, a total frustration. He was sullen, upset, pissed off at the world in general. He hated putting his mother into the nursing home even though she obviously couldn't live alone any longer. Taking Doris into their own home was never a real option, would have been a hideous mistake. He knew that, of course, but his heart was screaming "NEGLECT!" at him. He ached, and Julie ached with him, ashamed at her relief that it was his mother and not her own.

That was the season, too, of the terrible problem with tomato-spotted wilt virus, carried through the greenhouse by thrips. They were losing all sorts of plants. It wasn't an issue of organic vs. chemical, either. They were desperate. They'd have tried anything: dioxin, flamethrowers, the neutron bomb.

And on top of everything there was the continuing battle over reversing Adam's vasectomy. Julie's desire for a child was palpable, had reached a stage where she would awaken in the morning in tears after dreams of infants snatched away. Adam, already paying to support his kids in Stockton and his mother in Oceanside, found the notion of further responsibility terrifying. He became less interested in sex of any sort as she pressed the issue. To this day she was unsure what had finally caused him to change his mind, to have the reversal surgery.

She was certain, though, that the decision had saved her marriage.

Temporarily, at least.

But the surgery came later. Before that, in the midst of seemingly endless stress, Shane Pettigrew suddenly changed focus in her life.

Shane was the perfect antidote to Adam's grim depression. He had such a carefree way about him, such a joyous presence. It was so easy to be with Shane. He made no demands, shared no traumas, asked nothing but her time and body. Since Adam was showing no particular interest in either, it seemed perfectly reasonable to oblige.

What she remembered now about the stolen afternoons with Shane was not the physical passion, though certainly that had been satisfying enough. Shane was a happy lover, always giving her the sense that he was delighted to be with her, that their time together was perfectly glorious. He wasn't as gentle as Adam, nor as serious. Shane was just . . . fun.

No, what she thought about now was how her time with Shane was some kind of special secret gift, designed to get her through the difficult period with Adam. That sounded terrible, of course, had the hollow ring of an after-the-fact rationalization.

But it was true.

In the afternoon quiet of Shane's secluded condo, there were no problems in her world. Even motels had an isolated, dreamlike atmosphere. She particularly liked to recall the day they drove up to San Clemente and spent the afternoon in a balconied room overlooking the ocean.

It was one of the last times, and one of the best.

By the time she told Shane it had to end, she could sense his own relief. Shane wasn't a creature too terribly concerned with consequences, and she suspected that he regretted having started the affair in the first place.

So they parted friends, friends who had shared a special time and special secret. The idea that others had known all along—since when? and did it matter?—chilled her. Who *had* known, anyway? Margaret Whiting, according to Nan. But Margaret wouldn't have sent the letter.

Oh, well. It was too late to worry about that now. Too late for so many things.

Like too late for the damned red roses that refused to bloom in time for Valentine's Day. She and Adam had managed to get some stems out on schedule, rejoicing as the price climbed in the ten days before the critical holiday. But now it was February 16 and roses were bringing a fifth of what they had three days ago. No good to bundle them up for bouquets, either, since nobody'd buy much of anything for weeks now. Everybody'd be home watching their rosebuds open and eating chocolates out of heart-shaped boxes.

Damnation!

And now the obstetrician. It was bad enough to even be seeing an obstetrician. Julie's plan was quite simple: a natural, self-regulated pregnancy culminating in a home birth with a midwife.

Which wouldn't be a problem except that her body kept betraying her. Karen, the midwife, was worried about Julie's rising blood pressure. For two weeks Julie had cut all salt from her diet, gorged on bananas and other high-potassium fruits and vegetables, supplemented calcium. Avoid stress, that was the other instruction.

The amazing part was that Karen gave the instruction with a straight face. She knew what was happening in Julie's life.

So the two weeks were up, and so was Julie's blood pressure. Again. She was healthy, dammit, not even old enough for amniocentesis. She certainly wasn't old enough for high blood pressure, pregnant or no. She'd never even understood what it meant. Her image of a hypertensive was some red-faced blustery Type A man. Angus Pettigrew, for instance. Or an elderly lady with a rhinestone pillbox. Not Julie Robinson Chandler, hearty young lass. And it was too early for high blood pressure to be setting in as a normal (or at least predictable) part of the pregnancy. She was still in her seventh month.

So Karen had ordered Julie to see Dr. Greenberg, who recommended bed rest.

Bed rest!

How was she supposed to get everything done that needed to be finished in the next six weeks before Easter? Easter was impossibly early this year, the twenty-eighth of March. Given the damn roses' refusal to bloom on time for Valentine's Day, it was even more critical that the Chandlers get as much product as possible into the marketplace.

Bed rest!

Adam would have a fit. And then, having stomped and stormed and kicked the furniture for a while, he would

insist that she stay flat on her back. He'd order her to relax,
as if that were something you could just do when your husband was facing murder one and even you weren't entirely
certain he was innocent.

They never talked about that part of it. During medita-
tion, part of her independent campaign to bring down the
damned blood pressure, she had told herself repeatedly that
things were going to work out for Adam, that he would be
acquitted. But even as she heard one voice inside her head
say soothingly, *"Everything will be fine,"* there was another, more insistent voice hollering, *"Fat chance! No
way!"*

How could they defend Adam? Julie knew how flimsy
his alibi was, that he'd been home in bed with her. And
while she was prepared to swear up, down, and crosswise
that he'd never left, she knew deep down that he *could*
have slipped out while she slept.

Nan had started out as a real dervish, racing around, talking to people, stirring things up. But a month later, none of
Nan's ideas had come to much.

And poor Ramón. He was working so hard on this, had
put in so much time and felt so incredibly frustrated. He'd
been *shot* at. And now the surfboard leash business. Who
on earth could have cut that fool leash, anyway? Somebody
who knew Ramón's habits, that he'd be almost certain to
go out when that Alaskan storm raised the surf. But anybody who knew that much would surely realize that Ramón
could swim just fine.

So maybe the intent really *hadn't* been to hurt him. Perhaps it had been a genuine warning, just like the phone call
said.

But there was another thought scurrying through the back
recesses of Julie's mind, one she was terrified might move
far enough to the front that she'd have to actually articu-
late it.

Adam hadn't shot at himself, of course. But Adam had

been surfing with Ramón that day, had even splurged on breakfast at the Maui Cafe. He could easily have nicked the leash after breakfast or when Ramón parked back at the office. He'd know that Ramón would be safe when it broke. And then on the morning when it did break, Adam could have made the call to Ramón after they split up, before he came home.

Because it was Adam who had proclaimed most loudly that the entire episode proved his innocence.

She knew she could never let Nan know her own doubts, particularly since her sister finally seemed to believe in Adam's innocence. It was two weeks now since Nan's last visit, for the preliminary hearing. Julie didn't think she could handle her sister's anxious energy, not now. The simplest approach would be to just not tell her about the blood pressure. As soon as Nan heard that, she'd be back in a flash. She'd have endless ideas for treating hypertension, all well-intentioned but none likely to be very practical.

The one thing Julie knew for sure was that her mother could not be informed. The long-distance calls came at least twice a week and were horribly arduous, as Mom tried to be upbeat and Julie attempted to match the mood. They were a pair of frauds, neither very good at the deception. But awful as the calls were, Mom's determinedly cheerful presence had been much, much worse. If June Robinson were to return to Floritas, Julie felt quite sure that she *would* have that stroke that both Karen and Dr. Greenberg kept threatening.

First things first, however.

She pulled up the drive, parked the truck, and trudged back to the greenhouse to tell Adam about her visit to the doctor.

Julie was dozing on the couch two weeks later when the call came from Laura Belton that Adam had been arrested at the Flower Auction. At first, mildly groggy, Julie thought it was some kind of odd hallucination, some hideous form of déjà vu.

Then she realized it was worse. This was actually happening twice.

"I just wanted you to hear it from somebody friendly," Laura told her.

But it wasn't friendly news.

"What happened?" Julie asked carefully, taking a deep breath and sitting down on the kitchen stool. So much for stress avoidance.

"He got into a scuffle with Johnny Simpson. I saw Adam come in and waved hi, and then a couple minutes later I had my back turned when I heard shouting. I saw Adam take a swing at Johnny and Johnny slug him back, and by the time I got across the room, there were flower carts flying and Johnny was lying on the floor in a puddle of white spider mums." Laura gave what sounded like an involuntary chuckle.

Well, it *might* have been a funny image. Some other time. Right now, Julie fought nausea. She moved the stool closer to the sink, just in case.

"You all right?" Laura asked suddenly. "I hate to upset you."

"Swell," Julie answered. "Go on, tell me the rest of it."

"Problem was, somebody'd already called the cops, and when they got there and realized who Adam was, that he was out on bail, they hauled him in."

"Is Johnny hurt?" Johnny Simpson was a loud-mouthed moron who grew proteas out in Escondido. Julie didn't think she wanted to know just what he'd said or done to provoke Adam. It didn't have to be much. Adam was pretty thin-skinned these days.

"He looked fine to me," Laura said. "He was cussing about Adam attacking him and all, saying he'd sue Adam's ass off, but he wouldn't let them call the paramedics and he just drove on home."

So Johnny thought he'd sue? That vampire wouldn't find much around *this* turnip farm. "And they arrested Adam?"

"I can't say for sure they arrested him, honey, but they sure did take him away. Listen, I'll make sure all your flowers get brought in and taken care of. I took a peek at the truck and it looks like Adam was about halfway through. I'd bring you the truck, but Adam must have the keys. They're not in it."

"Damn!" Now she'd have to get down to the Auction somehow, and *see* people. Without warning, Julie burst into tears. It felt surprisingly good to cry, certainly more pleasant than throwing up. Great options her life had reduced to.

"Now, now," Laura soothed her. "It's gonna be all right, honey." Easy enough for her to say. "Listen," Laura went on brightly, "I could probably hot-wire the fool truck and bring it to you. Just back me up if anybody gives me a hard time. Don't feel like visiting Adam at the jail."

Julie laughed, a bit hollowly. Laura was certainly a creature of varied talents. "Be my guest. Hotwire the hell out of it. And Laura, thanks."

She hung up and called Ramón's office. It was no longer necessary to look up the number.

This time Adam didn't come back home. His bail was revoked.

But the worst part, Julie realized, was that it was a relief to have him gone.

Francisco Santos Hernandez was nineteen years old and eleven hundred miles from home.

When he had enough money, he would return and marry Rosalita, but the work was slow these days and it seemed there would never be enough money. He was unbearably lonely. He was the youngest in the camp here, and there was nobody he had known before, nobody from his village.

He missed home, missed it badly. He missed the friendly sounds and smells of his native town, the whitewashed church, the nieces and nephews playing everywhere. He missed the easy laughter. He missed knowing who everybody was. He even missed the dusty streets, the wandering chickens, crotchety Enrique's ancient balding burro.

This place was not as he had imagined, and he had no love for it. The nights were cold and long and the days when there was work were long and hard. When there was no work, he sat for countless hours on the side of El Camino Real under gray gloomy skies, attacked by chilly winds.

He had just worked for three days, digging trenches on a construction site, but it was the first work in weeks that lasted more than a few hours. When he sent back the money order to Rosalita, he had kept out more than before. He did not know when he would work again, and food was expensive, particularly on the silver truck that sometimes came by with hot foods.

He had no gift for the language here. The English words were full of hard, rough sounds that he could never tell apart. *Thank you* he knew, and *please* and *how much.* He had trouble with the money, too, but he was finally getting the hang of that, learning to pick out the number words. He always felt a fool when he had to hold his hand out like a child and let the shopkeepers take money from him.

Francisco wanted nothing more than to go home, but he was too proud to leave before he had what he had come for. In the spring it would be better. The men he shared his camp with had told him so, the ones who had come back and forth before, had seen the change of the seasons. Soon more strawberries would ripen, the main crop. There was always work in strawberry season.

But none of it was the work he had expected when he arrived in the country with a scrap of paper saying simply "Floritas." *Flower fields in Floritas,* the man had told Juan, who told Paco, who told Francisco back home. *Fields where they need help.*

But there were few fields and nobody needed help. Most of the flowers were inside, in the greenhouses, like those down below the camp here. The Mexicans who worked in that place all lived in town with their families, had apartments, worked year-round. They were legal, most of them. And no more help was needed.

So Francisco did what he could. He dug trenches. He chipped holes from the hard hillsides with the long digging stick so the Anglos could plant their big palm trees. He loaded boxes for two days at a warehouse once, never knowing what was in them. Not caring.

Mostly he sat by the side of the road and waited.

The nights were worse. He lay on the hard ground beside snoring Miguel and thought of Rosalita's warm brown eyes and gentle white smile. Her soft red lips. They made a handsome couple, everybody said. She would be a beautiful bride.

He was too proud to go back defeated, but on these lonely nights he sometimes wondered at the price of pride.

Tonight the wind rushed cold from the ocean, skimming across the tops of the hills, lingering in the valleys like this one where he tried to sleep. Francisco wore two shirts and the jacket that the priest with the station wagon had given him. Still he shivered under the thin blanket.

Better to move around since he couldn't sleep anyway.

He silently rose and crept away from the others, leaving the camp and climbing to the ridgetop. In the faraway night he could hear an owl. Even farther away a coyote howled.

The night offered only a sliver of moon, but Francisco was blessed with superb vision. *The Hawk,* they called him back home, *El Halcón.*

El Halcón looked out across the silent darkened hills. Down below, the big house sat dark and quiet. Beyond that lay the greenhouses, and then the deserted highway. A pair of headlights came down the highway, moving fast. He heard the sound as the car approached, listened to it fade away as it headed north.

Then something moved, closer. It caught his eye and he leaned forward, puzzled.

El Halcón slipped forward for a better view and squatted beside a rock. He watched for over an hour, until long after the figure below descended the hill and passed the greenhouses. He watched the dark shape of the car roll silently out of the greenhouse complex and turn to the highway, heard the distant catch of the engine and saw the lights go on as it roared off into the night.

He did not understand what he had seen. It could not be. It made no sense.

He could tell the others in the morning, Miguel and them. But they were not really friends, just fellow prisoners of the same sad choices. They would laugh and tell him he was having nightmares, imagining things. They would not believe that the eyes of *El Halcón* had never failed him yet.

He would have to think about it all.

He wished he understood what he had seen, that there were someone he could tell.

CHAPTER 15

Nan seethed as she sat in gridlock on the Santa Ana Freeway.

It had been a day of endless minor irritations. First she overslept. Then the morning paper was strewn across the entire lawn. Her bagel burned. The new bottle of her favorite shampoo was reformulated and smelled like strawberry soda pop. The cassette deck in her car devoured her favorite Bonnie Raitt tape.

And so on. An investigator misplaced a report she urgently needed. She got an inch-wide run in a brand-new pair of pantyhose. The Coke machine's motor burned out. Her pen suddenly blobbed and left a nasty smudge of bright blue ink all over her hand.

Now she sat in freeway purgatory, listening to some chipper bimbette describe what a mess rush-hour traffic was, with the glee of a sportscaster covering the season finals. There were two Sigalerts on Nan's immediate route, both the result of what the bimbette delicately referred to as "injury accidents." The phrase gave Nan the creeps, reminding her of her father's death. Just what she wanted to think about as she crawled toward yet another family emergency.

Nan was frantically worried about Julie, and absolutely furious with Adam.

Of all the bone-headed stunts her brother-in-law might

241

have pulled, getting into a fight and being arrested had to head the list. What on earth was his problem?

Even more alarming was the news of Julie's elevated blood pressure. "I didn't want you to get mad at me," Julie had whimpered on Tuesday night when she called and poured out everything: Adam's arrest, the hypertension, the bed rest, the threat to her planned home birth, the disintegration of what little remained intact in her world.

Mad? Did Julie really think Nan would be angry about a medical condition? When there were so many other things—like Adam's colossal stupidity—worthy of genuine fury?

"Look," she had answered, "the only thing I blame you for is not telling me when you first found out. If you were somebody who normally neglected her health, then maybe I could work up a little righteous indignation. But hey, you can only control so much in your own body. Everybody gets dealt some physiological wild cards."

"Then I want a reshuffle!" Julie wailed.

Nan laughed. "Look, it's like they say: after you turn thirty, your body decides it wants a life of its own. At least you were sensible enough to see the doctor. And listen to her."

Julie's sigh whistled down the line like a Santa Ana. "I want so much to have this baby at home, Nan."

Nan contained herself. "What you *really* want is to have a healthy baby, right?"

"Well, of course."

"So then what the hell does it matter if you have it in a hospital or a birthing center or a taxicab? Did you have in mind maybe setting up a little nest of sphagnum and rosebuds out in the greenhouse? You're not having puppies, Julie."

Julie laughed. "My sister the romantic."

To Nan's mind there was nothing remotely romantic about the idea of childbirth. From everything she'd heard it sounded perfectly dreadful, called *labor* with excellent reason. Long ago, she'd been left writhing in pain on the clinic floor while her body tried to expel a just-inserted IUD. If labor was any worse than that, it was a miracle the species survived.

But Julie and Adam always carried the issue of natural health to extremes. Nan remembered Adam's funk when his father suffered a fatal heart attack several years earlier. "He didn't have to die," Adam kept repeating, dirgelike, as Nan waited expectantly to hear about a delayed ambulance or mixed-up medications or misdiagnosis or some kind of hideous emergency-room screwup. What Adam meant, it finally developed, was that if his father had lost seventy pounds, given up bourbon, quit smoking, and stopped gnawing pork rinds, he might have lived a good deal longer.

"Look, lots of women get put on bed rest and they don't blame themselves, Jules. I have a friend who wrote contracts for four months with a laptop across her belly. She maintained that her cervix might be considered 'incompetent' but the rest of her damn sure wasn't. Just be grateful your midwife has the good sense to turn you over to a doctor when there's trouble."

"There's nothing but trouble, seems like," Julie said finally.

There wasn't much that Nan could say to that. Most frustrating of all had been the realization that she was swamped at work and couldn't get away to Floritas for another three days.

Now exhaust fumes filled the freeway as traffic bumped and ground through Orange County. I-5 was a nightmare, always giving the impression of being midway through a forty-year construction project. Near downtown L.A. narrow stretches permitted driving on the shoulder and featured a washboard finish that felt like at least two flat tires. The northern Orange County segments had stretches where traffic twisted and turned at seventy mph with concrete bumpers inches away. Overhead, pylons and supports and bits of roadway were jumbled willy-nilly. And then, without warning, the whole thing suddenly opened to seven and eight lanes.

It was hard to believe this had been agricultural land within Nan's lifetime, had actually been named for citrus groves. Now it was endless red tile roofs, interspersed with jillions of disgusting fast-food franchises.

She paced herself, did some deep breathing, tried to remember the lyrics to "Margaritaville." She would get to Julie's and have a couple of beers. Then together they'd figure out a way to work things out.

Not quite.

When Nan finally stepped out of her car three hours later in front of Julie's house, the cold night air was thick with the sweet smell of jasmine. Mr. Nashimora's vines bloomed in succession year-round across the front of the house. No matter what time of year Nan visited, there was always something flowering, and more often than not it smelled wonderful.

But she barely had time to inhale twice before Julie threw the front door open and stood there, wide-eyed and frantic. She wore a large embroidered workshirt with the sleeves rolled up and baggy khaki shorts, with her hair hanging in a long single braid over her left shoulder. She looked decidedly more pregnant than she had at Nan's last visit.

"Thank God you're finally here," Julie caterwauled. "Angus Pettigrew is dead!"

So?

"What happened?" Nan asked neutrally as she walked inside. Julie had a fire blazing, and the living room was warm and inviting. Nan set down the bag she was carrying and turned to her sister.

"He had a heart attack last night, out in his workshop. Lupe found him this morning when she went to take him breakfast. She didn't think much of it when she saw his bed hadn't been slept in. He'd stay out there sometimes for days when he was working. But this time . . ." Julie crumpled and began to cry.

"Now, now," Nan soothed. She said a few of the customary things about living a full life, and expecting old people to die, but inwardly she felt no particular sympathy. Angus Pettigrew had been unspeakably rude to Julie in Nan's presence and had presumed Adam's guilt automatically. He'd deliberately cut himself off from his only remaining daughter and cast aspersions on the pedigree of her son. Nan was going to have a tough time working up much sorrow that he was gone.

"Look," she said firmly, "no matter how bad you feel about this, there *is* a bright side. It should make things easier for Adam and Ramón. We've figured all along that Angus was exerting pressure behind the scenes against Adam. And now—drum roll, please—I have something for you."

"A get-out-of-jail-free card?" Julie wondered grimly. She'd stopped crying and now carefully wiped her cheeks with the back of her hand.

Nan chuckled. "Afraid not. But I did bring Squares."

Julie's eyes brightened. "What a great idea!" For the first time she noticed the bag Nan had set down. "Is this—" At Nan's nod, she ripped open the bag, pulled out a baking pan, and pried loose a chunk with her fingers.

Squares were a treat from their childhood, one of the first things Julie Robinson taught her daughters to bake. They were the essence of simplicity: crush a packet of graham crackers, then mix with a can of sweetened condensed milk, a small bag of chocolate chips, and a teaspoon of vanilla. Baked half an hour at 350, they were fabulously rich and crammed 3,000 calories into a modest eight-inch-square pan. Nan had, on more than one occasion, eaten an entire batch in an evening.

Nan quickly settled Julie on the couch by the fire with Frisky/Comatose in her lap, a cup of Sleepytime tea in her hand, and the Squares at her side. Then she went out and brought in the overnight bag she had packed last night. It felt like weeks ago. She thanked the impulse that had led her to stop for a six-pack before coming to the house as she opened a Molson Golden.

Julie was tired, and there wasn't much to say. Nan didn't feel like falsely mourning Angus Pettigrew, Adam's stupidity bore no comment, and the problems of the greenhouse could wait until morning.

So Nan sent her beleaguered sister off to bed half an hour later, then opened another beer and went outside. The fields of gypsophila lay ghostly behind the house. It would be a shame if this land really were converted into a shopping center. There were so few genuinely pretty places left along the Southern California coast, and so abominably many minimalls. Surely there was no need for such development, though developers tended to operate with a cockeyed, need-will-follow optimism.

Ramón was looking into the developer angle, but he hadn't come up with much and his local contacts were far better than Nan's.

"The company interested in that land is Shadetree Properties, and the name is apt. They're just a bit shady," Ramón had told her last week. "Nothing you can prove, but I know for a fact they pumped a lot of money into the last City Council election. Through stooges and intermediaries, to maintain the legal spending limits. Which were enacted to protect against the likes of Shadetree in the first place. They bankrolled Jake Catson's run for State Senate and he almost won, even though he's so dumb he can't get through the Pledge of Allegiance without writing it on his hand."

Meanwhile, Ramón had also explored his local contacts,

trying to determine the status of Fairy Tale World. There was an available tract of land, but it was on a flood plain and consequently would require all sorts of special work. Mr. Nashimora's property and the land around it, Ramón said, wasn't under serious consideration. There were too many small landowners, too many stubborn holdouts.

It was Angus Pettigrew's land they'd really wanted, land that was unavailable. Nan corrected herself. Land that *had been* unavailable.

What would happen now, with Angus dead?

On Saturday night, Nan and Julie went to dinner at Ramón and Victoria Garza's house, a meal that had been planned a week earlier. Julie assembled a fabulous bouquet of mixed spring flowers—snapdragons, daffodils, baby's breath, and Dutch Iris—and Nan added a bottle of wine.

The Garzas put on a brave front, but there was a chilly fog hanging over the evening. Ramón was melancholy and vaguely disoriented, shaken by Angus's sudden death. He wore a soft charcoal turtleneck over black jeans, the most casually dressed Nan had ever seen him. Frequently lost in thought, he would literally jolt back to attention when directly addressed. It was the first time Nan had seen him when he wasn't utterly composed. He had the air of a brooding poet.

Victoria compensated for Ramón's malaise by being even more hyper than usual. She was sleekly sophisticated in an Elizabethan magenta blouse with swirling sleeves, neatly tucked into tailored black wool slacks. Her earrings and necklace were faceted onyx. Even the hostess apron she wore—a vertically striped black-and-white number—seemed far too classy to ever actually see kitchen duty.

Still, plenty of kitchen chores had been accomplished, in a setting so spotless it suggested some fairy godmother had bibbity-bobbity-booed the whole works into position. An inveterate list-maker, Nan immediately noticed the three lemon-yellow sheets held on the otherwise naked refrigerator by complicated three-dimensional magnets of kitchen paraphernalia. They were written in a tight, precise backhand. The first listed the menu items for the evening, the second detailed advance preparation chores. The third, positioned by a miniature Cuisinart, was an honest-to-God timetable, a countdown to D-hour in fifteen-minute increments. The dining-room table, of course, was already set, a vision of stark elegance: Swedish crystal, bone china, sterling so modern it might have been mistaken for stainless. The centerpiece was a low concoction of anthurium and twisted twigs painted white.

Nan, who enjoyed the notion of entertaining far more than the reality, found the whole production mildly intimidating. On more than one occasion, she had offered Chinese takeout to her own dinner guests, careful to put everything in serving bowls and offer nice chopsticks and lots of Tsingtao beer. She always cheerfully accepted offers of help. Victoria unequivocally announced no help was necessary, which seemed plausible enough. There didn't seem to be anything left to do but check off "Set salad on table."

With dinner so obviously under control, Victoria had plenty of time to be solicitous toward Ramón and hover over Julie, fussing with pillows and doing everything possible to make her comfortably horizontal. The size difference between the two women made the situation almost comical; apart from Julie's swollen abdomen, she towered a good eight inches over Victoria. Victoria made enough anxious remarks about "the baby" to firmly underscore her own pain at being childless and give Nan a sense of chilly creeps.

The evening had the potential to be downright ghastly, but fortunately the Garzas had seasoned the stew with another guest. Male. Nan was accustomed to dinner parties where she was expected to make nice to some unattached man, but this hardly seemed a conventional setup. Bob was actually *Father* Bob O'Reilly, a priest from the jeans-and-workshirt school of theology.

Father Bob certainly didn't fit Nan's preconceptions, though she was no longer terribly sure what those were. The priesthood had always been a bit of a puzzlement. Spring Hill's Queen of Martyrs church and elementary school served the town's far-flung smattering of Catholics, with the bulk of the citizenry divided among a half dozen Protestant denominations. The Queen of Martyrs nuns wore terrifying habits and the kids wore ugly plaid uniforms and Nan couldn't remember ever even *seeing* a priest. Most of her childhood notions about Catholicism came straight out of Hollywood, via Audrey Hepburn and *The Nun's Story*.

There had been that brief confusing period then, when priests all seemed to be leaving the Church, marrying former nuns and getting busted for civil disobedience. But nowadays you mostly only heard about priests when they were involved in some kind of awful scandal. Paternity, pedophilia, maybe a little embezzlement or gunrunning.

Father Bob, however, seemed like a regular guy and probably didn't even have a criminal record. He was fiftyish, good-natured, and liberal with the wine. He still had a lot of salt-and-pepper hair, and a body that was soft but not fat. He was charming to Julie, and jovial about the inconveniences of a difficult pregnancy. While not insensitive to Ramón's mourning, his manner suggested that a fond celebration of Angus Pettigrew's life made more sense than a lot of glum breastbeating. Nan held little hope that the group might follow her favored third option, forgetting the old blowhard altogether.

"I really thought for a while that Angus was going to let us put a shelter on that land he owns in the southern part of Floritas," Father Bob said, with just the right tone of fond regret. He had already revealed a flexible elbow when pouring wine. "It was so suitable, centrally located but far enough away from businesses that we'd probably not have gotten too much flak about ruining the neighborhood."

"He might have," Ramón agreed halfheartedly.

Julie shook her head. She was reclining on a loveseat in the family room and looked quite lovely in an eggshell sweater embellished with pastel flowers, part of a shipment of expensive maternity duds from June Robinson. "If he wouldn't do it for you, Ramón, he certainly wouldn't do it for anybody else. And you tried hard enough to convince him, didn't you?"

Ramón nodded and sighed. "Many times. We need so much for someone like Angus to embrace the immigrant rights movement."

"We're doing all right," Father Bob interjected mildly. "It's a long and uphill battle, after all." He turned to Nan. "My parish is very upscale, almost exclusively Anglo. There's extraordinary resentment about migrants. I try to educate people subtly, of course. But they tend to hear only what they want to. So many people are afraid of these men, never realizing how gentle and kind they are." He shook his head with a wry grin. "And the economic arguments! With a dime for every discussion I've had with a parishioner who truly believes these men are stealing jobs from deserving American citizens, I could build a shelter myself."

Ramón gave a little snort. "When was the last time you saw Anglos willing to dig trenches in the hot sun for twenty-five dollars a day?"

"It all takes time," Father Bob said soothingly, "and we *are* making progress." He reached for the wine bottle again. He was going to need either a taxi or the Garza guest bedroom. "We may be pitifully short on tolerance and facilities, but we're reaching the men in the hills, and they know where to come for help." He turned to Nan again. "We have regular gatherings at the end of the workday, when the men are finished. Often Ramón will come and talk to them about their legal rights."

"They don't really *have* rights," Ramón pointed out irritably. "Just needs. Housing, and medical care, and regular food. And for somebody in the local power structure to accept responsibility. If only Angus would have done that. He could have made such a difference." Suddenly melancholy again, he held his glass to the light, looked through it, set it down.

"Angus meant a lot to you," Julie said softly. "It must be difficult to lose him."

Ramón nodded slowly and deliberately. "He was like a father to me. I never knew my own father. Only Angus. I can't imagine this place without him."

Which raised an interesting point.

"What happens to all of Angus's land and property?" Nan asked, perfectly willing to be the rude outsider. Enough of this maudlin nonsense about a man she still regarded as an overbearing bully. "Who inherits?"

"I didn't draw his will," Ramón answered, with a tinge of petulance. "I'm not sure he would have entrusted something so complicated to me. But as far as I know, most of it went to Shane, after some minor bequests. It'll be interesting to see how he handles Jeff Nashimora. If he even includes him. As for Shane's portion, I'd guess it will go to his boys, unless Angus changed his will in the last month."

Not unwelcome news for the heavily indebted Sara Pettigrew—or her hanger-on brother Frank Reid and the perpetually grinning entrepreneurial beau, Pete Hobbs. Even if everything were locked up in complicated trusts till the boys came of age, there'd almost certainly be some current income to use on their behalf. Plus Shane's portion of Pettigrew Nurseries and his life insurance, though Ramón had said that was minimal: Shane Pettigrew had been too full of life to give much thought to estate planning. Taken as a whole, however, the Pettigrew fortune would pay off whatever Sara owed and still buy a lot of skateboards.

Maybe even a chop shop or pancake house.

Jeff Nashimora was a real wild card here. And what about the "minor" bequests? Lupe, perhaps, and other old retainers like Margaret Whiting. That would square with Angus's particular brand of feudalism.

"You might be in his will, too," Nan suggested. "After all, he *did* raise you. And that would explain why he had somebody else draw it."

Ramón shook his head, his eyes suddenly hard and opaque. "Unlikely, Nan. He may have felt an obligation to me while he was alive, but it was blood lines that really mattered to Angus."

"What does his death do for the Fairy Tale World boosters?" Nan asked.

"Ooh," Victoria said, eyes widening. "I hadn't thought about that. Can Sara sell Angus's land?"

"I hope not," Julie interjected suddenly. "At least not if she plans to sell it to Fairy Tale World. That place would destroy what little's left of the character of this area."

"But it would bring in jobs," Victoria argued. "And tourist money. Just imagine what Floritas could do—a new community center, improved schools, maybe a new library to replace that dinky old one downtown. Those are all things that would benefit you *and* your children, Julie."

Julie shook her head. "Floritas has already grown too much for my tastes. When I first came here, it was still a charming little town. Now it's full of tract homes and Angelenos."

"Anything but that!" Nan laughed, faking a swoon. "Not *Angelenos!*"

"You know what I mean," Julie said. "Families with hundred-dollar sneakers and Volvo station wagons and kids taking fifty lessons a week. In everything but manners."

Father Bob's eyes widened. "Gracious! I guess they'll not be asking you to join the Welcome Wagon, Julie. Though with respect to our progress-oriented friends, I must admit I share some of your reservations. It's entirely possible that too much development and tourism could harm the area. I suspect Anaheim was once a delightful little place, before Disneyland."

"If Sara *can* sell, I bet she'll be under a lot of pressure from Pete Hobbs," Nan noted. "He's probably already worked out the whole menu for his Little House of Fairy Foods."

"A very enterprising young man," said Father Bob, who couldn't be more than five or six years older than the restaurateur. "But my goodness, Hobbs House does serve fine food!"

"Speaking of which," Victoria announced, "ours is ready."

They gathered around the glass-topped dining table, with Nan between Ramón and Father Bob. Victoria's culinary capability was equal to her organizational skills, and she still hadn't even smudged her apron. Angel-hair pasta was topped with basil cream sauce, served with scallops for all but Julie. The salad was picture perfect, mesclun with a hint of fresh basil in the dressing. Crusty baguettes gave off steam when broken.

"Now let me see," Father Bob said, after lavishly praising everything, "is cholesterol good or bad this week?"

Nan chuckled. "And do we care? My new policy is to ignore all breathless medical studies. First coffee's going to give you pancreatic cancer, then decaffeination involves deadly something or other, and then maybe it's just fine after all. Maybe caffeine's even *good* for you. Butter's terrible, but hydrogenated margarine is worse. Milk is either nature's perfect food or disastrous, only fit for baby cows. One week high cholesterol is going to kill you and the next week low cholesterol's supposed to make you suicidal."

"A mortal sin," Father Bob noted cheerfully. "I don't believe that's the direction where caring for your body is supposed to lead you."

"Everything in this meal is as low-fat as possible,"

Victoria put in, with a bit of a frown. Nan noticed that while the guests were plowing into their plates with greedy abandon, Ramón hadn't even picked up his fork yet, and Victoria was dispiritedly pushing around her pasta. Old pure-body-temple Julie, on the other hand, was almost ready for seconds on salad.

"My dear, the last thing I want you to think is that we're criticizing!" Father Bob told Victoria. "No one who's taken a vow of poverty could ever be disdainful of such a splendid repast. But I *am* inclined to agree with Nan. I'd just as soon go back to the old days when common sense was the guideline, and if a man chose to load up on fatty corned beef, he knew the price he'd pay."

"Arteriosclerosis," Julie said, speaking up for the first time since she'd admired the salad dressing, "and early death. Really, now! It's well documented that vegetarians live longer."

"It only seems like it," Nan retorted. "Come on, you guys. This is the best meal I've had in weeks and I don't want to feel guilty about enjoying it." Not to mention the delightful change it made from the customary pass-the-Beano fare at Julie's. There was a reason candles burned so regularly at the Chandler house, and it had nothing to do with romance, or being leftover hippies. "Now we need a new conversational topic, something light, bright, and noncontroversial. Father Bob?"

"Will the Auld Sod do?" he asked with a twinkle. "If I promise to leave out the IRA?" He then launched a succession of light-hearted stories about his visit to Ireland the previous summer. By the time Victoria brought out fresh strawberry cheesecake, Nan was stuffed. She managed, however, to polish off an enormous slice.

When they moved with coffee into the living room, Nan pulled Ramón aside. "Is there someplace we can talk privately?" she asked.

Ramón looked as if he'd rather chew ground glass. He

nodded grimly. "In my study." He turned to his wife. "Victoria dear, Nan and I will be back in just a moment."

Ramón's study was down the hall, and the difference from the rest of the airy, pastel-dominated house was astounding. This room was a return to Olde Mexico. Heavy dark furniture. Terra-cotta tile floor with scattered Indian rugs. Pottery nestled amidst the legal volumes on the shelves of a towering bookcase. In one corner, an oil painting of a beautiful young woman was lit by a discreet track spotlight. A simple wooden table underneath the painting held an arrangement of silk lilies, what appeared to be a small tattered Bible, and a much smaller black-and-white photographic version of the same picture, framed in silver.

Nan felt drawn to the painting of the young woman. It had a luminous quality, an otherworldliness. Her hair and eyes were ebony, her face a softly glowing bronze. She wore a lacy white dress, with a white flower in her elaborately swirled dark tresses.

"What a lovely woman," Nan said, taking in her coloring, her youth, the shape of her face and mouth. She knew what Ramón was going to say.

"My mother on her wedding day." He spoke with quiet passion. "I had the painting done from that photograph. It was the only picture I had of her."

"The artist did a beautiful job," Nan told him admiringly. "You lost her when you were very young, didn't you? It must have been terribly difficult for you."

"I was five," he answered shortly. He turned away from the painting and sat in one of two chairs on the opposite side of the room. "Now. What is it that you want?"

Nan sat in the other chair. A table inlaid with hand-painted tiles was between the chairs. It held an incongruous copy of *California Lawyer*. "I want to know how bad it is with Adam this time."

Ramón grimaced. "I can tell you the truth," he said, "though I've tried to downplay the situation to Julie, in her condition. It's very, very bad, Nan. Adam has a history of violence, but we could have argued that he's mellowed and changed. Now we have a dozen witnesses to a down-and-out brawl, not to mention a potential civil suit brought by Johnny Simpson. Although Johnny's mostly bluster, and I doubt that he'll follow through on that threat."

"There's no way to get Adam released again?"

"None whatsoever. If there's reason to think the community might be threatened by releasing someone, that's grounds to deny bail. He'll be in till the trial, Nan, and there's not a damn thing I can do to change it. Your mother, of course, is no longer financially responsible."

Small comfort. "Why on earth did he do it?"

Ramón seemed genuinely baffled. "Who knows? My best guess is that he just snapped. The pressure is enormous, after all. Julie, the baby, the trouble they had getting their roses out for Valentine's Day. Adam's always had a tendency to brood, to let things build up inside him. Of course that makes the D.A.'s argument for premeditation in Shane's murder even more compelling."

"Damnation! So where does that leave your defense strategy?"

He shifted his weight a bit uncomfortably. "We'll have to rely heavily on Julie's testimony that Adam never left the house that night. We'll come down hard on the place being open enough that somebody could slip into the greenhouse and remove the gun. There've been some greenhouse burglaries around here recently and we'll play that up, too."

"Burglaries? That's *great!*"

"Well, yes and no. What's been taken is stuff like pesticides, and the cops assume it's somebody in the business. But folks in the business are aware of Adam's organic inclinations." He grinned slyly. "We won't mention that in court, of course."

Nan smiled. "But surely not every potential burglar

would know how Adam and Julie feel about pesticides. And a gun might seem like a nice consolation prize."

"Exactly. Now, Julie and Adam were sometimes away together during the day. The folks who run that greenhouse next door probably wouldn't notice someone sneaking around."

"True enough," Nan agreed. A Marine battalion could launch a full assault unnoticed by Lucille and Kevin Ellison, though heaven help the spider mite that tried to sneak into their greenhouse. "And there's nobody at all there at night."

Ramón nodded. "As for the gun, neither Julie nor Adam remember actually seeing it for several weeks before the murder. And the gum wrapper is easy enough to explain. Adam leaves a trail of them. He chews that silly gum all the time and he's always starting a new piece. I've seen him switch gum three times in the course of an afternoon. Somebody could have picked up a wrapper anywhere and held it to implicate Adam."

"But none of this gets to the real question," Nan pointed out. "Why would anybody go to such lengths to frame Adam? And *who?*"

Ramón shrugged his shoulders, raising his palms.

"You mean," Nan said carefully, fighting panic, "that's the best defense we can muster? That there's nothing else to go on?"

"Reasonable doubt, Nan. In a criminal case, the jury has to believe guilt beyond a reasonable doubt. All we have to do is raise that doubt, make it strong and tangible."

It didn't seem at all tangible to Nan, and as for strong . . . the whole defense was like that big old spider web outside Julie's back door. It was pretty enough, but it would collapse the minute you touched it.

Ramón went on. "In criminal defense, this isn't at all an uncommon situation. The *'SODDI'* explanation—some other dude did it."

Some other dude did it. Swell.

"Then can't you get the trial postponed? In hopes that we'll be able to develop new evidence?" Nan had spoken recently with Lorne Presser, a law school classmate practicing criminal law in Ventura. Lorne had firmly advocated stalling as a defense tactic: let memories fade, witnesses disappear, issues grow fuzzy.

Ramón shook his head. "We did waive the sixty-day statutory limit to get our trial date. But now that Adam's back in jail, he says no more delays."

Nan thought about that for a moment. Why? Adam's trial was set to start April 5. The baby was due April 27. Was he hoping for a sympathy factor? "What if Julie's doctor won't let her testify?"

"We'd have to ask for a delay then. And I'm sure the D.A. wouldn't oppose it. That would also allow us to do blood tests on the baby and prove Adam's paternity. Though frankly, the less attention paid to that issue the better."

All in all the situation was pretty bleak. "Isn't there *any* way to develop something else? Some other kind of evidence?"

Ramón offered the shadow of a smile. "I'm working on it, I assure you. And I do have a bit more on Frank Reid, Sara Pettigrew's brother."

Nan snapped to, a starving wolf catching a whiff of fresh meat. "Tell me everything!"

"There's not all that much to tell, but it's vaguely promising. His alibi, you may remember, is that he was in an all-night card game in Oceanside when Shane was killed. The police checked it out kind of perfunctorily. Well, I had a P.I. look into it further, and the people who are vouching for him are all real lowlifes. Nobody who'd make a very attractive witness. They all have records, and one's back in jail already, on a parole violation."

"So how would you handle that? Put on evidence about

Frank beating up Shane? Wouldn't that make more sense if Shane killed Frank?"

"Shane," said Ramón, "wasn't one to carry a grudge. Or even to remember one. He was a very good-natured guy. Frank Reid, on the other hand, has a reputation as somebody who gets even. He also has a record."

"For drugs."

"And violence. He's got priors for assault. That's why it was such an act of charity on Shane's part not to press charges."

"I can see him as the sniper, too," Nan noted. "Did he have an alibi for that day?"

"Nothing concrete, and he was a sharpshooter in the Marines. Actually, about the only people in North County properly accounted for that afternoon were the three of you waiting at the house."

"He's got a pretty decent motive, too. Sara's in terrible financial shape." She hesitated. Ramón seemed enormously fond of Sara Pettigrew. "And Frank hangs out at Sara's—he came in unannounced when I was there. *And* he's got no money of his own. What if Frank and Sara were in cahoots somehow? Or even Sara and Pete Hobbs? He went bankrupt a while back, I understand. What do you know about his background?"

Ramón shrugged. "He's got an ex-wife and a couple of grown kids back in Ohio. Served in the Navy. Been in the restaurant business most of his life."

"He *says*. He also told me he moved here directly, but he actually stopped over in Nevada for several years, long enough to pick up a silent partner for Hobbs House. People reinvent themselves all the time when they come to California, and nobody ever checks up on them. We don't even know for sure he *is* Pete Hobbs. He could be an axe murderer on the lam. A spy. In the witness protection program. We'd never know."

"He's kind of high profile for any of those possibilities,

don't you think? And I've talked Navy with him. He knows what he's talking about there."

"A spy would," Nan noted.

"You're not serious, surely?"

"Well, maybe not about the spy stuff. But still, Ramón. Call me an old crank, but it's hard for me to trust somebody who smiles as much as he does. We *don't* know that his business is successful, only that it looks that way. He could be gambling away every penny—which would fit with living in Nevada *and* the bankruptcy—and we wouldn't know a thing about it. But we *do* know that he's really hot to expand, which would make Sara's money pretty appealing. And speaking of Sara—have you come up with anything to show that she might not have been home the night Shane was killed?"

"No," Ramón answered, a bit stiffly. "She and the boys were home all night. It was a school night, after all."

"Was there a live-in or somebody else there? Pete, maybe?"

"No."

Nan liked the sound of this. "Then she *could* have left in the middle of the night, gone to the greenhouse, shot Shane, and come back home with nobody the wiser." Sara's house was maybe five minutes away from Pettigrew Nurseries.

Ramón seemed offended at the very notion. "The boys would have awakened. They're light sleepers."

Said who? Their mother?

"I know you're very fond of Sara," Nan said gently. "But I'm very fond of Adam. And if we're accepting that he didn't kill Shane—which we are, aren't we?"

"Of course!"

"Then somebody else did. Frankly, I'm not too keen on this some other dude business. I'd feel a whole lot better if we could identify that dude. Or dudette. What about somebody who owes Frank Reid? Even if Frank's got an iron-clad alibi, his friends all don't. Hell, we don't even know who his friends might be."

"Nan, I'm doing everything I can," Ramón answered.

"I know, I know. And I really appreciate all your efforts. Do you think there's a chance that one of those lowlifes Frank was supposedly with that night might recant the alibi? Maybe the guy who's back in jail, as some kind of deal?"

Ramón smiled hopefully. "That's a real possibility, Nan, and I have the P.I. still working on it. I'll look a bit deeper into Pete Hobbs's background, too, okay? Anything else?"

Nan hesitated. "What's Jeff Nashimora up to these days, Ramón?"

"Working at Pettigrew, I presume. We ran into him at the movies last week. With Kimberly Wilkes."

Oh, *really?* "That sounds cozy."

"Don't make too much of it, Nan," Ramón suggested. "They're a couple of kids from out of town with similar interests."

How similar? Nan's mind was racing. "What about this idea, Ramón? Everybody says Jeff Nashimora's good at the business end of running Pettigrew. So good at business, actually, that it doesn't make sense for him to even *be* there. He ought to be putting together international transactions somewhere. Then there's Kimberly. She's a plant person, currently picking up valuable on-the-job training in tissue culture. Put them together—maybe throw in some valuable alstroemeria hybrids—and you've got a viable business. Shane and Angus are both gone from Pettigrew now. It's wide open and Jeff is family."

Ramón was frowning. "I really don't think . . ."

"No, listen," she went on excitedly. "They wouldn't even *need* the Pettigrew facility at first, if they had access to Katsumi Nashimora's greenhouse. And if Adam's convicted, odds are that Julie can't manage it alone. Mr.

Nashimora always wanted to keep the family business going. Jeff is his path to do that. His last hope, really."

"But why on earth would Jeff want to harm Shane? Shane's the one who brought him into the business in the first place."

"I don't know," Nan admitted. "But I'm panicking, frankly. The trial is so *soon*."

"Relax," Ramón told her. "We've got a whole 'nother month to pull the defense together. And we'll do it."

Nan certainly hoped so. She somehow doubted that Some Other Dude was waltzing into the Floritas police station chewing XyliFresh cinnamon gum, confession on his mind.

CHAPTER 16

Francisco Hernandez shuffled warily in front of the pay telephone, clutching his quarter and wondering. Was there any point to this? He had started to tell Miguel about the other night, but the older man quickly laughed him silent and opened another can of beer. *Mind your own business,* Miguel had told him. *It is no concern of yours what goes on there.*

So Francisco had stopped, without telling Miguel the most puzzling and troubling part of the experience. Perhaps he had really not seen what he thought anyway. Even *El Halcón* might possibly be mistaken. It had been very dark, after all.

But he had to know, had to find out. He dialed the number he had copied out of the *directorio de teléfonos,* then spoke hesitantly.

Five minutes later, hanging up the phone, Francisco smiled. It was not so difficult after all. And tonight everything would be made clear.

Shortly after eight that night, a dark Chevy pulled up at the spot where Francisco had been told to wait. The front passenger door swung open and the young migrant stepped inside at the sound of his name.

He barely had time to realize that there was a man sitting directly behind him before he felt a cord sweep down over his face and tighten suddenly around his neck.

* * *

Nan found the services for Angus Pettigrew an eerie replay of his son's funeral.

Once again it was a Sunday afternoon, once again the church was jammed with mourners, and once again the floral arrangements were overwhelming. Nan noticed several people carefully and professionally examining the arrangements. She hoped that some of the flowers would be funneled someplace other than the cemetery when the funeral was over. It seemed a colossal waste, though folks accustomed to dumping carloads of exhibition-quality blooms because the color turned out wrong probably wouldn't agree.

Of course everything wasn't *exactly* the same. Angus wasn't there to keel over midservice, and nobody else did, either.

This time Cassie Pettigrew sat on the aisle in the family pew, her son Jeff between her and Sara's boys, who looked truly lost. Then came Sara, the picture of contemplative composure, and Lupe, once again distraught. Ramón and Victoria rounded out the pew.

Pete Hobbs sat a few rows behind Sara, and for once he wasn't smiling. But there were a couple of people missing from the congregation. Kimberly Wilkes was nowhere to be seen, and Frank Reid seemed to have overslept. Or maybe he was back at Sara's house, cleaning his nails with a Bowie knife and flipping through the Sharper Image catalog.

The service was long and depressing. The minister detailed Angus Pettigrew's role in the development of North County floriculture and his major contributions to the town of Floritas. He dwelt upon the old man's fascination with his rockets, his desire to create something that would soar among the stars. He reminded the congregation of the devastating losses that the man had suffered: daughter, wife, son. Angus was reunited with his loved ones now, the minister said, where sorrow could no longer touch him.

By the time the service ended, Nan was more than ready

to go home to Venice. She had said good-bye to Julie before leaving for the church. All she had to do was change her shoes and hit the road.

Back home in L.A. Nan fretted, and being busy didn't help much.

She had a new file, a pair of Riverside attorneys charged with masterminding an insurance scam of appalling proportions. Nan had handled a lot of insurance fraud cases, mostly variants on the same general themes: cappers, phantom vehicles, whore physicians, greedy plaintiff's lawyers. This new case, however, moved far beyond reprehensible, right up to deadly.

It was literally a scam to die for.

Although many of the instances uncovered were far more complex, the basic scenario was breathtakingly simple: car darts in front of tractor-trailer barreling down the freeway, car slams on brakes, truck rear-ends car, injured car occupants sue trucker, claim settles for cash.

The big rigs were targeted because they were too heavy to stop quickly and carried million-dollar liability insurance. For Nan, who reacted with terror on seeing the giant maw of any eighteen-wheeler close in her rearview mirror, the idea of voluntarily being rammed by such a monster bespoke lunacy. Or, as was generally the case, total financial desperation.

Half a dozen different rings were currently under investigation by a bevy of law-enforcement agencies. So far, two of these had led to the Riverside law partners in Nan's file. In addition to dozens of counts of garden-variety—and hybrid—insurance fraud, they were charged as accessories to murder in one case. A refrigerated truck full of hams had jackknifed on the Golden State Freeway, crushing a Chevy Malibu carrying five Salvadorans, only two of whom survived.

For the most part, total immersion in the horrors of this

case forced Nan's mind off Adam and Julie and the mess in San Diego County. At stray moments, however, she would visualize the courtroom of her nightmares, the one with the hanging judge and American Gothic jurors.

Some other dude did it. Yeah, but who?

Wednesday night Nan met Tom Hannah for dinner at Versailles. Both of them loved the bustling Cuban restaurant, which was close enough to midway between their homes to make a logical and frequent meeting place.

Tom looked very prep tonight in a navy V-neck sweater and tan cords. He had twinkling brown eyes and salt-and-pepper hair that remained thick even as he closed in on forty. Nan took a close look at his hair, which seemed to have less gray in it than she remembered. Was he using some sort of hair dye, one of those manly comb-in preparations? He was certainly vain enough to. Nan had known Tom almost as long as she'd been in L.A., since shortly after she arrived to attend law school. At one point, long ago, they had slept together enough times to realize that they made better friends than lovers.

Tom was a hopeless romantic and a marrying man, currently on the lookout for wife number four. Tonight he had brought along a new girlfriend. Suki Moran was midtwenties, a lot younger than Tom. She was an engineer at Hughes, with the no-nonsense air of those post-feminist young women who genuinely believe they've never experienced sexual discrimination and never will. Her light-brown hair was cut in the sort of really short bob that requires trimming every three weeks, and her turquoise-framed glasses matched her eyeshadow and hoop earrings. She wore a long multi-colored harlequin-patterned sweater over black tights.

The three of them sat near a big black-and-white photographic poster of sugarcane stacked on carts waiting to be hitched to horses and carried away. Or maybe hitched to humans, Cuba being notoriously short of all sorts of basic supplies.

After much discussion about how one of these times they'd really have to try something different, Nan and Tom both bowed to tradition and ordered the roast chicken. Suki, in a display of daring, went for the roast pork.

"I've been feeling so disoriented these last couple of months," Nan confessed as the waiter returned with their beers. "Leon getting married kind of shook me up, and all this back and forth to Floritas is starting to get to me. I just feel so goddamned helpless about not being able to *do* anything." She turned to Suki. "It's too long and sordid a story, but my brother-in-law is in a horrendous legal mess and my sister's in the last trimester of a high-risk pregnancy and I'm just totally stressed out."

Totally stressed out? Nan listened in disbelief as the cliché slithered out of her own mouth. Which undoubtedly proved it was true.

"To stress reduction," Tom said easily, lifting his glass.

"Would that it were so simple," Nan answered. "So tell me, how did the two of you meet?"

"We took a screenwriting seminar together a couple of weeks ago," Suki explained earnestly. Of course. With the cold war thoroughly defunct, aerospace engineers with foresight were actively exploring new employment options these days. Sometimes even before their actual layoffs.

Tom had the good grace to look mildly embarrassed. "It's a new approach," he told Nan, "called 'The Overnight Screenplay.' "

"How interesting," she replied noncommittally.

How preposterous! Tom was a high school English teacher—and a truly gifted one, at that—but he could never quite accept that teaching was his career. He wanted to be a screenwriter. No, he *yearned* to be a screenwriter. After countless years of having exactly nothing happen with this by now thoroughly shopworn illusion, Tom couldn't cut loose the dream. He still actively nursed the fantasy that he would one day write a script so brilliant, so trenchant, so profound—and yet so fabulously commercial—that sleazoid producers with gold-plated septal replacements would beat a path to his door. He'd started a dozen such masterworks. The problem was that he never got any of them finished.

"I thought the Simmons Structure Seminar was more useful," Suki offered. Her script, Nan suspected, would be a zany comedy set at a defense contracting plant suddenly caught without an enemy. Lots of pocket-protector humor.

Bowls of black bean soup arrived, delivered by a handsome waiter in a white shirt with black pants. His thick black hair was combed straight back.

"This may make me a total racist," Tom said, when the waiter had departed, "but every single waiter in this place looks exactly the same to me. Like Ricky Ricardo."

Suki looked puzzled. She was far too young to remember *I Love Lucy*. Hell, she was probably too young to remember Mary Tyler Moore.

But Nan laughed, realizing just how true the statement was. None of the staff at Versailles even remotely resembled the Mexicans she'd seen on the street corners of Floritas. Or L.A.'s Salvadorans or Guatemalans or any of the other groups lumped together under the heading *Latino*. Of course *white* covered a lot of territory, too, from Sweden through Sicily.

Suki finished half her soup and then laid her spoon down with a sigh. "I'm beginning to feel almost human," she told Nan. "I spent the entire afternoon waiting at my apartment for this plumber who didn't show up till four-thirty. Then he took one look at the heater and said the whole damn thing has to be replaced."

Nan murmured sympathetically. L.A. heater complaints weren't uncommon, though they lacked a certain drama in a town which never froze, where a mercury dive into the fifties was considered a cold snap necessitating Beverly Hills matrons to break out the mink.

Suki continued. "Now I have to wait till Roscoe, my landlord, gives the go-ahead, and he's out of town till Thursday. He'll probably try to patch it up with Silly Putty or something to save a buck. Such a cheap bastard. He didn't seem the least bit concerned that Tom and I could both have been *killed*."

"What happened?" Nan asked. Tom hadn't mentioned any narrow brushes with death.

"I started noticing that whenever I had the heat on, I'd get headaches," Suki explained. "Though I really didn't make the correlation till I saw some family on TV with carbon monoxide poisoning being carried out of their apartment by paramedics. Then I thought, *Yikes!* So I called Roscoe, and he came over and looked at it and said everything was fine. He's this real patronizing SOB, very macho Eastern European and *very* cheap. I figured the hell with it and I just stopped turning on the heat. I'm from Buffalo, so it's no big deal. But Tom's kind of a wuss about cold weather, so when he was at my place over the weekend, I put the heat back on. We *both* started getting woozy."

"At first I thought it was just love," Tom said with an easy smile, "till Suki told me the back story. So I called the gas company and they came out and shut the heater off. Said it was filthy and not venting properly and we were lucky to be alive."

Suki took over the story now. "So I finally reached Roscoe up in Fresno where he's on vacation—"

"Wait a minute," Nan interrupted. "What kind of person vacations in *Fresno*?"

"Immediate kin to the California Raisins and Suki's landlord," Tom said. "Plus maybe the midget from the mayonnaise factory."

"Are you *sure* you're not exaggerating, Roscoe asks me," Suki went on, "like maybe the gas company can't tell a defective heater when they see one. Then he finally agrees to send out somebody and here we are. By the time Roscoe gets it replaced, it'll be August."

Their dinners arrived then, and conversation turned to current events. There was a juicy scandal breaking at one of the film studios, and Tom claimed to have the inside scoop. Nan listened halfheartedly, suddenly exhausted.

But by the time she got home, the coffee had kicked in and she was wide awake again. Nefertiti waited patiently on the doorstep.

"What am I going to do with you, girl?" Nan wondered aloud.

She would definitely lose face once her friends realized that Nefertiti seemed to have become a permanent resident, bearer of a kitty green card. But Nan was damned if she would admit to anybody that on two separate occasions, the cat had come around the corner of the house—her perfect new house, her charming walk-street bungalow—with a dead mouse in her mouth.

Nan was not proud of her fear of little rodents. It was irrational and stereotypical and embarrassing. It also left her antipathy toward cats in the dust.

What complicated matters was that Nan had actually started getting accustomed to Nefertiti's companionship. Had even begun to think of the animal by name instead of as *that cat*.

This was getting out of control. Before she knew it, she'd have an ATTACK CAT door mat and one of those floor-to-ceiling carpeted cat condos. A bumper sticker saying I ♥ MY CAT and a life subscription to *Cat Fancy*. There'd be awful little feline tchotchkes all over her house.

Nefertiti began rubbing Nan's ankles and purring loudly. She slipped inside as soon as Nan had the door unlocked. Perhaps Nan hadn't admitted to herself that the cat lived with her, but Nefertiti clearly had her own mind made up.

Had probably, indeed, already ordered stationery with her new address. She moved directly to her food bowl and began crunching.

"At least you're a lady," Nan told her, as she crossed the room to turn on the gas wall heater. The house was beastly cold. Nefertiti looked up, puzzled, then went back to her feed. "But my warning stands. The first time you scratch the furniture or piss on the rug, you're history."

The cat looked up again, and Nan would have sworn her yellow eyes had a hurt expression. Half an hour later, the two of them were in bed. Despite her initial attempts to keep Nefertiti out of the bedroom, Nan had come to realize that she actually *liked* the little patch of warmth at the foot of her bed. Besides—even though there was no evidence to suggest that mice had actually invaded the house—it made sense to have the bed under guard.

Tonight, when she crawled under the covers, the satiny black ball of fur was midway up the unused side of Nan's queen-sized bed, her little motor gently purring. Nan didn't move her. But as she lay awake in the darkened room, Suki's story returned to her.

She got out of bed and turned off the heater.

In the morning, Nan called Ramón.

"Do you happen to know if an autopsy was performed on Angus?" she asked.

"Why?"

"Just curious. Humor me."

"All right," Ramón answered. "There wasn't one, because there was no reason. Angus had a long history of coronary problems, and several hundred people witnessed his heart attack at Shane's funeral. Including me and you, remember?"

"So if there'd been any other cause of death, it wouldn't have been noticed?"

"I assume that his doctor examined the body before he

signed the death certificate. What's this all about, Nan?"
Ramón sounded mildly perturbed.

Nan neatly aligned the papers in the file she'd been reviewing. "It occurred to me," she said, "that if somebody were after Angus's money, a death which appeared natural wouldn't be checked too closely. Particularly since he just had that very public heart attack."

"I suppose that's true," he answered slowly, "but who are you thinking of?"

"Any number of people. Maybe Jeff Nashimora, who's lined up to take over two nurseries *and* Shane's girl. Or Cassie on Jeff's behalf—certainly there was no love lost for Angus on her part. Possibly Sara, with or without help from Frank Reid or Pete Hobbs."

"Nan, there's *nothing* to suggest that any of these people would kill Angus. Or that Angus didn't die of natural causes."

"Hear me out," Nan told him. "Angus had a lot of money, a lot of land, a lot of everything. What did you find out about his will?"

Ramón was silent for a moment. "I saw it on Tuesday. As I suspected, he hadn't changed it since Shane's death. If Angus had died first, it would have gone two-thirds to Shane, one-third to Jeff Nashimora when he turns twenty-five. After a few minor bequests. And incidentally, you were right. Angus left me five thousand dollars."

"I'm glad to hear that," she told him, though it occurred to her that five grand was chump change in an estate like Angus Pettigrew's. "What happens since Shane died first?"

"Because Shane predeceased Angus, his portion of the estate will be held in trust for his sons, until they're twenty-five. Just like Jeff's third is also in trust for the next few years."

"Who's the trustee?"

"Bank of America."

"Can they sell his property?"

"As trustee? Sure. A trustee can make whatever decisions he deems proper for the responsible management of the trust. If, say, an estate has a lot of stock in a company that's going down the tubes, the trustee has an obligation to unload it and put the money into something more stable. They have a fiduciary responsibility to do everything possible to preserve and expand the estate they're managing."

"Hmm," Nan said thoughtfully. Estate work had never interested her very much, and just that brief speech reminded her why. She'd long since forgotten whatever she'd been forced to learn in law school. "So at least until Jeff turns twenty-five, B of A runs the whole show. Do the beneficiaries get the income from the trust?"

"Yes."

"That's probably a nice piece of change right there." She thought a moment. "And there's *still* all that land, land the trustee might be persuaded to sell. Angus owned great big chunks of Floritas he refused to sell. A trustee bank might look at the big picture, sell some of that land to develop it as houses or an industrial park or . . . or Fairy Tale World."

"Oh, come on!" Ramón answered, laughing. "Nan, you can't be suggesting that Fairy Tale World would commit murder to put up a theme park. Why, they're so wholesome they sanitize fairy tales. The Big Bad Wolf doesn't eat Grandma, he just sticks her in the closet. That sort of thing."

"Yeah, but even if the Fairy Tale World people themselves are squeaky clean, there's a lot of locals really anxious to get that theme park's revenue base and ancillary business for Floritas. And at least one of them has a close tie to Sara Pettigrew. Have you found out anything about Pete Hobbs's background?"

"He seems to check out, Nan. But I'm not sure it's worth spending the money on an Ohio P.I. without something more to go on than that he smiles too much."

Put that way, Nan could hardly argue. "I guess not. Tell me this, though. A big part of Angus's estate is Pettigrew Nurseries. I'm thinking about the greenhouses here, not the undeveloped land. Surely Bank of America doesn't know anything about growing flowers."

"Of course not. But they'd either hire a management company that did, or rely on the structure already in place."

A structure that included Jeff Nashimora. Nan doodled on her legal pad, an ecologically correct white instead of the familiar old yellow. She drew a bouquet of dollar signs atop leafy stems. "Could the bank sell Pettigrew Nurseries? As trustee?"

"Maybe. But I'm not sure there'd be a market for it anyway. Flower growing is a healthy industry in San Diego County, but it's an expensive and risky investment for somebody who doesn't already own the land."

"So that if somebody bought the place, it might well be for other purposes?"

"It sure might. There's a saying around here that you can make a lot more money growing houses than roses."

Particularly, in this case, if they were made of straw, sticks, and brick—and belonged to the Three Little Pigs. Who probably, in the laundered Fairy Tale World version, invited the Big Bad Wolf in for cookies and a game of Old Maid.

"Okay, forget that for a minute. Let's say the greenhouse operation continues as it has been, and that the income goes to the trust. That would then be ... what? Divided two-thirds one-third, between Shane's sons and Jeff."

"Yeah. Jeff might get his outright since he's twenty-one, but Sara would control the boys' portion."

"Are there any restrictions on how Sara can spend it, other than some kind of general statement about 'for the benefit of the boys'?"

"Not really. Nan, what are you getting at here?"

Nan flipped to a new page of the legal pad and began drawing question marks. "Turn the situation around, Ramón. What if Shane's murder was a blind, a red herring designed to draw attention away from the really important death—Angus. All along, we've been fighting with the fact that nobody really wanted Shane dead. He had some minor enemies, but not the kind that would lead to murder. There just haven't been any credible *motives*. But what if the real target was Angus all along?"

"Oh, come on, Nan!" Ramón laughed. *"Angus?!"*

"No, listen. If somebody wanted Angus dead, but didn't want Shane to have control of his money and property, it would make perfect sense to kill Shane first. Frame Adam, then wait a while and kill Angus in some quiet way that would look like a heart attack."

"You're forgetting that he *did* have a heart attack."

"We don't know that for sure. We know he had *one* heart attack, at Shane's funeral. But his death could have been something else altogether, as long as it didn't leave marks. Some kind of poison, say. Or carbon monoxide."

Ramón didn't say anything for a moment. "Nan, I want to get Adam freed as much as you do, but this whole idea is just crazy. Poison? Come on now."

"Never mind the poison idea. I just threw that out as a possibility. What I'm really wondering about is carbon monoxide. Angus was found dead in his workshop, right?"

"Um hmm."

"Well, when you and Julie and I went to see him in that workshop, it was hot as hell in there. He had a gas heater blasting away. Those things can be dangerous, you know. Somebody just last night was telling me about one that malfunctioned and was filling her apartment with carbon monoxide. Suppose somebody fiddled with Angus's heater? He was out there alone most of the time. Carbon monoxide poisoning makes you drowsy, and if Angus got drowsy, he might well just lie down. He had a bed right there in the workshop." Nan pictured Julie lying on that bed, under attack from the old tyrant.

"So he'd lie down for a while," she went on. "And if the heater kept pumping out carbon monoxide, it would kill him. CO poisoning makes the victim's complexion red, I think, but Angus was florid and they might not have noticed."

"The whole idea sounds awfully farfetched to me."

"But it's possible, isn't it?"

Ramón considered. "I suppose it might be. But wouldn't there have been gas in the room, an odor that somebody would have noticed?"

"Carbon monoxide is colorless and odorless. That's what makes it so deadly. And people wouldn't have been looking for a problem, with his cardiac history. My guess is that whoever got in there first probably just turned the fool thing off and opened the doors because it was so damn hot. And then once the body was removed, that's that."

"Nan, this really strikes me as terribly silly." Ramón sounded mildly condescending. No, *very* condescending. "But I tell you what. If it will make you feel better, I'll call Larry Woodward and see if anybody with the Floritas police checked the heater. The workshop's probably been closed up since Angus died, so they can check it now if they didn't already. How does that sound?"

"It sounds great, Ramón. Thanks. Listen, I hate to bring this up, but have you gotten any more threatening calls? Since Angus died?"

He didn't answer right away. "Just one," he admitted reluctantly. "Yesterday afternoon. The same voice, telling me to drop Adam's case."

"And you weren't going to tell me?"

"What for?"

"Because it shows Angus wasn't behind the calls!"

"I never thought he was," Ramón said patiently.

"Then who is?" Nan considered the possibilities: Frank

Reid, Pete Hobbs, Jeff Nashimora, one of the loyal Pettigrew employees. Even Cassie Pettigrew had a deep enough voice to fit the profile.

"I honestly don't think it matters, Nan. I'm afraid I'm used to this. The calls I got during the Jesus Alcazar case were a lot worse, believe me. Listen, are you coming back to town this weekend?"

"Tomorrow night," Nan told him.

"Any chance you could stop by my office when you first get here? I'll be in court all day and then I'm going away for the weekend, leaving very early Saturday. I'm a facilitator for a leadership retreat up at Big Bear. Victoria's a bit annoyed, actually, since tomorrow's the anniversary of our first date, but I promised I'd take her out to dinner before I go. Fortunately Hobbs House stays open till ten."

Nan recalled Victoria's story of their arranged meeting and felt vaguely jealous. Would she ever again have somebody to celebrate anniversaries with? Other than Nefertiti, who was a notably poor conversationalist?

"Well, sure. But what do you need to do that we can't talk about right now?"

"I've been going over some of the statements my P.I. got from Frank Reid's friends about his alibi," Ramón explained. "We may have a shot at breaking that alibi. They're a pretty slimy bunch and there are some curious discrepancies. I'm hoping you'll have some ideas on how we can use them to Adam's advantage."

Nan thought for a moment. "Well, sure, I'll be happy to. Why don't you fax them to me so I can look over them before I get there?"

Ramón laughed. "I'd love to, but my fax machine is kaput. It gave a little sizzle yesterday and sent out a puff of smoke. Luckily we were here. Might have burned down the office otherwise."

"Yikes. Oh, well. Listen, I'll bring my things with me to work and just come straight down the Santa Ana. That way we can take care of our business and still be done at a respectable hour. You can get to your dinner date and I can make it to Julie's before she folds for the night. With luck and a tailwind I can be at your office by seven-thirty."

"Great! But listen, Nan, let's not build up Julie's hopes just yet. I'm so worried about her health, and the baby. And these ideas are still long shots, all of them."

"True enough," Nan agreed. "But hey, every now and then a long shot makes a basket."

CHAPTER 17

On Friday afternoon, Nan called Detective Larry Woodward at the Floritas Police Department and asked what he'd found out about the heater in Angus Pettigrew's workshop.

"Heater?" he replied. "Workshop? What are you talking about?"

Drat! Ramón must have forgotten to call, or maybe something had come up. He'd probably gotten stuck in court, or bailing out some juvenile delinquent. Nan explained her carbon monoxide theory and listened to the detective sigh.

"I'll grant you it's a possibility," he said finally, "but frankly it sounds to me like you're grabbing at thin air with this one, pardon the expression. Nobody else at the location was affected."

"But most likely nobody else was in there for any length of time," Nan argued. "Lupe, the housekeeper, wouldn't have stayed longer than it took to see that Angus was dead. And Lupe or somebody probably turned the heater off when they found the body. He kept that place at about ninety-five degrees. It was like walking into a pizza oven the time I visited. Julie told me once that Angus picked up malaria in Asia when he was in the service, so he kept everything really hot."

The detective said nothing for a moment. "Maybe next week I can check on it," he told her finally. "But right now I'm kind of tied up. Floritas is having what for these parts is a major crime wave. There's a string of odd burglaries, an eighty-year-old woman says she was kidnapped by aliens, and now we've got an unidentified migrant found stabbed to death in a gladiola field. So far we haven't even been able to identify the poor bastard. His compadres won't want to get involved for fear we'll ship them off to Immigration. And God knows where his family is."

Nan sympathized, both with the detective's frustration and the migrant community's fears. "You get murders like that often?"

The detective barked a mirthless laugh. "Well, contrary to your experience, we don't generally have a lot of homicides in Floritas. Maybe one, two a year. And the migrants tend to lay low in general. As a whole, they're a pretty law-abiding part of the population. Of course, eventually we *will* I.D. this guy. This has the earmarks of a crime of passion, so somebody will know something. Meanwhile, I can't say I've got a lot of time for your wild-goose chase."

Five minutes after Nan hung up, she heard a female shriek from somewhere down the hall. Welcoming the interruption, she opened the door of her office and found Danny Harrington running in her direction. This in itself was startling. Danny was a fiftyish investigator, and his customary pace was a languid saunter.

"Grab your socks and get your ass out of here," he barked as he hustled past, banging on the doors along the hallway. "Don't use the elevator. Somebody called in a bomb threat."

A *bomb threat?* To the State Bar?

It sounded ludicrous, but Nan had learned to take Danny Harrington seriously. She grabbed her purse, stuffed papers in her briefcase, and raced for the stairs, joining others pouring down the stairwell in a flood of adrenaline.

Outside, three black-and-whites were flashing lights, and a lot of uniformed cops were hustling people away from the building. A huge armored truck pulled up. The bomb squad. Seeing the truck made it somehow more real. *Very* real, in fact, and mighty disturbing.

Nan joined Danny and a group of other State Bar employees who were speculating about the threat. A lot of folks looked remarkably disheveled, considering that all they'd done was abandon their desks and climb down a few flights of stairs. One female attorney, who admittedly had a bit of a weight problem, was flushed and hyperventilating. Several of the men had left their jackets behind, and a couple looked as if they'd been roused from naps. Well, it *was* Friday afternoon.

"My guess is it's some poor sap who's taken the Bar forty-three times without passing," a male attorney was saying. "I always think it's a wonder more of those folks don't snap."

"There's always the proverbial disgruntled former employee," Danny suggested.

Nan snorted. "*Disgruntled?* This isn't the post office, Danny. People may not look back with aching hearts when they leave here, but I don't think they go away disgruntled. Disillusioned, now that I'd buy. But I don't think disillusioned people set bombs."

"Some pending case, perhaps?" Violet Thomas, the eternally proper office manager, did not look as if she had rushed from a building in fear for her life. She looked as if she were about to join the Queen for high tea. Every silver hair in place, lipstick fresh and precisely applied, a dress that might have just been slipped out of the cleaner's bag. Violet's clothes, Nan had noticed, never *dared* wrinkle.

"Oh, come on, Violet!" Nan didn't really want to consider the possibility. Which wasn't likely anyway. Was it?

Violet shook her head slowly and her eyes were sad. "People have so much to lose when their cases come to us. Just look at your insurance fraud case, Nan. Those horrible truck accidents. Those attorneys are charged with murder, facing years and years in prison."

"Which makes anything we might do pretty insignificant. We're the *least* of their problems, Violet. All we can do is take away their law licenses, after all, and where they're headed there won't be much opportunity to use them. Besides, we aren't even holding the criminal evidence."

"But you never know," Violet warned. "You just never know."

After the first flush of excitement, people began to grumble, remembering all the things they'd left upstairs—purses, wallets, checkbooks, briefcases. Nan was feeling pretty smug until a cold wind sprang up and she recalled that her jacket was hanging on the back of her office door.

Shivering, she wandered close enough to the police line to overhear a cop telling the building manager that a thorough sweep of the building might take five or six hours. The hell with it, she decided, and said her good-byes for the weekend. She might just as well leave early for Floritas. If her office was going to explode—a forlorn hope, really—being there to hear the muffled thud wouldn't be a particularly gratifying experience.

The traffic gods were smiling as Nan headed down the Santa Ana Freeway, and she sailed through Orange County with almost no trouble at all. There was barely even a slowdown at the notorious Mission Viejo bottleneck.

She reached Julie's just after five, and her sister greeted her joyously. Julie appeared very, very pregnant, in that odd way tall women have of looking as if they've swallowed a basketball. She was quite pale, but swore that her blood pressure was behaving itself. With a sort of gentle glee, she announced that the baby had become so active it was sometimes difficult to sleep. To emphasize the point, the baby periodically thrust a fist or foot outward, making definitely peculiar bulges in Julie's sweatshirt.

"Before much longer," Julie said, "there won't be room for her to move like that anymore. Things are getting pretty crowded in here."

"Her? Is this still conjecture, or do you know for sure?"

Julie smiled maternally as she stretched out on the couch. "Still conjecture, counselor. I convinced them that I didn't really need another ultrasound, since you wouldn't believe what they cost. All along I've had this feeling it's a girl, and my dreams are all about girl babies, for whatever that's worth." She rubbed her belly, which suddenly sprouted a sharp angle over her right hipbone. "But as long as it's healthy, that's all I really care about. Even though all this bed rest has made me half crazy."

Nan chuckled. "You were *already* half crazy, Jules."

"Precisely the problem!"

Hoping to get the meeting with Ramón over with early, Nan tried his office, but his secretary was gone and she got his service. No matter, she decided, and left no message. They had a specific appointment, and if he was expecting her at seven-thirty, he'd probably gone off to do something else.

Over dinner, Julie cheerfully reported on her marketing plans for Easter flowers. Lisa Tudor's husband Brad had just shipped out for six months, and Lisa was handling all of Julie's bouquet deliveries on commission. Lisa had even lined up some new accounts. So far, Julie announced, everything in the greenhouse and field was cooperating. There ought to be enough of all the right flowers to make up the Valentine's Day loss. Mother's Day would be tricky, coming less than two weeks after Julie's due date. But, Julie explained brightly, by then the trial would be over and Adam would be home.

Uh huh. Nan smiled noncommittally. By then it was far more likely that Ramón would be frantically researching grounds to appeal a guilty verdict.

But Nan didn't share her gloomy predictions. She

listened and smiled and nodded, grateful to see Julie so positive about her crops again. About her life, for that matter. Her sister's appetite was back, too. Dinner was a chewy conglomeration of grains stir-fried with fresh garden vegetables, with succulent sweet baby beets on the side. Julie's pantry resembled a feed store display, featuring shelf after shelf of giant glass bottles filled with stuff that looked as if it ought to be served to goats or cattle. That she and Adam managed to render so much of it edible was a source of continual fascination.

They moved out to the porch swing after dinner, Nan with coffee and Julie nursing a cup of camomile tea. Nan considered Ramón's admonition not to tell Julie about the possibly defective heater in Angus Pettigrew's workshop. Ramón was, she decided, being a fussy old lady about Julie's health. It couldn't possibly hurt to tell her sister, and Julie might well know or remember something about the workshop that could help.

Julie listened carefully. "It certainly opens up a lot of different possibilities, doesn't it?" she said finally.

"Wide open," Nan agreed. "If Angus was the real target, then we've been looking at everything backward. Angus lived a long time, and I'm sure he managed to get a lot of people pissed off over the years. Hell, I only met him once, and he had me furious almost instantly."

"But Angus hasn't been involved in anything much these last few years," Julie argued. "He's just been shut up in the workshop building rocket ships."

"But that could be the whole point. That he was obstructing progress by doing nothing." Guinivere, the pretty little calico, sauntered around the corner of the porch and jumped into Nan's lap. She automatically began to stroke the cat's ears. Damn, this cat business was out of control. "And of course we don't *know* there was anything wrong with his death. I sure wish the police would check out that heater. I hate to get all excited about something if it's not even possible."

"I don't see why not," Julie said. "It beats the hell out of being depressed and defeatist. And worrying about a trial that starts in three weeks." She considered. "Do you think it would help or hurt if I go into labor on the stand?"

Nan laughed. "I don't know. But I think I like the dramatic effect. Listen, think about all this while I go see Ramón, and if you're still awake when I get back, we can brainstorm some more."

"Absolutely! You know, I *do* have this feeling that there's something I'm not remembering. But the more I try to think of it, the farther away it goes."

"That happens to me all the time," Nan said, "and I never remember until I manage to put the whole thing out of my mind for a while. Go knit some booties or something."

The days were much longer now, the official start of spring only a week away. But it was still nearly dark when Nan parked behind the quiet building where Ramón had his office at the edge of downtown Floritas. His gold Cadillac was the only other car in the lot. The window had long since been replaced, the bullet hole in the fender filled in and repainted. As she got out of the Mustang, she could see a light on in Ramón's office behind the thick shrubbery and tiny patio.

She walked around to the front door. Locked. She banged a couple of times and Ramón appeared a moment later, apologetic. He wore a white shirt and the pinstriped pants from a charcoal-gray suit, classic courtroom attire. But the shirtsleeves were rolled up, and his green-and-gray-striped tie was loosened.

"My staff is all gone for the night," he explained, "and I try to keep things buttoned up when I'm here alone." He gave a little smile. "You work long enough in criminal law, you learn not to want surprises."

"I understand perfectly," Nan answered, wondering how the State Bar bomb threat had been resolved. Did she still have an office? Did she care?

Inside, the reception area was dark, the magazines in English and Spanish neatly arranged. The whole building was almost preternaturally quiet. Nan followed Ramón past the secretary's desk at the reception window and back into his office. He closed the door behind them and sat in the oversized burgundy leather chair behind his heavy oak desk, waving her to a client's chair.

Ramón looked tired, and seemed mildly agitated. He kept rubbing his left thumb against the fingers of his hand. He glanced at his watch which would tell him, Nan knew, that it was seven twenty-five. She'd checked her own in the parking lot. Why was he so antsy? Was Victoria waiting somewhere?

"I'll try not to keep you too long," Nan told him. "What have you got to show me?"

He handed her a stapled report from an Oceanside private investigator. She scanned it quickly. Apart from disheartening defects in spelling and grammar, the report didn't seem to say much of anything significant about Frank Reid or his cohorts. It touched on the night of Shane's murder only perfunctorily and it was certainly no alibi-breaker.

"This is it?" she asked, rather surprised. "It seems pretty weak."

He raised his hands, palms up, fingers flung wide. "What can I tell you, Nan? All we can do is hope."

Nan was starting to get irritated. If he had nothing to tell her, he could have done that on the phone yesterday. And why *didn't* he have something to tell her?

"We need to do a lot more than just hope, Ramón. Adam's trial starts in three weeks, and as far as I can see, he's a goner. Three *weeks* and we haven't got *anything* to work with that I'm aware of. You've simply *got* to stall the beginning of the trial."

Ramón assumed a stern and mildly patronizing expression. "I might be able to get us a few more weeks, Nan, but we'd be in exactly the same position then that we're in now. At the pretrial conference, I'm sure I can get the D.A. to knock out the special circumstances and the death penalty threat. They just plain haven't proven that. But I don't see what buying additional time would accomplish."

"It might keep Adam from being unjustly convicted!"

"Adam wants to go forward with the trial as quickly as possible. He's tired of being in jail."

Suddenly Nan snapped. "He'll be in jail for the rest of his life at the rate things are going. I don't understand this, Ramón. You're his friend, his attorney, his *advocate*. And you're paying less attention to defending his case than some public defender straight out of law school would."

"I've devoted the lion's share of my time to Adam's case since the moment of his arrest," Ramón responded sharply. "I'm defending him to the best of my abilities."

Perhaps that was the problem. "Then why didn't you call Larry Woodward and ask about the heater in Angus Pettigrew's workshop?" she shot back. "Surely that's the best possibility we have right now to break this case open."

"I didn't have time."

"Bullshit, you didn't have time. How long would a phone call take? Mine lasted about three minutes, and that counts looking up the number."

Ramón's eyes narrowed and his spine seemed to stiffen. "I was tied up all day, Nan. The enormous amount of time I've been devoting to Adam means that other aspects of my practice have suffered. I have to work very efficiently. It just slipped my mind."

This was crazy. And getting Ramón mad wasn't going to help.

"Look, Ramón," she began slowly, backing off, trying to placate him. "I appreciate how busy you are, how far this has stretched you. But I'm sure it's not too late to bring in co-counsel. Maybe all we need is a fresh perspective. We could get a continuance—"

"I will try this case myself," Ramón announced flatly, "as I've planned and as my client prefers."

"But, Ramón . . ."

"You don't think I can do it, do you?" His dark eyes blazed at her.

"I never said that."

"You didn't need to. Your meaning is perfectly clear." His voice was angry now, his delivery rapid and intense. "You're just like all the rest of them. You're thinking I might be all right to defend some Mexican, but not your precious Anglo brother-in-law."

The atmosphere was charged now, with an antagonism that went far beyond the moment, a fury that Nan found truly frightening. "Ramón, I never . . ." She was unsure what to say, how to react.

But Ramón didn't seem to be looking at her anymore. He was staring over her shoulder at the bookshelves behind her. Nan turned to follow his gaze and saw a small framed picture. It was the twin of the one in his office at home, a beautiful young black-haired woman with a gardenia in her hair.

Ramón's mother.

Ramón's dead mother.

Suddenly she knew, and was consumed with terror.

When she turned back to face Ramón, she was staring down the barrel of a shiny silver gun.

CHAPTER 18

Julie straddled the floor heater and felt the welcome warmth course up her legs. She'd have to have Nan bring in some wood from the pile behind the greenhouse later tonight. Heavy lifting was one of the many things she was forbidden to do these days, and while she sometimes fudged a bit if something needed shifting in the greenhouse, being chilly hardly constituted an emergency. The floor heater might not be terribly efficient, but it was a perfectly acceptable alternative to the fireplace.

Besides, sitting alone by the fireplace made her melancholy, made her miss Adam and the nights they sat together by the fire. There'd been a wonderful stone fireplace in the little house they first shared in Santa Cruz. The first time she and Adam ever made love was on a winter night in front of that stone fireplace.

She sighed, unwilling to think about the possibility that Adam wasn't coming home, and forced herself to find a cheerier topic for thought. Ramón and Victoria celebrating the anniversary of their first date—now *there* was something joyful and romantic. It didn't seem all that long since Ramón had first introduced them to Victoria. A Halloween party at Shane and Sara's, with Ramón a pirate, wearing a black eyepatch and a silly red paisley tie wrapped sash-like around his middle. Victoria, sleek and feline in black leotard and tights, had little whiskers drawn across her cheeks. She blushed furiously when Ramón confided conspiratorially that he'd known her only forty-eight hours but fully intended to marry her.

But wait a minute.

That was *Halloween*. This was March. Nan must have misunderstood. Maybe it was their wedding anniversary. No, Nan had specifically referred to the only successful blind date in history. Besides, Ramón and Victoria's wedding had been midsummer and beastly hot.

Strange.

Suddenly Julie felt dizzy and light-headed. She stumbled to a chair and tucked her head down over her swollen belly, felt the blood rush back to her brain. Her heart was pounding, though, and that didn't stop. *Wouldn't* stop.

She started remembering things, frightening memories all jumbled up: Ramón at her father-in-law's funeral, glaring into the coffin when he didn't realize Julie was watching, then telling Adam later, "I know how you feel. Now you know how *I* feel." Ramón's bitterness just last week as he discussed Angus Pettigrew's refusal to support migrant housing in Floritas. Ramón's reaction—more revulsion than surprise—when he first asked Julie about the affair with Shane.

No. It couldn't be. It was just too preposterous.

Still, Julie knew she had to talk to Nan, had to tell her *now*. She dialed Ramón's inside office line, the one he always answered when he was working late. The service picked up, said Mr. Garza would be out of the office until Monday. She left no message, but her hands were shaking as she dialed his home.

Victoria answered.

Julie fought to remain calm. "I wanted to talk to Ramón," she said, wishing she were a more fluent liar, "and I thought maybe I could catch him before you guys went out for dinner."

"Ramón's out for the evening," Victoria replied, sounding a bit confused. "He's at a dinner down in Chula Vista, a law school scholarship presentation."

Yeah, right. Julie swallowed before she spoke. "Silly me," she said. "I got all mixed up. Have him call me, would you?"

"Is anything wrong?" Victoria asked solicitously. "Can I help?"

She meant the baby, Julie realized suddenly. Poor Victoria. "No, no, I'm fine, the baby's fine," she gibbered. "Thanks, Victoria." Julie hung up quickly, shaking uncontrollably again and anything but fine.

Nan. She had to tell Nan. She had to *get* to Nan, find her and tell her.

Without thinking further, Julie grabbed her keys and dashed out the door.

The roads were quiet and almost empty as she raced into downtown Floritas. Should she have called the police? No, that was silly. If she was mistaken, she'd look ridiculous. But Julie was increasingly certain that she wasn't mistaken, that something was seriously amiss and that Ramón was at the center of it.

Ramón's office was on a side street, well removed from what little activity occurred downtown on a Floritas Friday night. Julie drove past the front of the building. Nothing remarkable. The waiting-room miniblinds were tightly closed, and she couldn't even tell if there was a light on. Rounding the corner, she started to pull into the lot behind the row of offices, then reconsidered and parked at the curb. Again she felt light-headed, and again she twisted to put her head briefly between her knees.

Nan's Mustang and Ramón's Cadillac were the only cars behind the office building. There was definitely a light coming from Ramón's office. Julie considered, starting to feel silly again. Maybe she should just sneak around and take a peek, then acknowledge that she simply had the prepartum willies and go home to bed. Nobody would ever need to know of her foolish paranoia and suspicions.

She turned off the engine and stepped down out of the pickup. Instinctively she closed the door just enough to have it catch without making any noise. Then she took a deep breath and slipped into the parking lot, staying in the shadows as she moved toward the lighted office.

Nan stared down the barrel of Ramón's gun. Logic told her that the opening at the end of the gun barrel was really quite small, but it looked enormous.

"You couldn't leave well enough alone, could you?" Ramón asked, and there was actually a tinge of sadness in his voice.

Nan couldn't find her voice just yet. She kept looking at the gun. It seemed to grow as she watched it, like some bizarre cartoon hallucination. Except this was real. This gun could very easily kill her as she sat here in her chair.

Just as Shane had sat in *his* chair.

Right before he died.

Could she possibly talk her way out of this? Nan fought panic as she tried to process what was happening, frantically sought a verbal escape route. She had used quick thinking and a facile tongue to wiggle her way out of difficult situations before: nasty work confrontations, unwelcome sexual advances, doorbell-ringing Jehovah's Witnesses. But the stakes had never been quite so high.

"Boy, this is some crazy kind of joke." She made a real effort to appear jovial, and was distressed to hear a quaver of panic in her voice.

Ramón heard it, too. "No joke," he answered shortly. "I'm sorry about this, as a matter of fact. But I'm afraid you leave me no choice, counsel."

Keeping the gun aimed steadily at her head, he reached into a desk drawer with his left hand and pulled out a small spool of telephone wire. Then he got out and came toward her.

"Kick your shoes off, please." *Please?* Well, he'd asked nicely. She slipped off the black leather pumps. "Now, go get that chair from the corner."

"And if I don't?"

"I'll have to shoot you right here and now," he answered matter-of-factly. "Which would be a pity, wouldn't it?"

Indeed. And it would mess up the rug, too. Nan stood and looked at the chair he referred to. It was a simple, straightbacked wooden one, but it looked mighty sturdy. She took the three steps required to reach it, trying to figure a way to overpower Ramón and get out of the room. He was small, not much larger physically than she. But she knew he was strong. And she remembered, spirits plummeting, that he'd been trained as a Navy SEAL. Those guys learned all kinds of specialized skills, like how to kill with their bare hands.

"Set it out in the middle of the room," he went on calmly. "Good. Now sit down and put your arms behind the chair. Stretch now, pretend you're at the gym."

She tried to keep as much slack as possible, but he yanked her arms further back, tight enough to really hurt both shoulders. In the reflection of the French doors that led to the patio, she could see him working behind her even as she felt the plastic cord tighten around her wrists. He tied a knot and left the cord dangling, then took a pair of scissors from a leather desktop accessory set and cut it. Next he cut two more lengths of cord, working with remarkable dexterity considering that he never set down the gun.

Nan was still in her dress from work, not exactly combat garb. But she had to do *something*. When he approached her right leg, clearly intending to tie it to the chair, she waited till he was just in range and then kicked out sharply, trying to trip him. His reflexes were good. Too good. He sidestepped, then smashed the gun down on her right knee.

The pain was excruciating. She yelped involuntarily.

"Stay put," he ordered, rapidly tying first her right and then her left ankle to the chair legs.

She tried to ignore the pain. *Think!*

Talk. That was the key. Keep Ramón talking—*get* him talking—and something might happen.

Like what? An earthquake, maybe? Now, *that* was an idea. Law books flying across the room to knock the gun out of his hand and conk him on the noggin.

When Nan was securely tied to the chair, Ramón went back behind the desk and picked up the phone.

"Dialing 911?" Nan asked. This time her voice was stronger.

He gave a chuckle and waved the gun at her. "Laughing in the face of death. I have to admire that." He spoke rapid-fire Spanish into the phone for a moment and then hung up. "That was an *amigo* who helps me with little problems. He'll be here shortly."

"I think you're making a horrible mistake," Nan told him. "I'm not a little problem."

"True," Ramón agreed cheerfully. "You're a great big one. And *you* made the mistake, counsel."

"But I thought we were on the same team," Nan explained, letting her tone be mildly apologetic. This was not going well. She suspected that she was not going to like Ramón's *amigo* at all. And it wouldn't occur to Julie to worry until hours more had passed. Assuming that her sister didn't just fall asleep. She might not realize Nan was missing till morning.

But at least Julie knew where Nan was. That was something, anyway. And Ramón didn't know that Julie knew. As far as he was aware, Nan had come directly from L.A. to his office, obeying his instructions of the previous afternoon.

Had he been intending to kill her even then?

"Did Shane laugh in the face of death?" she asked conversationally. Keep him talking. Pray for meteorites.

Ramón leaned back in his big burgundy leather chair and laid the gun on the gleaming wooden desktop in front of him. "You do know," he said.

"Not as much as I wish I did. But I can't think of any other reason why you'd pistol-whip me and tie me up to wait for some goon." She glanced down at her knee, which was swelling rapidly and hurt like hell. "You did kill Shane, didn't you?"

He nodded.

"Why?"

"Surely you've figured that out, counsel."

Nan spoke slowly. "I'm trying to put everything together, and it makes more sense by working backward. Starting with Angus and the heater. It *was* the heater that killed him, wasn't it?"

"He had a bad heart."

"Oh, bullshit, Ramón. It was something about the heater, because when I first brought that up, that's when everything started to go sour with you and me. And it was the heater because that's how your mother died. Am I right?"

He smiled appreciatively. "I didn't give you enough credit, Nan. Yes, you're right. What do you know about how my mother died?"

Nan tried to remember what Julie had told her. She recalled the setting more clearly than the information: Adam had just been arraigned and they were waiting in Angus Pettigrew's sterile living room while Ramón was off arguing with Lupe. "Almost nothing, really. That she was here, working for Angus Pettigrew. That a heater malfunctioned."

"She was living in a shanty," Ramón said bitterly. "A crappy little shack in a row of crappy little shacks where Angus kept his slaves."

"But the shacks had heaters?"

"There was a gas line that extended out from the

greenhouses. The shacks tapped into that. If it hadn't been convenient, Angus would never have bothered. Same thing with the running water. There were sinks but no toilets. Because the water line passed by on the way to the greenhouses. He always cared more about the plants than the slaves."

There were headlights on the street out beyond the parking lot, headlights that stopped, then abruptly turned off. Surely there hadn't been enough time for the goon to arrive. Nan fought panic, kept her voice even. "Why do you keep saying slaves? Did he keep people there by force?"

Ramón's laugh was bitter. "Not chains and locks, not that kind of force. But anyone that Angus brought in had to work off the expenses of getting here. At the wages he paid, that could take a long, long time."

"That was how your family came here?"

He hesitated. "That was how my mother came. My father . . . I don't know. He went before my mother, so long before that I don't have any memories of him at all. That was one reason my mother came, you see. She was trying to find my father." He gave the same bitter laugh. "She knew he'd come to California and she thought that was enough to be able to find him."

"But she came to Angus . . ."

"Someone brought her to him, a cousin who died when she did. Angus liked to have families working for him. He always claimed to be a big believer in family, Angus. But really what it came down to was that it was harder to leave if you had others with you, if you had too many responsibilities to just walk away."

"Did you ever find out where your father went?" she asked with genuine curiosity. It occurred to her that nobody had *ever* mentioned Ramón's father before.

He shook his head. "No. I've never been able to find out anything about what happened to him. In those days, you see, records were very scanty and the border more open.

When people were deported, they just piled them on a bus and shipped them down to Mexico without even taking names. I tried to look for him, but . . . I've always assumed that he died somewhere without identification. For whatever it's worth, Angus always swore my father never came to Pettigrew Nurseries."

Nan thought about that for a moment. "And you didn't believe him?"

"I didn't know what to believe. I still don't, and I never will. The others who were here when I came, after my mother died, they all said they didn't know my father, either. That my mother hadn't been able to find him. But I did know where my mother came, and that I was coming to meet her."

His voice slowed, became almost dreamy. "I was five years old, living in a little Mexican village with my aunt and my great-aunt, dreaming about when I would go to be with my mother in America, that magical place. My Aunt Elena and I, we planned to be here in time for Christmas that year. On our way to America—I can still remember how excited we both were. But it was very cold that December. Bitter cold." His delivery was faster now, very intense. "There was one of those old-style open-flame gas space heaters in my mother's shack. They're illegal now, but poor people still have them some places. The flame went out in the middle of the night and she was asphyxiated. They all were. Seven people died that night."

Julie stood at the edge of the parking lot, clenching a branch of the hedge so tightly that she felt thorns pierce her palm. Through the shrubbery she could see clearly into Ramón's office, see Nan trussed in a straightbacked chair, facing Ramón's desk. She could see the corner of the desk, see a shiny gun resting on it.

Where was Ramón? At the desk? As she swayed, fighting recurrent waves of dizziness and nausea, Julie saw her sister nod and speak. She couldn't hear the words, but Nan's face was calm, her expression concerned.

Help. Julie had to find help. There was nothing she could do here on her own. Ramón had a phone in his car, but he also had an alarm system that would shatter the night silence before she could even figure out how to use the phone to call for help. On the brighter side, though, she realized suddenly that there might be a gun in his glove compartment. She'd seen one there when he drove her to the courthouse one time, when she started to cry and Ramón reached over to open the glove box and hand her a Kleenex. Seeing the gun there, all big and cold and shiny, had startled and frightened her. She could go for that gun now.

But suppose she broke into the car, smashed the window with a rock or something and got the gun. Then what?

And what if it wasn't even there?

This wasn't something she could do herself. She remembered a pay phone a block away, outside a little diner that was only open for breakfast and lunch. Her heart lurching, Julie began to run and fell headlong as she tripped over a crack in the pavement. She thrust out her hands to break the fall, felt the flesh scrape off her palms in the searing unforgettable skinned-knee sensation of childhood. She lay still for a moment, out of breath, fearful that the fall had harmed the baby. Fearful for Nan. Fearful for Adam.

Then she struggled to her feet.

It had to be done. She would find a way to do it.

CHAPTER 19

Nan felt like a high-tension wire, crackling electricity through every cell of her body. It was a speedy, racing kind of feeling, mind zooming out of control. Like the time she'd tried speed during college exams and found herself flitting around wildly, unable to even sit to study. Her personality was already too speedy, she'd decided then. Never again.

Now she sat six feet from the man who planned to kill her. Someone who had already killed twice, crimes so carefully planned that he was actually going to get away with them. Whatever he had in mind for her, Nan realized, was probably planned just as well. Lawyers tended to be compulsive that way.

She frantically calculated distances to doors, surreptitiously flexed her bonds. No good. No way.

She was stuck physically as long as he remained in the room. And he didn't look as if he was planning to go anywhere.

He continued speaking, and she watched his face. Ramón had always seemed so very handsome. She'd admired the golden warmth of his complexion, the thick wave in his black hair, the anthracite glitter of his eyes, the strong Indian lines of forehead and cheekbones. Now bitterness contorted his features, all but obliterated the handsomeness.

"Your mother was . . . gone when you got here?" Nan asked gently.

He nodded. "She died four days before we arrived. I couldn't understand at first. I thought we were at the wrong place, that this was just another intermediate stop, that she was still waiting for me somewhere else. But this was the end of the line, and she was already buried."

"I'm sorry," Nan said softly.

Her mental processes were bifurcating, she noticed suddenly. One small portion of her conversed with Ramón, remained calm and empathetic, even found herself hurting for the small, wide-eyed boy so anxious to be reunited with his loving mother. In the rest of her brain, however, the mental fibrillation continued, that speedy, out-of-control sensation.

She was going to die. *Die.* Dead. Cold. Final. She would die alone, away from everyone who had ever loved her. With no chance to say good-bye, or thank you, or I love you. To anyone.

Ramón went on, as if he hadn't heard her. "Aunt Elena wanted to just go back home to Mexico, but Angus convinced her that he would take care of us. He knew his guilt." The last statement had the finality of a judicial pronouncement.

"And he did take care of you, didn't he?"

Ramón practically snarled. "The way he took care of his dogs. Elena and I, we became house dogs. When I studied American history, I noticed all the parallels in our lives to the antebellum South. We were house niggers, Elena and I. Separate and not even remotely equal. We lived in the servant quarters of the big house, and she was the maid. I was some kind of little mascot, I guess. Son, Angus would call me sometimes, with a kind of lordly largesse. We're all one big family, he'd say. Sure. Hypocritical lip service. The reality was that only his blood family really mattered to him. Shane. Cassie. And Amelia."

What would he do? Just shoot her and leave her somewhere? Take her down to the border and abandon her battered body for *La Migra* to find? Or would he arrange for her to simply disappear? Disappear . . . like Amelia?

She spoke without thinking. "Amelia. Did you . . . were you . . ." His head jerked and she had her answer, knew also she had gone too far.

He cocked his head and narrowed his eyes. "You're the first person who ever figured that out," he said slowly. "The first who ever credited me with the intelligence."

Nan listened, horrified. Intelligence did not seem remotely relevant here. "But *why?*"

"To punish Angus. To show him the pain of loss. What it meant to have a hole in your heart."

"But to kill a *child*, Ramón? And when you were only a child yourself?" How old would he have been? Twelve? Thirteen? "I don't understand."

"I didn't hurt her," he said shortly. "She didn't suffer. Only Angus suffered."

"And her mother," Nan reminded. "And Shane and Cassie. Cassie told me it made her wild, made her act out."

"Cassie was a slut," he snapped, "and a tease. She was already after Adam then, not that he was fighting her off." Nan remembered Cassie's offhand braggadocio about her "multicultural program," her nonchalant reference to Ramón on her list of high school lovers.

But it wasn't just the Pettigrews who'd suffered. Nan thought of all the little girls in the area—like Sara Pettigrew, then Sara Reid—who cried at night and looked at the picture of the little girl with the Dutch-boy haircut and feared for their safety at the hands of a madman on the loose.

A madman who was actually a twisted little boy. Nan shuddered involuntarily. She realized suddenly that she was bathed in sweat. When had that happened? "So that's why there was never any ransom demand, any real one." Good God, she thought, that makes *three* people he's killed. Soon to be four if she didn't come up with some kind of plan. Fast.

"Of course," Ramón answered. "There was no need. The whole point was the uncertainty. I planned it for a long time, waited for just the right day. I wasn't sure, for a while, whether I would leave her body to be found, like he had left my mother. But then I decided that not to know was even worse. I never knew what happened to my father. He would never know what happened to his daughter. She would never be found."

And she almost hadn't been, Nan remembered. Her remains were discovered only after a freak rainstorm washed away land at the side of a road cut by a developer. A developer to whom Angus had sold land in order to finance his rocket-building hobby. A hobby he embraced only after his cherished daughter disappeared without a trace. Everything twisted around and turned back in on itself.

The hatred was so deep, so convoluted. And so strangely unrelenting.

"But that was so long ago," Nan said. "Why Shane? Why now?" And why frame Adam? she was wondering. But that would have to come later. Ramón seemed to relish telling his tale, spilling his horribly tangled version of reality. Surely he would come to that part. And the longer she could keep him talking, the more hope there was.

Hope? For what? That the goon would have a flat tire?

"To punish Angus again," Ramón answered simply. "Angus was the worst kind of racist, you see. He would tell people I was like a son to him, but of course that wasn't true and everybody knew it. Especially me. He was buying me off, paying me off, because of his own guilt. Yes, he gave me a home. Yes, he gave me an education. He even somehow bought me citizenship. But he always made a big point of how generous he was, how gracious. He never would admit it was because he and Jack Chandler didn't take decent care of his workers' housing. Jack used to tell me I was a reminder to him, and from everything I understand, after my mother died, Jack *did* do a better job maintaining the shanties. But that still didn't make them more than shanties. And it didn't exonerate him. Jack may have realized that, but Angus never did."

Nan took the opening. "Is that why you framed Adam?" she asked. "To get back at his father?" His father who was dead, for God's sake. Where did this all end?

"No," he answered. "I framed Adam because it was the easiest way. Because I knew Shane had been sleeping with Julie. But I always knew I could get Adam off, later."

"How?" It seemed to Nan that this whole conversation, this whole deadly situation, had begun precisely because Ramón *couldn't* get Adam off, had in fact framed him so tightly that acquittal was all but impossible.

"Oh, there are ways," he answered airily. "Some new evidence might turn up, someone might confess in a suicide note."

"Jeff Nashimora," she suggested. Of course. And that would complete Ramón's retaliation against the Pettigrews by annihilating Cassie. The slut. Who had, at a guess, used and discarded him far too casually long ago.

"It could happen," he agreed.

"Well, it all makes sense, I suppose." In a sick, contorted way. "But this was all so long ago. Why now? Something must have happened to trigger all this."

"You continue to impress me," Ramón said. "And I wouldn't have told you this, but it doesn't matter. You won't be able to pass it on. We had dinner with Angus and Shane last Thanksgiving, Victoria and I. Angus was drunk. He kept asking Victoria when we were going to have children."

Nan winced. "Oh, no!"

"So you know, too," he said resentfully. "There's no such thing as privacy anymore, not for anything."

What to say? Fertility medicine more often than not was hell.

"I'm sorry," she answered simply.

"Angus wasn't," he replied. " 'Mexicans are breeders,' he told Victoria. 'Can't see what's keeping you from whelping.' Like a *dog*. We were just animals to him. Victoria's Puerto Rican, besides. That he should humiliate her that way! She was so hurt, so mortified."

Nan remembered, suddenly, the flash of anger that Angus Pettigrew had shown when his workshop was invaded after Shane's death. *That damned Lupe,* Angus had said. *I'll wring her brown hide.* She remembered, too, the flush of anger on Ramón Garza's neck as he heard those words.

"So you planned to kill Angus all along?"

"Of course." Ramón might have been discussing the lease of a photocopier, he was so matter-of-fact. "And I would have waited longer, but the heart attack worried me. I wanted death to creep up on Angus just as it crept up on my mother. It was easy enough to manage. I just blocked the outside vent to his heater and later, when I was sure he was dead, I cleared the blockage. Your idea that the room was inadvertently aired out was a good one, but it was too risky to assume that would happen. By the time Angus was found, the heater was running properly and nobody was the wiser."

Which meant, Nan realized, that even if Detective Woodward got around to checking the heater, there'd probably be no way to prove a malfunction had occurred.

"Very clever," she told him. "You seem to have thought of everything."

He frowned. "Actually, there was one minor glitch, a migrant who saw me removing the plug from the heater vent in the middle of the night. He'd heard me speak to a group of the migrants and recognized me. When he called, he wanted to know what I was doing outside the big metal house in the middle of the night. It was unfortunate that he was watching."

"You killed him, too?" That would bring the body count to four. Holding for five.

"Not me personally, no."

Of course. The goon. Nan remembered Detective Woodward's comments about the migrant found dead in a gladiola field. A crime of passion, Woodward had said it looked like. Well, at a distance.

"And I guess you didn't shoot at yourself, either."

"Nope."

"Another of your friends?"

Ramón's smile was twisted. "The gentleman who's joining us is very loyal." Apparently, if Ramón trusted him to shoot at a moving vehicle and miss the driver. "I managed to get him off on some very nasty charges a while back. He obliges me with the occasional favor."

"But you wouldn't have needed him to cut the surfboard leash . . ."

"Of course not. I took care of that in the privacy of my own garage."

Something didn't fit. "The phone call at Julie's. After you were shot at."

"I asked him to call. He obliged."

"And the other threatening calls?"

He smiled again. "A bit of an exaggeration. But I know what they'd be like. I *have* gotten threats in the past, after all."

Nan was starting to feel truly panicky. The goon would be here any minute. She looked past Ramón onto the small private patio beyond the French doors. There hadn't been any more headlights.

But wait! Was something *moving* out there? Just beyond the bushes?

A loud banging on the front door jolted her back to the inside of the room.

Ramón smiled. "*Mí amigo.* Don't go away, counsel." He crossed behind Nan and went through the reception area. Leaving the gun on the desk.

Yes!

Now! Do something while he was gone! Nan could hear the door opening, hear Ramón and another man speaking Spanish. Get the gun, that was it. She had to get the gun. She tried to stand, chair and all, to get to the shiny weapon on the far corner of the desk.

But she was overbalanced. She teetered precariously and then fell forward, smashing painfully onto her swollen knee.

She turned her head sideways, frustrated and frantic, unable to move or even to right herself. Then she saw something on the patio that stopped her heart.

Julie.

Julie! She came through the bushes, crossed to the wrought-iron table and chairs and moved one chair close to the French doors. Then she caught Nan's eye, held up one finger briefly, and slipped away. It all happened so quickly that Nan might have imagined the whole thing.

Except that the chair was in a new position.

How? What? Nan had thought, till now, that she couldn't possibly be more frightened. But seeing Julie on that patio—her pregnant, vulnerable, hypertensive sister—multiplied the terror exponentially. He'd kill Julie, too, if she got in the way. Maybe he already planned to kill her anyway. This was a man with a definite agenda.

More footsteps as Ramón and the other man returned to the room. "My, my," Ramón said sardonically, "were we trying to make a break for it?" Nan felt him take the chair back in both hands and right it effortlessly in a single fluid motion. Just in case she'd forgotten that he was strong.

Upright again, she could see his companion. A savage-looking Latino thug dressed in black T-shirt and loose, dirty jeans. Lots of bulging muscles and a thick shock of greasy black hair. Eyes opaque and cold. Nan knew this was nobody she could sweet-talk in any language.

Her heart sank even further. She wasn't in the habit of prayer, wasn't even entirely sure she believed in God. But just in case, she opened mental negotiations. Let Julie get away, that was what she asked for. Dear God, just let Julie get safely away. Oh, and after that, could you maybe give me a hand, too?

"You're going to take a ride with my friend here," Ramón said, making it sound like a family excursion through blooming ranunculus fields. "Down toward the border."

Well, she'd called that one right. "Surely we can discuss this," she said carefully. She was very much afraid that she would cry. It seemed extremely important not to.

He shook his head firmly, finally. "There's nothing more to say."

Suddenly the blare of a car alarm erupted just outside the patio. Ramón and the thug swung around toward the window, stunned. Ramón lunged for the gun he'd left lying on the desk.

Nan watched in breathless horror as Julie dashed up onto the patio, picked up the wrought-iron chair, and hurled it through the closed French doors. The glass shattered and the inner wooden window frames splintered. Everything seemed to be in slow motion.

But then, when Julie pulled a gun from underneath her jacket, things speeded up instantly.

A *gun?* Julie?

For one fleeting second Nan gaped at the incongruity of her pacifist sister braced on the patio, holding a gun in both hands the way cops did on TV.

No! Ramón would kill her!

"Don't shoot her!" Nan screamed.

Ramón hesitated for a fraction of a second, then barked a command in Spanish. The loathsome thug rushed toward

Julie. Thoroughly immobilized, Nan was powerless to do anything but scream. And so she did, a piercing lungbuster that was swallowed moments later in the sudden stunning boom of a gun.

Julie's gun. She fired point-blank at Ramón's *amigo*. His chest blossomed scarlet as the impact of the shot threw him backward onto the floor.

He lay motionless. And all of them froze for a moment in the new and chilling silence.

Then, in the shattered patio doorway, Julie began to sway slightly. She released the gun with her left hand and grabbed at the door frame. With her right hand she swung the gun and aimed it at Ramón.

"No more," Julie whispered into the heavy silence. From far away, Nan could hear a siren. "Please, Ramón, no more."

Nan looked at Ramón's fingers, tense and pale, clenched on his own gun. She wished she knew more about guns, about things like safety and how could you tell if it was cocked. His finger was definitely on the trigger, however. That much she knew for sure.

There was another endless frozen moment.

Then he suddenly jumped behind Nan's chair, crouching behind her and bringing his left arm up tightly around her neck. Nan felt the chilly steel of his gun on her temple, felt a shudder of sheer terror run through her body, saw Julie hesitate. Did Ramón still have his finger on the trigger, that tense, twitchy finger?

Tears poured down Julie's cheeks, but her right arm remained steady as she supported herself on the door frame. The gun was now pointed at Nan and Ramón. *Two* guns on her. She felt Ramón's harsh steamy breath against the back of her neck, saw beads of glistening sweat form on the tawny forearm that crushed itself against her chin.

The siren grew louder.

But Julie was fading fast. Nan could see her face grow

pale, as it had that afternoon in Angus Pettigrew's workshop. She swayed again, then slowly collapsed to the ground. Her gun gave an awful clank as it fell to the patio floor and bounced once.

"Don't shoot her!" Nan pleaded in a low urgent voice. "Please, Ramón."

Slowly he released the pressure on her neck. Then she felt the gun leave her temple. Julie lay on her side, frighteningly still.

"Got to get out of here," Ramón muttered. He paced to the patio door, looked down at Julie for a moment, then turned and faced Nan.

This was it, she realized. She was going to die. Right here, right now.

And for nothing. Ramón could never get away. The siren grew even louder. She forced herself to look him in the eye. He might kill her, but he'd have to face her as he did it. At least she could do that much.

But then he was in motion again. He leaned down over the body of the dead thug, pulled keys from the man's pocket. He snatched the scissors from the desk and began to cut the bonds that tied Nan to the chair.

"We're going out the front door," he told her. "Any trouble, any time you try to get away, I'll kill you right then and there. No second chances. Understand?"

"Yes." Her voice was shaky.

He had the cords off now and was pulling her to her feet. The siren was impossibly loud and now she could see red and white lights swirling as a police car squealed into the parking lot beyond the bushes.

Ramón shoved Nan roughly toward the front of the office, holding the gun in the center of her back. She stumbled once as her injured knee buckled, felt him forcibly pull her upright.

She staggered on, determined to ignore the pain. At least she had a chance now. She had survived what she was certain were her last minutes, had one more opportunity to live.

At the front door Ramón moved her to the side and cautiously opened the door inward, looking out and twisting his head from side to side. Outside, the street was dark, deserted. A dark old Chevy sedan was parked directly in front of the office.

"You'll drive," he hissed, pushing her across the sidewalk. Her shoes were somewhere in the office and the cement was cold against her stocking feet, a startling sensation. But it was a sensation, a physical feeling after she'd thought she would have no more physical feelings ever.

Ramón opened the passenger door and gave Nan an impatient shove. She got across the console somehow and settled herself behind the wheel. A set of pink furry dice hung from the rearview mirror and the car stank of cigarettes.

Now he was beside her, pulling the door closed, jamming the keys into the ignition. "Go!" he ordered, and she turned over the engine, slammed the car into gear, groped for headlights. She turned the wheel away from the curb just as she heard the office door crash open again.

A male voice yelled, "Police, *freeze!*" She ignored it and smashed down the gas pedal, jerking away from the curb. The unmistakable sound of a gunshot followed—once, twice, three times.

"Just get out of here," Ramón commanded. "Left up ahead. Then right. Get on the freeway going north."

Toward where? Nan tried to concentrate on the car, the road, the simple mechanics of moving the vehicle forward. The Chevy was enormous and the suspension was shot, but there was something powerful under the hood and the car surged ahead as she accelerated. She ran a red light in quiet downtown Floritas, blew a stop sign, then pulled onto the freeway at the Pettigrew Road entrance, momentarily considering the irony.

"Keep it at sixty-five," Ramón ordered. "Number two lane."

Nan obeyed, settled into the lane and then glanced over at him. His brow was knotted and he seemed closer to total panic than she had ever seen him. For the first time she realized the incongruity of their clothing. They were dressed for court, both of them. Ramón was still in his suit pants and white shirt, tie loosened around his neck. And she wore a silk dress. A couple of Southern California lawyers, hanging out on Friday night.

"Where are we going?" Nan asked. It was the first time she'd spoken since they were in the office. But now, for some reason, she felt almost comfortable—even hurtling down the freeway in a stolen car with a murderer. He couldn't shoot her here without risking his own life.

"I haven't decided yet," he said. "Just shut up and keep driving."

So she did, moving north through Camp Pendleton, through the familiar dark landscape she'd traveled so many times in the past three months. She was going seventy now, being passed on both sides. Traffic grew heavier, but they passed under the signs for the immigration checkpoint without slowing noticeably.

"Good," Ramón muttered. "Closed."

Then, without any real warning, traffic slowed dramatically.

"Shit!" Ramón hissed. He swiveled his head, peered ahead. "They've opened the checkpoint. And there's no turnarounds till after we go through. We'll go through nice and cool and easy. Don't get any ideas about being a hero. Whether or not you can see the gun, I can kill you in an instant."

Nan's heart was racing. The potential for disaster here was enormous. There were armed officers at the checkpoint, far too many people with guns. One of them sat right beside her and had nothing to lose.

Had the checkpoint been warned to watch for them? Was that why it had suddenly opened?

Ramón went on. "Now. Get in the number one lane. If there's no trouble, keep on toward L.A. Anything goes wrong, take the crossover just past the checkpoint and make a fast U-turn."

Nan pulled into the number one lane, gripped her hands on the wheel as traffic inched forward. They were four cars back. A Border Patrol officer stood between the lanes on Ramón's side of the Chevy, looking vaguely bored. A lime-green Border Patrol van was parked across the shoulder, doors open. No driver.

Three cars back now. The officer between the lanes was young, fair-skinned. He glanced into cars, waved them through. Nobody was stopped. Two cars back. No change. The officer kept waving them on. One car.

Nan crawled forward, held her breath as they drew closer to the moment of reckoning. She had never been stopped here, never been subjected to more than the most cursory glance. Ramón had his hand with the gun down between the seat and the car door.

Now they were at the head of the line. The car on the right was waved through and moved forward. The officer looked at the Chevy. Nan estimated her pulse at about three hundred.

He waved the car on.

Nan felt a flood of relief. She stepped lightly on the gas, began to move forward again. And then, in the rearview mirror, she saw an officer run across the road in front of the stopped cars, speak to the man who had waved them through. They were both looking at the Chevy.

Ramón was turned partway in the seat, looking back. "Turn around!" he ordered. "Do it!"

Nan stepped on the gas, headed for the turnaround,

marked by an emphatic international sign prohibiting all turns. She slowed, went through, turned to merge into the fast lane of the southbound traffic. Behind them, one of the officers had jumped into the van, which was heading toward them down the shoulder, lights flashing.

"Come on, get out of here!" Ramón urged, sounding panicky.

Traffic raced southward, whooshing past the hood of the Chevy. There was no way to break into traffic this heavy. The Border Patrol van was closing in.

"Just do it!" Ramón snarled.

"I can't go till there's an opening," she snapped back. The van had almost reached them. "We'll be creamed."

And then came a miraculous clearing in the southbound traffic. Nan swung the big car into the number one lane, gunned it up to speed, and then cut back into the number two lane. In the rearview mirror, she saw the Border Patrol van stop, wait for several cars to pass, then enter traffic.

Ramón was turned around in his seat watching. The gun had reappeared, was in his lap pointed at Nan.

"Floor it," he ordered, and she obeyed, feeling the strong engine respond and watching the speedometer rise. Seventy, seventy-five, eighty, eighty-five. She was cutting people off now, switching lanes, racing to elude the van. It held steady, however, switching lanes as she did, moving right along. It was three cars back, then two, then one, now directly behind their car, furiously flashing its lights, siren blaring. Cars moved out of the way, dodged over, switched lanes to get out of the van's path.

Nan was doing ninety-five in the number one lane when she saw the men crouching on the median far ahead. There were two of them. Obviously they'd been dumped by their drivers, told to cross and reconnect up north. They were stunningly exposed. There was no shrubbery here, no concealment, nothing between the northbound and southbound traffic but solid low metal barriers on one side, metal spikes on the other.

Not now, she silently willed them, for God's sake not now! Wait, cross later. Go back to Mexico, don't be crazy!

She hurtled past the men, the van closing in on her, saw them poised to spring across the freeway. She cut over two lanes suddenly, saw the van swerve to follow, and then heard the horrendous crunch of crashing metal behind her.

"What's happening?" she asked Ramón urgently. He was craning his neck. The van was suddenly gone from the rearview mirror, stopped on the shoulder. Lights from the headlights behind them were pointed every which way. And they weren't moving forward anymore, any of them.

Nan eased up on the gas pedal, dropped the Chevy's speed to seventy-five. Up ahead there was another clot of traffic, oblivious to the drama acted out behind them.

"They tried to get across the freeway," he said, peering back. "I think. I can't tell if they made it. Looks like a chain reaction: somebody swerved to avoid them and crashed, then people smashing into them. There's cars spun out all over the place. Shit!"

"What about the Border Patrol van?"

"It stopped. Slow down, Nan. Get it back to sixty-five, seventy."

She obeyed. The Chevy seemed to crawl at the reduced speed. Which was still fifteen miles over the limit. She moved sedately over into a slower lane. This was not the time to wonder if the men had made it across the freeway. What on earth had they been thinking, anyway? That the flashing lights were coming for them?

This was also not the time to wonder how badly the other drivers had been injured, if anyone had been killed. The litigation would run on forever. If Nan survived, she'd spend years being deposed.

"Now what?" she asked, Bonnie to his Clyde. There had been something genuinely exhilarating about being in a

high-speed freeway chase. And surviving it. A chilling realization that it could almost be called fun.

"Keep heading south. Let me think."

Nan thought, too.

She wondered about Julie. Was she all right? Was the
baby all right? Was it a stroke that toppled her? Nan shook
her head, not daring to really consider that possibility.
Surely it was just a faint. The stress, the incredible shock of
shooting and killing a man.

And the police had been right there, Nan reminded herself. They'd have called paramedics, rushed her to the hospital. Oh, *hell*. They'd probably *arrested* Julie. She was
lying beside a recently fired gun and there was a dead man
six feet away.

But, still. She was female, pregnant. Surely they'd worry
about her medical condition first.

And what of herself?

As if to answer, Ramón stirred beside her. "Take Poinsettia," he instructed as they neared the exit. She pulled off
and drove toward the beach, following his directions, turning south and driving past the campsite at South Carlsbad
State Beach. There were a few RV's parked there, some
tents. She could see a campfire through the trees.

They continued south, drawing nearer to Floritas. "Pull
into the overlook," Ramón told her. She obeyed, drove
through to the far end of the lot, past a few cars parked at
discreet intervals. Teenagers, probably, getting romantic.
She willed them to stay put, or, even better, to all go home.
Right now.

But none of the cars moved. She cut off the engine at
Ramón's command and the silence was deafening. Far below them, under the bluffs, waves crashed into shore.

On the day Adam was arrested, Nan realized suddenly,
she and Julie had sat in this lot eating tacos. Dear God, let
Julie be all right, let at least some good come out of all of
this.

"We need another car," Ramón said abruptly.

"Let me go," Nan pleaded softly. "Ramón, you don't need me. You'll travel faster without me. You know people, there are places you could hide. The men in the hills would take you in, keep you. You could get away to Mexico then."

He shook his head. "I can't let you go. You'd have them on me in a flash."

"What if I promised I wouldn't?"

He laughed, and the sound was jarring. She couldn't remember the last time she'd heard him laugh. "You think I'm dumb enough to trust you?"

"My word is good," Nan told him. She tried a chuckle. If he could laugh, maybe she could, too. Perhaps if she could just lighten the mood. . . . "I'd tell you to ask around, but I guess we're under a certain time pressure here." She thought for a moment. "Tie me up. Put me in the trunk. That'll give you plenty of time to get a head start. And I really *don't* have any idea where you're going anyway."

"You sure you never did trial work?" Ramón asked. He was smiling, seemed almost relaxed. But he was still pointing the gun at her.

"Not yet," she said, with forced bravado. "Maybe I'll give it a try." She paused, spoke more forcefully. "I'm sorry about all of this, Ramón. Honestly. But it doesn't have to get any worse. And I really believe you can get away, get *totally* away if you want to."

He seemed to be thinking about it for a moment. Then he shook his head. "Nice try," he said. "But overruled. Here's what we're going to do. You're going to approach that Subaru pickup, come in nice and unthreatening at the driver's side. They roll down the window, you tell them you've got car trouble. I'll come up from behind and then you just get out of the way."

"Don't kill them. There's no need."

"Hey," he said, "this is *my* show."

"Then try to run it with a shred of dignity," Nan told him angrily. "God knows how many people were hurt or killed on the freeway back there. It was one thing when you had a *reason* to hurt somebody. But those people hadn't hurt you, and neither have these. Tie *them* up, leave them in the trunk."

"We'll see," he answered. "Let's say that what happens to them is entirely up to you. You make trouble, try to slip a message, do anything cute—they die. You, too. I'll be right behind you, and I'm a damned good shot."

Nan looked at him, considered. She didn't exactly have a choice, other than immediate death. And she hadn't for a while. There'd been a gun trained on her without interruption for what felt like forever, at least an hour and a half. What's more, Ramón had proven to her total satisfaction that he was willing to do anything.

The asphalt of the parking lot was rough and hurt her feet as she padded across the chilly surface in her shredded stockings. Her knee was protesting every inch of the way, and she limped badly.

She would do this straight, just as Ramón had instructed. And then hope that somewhere down the line . . . What?

Never mind down the line, she told herself as she walked up to the driver's window of the red Subaru. Just concentrate on right now. *Carpe diem*. Seize the moment.

The car was fogged up and the radio was on. "Stairway to Heaven." Nan hoped not. She had a sudden fleeting memory of high school, of parking and making out down by the cemetery in Spring Hill, on the stretch known as the Passion Pit. But nobody in her circle had ever driven these little pickups that the California kids so loved. This one had a mess of junk tossed in the back: roller skates, a skateboard, a massive cooler, the detritus of adolescence.

The cab rocked slightly. Somebody in this car was seizing the moment, all right, and probably a lot more, too. But wait. There was a female voice now, shrill and urgent. "Jason, I said *no!*"

Nan rapped hesitantly on the window, heard the music soften and an angry young male voice say, "What the fuck? Shut up, Cindy."

Nan rapped again. "Excuse me," she called softly. "I need help."

Ramón crouched motionless at the rear of the pickup, moonlight glinting off his gun. He nodded encouragement.

The Subaru's window rolled down partway and Jason turned his head. It filled most of the window. He was a big kid, with a short haircut and a huge square solid head. Nan looked past him and saw a girl backed against the passenger door. Cindy. She looked young and pretty and scared. She wore an oversized Floritas High Football sweatshirt and was surreptitiously tugging at her jeans. They were scrunched partway down her thighs.

"What the fuck?" asked Jason again. Probably a linebacker. The kind of kid who always sat in the back row in high school, making rude noises and obscene remarks. Ungrammatically. Then segued into an adulthood full of twelve-packs and bitching about not getting enough overtime.

"I've got car trouble," Nan told him, offering her most sincere smile. "The battery's been low and I've got jumper cables. If you could possibly just give me a jump . . ."

But the jump came on the other side of the car and took Nan totally by surprise. Cindy opened the door and hopped out, giving one last upward yank to her jeans.

"He tried to rape me," she squealed. "Get me away from here!"

"Oh, shit," Jason muttered loudly. He suddenly opened his own door. Nan barely was able to get out of his way before the truck's door slammed into her.

"Don't move," Ramón ordered. He was standing now, the gun aimed at Jason's midsection, which was enormous.

Jason stopped in his tracks, stunned and confused. Cindy, meanwhile, began inching back into the darkness on the passenger side of the truck. She probably couldn't even see the gun.

But Ramón noticed her. "You! Get back here!"

Cindy had apparently had enough instructions from the male gender for the evening. "Forget it," she told him.

He waved the gun at her. She gave a piercing shriek and started to run.

Ramón turned to fire in her direction, but then Jason was on him like some huge furry hound. The gun fired once, off into nowhere, and then it came flying past Nan's head as the two of them fell to the asphalt.

She limped over to the gun, picked it up, and stared at it a moment. She fitted her hand to the trigger. Nan had never fired a gun, never before even held one. It was heavy, alien. She pointed it at the two men fighting on the ground. It would be madness to fire now. She could kill them both, or miss Ramón altogether.

She stepped back then, and waited. The two men were surprisingly well matched. Ramón was lithe, fit, trained to kill by the United States government. But Jason had youth on his side, and anger, and sheer bulk. He was a full head taller than Ramón and half again as heavy.

At the other end of the parking lot, two cars abruptly started their motors and sped out of the lot, driving the wrong way down the entry lane. Cindy had totally disappeared. Only one car remained, at the far end.

As Nan watched, she saw Ramón wiggle loose from Jason's bear-hug, slip his arm around the young behemoth's neck, and jerk. The boy went immediately slack.

Good God, another one dead.

Ramón rose slowly to his feet, faced Nan. She held the gun in both hands now, the way Julie had. She was too far away to be rushed and he knew it.

"Let me leave, walk away," he told her. "Like we talked about before."

"I don't think so," she answered. She had just watched him kill a boy guilty only of raging hormones and trying to protect his girl.

He began circling then, staying at the same distance but moving slowly toward the bluffs.

"Lie down," Nan told him. "Stay put or I'll shoot you."

"Somehow I doubt it," he said. He kept moving sideways. What was he trying to do?

Nan tightened her finger on the trigger. It would be so easy, a little squeeze. But could she do it?

He had gone a full ninety degrees now, had his back to the ocean. He was beyond the sign warning that the bluffs were unstable, forbidding foot traffic. The crashing waves below sounded louder, the wind stronger.

"Don't press your luck," Nan warned him. She moved forward at the same pace, matching him step for step, passing the warning sign. She should have shot him by now if she intended to. Maybe he was right. Maybe she *wouldn't* be able to.

Then he sprang, coming straight at her, leaping for the hand that held the gun. Without a moment's thought, she tossed it out over the bluffs and it disappeared into the night. She dodged as he tackled her, but he had her foot, was grabbing her left ankle. He was strong and heavy and the impact hurt, made her completely forget the pain in her right knee for a single fleeting moment.

Then suddenly the edge of the bluff began crumbling. Nan felt the earth beneath her tremble as a chunk of the unstable land broke loose.

He was closer to the edge. She looked back and saw him sliding, saw the ground beneath his legs disappear. He was pulling her with him as he slid toward the edge.

And then as suddenly as he had grabbed her, he let go of

her ankle. He lunged sideways at a scrubby bush, maybe two foot tall.

Nan didn't stop to look at what he was doing. She crawled inland as fast as she could, scrabbled along, desperately fleeing from the crumbling bluff. Now that it had started to give way, anything could happen.

When she was maybe ten feet in, she cautiously raised herself, tested her bum knee and newly twisted ankle. They both worked, though just barely and certainly not well. She slowly moved back toward the parked cars. When she was twenty feet from the edge of the bluffs she finally felt safe enough to look back.

He had caught onto the scrubby little bush and miraculously its roots had held. But his knees stuck out over the edge still, the land beneath them completely gone. He tried to bring his body sideways, and Nan saw another chunk of the cliff edge vanish.

Think. There'd been rope in the back of the Subaru pickup, mixed in with all the skateboards and junk. She supported herself on the hood of the truck and worked her way around on the passenger side, avoiding looking at the big motionless body that would never play football again.

Was it worth trying to save him?

She kept moving as she wondered, knew she had to at least make an effort. The rope was there, and a toolbox, too. She opened the toolbox, a jumble of odd items, dug till she found a pair of wire-cutters. She tested the cutters on the rope, found it cut effectively, if not easily.

Then she retraced her steps to the front of the truck and tied one end of the rope to the bumper. She estimated the distance to Ramón, cut a length of rope maybe four feet longer. He was hanging on to the bush and watching her.

Silently. With no expression on the face that was once again handsome.

She took a deep breath and tossed the end of the rope

toward him. "You know knots," she said. "Tie it around your wrists or whatever it will take to hold you."

Ramón reached tentatively with one hand, brought the rope in toward him. He tested its strength, pulled it taut and found that it held. "Thanks," he said. He held the bush with his left hand, looped the rope around his right wrist several times. Then he gingerly let go of the bush and grabbed the rope with his left hand.

"Don't get any ideas about pulling yourself closer," Nan told him, as she painfully lowered herself to the ground beside the bumper. She positioned the wire-cutters on the rope, made sure he could see them. "You make any kind of moves to get closer, and I cut the rope. Guaranteed."

Then she leaned her head back and screamed, *"Fire! Fire!"*

Southern Californians might not respond to a cry of *Help!*, but fire was the universal enemy. If anybody could hear, they would surely react. Of course, everybody seemed to have fled. Even the last car down on the end was gone now. The only vehicles remaining in the lot were the Subaru truck and the Chevy.

She pondered alternatives. Maybe throwing away the gun hadn't been such a great idea after all. Maybe she should just get in the Chevy and leave, go for help herself.

But he would get away if she did that, she was certain. And letting him get away was no longer an option, never really had been. She would wait till morning if she had to.

Finally she heard the faint whine of a siren come through the night, growing louder and clearer and brighter. Somebody *had* called for help. Moments later a police cruiser careened into the lot and she heard the doors bang open.

"Police!" somebody yelled. "Nobody move!"

No problem. She was too tired to move, unwilling even to try to stand again. "Over here," she called. "In front of the truck."

Two officers approached cautiously, working their way

along opposite sides of the truck. And then Nan saw what was happening at the edge of the bluff.

He had untied the knot that tethered his wrist to the bumper of the car, held the rope in both hands as if playing tug of war.

"Sorry I can't stay," he said, looking straight at Nan. Smiling.

Then he let go of the rope with both hands and slid backward over the precipice into the darkness. Far below, the surf crashed.

EPILOGUE

Mother's Day in Floritas began gloomy and overcast, but by eleven the fog had burned off and the sky was a glorious blue. The picnic table on Julie's back patio was set with a tablecloth fashioned from a bed sheet and plates and glasses that sort of matched. A vase of late ranunculus sat in the middle. Cottage cheese pancakes with blueberries were coming up, and after brunch, they would all go visit the ranunculus fields in Carlsbad. June Robinson, who was staying at a nearby motel for what Julie claimed was eternity, had bought a special panoramic camera to take pictures of the bands of red and pink and yellow and orange. And she'd already shot seven rolls of the baby.

Nan sat with her right leg propped up on a chair. Pampering the knee was no longer essential, but had become something of a habit. The knee still hurt her some, but not enough to really worry. She'd been lucky, all told, and so had the folks in the other cars at the checkpoint pileup. Nobody had been killed, no one seriously injured. And the migrants who'd made the foolhardy dash across the freeway had gotten clean away.

Nan looked around at her assembled family and loved them all fiercely. Even Adam.

Julie moved slowly back and forth in the glider, nursing Colleen. At almost eight weeks, Colleen was growing rapidly, making up for lost time. She had been born six weeks early. On Saint Patrick's Day, which pretty much sealed the matter of her name.

Julie had been admitted to the hospital in the early stages of labor on the night of the shooting. There'd been no stroke, only another faint on the patio, and by the time the police arrived, she was already starting to come around. They kept her hospitalized for five tense days, monitoring the skyrocketing blood pressure, trying to halt the labor. Defiantly, Colleen insisted on making an early arrival. And once her baby was born, Julie's blood pressure promptly sank to its healthy normal level.

Nan enjoyed watching Julie fuss over the baby. She seemed a natural mother, serenely confident of her abilities. While Nan was terrified, certain she'd drop her poor niece smack on the soft spot of her head if she even tried to hold her. Colleen seemed so tiny and helpless and fragile. But sometimes Nan did hold her, carefully seated, lost in wonder.

Adam was besotted. There was no other word for it. He would stare at his funny wrinkly little daughter for hours, Julie said. Carried her around the greenhouse strapped tightly to his chest in a Snugli. Even changed diapers. Adam seemed almost a new man, and it was definitely an improved model. All charges against him had been dropped, even the assault at the Flower Auction. He was free now, as free as any father is. His older children had come to visit the previous weekend, bringing an enormous panda bear.

Mom came outside now, fretting that Colleen would be sunburned if her head weren't covered, holding a ridiculous frilly cap. Mom had filled the house with baby stuff—cradles and swings and lacy bedspreads and a wardrobe worthy of royalty. Nan, ever the pragmatist, had contributed a top-of-the-line car safety seat and an intercom so Adam and Julie could hear Colleen's waking cries when they were working in the greenhouse.

Julie smiled maternally as she took the lacy cap. She used her free hand to slip the hat carefully on her daughter's tiny head, then popped an early raspberry in her mouth from a bowl of fruit beside her.

"I think," she said to nobody in particular, "that I'm going to like this mother business a lot."

Get to know
Jesus Creek, Tennessee,
where fiction and fatality collide.

"DEBORAH ADAMS'S books perfectly
capture the rhythms of life in a small
town, where everyone sees it as a
God-given right to know everybody
else's business."
—*The Baltimore Sun*

Published by Ballantine Books.
Available in your local bookstore.

Turn the page for an entertaining
sample of Deborah Adams's
Jesus Creek, Tennessee, daily life....

The town of Jesus Creek occupied two blocks along Main Street. Most of the buildings still bore the names of the original businesses from the time the town was incorporated in 1840, with only a few minor changes on the facades.

The courthouse stood on a grassy square in the middle of the other buildings, so that it was possible to walk the entire town and around the court square in less than five minutes. In decent weather it was also possible to take one's time, observe a game of checkers being played on the courthouse lawn, stroll through the miniature memorial park, buy vegetables from Mennonite peddlers in front of the movie house, or sit on the steps of Marion's Dance Studio (formerly Hansen's Feed and Grain), and watch motorists ignore the town's only traffic light....

"So, tell me about your charmingly bucolic community."

"What would you like to know?" Kate didn't like his attitude, but she supposed he was trying to be civil. Some people never could get the knack of it.

"Where did the name come from?"

"The story is that a group of religious dissenters left their community up north, looking to settle their own version of Paradise. When they got here, the leader, a Mr. Wicken, said 'Unload the mules,' or words to that effect. And they all waded into the creek and baptized each other. So then the settlers who were already here started to call it Jesus Creek. The name stuck—and the town itself got rechristened."